MEET JAKE TANNER

Born: 28.03.1985

Height: 6'1"

Weight: 190lbs / 86kg / 13.5 stone

Physical Description: Brown hair, close shaven beard, brown eyes, slim athletic build

Education: Upper Second Class Honours in Psychology from the University College London (UCL)

Interests: When Jake isn't protecting lives and finding those responsible for taking them, Jake enjoys motorsports — particularly F1

Family: Mother, older sister, younger brother. His father died in a car accident when Jake was fifteen

Relationship Status: Currently in a relationship with Elizabeth Tanner, and he doesn't see that changing, ever

By The Same Author

The CID Case Series
Toe the Line
Walk the Line
Under the Line
Cross the Line
Over the Line
Past the Line

The SO15 Files Series
The Wolf
Dark Christmas
The Eye
In Heaven and Hell
Blackout
Eye for an Eye
Mile 17
The Long Walk
The Endgame

The Terror Thriller Series
Standstill
Floor 68

TOE THE LINE

BY JACK **PROBYN**

ISBN: 978-1-80520-001-7

eBook ISBN: 978-1-80520-000-0

First Edition

Visit Jack Probyn's website at www.jackprobynbooks.com.

For Nana.

| PART 1 |

CHAPTER 1

PLAY DIRTY

SIX MONTHS AGO

Two years had passed since the world's media had last uttered their name. In that time, they'd been forgotten, disregarded and pushed to the bottom of the history books – more importantly, pushed to the bottom of the nation's police forces' unsolved case files. Where they should be.

There was a reason they were the best in the business and had already taken home more than two million pounds' worth of jewellery and money from their previous four heists. Their methods methodical, their planning meticulous. And with a certain amount of help from friends in high places, they were almost untouchable.

With each heist the pressure and risk grew exponentially, and every possible outcome had to be accounted for. And in the past it had – except in their last heist. Cock-up from start to finish. Oxford, 2006, HSBC bank on the high street, 9 a.m. Charge in, siege the place, force everyone into the centre of the room and destroy any and all means of communication, then pilfer the contents of the safes and ATM machines until their gym bags were brimming with sweet, sweet paper. Easy. At least it should have been.

The one thing they hadn't planned for was what they liked to call in the business a Good Samaritan: someone dumb enough and brave enough to stand in the way of sub-machine guns and shotguns and defend the bank until the police arrived. The name of that individual would forever be etched in their memories, including the minute details of his face. Not because he was instantly recognisable or because they all had photographic memories – far from it – but because the man had instantly earned himself some notoriety. Following the event, and the subsequent arrest of their former leader, the media had a hard-on for the Good Samaritan and gave him more airtime than they should have – far more than he deserved.

What the Good Samaritan was doing now, nobody knew, but they'd each resolved to make sure nothing like that happened again.

Next time would be different. Next time they would set the world alight and make sure their names were burnt into the retinas of anyone who saw them or dared cross them. They wanted to go rogue. Off the books. Off the radar. To commit the worst robbery ever seen and be immortalised by the media coverage that had followed them throughout their nine-year career. And they were going to make it exceptional.

It was time to forget the rules and play dirty.

CHAPTER 2

MEAN STREETS

SIX MONTHS LATER: JUNE, 2009

Jake Tanner had never been fond of first days. As far back as he could remember, they were always filled with awkwardness, facetious grins, overbearing smiles and greetings, and a solid case of nervy runs. But the one thing that stung him badly was shyness. The first day of school where you didn't know anyone in the playground and all the rest of the kids seemed to have made lifelong friends already. The first day of university where you were a day late to freshers' week because you were respecting the anniversary of your father's death, and everyone was beginning to get on like a student kitchen fire and build lasting relationships.

And today was no different: the first day of a new job, a new start to his professional career as a detective constable. New names, new faces, new personalities.

The sun beat down on the windshield of Jake's Mini Austin Cooper; he was barely able to fit into it, but it was his pride and joy nonetheless. The air conditioning was beat – the latest in the long list of repairs the car required – and the windows were having little effect against the monstrous and offensive heat that opened his pores and covered his body in a thin veil of sweat. The world outside the car was still – the trees, bushes on the side of the road, even the air. So far so good.

Jake glanced down at the satnav, wiping a layer of liquid from his top lip. *In a hundred yards, please turn right.* Easy enough. But if he needed a reminder, the sign bearing the words MOUNT

BROWNE, SURREY POLICE he saw a few seconds later did its job. He slowed, turned and idled the car past a row of detached properties, his eyes searching for the correct entrance. There was no mistaking it. At the end of the road was an even bigger sign than the first. Between the two lanes sat a booth that reminded him of the ones at Dartford Crossing that he and his family used to drive past on their summer holidays to the Norfolk coast – the only time of year when his dad was allowed time off from work.

He rolled the car to the booth, held his warrant card beneath the digital scanner and waited for the bar to lift, granting him access.

While the internal systems of the scanner worked quietly in the background, cross-referencing his face and his data with the police force's databases, he tilted forward and stared into the camera lens aimed directly at him. He thought about smiling childishly but suppressed the thought, remembering his place and where he was. Nerves did funny things to people.

Shortly after, the bar lifted and Jake drove up the steep incline towards the headquarters of Surrey Police, ignoring the agony of the engine running at five thousand revs in second gear. As he climbed over the lip of the hill, the knot in his stomach tightened, forcing pressure on his abdomen. He manoeuvred his way into the nearest parking space he could find: at the opposite end of the car park. It was only 7:50 a.m. and already the entire force was making him look bad.

He wasn't sure he could even plead innocence of it being his first day.

Mount Browne was a vast building and looked as though it had once been a stately mansion in a former life, a host for aristocracy and the wealthy, with its eaves, vaulted walls and several chimneys dotted along the roof. Now, however, it had been transformed into the hub of a vibrant and buzzing police force, the home of one of Surrey Police's satellite Major Crime Team divisions. The brick was a combination of black, brown and red, and stood front and centre, proud, against the backdrop of paradise green and sky blue.

With nothing but his backpack – which contained a packed lunch his wife Elizabeth had made for him and a reusable plastic bottle filled with water in anticipation of the heat – along with his phone, wallet and keys, Jake climbed a small flight of steps and entered the foyer. Inside he looked for signs of someone waiting for him, like he was stepping out of the arrivals lounge at Heathrow. There was nothing of the sort. Instead he was welcomed by an unenthused member of staff sitting behind the front desk at the far end of the entrance. A pen chained to the surface dangled over the edge, and a few police leaflets were fanned across the surface.

'Morning,' Jake said, feigning an excitable, I'm-so-happy-to-be-here smile. In reality that would only be genuine when the stomach cramps left him.

'Name?'

'Temporary Detective Constable Jake Tanner,' he said. 'Here to meet with DCI Nicki Pemberton.'

Jake removed his warrant card from his pocket and flashed it in the man's face, who immediately dismissed it and reached for a clipboard and slid it across the desk's surface.

'Sign in.'

Jake did as he was told and scribbled his name, rank and sign-in time on the sheet. Passing it back to the reception officer, he asked, 'Is there a coffee machine anywhere?'

The man grunted and pointed to Jake's right. Then he leant over the arm of his chair, disappearing beneath the desk and returned a moment later with a polystyrene cup. 'Put it in the bin when you're finished. Nicki will be down in a few minutes. You can wait over by the seats.'

Jake thanked him and moved over to the coffee machine. *Smart one, Jake. Have a natural laxative – that'll make you feel better.* He prodded the button for a latte and waited. As the steaming milk filled the cup, Jake read from the dozens of leaflets dangling from the corkboard on the wall. 'An Introduction to Your Rights'. 'So, You've Been Arrested'. 'How to Report a Crime'. 'How to Report a Police Officer'. Jake had read them all. Back to back. Cover to cover. Police training 101. But there was only so much you could learn from a manual, and there was no substitution for experience.

Once the coffee machine finished, Jake found himself a seat on a small armchair so old and dirty that when he sat down, a plume of dust billowed in the air. Fighting to keep his dust-induced sneeze down, he took a sip of the coffee and instantly wished he hadn't — it was bitter, too hot and made him gag. But it was enough to perk him up in the morning, even if it was going to haunt him in a few hours' time after the contents had mades its way through his stomach.

Jake bent forward to place the cup on a wooden table in front of him that looked older than the building. He'd seen that type before and, for a moment, wondered whether all police stations shared the same coffee tables as those commonly found at doctors' surgeries – whether the public services budget extended as far as differentiating any of them. He didn't think it likely.

Someone called his name from behind, distracting him from his thoughts.

'DC Tanner.'

He flinched, almost knocking the cup to the floor, then composed himself before rising from the chair.

DCI Pemberton, a slim, experienced-looking woman with a lob haircut, stood with her hand extended. She was dressed in a full suit with trousers and a look on her face that told him even though she was happy to see him, he'd already taken too long in addressing her. Jake, in a frantic rush, as if he'd just locked eyes with a celebrity, wiped his hand on his trousers and took hers. With his other hand, he brushed his black-and-grey-striped tie down, centred it and pushed it deeper into his collar.

'Thank you for joining us,' Pemberton said. Her grip was powerful and firm, and she spoke with a certain authority he hadn't heard in a while.

'Thanks for having me as part of the team. I hope to learn a lot, and hopefully I can be of some assistance!'

'From what I hear, you already are. I've heard some exciting things about you. You travelled far this morning?'

He shrugged. 'Only Croydon.'

'Park all right?'

'Just about. And I thought I was here early this morning.'

Pemberton's gaze turned towards the building's entrance and then back to Jake. 'It's a free-for-all in the mornings. You should see the amount of fights that have broken out. We don't have designated spaces, but having said that, if you park in mine, I can assure you that your days with us will definitely be numbered.'

A P45 threat within the first minute. Well done, Jake. At this rate you'll be gone by lunchtime.

'Good coffee?' Pemberton asked.

Jake glanced over his shoulder at the bead of brown liquid abseiling down the length of the cup. 'Yeah, it was nice, thanks.' He rubbed his cheek, massaging his fingers over the small scar that prohibited any facial hair from growing around it.

Pemberton smirked, drawing Jake's eyes to her mouth and then down to her shirt collar covered in make-up residue. 'You're a superb liar,' she told him. 'You should fit in fine here. Come on – I'll take you up and show you to the rest of the team.'

The rest of the team. The cliques at school. The university accommodation where all the bonds had already been formed.

Pemberton started off towards a set of double doors at the back of the lobby. Jake shot one last look at the cup of coffee, checked he hadn't left anything else behind and followed. At the door, Pemberton scanned her card, and they both waited until a green light flashed above the reader.

Then she led Jake through a myriad of corridors and offices until they eventually stopped by a lift at the back of the building. Pemberton pressed the button, then, once inside, chose the fourth floor. Jake stood slightly behind her, his head craning at the red bar above the doors that moved from left to right as they climbed the building.

A surprise yawn attacked him and broke free, stretching his mouth wide open and filling his brain with oxygen. He threw his hand over his mouth.

'Boring you already?' Pemberton asked with a smile that put him at ease a little.

'Not at all. Hardly slept last night.'

'Nerves?'

8

That and everything else going on.

'The opposite.'

'I think you'll find Surrey's a little calmer than the mean streets of London. We don't have that much going on.'

Jake disagreed. 'There's *always* something going on.'

CHAPTER 3

IRONY

For the first time in their career, The Crimsons were ready on time, and things were beginning to settle in place.

'Even the sun's out, lads!' Danny Cipriano shouted from the garage doorway, soaking up the rays as they beat down on his face. He closed his eyes and listened to the sound of birds singing, a welcome break from Michael's heavy metal music, which always threatened to make his ears bleed. He exhaled deeply. 'Today's going to be a fucking good day.'

'Don't be a tit,' Michael, his younger brother retorted, coming to a stop by the back of the van, his broad shoulders and thick arms almost as wide as the door he was standing in front of. 'You'll jinx us if you ain't careful.'

Danny scoffed. 'Since when did you believe in all that bullshit?' He shut the garage door and returned to the van's rear.

'Ever since you came up with the idea for that—' Michael pointed to the device laid flat in the back of the Transit. It was covered in a piece of tarpaulin, and to the unsuspecting eye it looked like nothing more than a square box. But the reality was far more deadly.

Danny turned to his brother, making no attempt to hide the smile on his face. 'You should feel my cock right now. I've got such a hard-on.'

Michael looked at him in disgust. 'If you don't shut up I'll punch *you* in the cock. Freak. Now help me with these.' Michael hurried over to a storage unit against the garage wall. Resting atop it were three sub-machine guns – Mini-Uzis, to be precise. Their preferred weapon of choice for proceedings: compact, comfortable, capable of firing rounds at a rate of 950 a minute. The perfect machine for the job.

As Danny was about to pick one up, Luke, the youngest and smallest of the brothers, stepped in from the other side of the garage. The three of them were suspended in a moment of darkness after he'd shut the door, while their eyes were left to adjust to the weak beam of light hanging overhead. Luke walked with one arm in the oversuit and the other rummaging around the waistband, rearranging himself.

'Don't know what's going on with me this morning, but that's the third time I've been.'

'Told you you shouldn't have had that curry last night,' Danny replied.

'You're the one who broke the tradition.' Luke stopped in front of his brothers. He may have been the smallest and scrawniest of the three, but what he lacked in size and strength, he more than made up for in speed – the way his little legs spun, it was like watching a real-life version of Road Runner.

Danny threw his hands in the air, looking between his brothers. 'Seriously, since when did you both become superstitious?'

Neither of them chose to answer. Instead they offered him an admonishing glance and then turned their attention back to the guns. Danny picked one up and bounced it in his hands, gauging the weapon's weight. It felt lean. He opened the cartridge, checked that the magazine clips were full and then shut it with a satisfying *tsck* that sent a wave of euphoria rolling over his body.

Less than an hour to go. Less than an hour until he got to use them. And the irony was the Mini-Uzis weren't even the deadliest thing they were taking with them.

CHAPTER 4

INITIATIONS

The lift doors opened and revealed Jake's new home for the foreseeable future. Jake Tanner, Major Crime Team, Surrey Police. He liked the sound of that – there was a certain ring to it.

The beating heart of the building stretched sixty feet wide and nearly eighty deep and bustled with life. To his right was a series of offices. Closed-off. Private. Beyond that, in the far-right corner, was an even larger office space. Jake recognised it as the Major Incident Room, the hub of any large-scale investigation, and through the floor-to-ceiling windows, he saw a wooden table in the centre, making the room look like a horseshoe. Surrounding the table was a series of corkboards hanging from the walls, a television and portable whiteboards on wheels in what was left of the available space. The other side of the office housed the rest of the Major Crime Team.

Jake counted another twenty bodies in the department, busy tapping their keyboards and mice, hunched behind their computer screens. A lot of new names and a lot of new faces to remember. He soaked in the atmosphere. There was a liveliness to it, a raw energy that enthused him.

'Welcome to Major Crime,' Pemberton said, casting her gaze out at her well-oiled machine. 'I'll introduce you to the important people first, and then I'll let you get settled in.' She lifted her wrist and checked her watch. 'If we've got time before the mid-morning briefing, we'll see about taking you into town to get a flavour of the place and maybe a coffee.'

Jake thanked her with a smile and a nod. Just what he needed – more laxative.

Before Pemberton conducted the tour, a door behind them opened and a man exited, brushing past her. He was tall and well dressed, wearing an expensive designer suit judging from the texture of the material. Possibly Boss, Gant, something Jake couldn't dream of owning, let alone afford. A thin line of hair that looked like it was an early attempt at Movember sat above his top lip, and his Adam's apple was the size of a golf ball. The man looked no older than early forties, yet there was something about him that immediately startled Jake; he just didn't want to admit what it was.

'Elliot.' Pemberton flagged him down with a wave of her arm. 'Glad to see you finally arrived this morning.'

'Sorry, guv,' Elliot said, standing with his hands in his pockets, tilting backward slightly, crotch thrust forward. 'Parking was a nightmare. Some Mini Austin Cooper parked in my spot.'

The knot in Jake's stomach tightened. He cleared his throat. 'That'd be mine,' he said sheepishly.

Elliot turned to face Jake, scowling down at him. And then his expression flipped on its head and he burst into a laugh. 'It's all right, mate.' He slapped a firm hand on Jake's shoulder and kept it there. 'Can't argue with someone who's got a wicked car like that. Always wanted one myself. You're only supposed to blow the bloody doors off!'

If Jake had a pound for every time he'd heard that, he'd probably still be nowhere near as rich as Michael Caine. He chuckled awkwardly and stood still, allowing Elliot's hand to remain in place.

'Elliot,' Pemberton began thankfully, 'this is Temporary DC Jake Tanner. He's joining us from Croydon on a probationary period for now. But from what I'm hearing, he'll be with us for a long time.'

Jake's cheeks flushed at the praise.

'Fresh meat, eh?' Elliot removed his hand from Jake's shoulder and extended it for him to take. He did. 'Bet you're glad to be getting away from the city, eh? Welcome to the best team in the country – and don't let anyone tell you otherwise. If you need anything, you can come to me. Oh, and don't call me Elliot – only the guv can get away with it. Everyone else just calls me Bridger.'

Jake immediately felt a sense of calm around Bridger, like the man had the ability to wrap his arms around him with the same strength as his handshake and lead him along the right path, put him at ease.

'I'm excited to get started,' Jake said, this time believing it.

Pemberton swivelled on the balls of her feet and addressed Jake. 'Elliot's one of our best detective sergeants and will be your immediate senior. Anything you need, he'll be able to help with.' She turned back to Bridger, and said, 'Get yourself settled. I'm going to show Jake around and then we can take him and Danika out for a coffee.'

Jake's ears perked up. 'Danika's here already?' He craned his neck in search of his former colleague and Croydonite, the one friendly face in the office he could depend upon. 'I thought she was due tomorrow?'

'Apparently not. We're happy to have her though. We could do with the help right now.'

Pemberton ended the conversation with a smile and started leading Jake through the office, firstly showing him where everything was – the toilets, the kitchen and the supplies room – and then to his desk, which was situated in the far-left corner of the office, beside the communal printer and photocopier.

'Danika's sitting next to you, but I don't know where she's gone right now,' Pemberton added.

With the brief tour concluded, it was time for Jake to meet the rest of team. First on the list was DI Mark Murphy, a man who looked as though an entire tub of hair gel – or perhaps it was superglue – had been rubbed onto his head to keep the short quiff he'd given himself in place. Also attached to his head were a pair of headphones. As Jake and Pemberton approached him, he finished what he was doing and slid the headphones down to his neck.

Pemberton introduced them to one another.

'So this is the whiz-kid?' Murphy asked, leaning back into his chair and bouncing on the support, testing its durability.

'Nothing like that,' Jake remarked. His eyes leapt between Murphy and Pemberton.

'Anybody told him about the initiation yet, guv?'

Pemberton seemed to ignore the question, but Murphy continued anyway. 'It's customary for the newcomers to make everyone in the office a drink on their first day.'

Jake was no stranger to initiations. The word alone was enough to trigger his gag reflex. He recalled signing up to a bunch of different clubs and societies at university, and each had contained an initiation process featuring one thing: booze. And a lot of it. In a bizarre way, he felt more prepared for that than anything else. And he was in no position to decline it either.

Fifteen minutes later, Jake found himself in the kitchen, ten mugs in front of him, the kettle boiling beside him. Four black, six white, two with sugar, the rest without. Perhaps in another life he could have been a barista.

The tour had finished after he and Pemberton had spoken to DI Mark Murphy, and Pemberton had allowed him some time to wander around the office and introduce himself to the rest of the team. It was comforting to know that the most important people within the team were Murphy and Bridger. It was familiar and reminded him of his time in Croydon, where the only people he'd needed to impress were the Detective Chief Inspector and Detective Inspector.

As he waited for the kettle to finish its boil, Jake repeated the names of his new colleagues in his head. He was almost certain that one of them would escape his memory, but he would never forget their faces. Names, he wasn't so good at; faces, on the other hand, he was usually excellent with. Not only was it helpful for catching criminals, it was handy when he recognised someone he'd known from secondary school in the supermarket, so that he could find ways to avoid them at every possible aisle.

He finished repeating the names for the third time when the door to the kitchen opened. Bridger was standing in the frame, frozen, the handle swallowed in his hand, as if caught in an uncompromising position.

'What's happening in here?'

Jake glanced down at the mugs of coffee and then back to Bridger.

'Oh, you haven't, have you?' Bridger stepped into the kitchen and placed a hand on Jake's back. 'I was wondering if you'd fall for it or not?'

'Fall for what?' Jake asked, realising there was something he should know but obviously didn't.

'Mark… he does this to everyone so he can see how you react.' Bridger leant across Jake and killed the kettle. 'These people are adults; they can make their own drinks. Anyone tells you otherwise, you can send them my way.'

Jake smiled and laughed, but it wasn't enough to hide the humiliation he felt.

'Don't worry about it,' Bridger continued. 'Because I want you to grab your things – the guv and I are taking you and Danika into town, show you what Guildford's all about.'

Bridger removed his hand from Jake's back and left the room. Jake didn't mind Bridger's physicality; it reminded him of the way his dad used to console him, congratulate him, hug him. And it had been such a long time since he'd last felt that, he almost didn't want it to stop.

After Bridger had left, Jake grabbed the mugs from the counter, returned them to their respective owners and headed over to his desk to retrieve his things. The Holy Trinity: phone, wallet, keys. Without it, he felt naked.

'About time you got here, no?' a voice asked behind him as he logged in to the computer, testing the details that had been left on a Post-It note beside his keyboard.

Jake looked away from the monitor and saw Danika, his closest friend from the Met during his brief spell in Croydon. They'd worked the same streets together, and now they were working in the same office together, compounded by their mutual desire to progress through the plainclothes ranks. She was dressed in a white shirt that was tight against her chest, and a black blazer that hugged her shoulders and arms. It matched the colour of her hair, which, for the first time since Jake had known her, was tied in a ponytail, leaving two thick strands of hair framing her face.

'I was beginning to think you'd got cold feet,' she said. Her voice was thinly laced with a Slovenian accent that had assimilated over the years since she'd moved to the UK.

'Traffic was a nightmare,' he lied but then realised she'd see right through it.

If she did though, she gave no indication. Instead, she set a piece of paper on her desk and stood with her hands on her hips.

'Busy morning?' he asked before giving her a chance to say anything.

'Like you wouldn't believe. Who knew there was this much admin in being seconded?'

Jake flashed a grin, as if he knew what she was talking about. If there was a leader board of first day impressions, he was sure she was making a better one than him. Purely for the fact that she was over a day early for her first shift.

He had some climbing to do.

CHAPTER 5

DRAWING BLANKS

The still summer air, thick with endorphins and memories of holidays and happier times, swathed the streets of Guildford. Residents dressed in floral dresses, tank tops, shorts, and those brave enough to break the social boundaries of going topless – mostly the men – wandered up the cobbled high street. A wave of heat slapped Jake in the face as soon as he stepped out of Pemberton's car. She had driven himself, Bridger and Danika into the centre of town for a morning drink at a local cafe. According to Bridger, it was the team's regular haunt, and they each took it in turns to get a round in, like it was a daytime version of a trip to the pub. Jake was pleased to learn it wasn't his turn to buy a round – that gauntlet would be passed to him in a couple of weeks, soon after he'd settled in.

The cafe was called The Coffee Company and was situated down Angel Street, a small avenue barely wide enough for two people, let alone four. Entrance into Angel Street was through an archway, and the entire stretch of cobbled stones was sandwiched between two tall buildings that shaded it completely, long strips of wood climbing the walls like it was part of a K'nex structure. Jake was grateful for the protection from the blistering elements. It was only 8:40 a.m. and his back was already as wet as it was when he first stepped out of the shower.

'What're you having?' Pemberton asked as they made their way to the counter.

'Latte,' Jake said. And then remembered to add 'please' on at the end.

The rest of them ordered, and within a few minutes, the drinks were made. Jake took his from Pemberton and, following Bridger's orders, found a seat outside. A gentle breeze rustled through the alley, brushing against Jake's hand and face, and he shivered slightly as his sweat cooled. Danika, Pemberton and Bridger joined a few seconds later.

'Thanks for this,' Jake said, feeling obliged. 'You didn't have to.'

'Oh, please,' Pemberton said. 'It's no bother at all. I just hope you're prepared to jump into the deep end.'

Jake took a sip. The liquid scalded his lip and tongue, but he covered it well with a lick of his lips. It was like he was drinking from the sun.

Bridger cleared his throat, announcing he wanted to speak. 'So what sort of experience have you two got?'

Jake and Danika glanced at one another. She was in the middle of drinking, so he opted to respond. 'A couple of years on the beat, and about six months working in CID at Croydon.'

'You'll fit right in,' Bridger replied.

'That's what I said,' Pemberton added as she wiped the sides of her mouth clean.

Jake relaxed a little. The more he spent time with them, the more he realised he had less to worry about. Everything was going to be fine. Beside him, Bridger removed the safety sleeve from the cup and ripped small slits into the top of it before setting it down on the table. Jake observed him, oblivious to the conversation going on around him – that was exactly what his dad used to do.

'Thanks for sorting that out so quickly, Danika,' someone said as he gradually came to, joining them at the end of the conversation.

Danika blushed slightly and shook her head. 'That's no problem at all. Honestly, I was happy to do it.'

Jake didn't know what they were talking about, but whatever it was, it sounded like the gap between them on the leader board had distanced even further.

A few minutes later, after Danika and Pemberton had both finished their drink, Bridger checked his watch and suggested they leave. Noticing they were wearing the same timepiece – a G-Shock – Jake downed the last of his coffee, grimaced as the bitter taste blasted his tastebuds and placed the disposable cup in the bin.

The four of them left the privacy of the alleyway and burst into the sun. As they wandered down the street, Jake minding his ankles on the cobbles, he observed those around him. The retail workers rushing to get to work on time; the Royal Mail postman lugging his bag of letters and parcels over his shoulder; the labourers getting their things together for their latest project. And then there was them: four individuals dressed smartly. For all anyone else knew, they could be anyone and anything. In the short space of time he'd been training as a detective constable, Jake had learnt he adored the anonymity of wearing the suit. It covered him in the guise of being someone completely different and came with the added bonus of allowing him to get closer to unsuspecting criminals.

They reached the bottom of the high street where the cobbled road ended and the tarmacked part of the street bent round the corner. In front of him, connecting the tarmac and the cobbles, was a wooden gate. As Jake rounded the gate, heading back to Pemberton's car, he completely misjudged the black van heading directly towards him. It slammed on its brakes, the nose of the vehicle bowing under the momentum. Only aware of it at the last minute, Jake panicked and skipped out of the way, his heart racing. He raised an apologetic hand in the air, aware that he was in the wrong, but as he started to turn away from the van, something caught his eye. Through the glare of the sun and the reflection of the sky on the windscreen, he thought he recognised the driver and passenger. They looked oddly familiar, as if perhaps he'd already seen them around town in the ten minutes he'd been there.

Before he could dedicate any more thought to it, the van slipped into first and climbed the steady incline up the high street.

Jake hurried over to Pemberton's car. As he climbed into the back seat, he closed his eyes and attempted to recall the snapshot he'd taken of the driver and passenger.

For the first time in his life, he drew a blank.

CHAPTER 6

BRIDGEWATER JEWELLER'S

Fucking idiot, stepping out like that. Did the man have a death wish? Luke's hands tightened around the back of Michael and Danny's synthetic plastic seats as Danny eased his foot on the accelerator and slowly started the steady incline up Guildford High Street. The black Ford Transit rocked and swayed and jolted, knocking Luke off balance.

'Thought we weren't supposed to be drawing attention to ourselves?' he said.

'I can't help it when people step in front of me like that. Natural selection,' Danny replied.

Luke noticed in the rearview mirror a menace behind his brother's eyes, and he knew exactly what he meant by 'people like that'. The middle class, the upper class, the wealthy and arrogant suit-wearing city boy who snorted all his money up his nose on the weekdays and shared what little he had left of it with his wife and kids on the weekend. The modern-day family man.

Luke, Michael and Danny detested everything about them.

They were less than thirty seconds away, and a seed of emotion had crept into Luke's mind. This time, however, he was sure it wasn't the excitement or adrenaline that usually accompanied him on their heists. It was different. Emotions that he'd never felt before. The adrenaline of a job usually ravaged his body, made him shake, made him smile, made him feel alive. But this time he was filled with worry, regret and a terrible premonition that something was going to go wrong.

And, right behind him, was the reason for it.

The device. It was diabolical. Evil. Vicious. Luke hadn't even been aware that sort of sinister equipment existed. But it did, thanks to Michael's research and Danny's handiwork.

'You sure this is going to work, Dan?'

Danny veered the car to the left and then came to a stop. They were here. 'Wouldn't be doing it if I wasn't, Lukey. Not flaking out on us now, are ya?'

Too late now, even if he was.

Luke glanced out of the windscreen then checked the dash – 9:03 a.m. A few minutes behind schedule. By now, all the shops had opened, and small masses of keen shoppers had started to form outside the big chains like Jack Wills, Gant and Topshop. While dog walkers returned home from their early morning stint in the local field or woods.

On their left was Bridgewater Jewellers. Their next hit. Independently owned. Hand-crafted jewellery. Made with emotion and love. All that crap.

'All right, lads,' Danny said, sliding the handbrake in place, 'this is it.'

Game time.

Michael leant forward into the footwell, reached inside a gym bag by his feet and produced three masks. Their trademark. The masks were made from latex and depicted the face of the devil. Two large white horns protruded from the top corners of their heads, and a black snake climbed between a set of fangs, exited the mouth and made its way up the cheek, the tongue licking the eyelashes beneath the slits in the mask.

Michael passed them round, and they each took one. Danny donned his then pulled his hood over his head, Michael tucked away what little of his fringe remained, and Luke pulled his full head of hair from his face, snapped the elastic band against the back of his skull and zipped his coat to his neck. They each wore crimson-coloured overalls, covering them from head to toe.

Simultaneously, Michael and Danny jumped out of the car and ran to the rear. A second later, the double doors opened, flooding light into the small space. Through the slits in the mask, Luke blinked away the brightness and restored his vision to normality. By his leg, lying on the floor, was a row of three Mini-Uzis, clamped down by cable ties to keep them in place. Beside them, a Stanley knife. Luke grabbed the knife, severed the ties, and handed them a weapon each. He then loaded the magazine into his clip, aimed down the sights for good measure and hopped out of the van. Shutting the doors behind him, he left the device in the back, ready and waiting to be used for the next part of their operation.

Bridgewater was open, as they'd expected. Danny strolled through, keeping his arm down by his side. Michael followed immediately after, then Luke. Neither of them protested that he'd disrupted the usual working order of things where Michael, with his sheer size, would enter first and intimidate everyone in the vicinity. This was Danny's heist – he was in charge – and if he was going to break the mould, then so be it.

The inside of the jeweller's was empty save for two cashiers behind their desks and another who sat in a half-opened booth in discussion with a client.

'Hands in the air!' Danny shouted, raising the gun. 'Now!'

'Move!' Luke screamed. 'Get down on the ground now!'

Danny made a beeline for the two workers standing behind the cash desk on the left-hand side of the room, while Luke rushed to the booth on the opposite side, pointing the gun at a brown-haired woman and a balding man. Luke's breathing raced and the sound of his heart pounded in his ears, drowning out the screams and shouts surrounding him. All thoughts of fear and guilt had quickly dissipated, as though they had never been there in the first place, and were now replaced with pure, animalistic adrenaline.

'Don't even think about it,' Danny said.

Luke snapped his head towards Danny; one of the employees had her finger hovering over a panic button on the underside of the desk. If Danny's reactions had been a fraction slower, she would have pressed it and within seconds, their worst fears of being caught would have come true.

'Put your hands in the air now!' Danny screamed. 'Or I'll blow your fucking face off.'

The woman stared at him defiantly. She was blonde, portly and had a look on her face that Luke knew meant she had an attitude. Luke glanced at the badge on her left breast. Her name was Candice.

In the background, Michael was making his way around the shop, pilfering the contents from the cash register and window displays. Shards of glass splintered into a thousand pieces and rained down on the soft carpet, scattering across the floor. Michael lifted his gym bag to the edge of the cabinet and, with a sweeping motion, slid his bounty into the bag, scattering some to the floor. Watches. Rings. Earrings. Diamonds. Necklaces. Charms. They had everything.

Luke's gaze danced between his hostages and Danny. Danny still held the gun inches from Candice's face, but his brother's arms were shaking. Something wasn't right. Something was happening that hadn't been part of the plan.

'Hey…' Luke said, snapping his head back to the woman and man in front of him. He switched the gun between them both, left and right like a tennis match.

'There's no need to panic, people,' Danny said, keeping his eyes on Candice. 'This will only take a short while, and all you need to do is stand still and put your *fucking* hands in the air.'

Out the corner of his eye, Luke noticed Candice gradually raise her hands and he breathed a sigh of relief. In all their years, in all their heists, they had never fired a shot on a single person. It was a part of their mantra. Though, for a brief moment, Luke thought that had all been about to change.

'There was nothing difficult about that, was there?' Danny said through gritted teeth.

Candice spat at him, globules of phlegm landing on his overalls and on the cheek of his mask.

Before anyone could react, Michael shouted, 'We've got everything, now let's go.'

Nobody said anything. Nobody moved.

Luke's heart pounded in his chest. By now, his attention was entirely focused on the dynamic between Candice and Danny. He lowered the gun without realising it and grabbed Danny by the shoulder. 'Come on! We've got everything. Let's get the fuck out of here!'

Danny remained still. The gun had stopped shaking in his grip. 'She's coming with us,' he said calmly.

'No! You can't!' came the cry from the staff member standing beside Candice. She lowered her hands and reached out for the gun, protecting Candice's face. 'Please, don't—'

Before she finished, Danny spun on the spot, pointed the gun at the employee's head and pulled the trigger. The deafening sound split Luke's head in two. His body jolted and he blinked, stepping backward as the bullet tore through the woman's neck and buried itself in the wall at the back of the room. Blood sprayed against the shattered glass and metal stands, sparkling in the fluorescent light overhead. Screams emanated from the booth in the corner of the room, and both the man and woman cowered underneath the table. But Candice did nothing. She remained perfectly still, her face freckled with flecks of the woman's blood.

Danny groaned, lowered the weapon, grabbed her arm and yanked her towards Luke and Michael. Michael hooked her other arm, and the four of them hurried out of there. As they exited, Candice wriggled and writhed against their grip, but she was no match for them all, so she kicked and screamed, letting her body fall to the ground as if she were a deadweight. Michael stopped, handed Luke his weapon and shoved him away from her. Then he bent down, picked her up and hefted her over his shoulder in a fireman's carry.

Luke raced to the back of the van, his pulse racing, swung open the doors and held the nearest one open with Danny. Michael bounded over – ignoring the punches that Candice threw into his face as she struggled to break free – bent his legs and launched her into the back of the vehicle, throwing her into the chasm of uncertainty and despair.

As they were about to close the doors, in the street, a middle-aged man with thinning brown hair advanced towards them.

'Hey! What are you doing?' he yelled, holding a phone to his ear in one hand and a coffee in the other. 'I'm calling the police!'

Not another Good Samaritan, Luke thought, and as the man approached them, Danny smacked him in the stomach with the butt of his gun. The man doubled over, dropped the phone and staggered forward; Danny grabbed him by the shirt and launched him into the back of the van to accompany Candice. In the background, a high-pitched scream pierced the air.

'Roger!' somebody called.

Panting, breathless, Danny threw the door shut.

Luke stared at him, his eyes wild behind the mask.

'What are you—?' Luke began.

'Shut up and get in!'

Luke did as instructed. He climbed into the back of the van with Candice and the Good Samaritan, and pressed his back against the van's doors, pointing his gun at them both. Less than two seconds later, Danny hopped into the front, started the engine and pulled away just as the sound of sirens filled the high street. The tyres screeched on the cobbles and the van shot off.

They had just robbed hundreds of thousands of pounds' worth of jewels and diamonds.

They had just kidnapped the woman they needed for the next part of their job.

But there was a problem: they had another hostage with them.

And they were going to have to deal with him one way or another.

CHAPTER 7

TIME TO GO

The journey back to Mount Browne took only seven minutes, traffic permitting. By the time Jake and his lift arrived at HQ, his stomach was growling at him, the weight on his abdomen felt as though it was made of lead and the layer of sweat on his body had doubled. Not to mention his arse had never been so clenched.

Pemberton was the first to enter the Incident Room, followed by Bridger and then himself and Danika. The natural pecking order of things.

As they entered, they were greeted with a flurry of activity. Constables and sergeants hurried from one place to the next, some holding phones to their ears, others carrying folders under their arms as they centred around the Horseshoe at the back of the office. At the head of it all, orchestrating them into action, was DI Mark Murphy.

Pemberton called him over.

'What's going on?' She gestured at the office space, suggesting to Jake this was an unusual circumstance.

'There's an armed robbery in progress on Guildford High Street, guv,' Murphy said, his eyes focusing on Bridger and Pemberton. 'Bridgewater Jewellers. Reports of gunfire and a potential murder. First responders are already on the scene with paramedics. Scenes of crime officers are pulling in as we speak.'

Jake wasn't sure whether his internal reaction made its way onto his face, but he was stunned. He'd just been on the high street – they all had. A series of what ifs raced through his mind. What if they'd left later? What if Jake had asked to stay to finish his coffee? And then an image slapped him across the face. The van. The driver. The passenger. Had there been another one in the back too?

Jake stepped back slightly and allowed his mind to work while Pemberton and Bridger started organising the team into their necessary actions. He recalled the image in his memory again, this time willing it to focus more clearly. The van. The driver. What he'd been wearing. Was it red? Or orange? Or was he imagining it all, hoping that it *was* red? The face. He remembered that face now.

No, he told himself. *Stop it. It couldn't be.*

The next thing he felt was a hand on his shoulder. It was Danika. She looked at him, concerned.

'Are you OK?' she asked, lowering her arm.

Jake shook himself back to reality, cast his gaze around the room. 'I'm fine,' he told her. 'I just can't believe it, that's all.'

'What a start to our first day, eh!' Danika said with notable excitement in her voice.

The feeling in his stomach had subsided and the ravages of adrenaline were finally beginning to take hold of him. Bridger hurried over to them with an elderly officer – Jake remembered his name was Carl – in tow.

'Grab your things, you two,' Bridger said. 'It's time to go.'

CHAPTER 8

PROMISES

Bridger and Carl had ventured down to the bottom of the high street in their own cars while Jake was riding shotgun in Danika's Ford Escort. They arrived thirty seconds later at the road that bent round the bottom of the high street. An outer cordon had been set up a few feet short of the gate where, only minutes ago, Jake had nearly been knocked down by a one-ton vehicle. Sitting in front of the cordon were four police cars and two ambulances positioned awkwardly at different angles on the road. In front of the white and blue police tape stood a uniformed officer, his hands folded in front of him, his police cap pulled low over his eyes, his high-visibility jacket reflecting the early morning sun beating down on him.

After exiting Danika's car, Jake shuffled to the boot. Inside she had two forensic scene suits consisting of mask, hood, gloves and overshoes. Jake hated wearing them – they always rubbed and chafed his hands and neck – but he also knew their importance at the vital early stages of an investigation. Once they were all suited and booted, they made their way towards the uniformed officer where they flashed their warrant cards, signed in on the attendance log and ducked beneath the tape.

Jake paused a moment to look up and down the high street, to absorb his surroundings. Rows of shops and other businesses ran up the length of it on either side. Overhead was a string of bunting advertising a farmers' market due to take place in a few days' time. And, just beneath it on the left-hand side, was the Guildford Clock, one of the few landmarks that Jake had researched after a quick online search in preparation for his stint here. At either end of the high street, a small army of uniformed police officers and police community support officers were in the middle of herding the streets' employees – replete in their multicoloured uniforms – and shoppers out of the shops and on the right side of the cordon. Human curiosity prevailed however, and the sound of gossip and buzz and excitable conversation permeated the air like a dense fog.

Bridgewater Jewellers was situated halfway up the street, a few shops away from another small alleyway that led to North Street, the main road that ran parallel and dissected Guildford. The company's logo was emblazoned on the front of the store, in golden serif font that melted into the cream paint surrounding it. The main fascia of the jeweller's consisted of a series of window displays that had once been home to hundreds of pieces of luxury, waiting to create as many romantic moments as possible, but had now been decimated.

As the four of them arrived outside the jeweller's, Bridger turned to face them and said, 'SOCO have confirmed it's OK for us to have a look. But we've got to be brief.'

Entering the store, treading lightly across the stepping plates that the scenes of crime officers had placed on the ground, glass crunched underfoot, and the sound sent shivers up Jake's spine which branched out to the rest of his body like the splintered window displays around him. Three more scenes of crime officers were huddled together in the centre of the shop, hovering over a body, snapping photographs of the gunshot wound to her neck. One of them moved closer to Jake and set an evidence marker down by the shell casing in front of him. Jake averted his gaze from the body and chose to observe his surroundings instead. Until this moment, it had seemed like a normal armed robbery: guns, jewels, a getaway vehicle. But now there was another dynamic to it that Jake hadn't expected.

The shop was no larger than his living room at home. On the left was a desk. Resting atop it a computer, a cash register and a telephone. Behind that, a cabinet. And, on the right-hand side, a small booth with a desk in between the seats. Spread across the back wall was blood, dripping, forming streaks down the faces of the cabinets – reminding Jake of a scene from *Carrie*. A few sparkling rings and bracelets and necklaces that had been dropped and abandoned on the floor shimmered as Jake and the rest of his party distorted the ambient and artificial light above, although it was difficult to discern high-end jewellery from the mess of shards on the floor.

'Doesn't look like they were being too careful,' Bridger remarked, looking at the debris on the floor. 'Looks like they've thrown half of it about the place.'

A voice came from behind them, startling Jake. He spun on the spot and searched for the owner. On the other side of the door, standing on the pavement, was a uniformed officer. The four of them headed for the exit, shuffling past the investigators in the doorway, and moved over to the officer.

'Good morning,' he said, introducing himself. His voice was gruff and raspy, like it was carrying the weight of a thousand cigarettes behind it. 'I'm PS Byrd. Some of my team were the first responders.'

'Excellent,' Bridger said, brushing past Jake to get closer to Byrd. 'What have you got for us, Sergeant?'

'Armed robbery. Witnesses report a group of armed robbers stormed the building just after nine, looted the contents and opened fire on one of the employees. The witnesses' clothes have been taken for further examination. Paramedics announced extinction of life as soon as they were on the scene. SOCO are securing the body and preserving as much evidence surrounding the body, as you can see. And the witnesses are currently being seen to by a paramedic. Reports suggest the robbers evacuated the scene in a black van and their exit route was at the top of the high street.'

'Very concise, Sergeant,' Bridger replied. 'Have you got scene logs for both of the cordons?'

Byrd nodded.

'House-to-house enquiries conducted and collated from the shops on the high street?'

Another nod. 'Conducting those as we speak, sir.'

'What about first accounts – have you obtained those yet?'

This time Byrd shook his head. He'd made it two for three, and from the discouraged look on his face, Jake assumed the officer had been hoping he'd be able to make it a full house by the time the plainclothes officers arrived.

'Where are they?' Carl asked, his deep, monotonous voice booming from a set of big lungs.

Byrd stepped to the side and gestured at a man and woman sitting on the back of an ambulance at the bottom of the high street.

'Thank you, Officer. We'll take it from here.' Bridger turned his attention to Jake and Danika after Byrd had wandered back up the high street. 'I want you two to go with Carl. Speak to the key witnesses and take their first accounts. Nothing like learning on the job.'

Jake replied with a nod. So far he was happy to sit back, watch and learn, step in only where absolutely necessary. He hadn't earned the respect nor the right to tread on anyone's toes just yet. Even though he and Carl were the same rank, it was evident from Carl's age that he'd experienced more than himself, Danika and Bridger combined.

The key witnesses were dressed in matching tracksuit bottoms and jumpers, their faces ashen, their arms folded across their chest. The woman shuddered, and she rubbed her arms as if she were cold despite the oppressive heat radiating from the sun.

Carl was first to approach them. He held his warrant card in his hands. 'My name is DC Jenkins, and these are my colleagues. We're here to help you and make sure that you're OK and safe. I know this is a very stressful time for you both, but I'm going to need you to tell me what happened here.'

For a long while neither of them said anything.

'Anything you can remember now will be greatly appreciated.'

'It all happened so fast…' the woman replied slowly, keeping her head low. Two black snakes ran down her cheeks, and red rivers warmed her eyes. 'We… We opened at nine. Just like every morning. This gentleman wanted to buy a ring, so I offered to help him. Just as we sat down, a black van pulled up outside. Three men came in with guns. They screamed at us. Told us to put our hands up. And that… if we didn't, then they would…' She paused; there was a catch in her throat, and she coughed, clearing it. 'They shot Rachel. They took everything. All the money. All the watches, rings… everything. And then… And then…'

'Go on…' Carl urged gently.

'They took our manager. Candice Strachan. They drove off with her in the back of the van.' A tear slid down her face, and she wiped her cheek with the back of her hand.

'Took her?' Danika repeated, stepping into the conversation. 'What do you mean?'

'They kidnapped her. They put her in the back of the van and then drove off.'

'Did you see which way they went?' Danika asked again. She seemed to be getting a feel for it now. What surprised Jake was that Carl didn't object to her intrusion.

Both witnesses shook their head.

'How many of them were there?'

'Three,' the witnesses replied simultaneously.

Shit.

'What were they wearing?'

'They were dressed in these big red overalls. Like prison outfits.'

Double shit.

'Did you get a clear look at their faces?' Danika continued with the onslaught of questions. 'Any defining features? Characteristics?'

The woman replied with another shake of the head. 'Sorry, I wish I could be more helpful.'

Danika took a step forward and placed a comforting hand on her shoulder. Woman to woman. 'There's no need to apologise,' she said.

Carl stepped to the side and moved in front of the witnesses' vision, taking control of the situation. 'What can you tell us about Candice? Anything you know about her? Any friends? Family? Someone who might know where they could have taken her?'

The woman nodded. 'We have employee files. She made us have one as part of our personal development. They're inside the office.'

At once, Carl called a SOCO over and instructed them to go inside the office, retrieve the folder and submit it as evidence as soon as possible.

'There's a lot of weird information in there,' the woman continued. 'But she never really mentioned anything about any friends to us.'

'Family?' Carl asked.

'I think she had some a long time ago. She didn't like talking about them that much. She spent most of the time telling stories about her past, business strategies and that sort of stuff. I think she said she was writing a book on it.'

'Have you got an address?'

'Yes. Manor's Keep. It's in Farnham. I pick her up on my way to work every morning.'

Jake pulled out his pocketbook and scribbled the address down.

'Thanks,' Carl replied, reaching into his pocket. 'Listen.' He produced a contact card which had his mobile number and email address on it. 'You've been incredibly helpful. Really, you have. These are my details. Please call me if you need anything. Or if you think of anything else. Soon I'll be getting some members of my team to come and bring you into the station for a full witness statement. They're going to make sure you're well looked after. And you'll have your parents or other family members notified about what's happened. Does that sound OK?'

Both witnesses nodded.

With that, Carl turned his back on them and, as he brushed past Jake, told him to collect their personal details. Jake nodded and smiled ebulliently, but it felt like it was the shitty job he didn't want to do himself or palm off on Danika.

'Head back to the station once you're done,' Carl finished before heading up the street to find Bridger.

Instead of staying with him, like he'd expected, Danika wandered off with Carl, leaving him to do it alone, as if he was the runt of the litter.

Jake feigned a smile as he noted down the man and woman's contact details, addresses and next of kin.

'Thank you, both,' he said before heading towards the car.

'Detective…'

Jake stopped and spun on the spot.

'You'll find her, won't you?' Fresh tears filled the employee's eyes, and another lump caught in her throat. The man beside her placed his arm around her in a feeble attempt to comfort her. 'You'll find her, won't you?'

Jake swallowed before responding. 'Yes, we'll find her. We'll do everything we can.'

CHAPTER 9

THE DEVICE

Danny killed the engine.

'Nobody move,' he told them.

He slid himself out of the driver's seat, rounded the van and opened the back doors. The light poured in, forcing Candice and the Good Samaritan to shield their eyes with their arms. He leant in, reached for Candice, hooked his hand in the nook of her armpit and pulled her out of the van. As Danny hefted her to her feet, she stopped squirming, and he gazed out upon the mansion in front of them. They were outside Candice's house; for the next phase in their operation, they had forced her to give them directions. They had driven down winding, narrow country lanes, past large fields of green, and through a security gate to get there. The mansion before him was magnificent. Georgian. Elizabethan. Victorian. He didn't care. It was from one of those periods, and it was one of the most elegant properties he'd seen. Almost as large as the estate that he and his brothers had grown up on.

'Looks like we hit the jackpot here, lads,' Danny said, pulling Candice forward until she was in front of him, making them look as though they were new homeowners gazing out at their latest purchase.

Behind him, Luke shuffled out of the back of the van and grabbed the Good Samaritan by the collar. Luke groaned as he heaved the man out and up onto his feet.

'Please,' the man whimpered. 'Please, I… I don't want— You can't—'

Danny stopped and turned to face him, squinting behind the mask. Dressed in a pink Barbour polo shirt and cream shorts that painfully highlighted the fact he'd pissed himself during their journey, the man clasped his hands together and shook uncontrollably.

'What are we going to do about him?' Luke asked, pointing the gun at the babbling mess.

'I don't know,' Danny replied. 'Kill him.'

'No! Please! Please! No!' The man fell onto his knees and begged.

'You were the one who wanted to be the hero, mate. You've done this to yourself.'

'I didn't mean to. I'm sorry. Please don't hurt me.'

Michael rounded the back of the vehicle, sidestepped over the man and pulled out the device, wrapping it tightly in the tarpaulin. He clutched it in his arms and held it as though it were a cushion bearing wedding rings. Priceless. Delicate.

'Just carry on as planned, Dan. We'll leave him behind,' Michael added as he joined Luke's side.

'Names, you fucking idiot,' Danny snapped. 'What did I say about using names?'

Danny shut his mouth and exhaled deeply through his nose, feeling the tension in his body release. Sometimes he wondered whether he needed his brothers at all or whether he could do it alone. But there was still a long way to go – especially if he wanted to continue with the next phase of his plan, and so he reckoned he could keep them for now.

He turned his attention to the house, bathing in its grandeur.

'How'd someone like you afford a place like this?' he asked, only then realising that Candice was still locked in his grip.

'Husband,' she said. 'He was an art dealer. Somehow managed to sell art to Russians and other wealthy Eastern Europeans. Then he left it all to me in the will.'

Danny led Candice to the house where she let them inside using a spare key hidden behind a brick in the wall.

The interior of the mansion was just as luxurious and opulent as the outside. Marble floors. Grand staircases. Glistening chandeliers dangling from thirty-foot-high ceilings. Mahogany cabinets housing glasses and plates and cutlery. The majority of the interior was old-school, old-fashioned, collectible. Something, Danny felt, that was out of the Middle Ages. Nothing too high-tech. No seventy-inch plasmas, million-pound fish tanks, self-flushing toilets, pool tables, indoor swimming pools, or Lamborghinis or Ferraris hidden in an underground garage. Nothing that would be worth stealing and selling on afterward.

'What the fuck is all this? Can't take anything in here,' Michael said as he adjusted his grip on the device.

'Shut up,' Danny snapped. He stopped paying attention to the opulence of the house and the paintings that hung on the wall. There was a job to do, and time was running out. He didn't know how long they had left until the police arrived. And he wasn't going to start pissing about to find out. He pointed to a spot in the middle of the foyer.

'Sit down,' he told Candice.

'Why?'

'Because I told you to.'

'You're not going to hurt me, are you?'

'Not directly.'

'What's that supposed to mean?'

Danny turned to Michael, then gesticulated with his finger, beckoning him over. Michael removed the piece of plastic sheeting protecting the device. At the sight of what was beneath it, Candice's eyes widened, and her mouth fell open. The colour ran away from her cheeks, and she shuddered.

Perfect, Danny thought – it was the same reaction Luke and Michael had given when he'd introduced them to the idea of it.

'What… What is it?' Candice asked, lowering herself to the floor; beside her, Luke pushed the man to the ground. He fell and landed hard on his shoulder, letting out a monstrous groan as he coiled on the ground. Danny paid him little heed; he had no need for the man, but he wasn't in the mood to kill him and give him any more attention than he deserved. The Good Samaritan could wait with Candice.

Returning his attention to Michael, Danny took the device from his brother and felt the immediate strain in his bicep.

'This… is a spike collar.' He opened the mechanical lock and snapped it shut; it closed with a frightening *crack*.

'What does it do?'

'It fits round your neck. It should be a nice and snug fit. There's a countdown inside. And four locks. Each lock requires a key. The keys are scattered around the place – if you can find them and remove the device *before* the countdown finishes, you'll live. If not, the tiny charge inside this' – Danny knocked on the rectangular box of metal connected to the collar of the device – 'will spring ten spikes into your neck and kill you instantly.'

Candice's body tightened. His invention was having its desired effect. This was going to be his final moment of evil. The part that everyone would remember The Crimsons for. This callous, destructive device that would impart doom on the bearer. It was genius.

He was a genius.

'Please,' Candice said, her fingers clawing at the smooth surface of the marble flooring, searching for grip. 'No. There must be something else. Some other way. What do you want? Money? I have loads. Just take it. All of this stuff may look like a load of shit to you, but I promise you it holds its value. Take it now. Keep it. Sell it in a few years' time and you'll have hit the lottery. Please don't do this. I've got children. They depend on me.'

34

Danny smirked behind the mask.

'You don't get it, do you? It's too late. Soon, you'll be just as famous as us. You'll be the one people make documentaries about. Your face will be on the news. You'll be an icon – along with us. The final member of The Crimsons. Maybe they'll call you The Faceless Crimson because they won't even be able to identify you when that thing detonates. No one will know who we are, but they'll know you, and they'll know your name for all the wrong reasons.'

'B-But… do you not want them to know yours as well?'

'Did Jack the Ripper want people to know who he was? We want to be bigger than that. Bigger than him. We want to create a legacy. And you're going to play your part.'

Danny snapped his fingers, and Michael took the collar bomb from him and stuck the device around Candice's neck. She screamed and tried to wriggle away as Michael sealed the device shut, but her efforts were futile against the man who outweighed her two to one. Once the device was clamped around her neck, the corners of Danny's mouth rose.

'Don't panic. You'll have help soon – providing they can do their job properly and get here in time.'

Candice's chest heaved, the metal plate rising up and down against her breast.

'We'll make it easy for you,' Michael said, crouching down by her side. He reached inside his pocket, removed a piece of paper and handed it to Danny.

'The clue for the first key is written on here. The location for the others will be revealed as you discover the rest of them. Read the clues and decide for yourself whether it's worth the risk of going alone or waiting for the officers of the law to help you.'

Danny passed the letter to Candice, who inspected it for a beat. While she looked at the paper, Danny gave the signal to Luke, and at once his younger brother disappeared deeper into the mansion, climbing the steps behind Candice.

'How long?' Candice asked, raising her head.

'Till the boys in blue arrive?'

'No.'

'Until it detonates?'

Candice's expression remained impassive.

'You'll just have to wait and find out.'

Out the corner of his eye, Luke returned. At the sight of him, Danny rose to his feet, picked up the tarpaulin from the floor and ordered his brothers to leave the house. They had done it. Now all they needed to do was to get out of there without being seen or arrested, and then head south, where, in a matter of hours, they'd be free.

CHAPTER 10

INTUITION

Back at Mount Browne, Jake had been afforded a small opportunity to empty his bowels while the rest of the office continued with the investigation. It was in its infancy, and right now everyone was set on ascertaining as much information as possible. Who was behind the attack. Where they went. Who saw what. When Jake returned to his desk, his body and mind feeling clearer, he found Danika sitting at her desk, eyes glued to the computer screen. Apparently, in the time that he'd been gone, she'd been given a series of tasks to do.

'They were looking for you, but I didn't know where you were,' she said quickly before returning her attention to the computer screen.

How long was I in there?

'Who did you speak to?' he asked.

'Can't remember. Sorry.'

Either she was being an arsehole deliberately, or she genuinely had no idea. In this instance, he decided to give her the benefit the doubt.

'Maybe try Bridger,' she said. 'He seems to know what's going on.'

Yes. He would do that. But first, there was something on his mind. Something that sitting on the toilet had allowed him time to think about.

As Jake opened his mouth to speak, an officer brushed past him, rushed down the corridor and made a right turn into the kitchen. Returning his attention to Danika, he kept his voice low, and said, 'Can I talk to you about something?'

Danika sighed viciously. He wondered if that was the way she treated her children. 'Is it important? I'm busy.'

'I think it is.'

Danika dropped her pen and took her other hand off the mouse, giving him her undivided attention. Jake cleared his throat and stole a glance at the rest of the office before beginning. There was no one else within earshot.

'I was doing some thinking,' he said. 'This all sounds a bit too familiar to me. The van. The red overalls. The guns. Even the heist in the first place.'

Danika's face remained impassive, as though he were talking to a brick wall – it was clear she didn't appreciate him wasting her time like this.

'I don't think this was any old robbery. I think it might have been done by The Crimsons.'

Jake felt a slight weight lift from his shoulders. It was something he'd considered ever since he'd recognised the men in the van. Those faces. Those eyes. Ones that had given him many restless nights in the past.

Danika scoffed. 'Convenient.'

'Excuse me?'

She swivelled on her chair. 'First day here and look who chooses to rob a jewellery store at the same time.'

Jake stared at her in disbelief. He perched himself on her desk and leant closer, resting his left arm on top of her computer screen. As he neared her, he caught a vague whiff of her perfume. Jo Malone. One of Elizabeth's favourites. Back when they'd been students relying on loans as their only source of income, he'd bought a bottle for her birthday. Since then, the realities of adult life and their ever-struggling finances had prohibited them from treating themselves to such luxuries. It was something he hoped to change in the near future.

'You think I don't realise how strange it is? It's just too much of a coincidence.'

Danika shrugged, instantly dismissing him. She didn't give him the middle finger, but she might as well have. And he felt like giving her one too. Why didn't she believe him? The signs were there. The entire process was the same as their previous heists – he'd studied them fastidiously after what had happened last time, and he knew them inside out – better than they knew themselves. First, they started their raids at 9 a.m., when the jeweller's and banks had just opened and were less likely to be busy. Second, there were three of them, dressed in red overalls and wearing devil masks. Third, they were carrying firearms, and fourth, they'd been in and out within a few minutes. Textbook.

The only deviations from their norm had been the shooting of the employee and the abduction of the branch manager. Those aside, he was almost certain in his estimations.

Jake propelled himself from Danika's desk and moved towards

the kitchen. He'd just seen Bridger hurrying inside. The man was fetching a snack from one of the kitchen cupboards above the fridge.

'Jake,' Bridger said, sounding both happy to see him and stressed at the thought of what Jake was about to distract him from. 'Everything all right?'

'There's something I wanted to talk to you about,' he began.

'Can it be quick?'

Jake swallowed. Paused. Explained his theory.

Bridger set the packet of rice cakes on the counter and rested against it, moving his gaze away from Jake and focusing it on the sink on the other side of the kitchen. 'Why didn't you say anything earlier?' he asked.

'Because… because…'

Jake didn't know why. Perhaps it was because of everything else going on inside his head. The first day nerves. The little daughter he had currently in the doctor's surgery being tested for pneumonia. Maybe it was because he needed time to figure it out in his head, solidify the connections in his mind. Or perhaps it was because he was at risk of embarrassing himself by offering crazy suggestions. What did he know? He was just a temporary detective constable. In the grand scheme of things, he was still wearing nappies in comparison to some of the other minds in the office.

Bridger shimmied himself away from the counter and wandered up towards Jake. He placed a hand on his shoulder. That same feeling of being transported back to when he was fifteen again rolled over him.

'It's a good theory,' Bridger began, 'but nobody's seen them for years. I don't think it's a terrible idea, but right now that's not what we're focusing on. I'll raise it with DCI Pemberton, and we can put it on the back-burner, OK? Leave it with me.'

Nice try, son. Nice try. Good effort. But you can't win them all. His father's attempt at consoling him echoed through his head.

Jake felt slightly dazed as he sauntered back to his desk. Questioning himself was something he'd never had to tackle before, and it wasn't a pleasurable experience. It wasn't until he was at his desk that he realised the entire department had disappeared and was standing in the Horseshoe. *Last to know, last to be involved – again.* Even Danika was in there, climbing higher and higher. Soon, she'd be out of reach and would have claimed the championship title.

Jake slowly filtered in, standing in the doorway, out of the way and out of sight.

'Right, team,' Pemberton began after acknowledging his arrival with a quick unimpressed glance, 'I trust you all know your positions and what your roles are throughout this investigation by now. And if you don't, then I want you to speak to DI Murphy – he's in charge when I'm not. We're now treating this as a critical incident and Category A+ murder investigation. Bridgewater Jewellers is the location of the incident. At 09:03 this morning it was raided by a group of armed robbers. They've shot and murdered a civilian, IC1, and have abducted another – our second Nominal One, Candice Strachan.'

'Make that two abductions, ma'am,' someone from the other side of the Horseshoe called out, their hand raised. 'More reports are coming in that a middle-aged man was thrown into the back of the van with Candice Strachan.'

Pemberton nodded. 'Do we have a name for our second hostage?'

'Roger Heathcote.'

'Right… one confirmed fatality, two abductions. We can't let that number get any higher, guys. Whoever's the researcher in the team, I want you to create a victimology report on Candice Strachan in as much detail as you can. Why have they abducted her? Find out who she is, where she lives, what her skills are, education, qualifications, marital status, any relationships she might have, kids she doesn't know about, what she does for fun, whether she's ever had an STI in her life – I want to know everything about her.' Pemberton paused to catch her breath. 'Then we're going to need ANPR on the registration for the vehicle they were abducted in, and any CCTV footage we can get our hands on. As soon as we get a hit, I'm coming with you all on the ground – I want to make sure Candice Strachan and Roger Heathcote are returned to their friends and families safely.'

Before Pemberton continued, another officer raised her hand. She stood, juggling several documents. 'Ma'am,' she said, 'preliminary reports are coming in on Candice Strachan. That file from the jeweller's is a gold mine.'

'What does it say?' Pemberton urged.

The officer cleared her throat then continued, 'Years ago, she had a couple of stints as an actress. Performing in plays and all that sort of stuff. Says here that her next of kin is her husband, an art dealer, but a quick check on his name shows that he died a couple of years ago from a heart attack and left everything to her in his will. He had some sort of investment in Bridgewater Jewellers, and eventually she bought the company out and now owns it.'

'Bet that was a comfortable inheritance fund,' DI Mark Murphy jibed. He stood with his arms folded, and as he said it, he swivelled on the spot and glanced at Jake, a smile on his face. Jake didn't know why he'd looked over to him, but he didn't reciprocate.

'All right, Mark, that's enough,' Pemberton snapped, immediately stifling any disturbance that the comment was likely to provoke. She gazed around the Incident Room and waited until there was complete silence before continuing. 'While you're trying to find her, I want a small unit dedicated to focusing on her husband too. He might have pissed someone off in the past and they're coming to collect an old debt. Also, it's worth checking out Candice Strachan's financial history. Whether she's run out of money in the past. Whether she's done anything corrupt or has any dodgy dealings outstanding.'

'What are you insinuating, ma'am?' Murphy asked.

'Insurance fraud. She might be overdue on payments, and with an elaborate robbery like this, she'll get an insurance payout that's second to none. That'll clear any debts she's got outstanding and then some.'

Murphy shook his head. 'It's quite sophisticated—'

'But then the ones that always pass under our noses are,' Pemberton interrupted.

In the distance, the double doors to the Major Crime Team area opened, and a few seconds later, a woman wearing a blazer appeared in the Incident Room's door frame. She looked flustered, and her exasperated breath echoed over the silence that had befallen them. In her hand she held a piece of paper.

'Ma'am, had a ping on an ANPR camera. It matches the vehicle reg used in this morning's robbery. And we've had more eyewitnesses reporting seeing it on the road, driving erratically,' she explained as she handed the sheet to Pemberton.

'Where?' Pemberton asked, still keeping her gaze fixed on the officer.

'Farnham.'

'Where's that in relation to?'

'Candice Strachan's house is just down the road from the ANPR ping, ma'am.'

CHAPTER 11

THE INSTRUCTIONS

As soon as the front door creaked shut, Candice dropped the paper to the floor and her body convulsed. Her breathing sped up, rapidly filling her brain with oxygen until the room began to spin, left and right, left and right, left and right, the sensation unrelenting. The metal collar around her neck drowned her, its weight pushing down on her chest. The sharp, coarse edges of the metal from where it had been poorly cut dug into her flesh and reminded her, with each passing second and each exasperated breath, that it was there, suffocating her, asphyxiating the oxygen in her brain, waiting to pounce and spring into action. Her fingers clawed at the collar in a weakened attempt to alleviate the pain and pressure of it wrapped around her throat, but it was no use.

It was settled. She was going to die.

Then she closed her eyes and tried to control her breathing, tried to calm her nerves and staunch the overflowing emotions and thoughts bursting from her brain. But they wouldn't stop. And in no time at all the nausea returned with a vengeance. Candice rotated to the side and projectile vomited on her mansion floor, the orange liquid spreading across the white and great-streaked stones. It dirtied the collar and some of her clothes, though the latter was the least of her worries.

For a moment, she toyed with the idea of fainting, of allowing the veil of unconsciousness to descend over her and drag her down so she wouldn't have to face her imminent death anymore. But did she want that? No. Of course not. She had a family. She had a life. She had children. She didn't want to imagine how they'd react if they heard their mother had died after being impaled by ten spikes.

Worse, she didn't want to imagine how they'd react after they found out that she'd done nothing about it; that she'd sat idle; that she'd died defenceless.

No. She wasn't going to let this thing defeat her.

Candice rolled onto her shoulder and lifted herself to her feet. But the stranger inside her house had already beaten her to it. The man was half-standing, his arms flailing as he clawed at the ground, trying to find a grip on the smooth surface. As their eyes locked on one another, he charged towards the front door.

'Hey!' Candice screamed after him. 'Where are you going? Help me!'

The man fumbled for the handle, stopped, babbled incoherently and, within a few seconds, opened the door and sprinted out of the house. As the door swung closed, it left a large-enough gap for Candice to watch the man reach the end of the gravelled driveway and disappear up the road.

Just like that, he was gone.

Stunned that she'd been left in this situation alone, left to die, Candice searched the floor for the note. She grabbed it, and, using her arms to balance herself, struggled to her feet. The blood rushed to her head, and she swayed from side to side, teetering on the edge of collapse.

A few seconds later, she regained steadiness and controlled her breathing once more. With the taste of acid burning her mouth and throat, she read the letter. It was folded in four and had been handwritten, but the writing looked as though it had been stencilled over a printed version of the document. It was too neat and immaculate to be someone's own handwriting.

TIME TO PLAY A LITTLE GAME. YOU'VE BEEN CHOSEN AS THE STAR CONTESTANT. YOU HAVE NO OTHER CHOICE BUT TO COMPLY. FAILURE TO DO SO WILL RESULT IN DEATH. YOU HAVE A SPIKED COLLAR EXPLOSIVE STRAPPED AROUND YOUR NECK. INSIDE THE COLLAR ARE TEN SPIKES THAT, WHEN DETONATED, WILL KILL YOU. TO UNLOCK THE DEVICE, YOU NEED TO FIND FOUR KEYS. YOU HAVE AN ALLOTTED TIME OF JUST OVER SIX HOURS TO FIND THE KEYS AND SAVE WHAT'S LEFT OF YOUR LIFE.

HERE ARE THE RULES, BEFORE WE BEGIN.

THE DEVICE IS BOOBY-TRAPPED. SO IF YOU TRY TO REMOVE IT BY ANY MEANS OF FORCE, IT WILL DETONATE AND KILL YOU INSTANTLY. OR IF YOU TRY TO CUT ONE OF THE WIRES INSIDE THE DEVICE, YOU WILL MEET A SIMILAR FATE. DO NOT TAMPER WITH THE DEVICE. TO DISARM THE DEVICE, YOU

MUST FIND THE KEYS.

THE KEYS MUST BE COLLECTED IN ORDER: 1, 2, 3, 4. THE FIRST KEY WILL LEAD YOU TO THE SECOND, THE SECOND WILL LEAD YOU TO THE THIRD AND THE THIRD WILL LEAD YOU TO THE LAST ONE. YOU CANNOT SKIP ANY OF THE ABOVE STEPS. YOU MAY SEEK HELP, BUT WHOEVER AGREES TO HELP YOU IS ALSO BOUND BY THESE RULES. THERE IS NO NEED TO CALL THE POLICE, AS THEY WILL FIND YOU SOON ENOUGH. ALTHOUGH, IF YOU DECIDE TO GO ALONE, THEN THEY MAY NEVER FIND YOU. YOUR LIFE IS IN BOTH YOUR HANDS AND THEIRS.

AND, SURREY'S FINEST, IF YOU'RE READING THIS NOW, GOOD LUCK. SHE'S GOING TO NEED IT.

I HOPE THESE INSTRUCTIONS HAVE BEEN CLEAR, AND I HOPE THAT YOU UNDERSTAND HOW SERIOUS WE ARE. IN LESS THAN SIX HOURS' TIME, SHE IS GOING TO DIE.

THE GAME HAS BEGUN.

HERE'S YOUR FIRST CLUE.

THE FIRST KEY: WHERE CLOTHES ARE LEFT TO HANG AND DRY LIKE OLD FRIENDS.

Candice stopped reading. She had just over six hours to save herself. And in her current mental and physical state, she would never make it.

That thought made her nausea return. The world turned grey, and everything inside the house spun in a carousel of white and black. Her head felt light, and she vomited again, this time more violently.

As she wiped her mouth clean of stomach lining, a duvet of darkness descended over her, wrapping her gently around the body and pulling her into a void of sleep.

She was unconscious before her head hit the floor.

CHAPTER 12

RESCUE

Candice awoke drearily. For a moment she wondered where she was, but then as her surroundings gradually came into view, she realised. She was lying on the floor, her legs and arms sprawled in every direction. Her face had frozen to the solid marble that her husband had insisted on purchasing, and she groaned as she peeled her skin away. Her body felt weak. Her breathing. Her muscles. Her bones.

Her arms shook in an attempt to support her weight. And then she remembered why.

The spiked collar.

It was heavy, weighing her down, slowly beginning to suffocate her.

As soon as she realised what it was, panic set in again. The envelope of unconsciousness hadn't afforded her an escape from reality. It hadn't been a dream; it was indeed very, very real. In her head she heard the invisible sound of the countdown ticking down.

Tick. Tock. Tick. Tock.

Bleep. Bleep. Bleep.

Seconds were passing her by rapidly, and she was doing nothing about it. She had no idea what time remained on the countdown. It could have been three hours. Two. One. Twenty minutes. Candice couldn't afford to wait around for someone to come and save her. If she was going to get out of this situation, then she was going to need to get herself out of it. She had never been defeated by anything else thrown at her in life before, so why should she start now?

Candice looked around, her eyes taking in everything but

focusing on nothing. She stared at the spot where the man had been – the same one who had left her in the middle of her house. The same one who had left her to die. Before she could unleash a torrent of abuse directed at him for abandoning her, the white letter on the floor flashed in her eyes.

The instructions.

Her instructions.

Candice reached over, grabbed the paper and inspected it. She needed to read it again – the panic had stripped the details from her mind – but her hands shook violently, and she struggled to decipher the dancing letters on the page. The document felt thin in her hands, as though the paper had been the cheapest they could buy. Like even the slightest movement would rip it in two and destroy any hope she held of finding the first key.

Eventually, she managed to hold it steady enough and read through what it said.

THE FIRST KEY: WHERE CLOTHES ARE LEFT TO HANG AND DRY LIKE OLD FRIENDS.

That was good. Very good, in fact. It was closer than she thought. She was sure she had seen one of her attackers disappearing off upstairs somewhere. Feeling a new lease of energy and adrenaline, Candice started up the stairs as fast as her legs would carry her. She held on to the banister for support, lest her knees buckle under the weight of the device and send her cascading down the steps.

At the top of the stairs, Candice tore into the master bedroom – the place where she'd spent every evening for four months mourning the loss of her husband. Every time she entered this room, it reminded her of him. The side of the bed that he used to sleep on. The family heirloom alarm clock that he'd owned for half a century and repaired more times than they'd had sex. The slippers that he'd placed on the floor, ready for him every morning after he'd swung his legs out of bed. She hadn't had the heart, or the courage, to move any of it then, and she certainly wasn't going to start now. Since his passing, Candice had slept in the only room that faced the driveway, which was also much smaller. Perhaps it was because she felt safer there, as if the close proximity of the walls could protect her. Or perhaps it was because she was frightened that, every time she went to sleep, there would be someone trying to break in. Not that she would admit it.

A king-sized four-poster bed rested in the centre of the master bedroom, with bedside tables either side of it. To her left, on the other side of a beige door that matched the painted walls, was her walk-in wardrobe.

Candice approached it rife with apprehension. More than three quarters of the stuff inside was her husband's, and served as a constant reminder of their time together and the love they'd shared before he was taken from her too soon. Forcing thoughts and images of him from her mind, she began to tear at the clothes and shoes and jumpers and jackets and underwear inside the shelves and boxes and drawers. She overturned everything, searching each item of clothing first for the key before launching it to the ground. She poked her fingers into the nooks and crannies of the carpet and ran them over the skirting boards. After she'd overturned everything inside, she screamed. She'd found nothing.

Dejected, and becoming increasingly aware that time was running out on the invisible clock, she moved into the hallway to decide which room to inspect next. There were three more to choose from, including her own. In the end, she tried her room. It was the only logical location that had another wardrobe in use.

She stormed into the room, flung open the wardrobe doors and thoroughly searched inside. After decanting the contents onto the bed, she stopped. Panting. Her chest heaving. There was still no sign of the key.

'Where the fuck are you?' she yelled, gritting her teeth, small bits of spittle landing on the carpet. She sounded demonic, almost possessed. 'This is ridiculous!'

Her heart raced, and she became more irate, more impatient with every passing second, and just as she was about to leave, the gravel in her driveway crunched. Candice clambered onto the dust-covered windowsill and stared ahead. In the distance, the gated entrance to the house had been left open. Four individuals – two dressed in police uniform, the other two in suits – stalked across the driveway, the sound of their feet moving on the gravel reaching her behind the window.

This was it! They were finally here! They had finally come to help her!

Candice charged downstairs, heedless of what effect it would have on the device; she was just glad to have someone there who could save her. She skipped down the steps and bounded to the door. Her foot slid on a small patch of vomit, and she bashed her shoulder into the door. It hurt – a lot – but now wasn't the time to acknowledge the pain. She needed to let them in. All of them.

Candice fumbled for the handle, found it and then yanked the door. She breached into the open and stumbled over the front doorstep.

'Please!' she screamed, picking herself to her feet. 'You have to help me! I'm going to die!'

CHAPTER 13

SITUATION

Candice Strachan's Farnham mansion was a twenty-minute drive away, just over half that with the blue lights and a police escort leading the way. The mansion was situated in the middle of nowhere, surrounded by rows of elm trees and swimming pools of green fields in the distance. The driveway to the mansion was shielded by a tall row of hedges. Entrance to the property was guarded by a metal gate. Lying open.

The police escort was first to arrive, parking outside the front gate, just a few feet shy of the row of Portuguese laurel hedges. Bridger pulled in behind them, leaving the stone driveway clear between them. The road was barely large enough for two-way traffic, and they hadn't seen anyone coming against them on the way down, yet it was force of habit for Jake to check both ways when he disembarked the car. A dose of cool fresh air, heightened by the shade offered by the overhanging arms of the trees, graced his cheek and descended his throat.

Following Pemberton's orders, Jake and Bridger had been sent to investigate the property and search for any signs of recent activity. And Jake wasn't sure he was comfortable with the decision. There were better qualified people to be in attendance, yet he'd been chosen. Better, Bridger had chosen him.

'Be a good little bit of experience for you,' Bridger had said on the drive down. 'I know you've got some history in this type of thing, so I thought it might be good to see what you've got.'

Experience was last on his mind. Instead he was focused on what lay round the corner, what they might find as soon as they set foot on the driveway. Nothing, he hoped selfishly.

The two uniformed police officers were first to make the step. The sound of crunching stones reminded Jake of Maisie, of breakfast time, the way her growing teeth chomped down on her cereal and her face illuminated as she experienced a new sensation.

Maisie. He missed her, worried about her, and the knot in his stomach returned as he briefly thought about her.

The front of the driveway was split in two by a shadow cast by the hedges. On one side, nearer to Jake, the stones had been tinged a shade of grey, and on the other, closer to the mansion, they glowed gold beneath the sun's rays. Jake felt, as soon as he crossed the line and stepped into the sun, there was no going back.

Ahead of him, parked just outside the front of the house, was a black Ford Transit van. The front left wheel of the vehicle was tucked under the wheel arch from where it had been turned at the last minute, the back doors were open, and the passenger window rolled down. From his position, Jake could see the inside of the rear space. Empty.

But then everything changed.

A scream, the sound of a bird's cry, pierced the still air. Jake gazed around him, searching for the source. He found it emerging from behind the Transit. Candice Strachan. Dressed in her uniform: a smart, light-grey pencil skirt, a blazer, a white shirt buttoned up to her chest. She was shoeless, and her blonde, slightly sun-kissed hair radiated warmth against the coldness of her face.

'Help! You have to help me! Help!' came the plea, but Jake paid her little attention. His eyes were too focused on the thick piece of metal wrapped around her neck that looked like a giant handcuff. Attached to the bottom was a small metallic box, resting atop her collarbone. At the bottom of the metal box, on the underside, was what looked like a countdown timer and four holes.

All four officers froze.

'Please!' Candice yelled from across the driveway. 'They said it's a spike b-bomb. They said it was going to k-kill me. But I don't know when it's going to g-go off.'

The words raced around Jake's head. Spike. Bomb. Kill. Spike. Bomb. Kill. Until they became nothing but white noise. Soon, all other sounds around him were drowned out by the furious thumping of his heart against his ribcage, of his ballistic blood raging through his body. And then it started. It had been so long since the last one that he'd forced the memory to the back of his mind, but now it was coming back – and it was coming back with a vengeance.

Jake stumbled backward, vaguely aware that his mouth was opening, muttering something illegible. He retreated back to Bridger's car and bent double over the bonnet. He didn't dare close his eyes, because he knew what would happen if he did: his entire body would be transported back to that day – the day *they* began.

Hands planted firmly on the blistering bonnet, ignoring the

pain, Jake panted heavily in a vain attempt to regulate his breathing. It was useless, as usual. A great pressure forced itself down on his head, crushing him, crippling him to the floor. A second later, he was sitting on the grass, legs propped against his chest, back resting against the grill and number plate. With every frantic breath, the pressure in his head spread to the rest of his body. The sensation of being trapped washed over him almost as quickly as the blanket of white across his vision. This time his eyes didn't need to close for that to happen. He was really in the throes of it now. Surrounded by white, his skin turned to goose flesh and he was transported back to that day.

It had been sunny, just like it was now, except the temperature had been a few below and the altitude of several thousand feet meant it had little impact. There were five of them, absorbing themselves in the adrenaline of racing down the side of a mountain tucked deep into the heart of the Alps. One wrong carve in the snow had picked his board up and, within seconds, he was trapped, upside down, sentenced to death in a tomb of snow.

He felt a hand on his shoulder – strong, firm, yet slightly tender and gentle, like it was usually reserved for a woman or a lover. It roused Jake back to reality. As he opened his eyes, the white melted into blue and green and gold and the image of Bridger crouching in front of him appeared.

'Jake,' he said. 'Are you OK? What's wrong? What's going on?'

Embarrassment jabbed at him from every angle, mocking him. Three years, three years since his last panic attack, and he thought he'd finally started to get control of them.

'Nothing,' he lied, climbing to his feet with Bridger's assistance. 'Just in a bit of… shock. That's all.'

He was just grateful there was no firework display of vomit on the front of Bridger's car or the driveway.

'I think you need to sit.'

Jake brushed himself down, inhaled deeply, regained himself. 'I'm fine, honestly.' He peered behind Bridger and saw Candice and the uniformed officers in the driveway, left in the same positions they were in before it had happened. 'What's going on?'

'It's worse than we thought,' Bridger replied, looking over his shoulder at her. 'She says that thing around her neck contains metal spikes and, as soon as the detonator goes off, so will those spikes.'

'In her neck?'

Bridger turned back to face Jake and nodded.

Jake blinked away another wall of white. 'What happens now?' He hoped he wasn't the only one who was feeling well out of his depth.

Bridger reached into his pocket and waved his phone. 'Time to make a call.' He dialled a number and held the device to his ear. A few seconds later: 'Pemberton, it's me. I think you need to get down here – we've got a bit of a situation.'

CHAPTER 14

MUSIC

Candice Strachan's Mercedes GLC was unable to tame the never-ending, winding country roads of the Surrey Hills. Luke's grip tightened around the leather upholstery and he closed his eyes, willing the nausea in his gut to evaporate. Before leaving, they had stolen the keys from her, changed the number plates using a set they'd already prepared in the back of their van and hijacked the vehicle. For the next part of their operation they needed to be in something more inconspicuous, something that wasn't wanted by the police. Right now, with all the technology and knowledge that the police had available to them, the GLC was rapidly becoming a very expensive beacon pointing towards them from every direction. For now, however, it would suffice.

In all of their previous heists, The Crimsons had had an elaborate getaway plan, something they'd spent weeks, months preparing meticulously. It had been drilled into them very early on, the importance of escape. It was all well and good being able to rob a bank or a jewellery store in the first place, but if you couldn't get away with it, then what was the point? And so they arranged a series of stolen vehicles strategically parked on the sides of the road, acting as a long trail of breadcrumbs for the police to follow. Inevitably, the trail would become too long and confusing, and at the point when they thought it was clear, they would then trickle back into civilisation as decent serving members of the population.

By now, they would have normally been on their second vehicle change, having parked the last one in a remote location somewhere only dog walkers and doggers would find it. Now, however, everything about the heist was different. The dynamic had changed. And it was Danny's plan they were all supposed to follow, put their trust in. Luke was hesitant. He trusted his brother but not enough. Freddy, their old leader and Luke's closest friend, had been the one responsible for pulling off their previous heists. Danny's way of doing things was different.

And different didn't always mean good.

Danny swerved the car round a roundabout.

'Slow down,' Luke said, massaging his forehead. 'I'm going to heave in a second.'

'Do it on the back seats.'

'But I—'

'Look at the cars in front of us or something. That usually helps. We've got a couple of hours to go. You're a big boy – I'm sure you can last that long,' Danny said, throwing his hands in the air. 'Or you can start putting the diamonds in the bags if you want?'

'Do you want me to pass out? I'm useless if I'm unconscious, aren't I?' Luke replied, swallowing hard, fighting to allay the bile that rose in his throat.

Without warning, Danny slammed on the brakes, launching Luke forward in the seat. The seat belt dug into his shoulder. 'If you don't slow down, we'll get pulled over. The cops'll be all over this car soon, remember?'

'Yes – thanks, Luke. I *have* done this before. I know what I'm doing; I don't need a kid like you telling me what to do.' Danny gripped the wheel harder and rolled his knuckles back and forth.

Michael chimed in. 'A moment ago, you said he was a big boy, and now you're—'

Danny pointed his finger in Michael's face and then punched him in the arm. 'Don't start, Micky. Now ain't the time.'

'Never seems to be a good time with you recently. You've been uptight the past few days. Ever since you had to let that bitch go.'

'I did that for you boys. You lot should be thanking me.'

'Where'd you get that idea from?'

'Louise told me to sack you lot off, but I said no. Nobody splitting me and my brothers up.'

'Good riddance to the slut. I certainly ain't gonna miss her. Now, enough of her – she ain't worth our time.' Michael twisted in the seat and grabbed the open gym bag beside Luke in the back. 'How much you reckon we got here, boys? Hundred grand? Two? Three?'

'Easy five,' Luke added.

'Music to my ears, Luke. Music to my fucking ears.' Michael dropped the bag, clapped his hands, and switched the radio on – Radio X, blasting the latest rock track that Michael seemed to already know the words to.

Usually, Luke hated listening to Michael's taste in music – he was more of a drum and bass fan, garage music, something with heavy, repetitive beats – but on this occasion, he accepted it.

Luke had never been through a break-up – he'd never even had a girlfriend – and he was aware that they were hard, but from the way Danny continued to speak about Louise, it sounded almost as if they were still together. And that was beginning to piss both Michael and himself off. Danny was supposed to be the fearless leader of an organised crime group, not some wet-behind-the-ears drooler, pandering after his ex-girlfriend.

Luke eased himself into the chair, allowing the music to wash over him and offer a respite from any more episodes of the Danny and Louise Show.

CHAPTER 15

FRIENDLY FACES

A wall of smoke lingered in Danika's face. The air was still, and the smell of chemicals and tar in the tobacco climbed her nostrils and plunged down her throat. She inhaled hard, her mouth tingling as she absorbed the toxins. She cherished the taste, the feeling, the relaxing sensation the cigarette incited every time she took a drag. It helped vacate her mind and offered a momentary release from the angst and stress of life, of everything going on. She wanted more but knew she couldn't. Her husband would be able to smell it on her when she got home. No matter how much perfume she applied, the smell and taste lingered like burning rubber. And the less ammunition she gave him to use against her, the better.

Mount Browne's wooden double doors opened beside her, and DI Mark Murphy – the first person in the office who'd made a point of introducing himself – stepped out. He was handsome – his cheekbones prominent on his face and his jawline chiselled. He was dressed in a waistcoat with his tie tucked just beneath the buttons, and his navy shirt hugged the contours of his shoulders and arms. It was clear to see that he was in good physical shape. A man who took care of himself. His only obvious flaw was the receding hairline that looked as if it were running away from his eyebrows, even though he tried to hide it with copious amounts of hair gel.

Murphy reached into his pocket, produced a cigarette and placed it in his mouth. It dangled there as he frisked his chest and thigh pockets.

'Don't suppose I could borrow your lighter, do you?' he asked. 'Sorry. I left mine at my desk.'

Saying nothing, still reeling in the euphoria from her last hit,

Danika reached into her pocket and pulled out a lighter. She ignited the flint and held the flame beneath Murphy's cigarette. He inhaled and the end glowed orange like a small firefly dancing in the night.

'Fourth one of the day, and it's not even noon,' he said, ejecting a cloud of smoke into the air. As he did so, the wind picked it up and wafted it into Danika's face. Two for the price of one. 'How many you on this morning?'

'Just the one.'

'Good. If Pemberton saw, she'd kill you. Hates fag breaks. But I'm a little more lenient. Can't blame her really. Filthy habit. I've been meaning to quit. It's on my to-do list.'

'It's like that for everyone, no?'

Remember, Danika, he's your boss. Keep it civil and professional. Tony's not here – he won't know a thing.

'I like to think so.' He smiled at her and lowered the cigarette from his mouth. 'Interesting start to your first day. How you finding it? How'd the witness statements go just now? Get some solid reports?'

'Good, I think,' she replied. 'They didn't tell us anything we didn't already know, which was a shame.'

'That's not always a bad thing. Means that the rest of us are doing our jobs properly. Although I must admit I don't think I've ever seen anyone turn up to the office as early as you did.'

'I'm well trained,' she said with a smile. 'Had to make a good first impression somehow.'

'I'm sure you'll be able to keep it up. So far you seem to be pulling your weight just fine. What're you thinking about it all at the moment? Any suspicions?'

Danika hesitated a moment to collect her thoughts. It wasn't something she'd actively thought about. There were no hypotheses floating around in her mind, guiding her in a particular direction. That was for the senior detectives to decide. Unlike Jake, who'd taken it upon himself to jump ahead of everyone else.

That reminded her.

'I've noticed there are similarities,' she began.

'Between?'

'Have you ever heard of The Crimsons?'

Murphy's face changed slightly. His eyes narrowed and he took another drag on the cigarette. 'Should I have?'

'It looks to me like it could be them. From the witness reports, their uniform is consistent, as is the use of firearms.'

Murphy pursed his lips, nodded. 'Interesting, but how do you explain the abduction and murder?'

That was as far as it went. The hypothesis well had dried up. If only she'd listened to Jake more, she might have been able to impress Murphy better.

'It's a good theory,' Murphy said as he scratched the underside of his chin when she didn't respond. 'One that I definitely think we should focus on, but right now the priority is not who these guys are, but *where* they are.'

Danika took a drag of her cigarette; she'd lit a second one without realising.

'I can tell it's going to be a busy day,' Murphy said, nodding to the second stick she'd just sparked. 'What made you get into it?'

'My parents – they both smoked.'

'No… I meant the police. How did you become an officer?'

'It's a long story.'

'We've got some time. I like to make sure I know the people I'm working with. Make sure I can trust them.'

Danika hesitated. She was reticent to share the details with him. Not least because it involved the man who was currently making her life hell, and any mention of how she got involved with the police was enough to drudge up the feelings of repugnance she felt towards a man she'd once loved. In the end she ceded.

'My husband,' she began, 'he was a police officer. He joined when he left school. I met him a few years later when I moved from Slovenia. We worked together. Started a family together. A year after our kids were born, he was involved in an incident. Somebody threw him from the top of a building. Broke both his legs. He was forced to medically retire. He's been looking after the kids ever since.'

'That's heavy. I'm sorry.'

'You asked.'

A moment of silence washed over them. Danika enjoyed it. Relaxed in it. But Murphy… well, it was clear to see he was hating every second. She sensed from his body language – his posture, his eyes, his mouth – that he had an arsenal of questions he wanted to fire at her.

He fired the first shot from the barrel.

'Would you like to talk about it?'

Danika shook her head. Of course she didn't.

'Well, if you need someone to speak with, come and let me know. I'm always around. And it helps to know a friendly face in the office once in a while.'

CHAPTER 16

KEYS

Fourteen minutes later, Pemberton arrived with an entourage of police officers: four liveried police vehicles, a black van containing six authorised firearms officers, a dog van and two detectives pooling together in their Volvo. Within minutes, both ends of the street were sealed off and entrance to the road was blocked by one of the vehicles. Nobody in. Nobody out.

Up until that point, Jake's orders had been to sit back and wait. Bridger clearly didn't think he was much help, and Jake could hardly blame him. But as he watched the firearms team shuffle closer towards Candice Strachan and the device around her neck, he felt himself relax a little, less overwhelmed. The situation was beginning to feel like it was in safe hands, and he was happy to keep it that way.

Jake climbed out of Bridger's car and rounded the front, joining Bridger and Pemberton as they discussed the next plan of action. She'd been good on her word and got herself on the ground, and Jake respected her for that. He was sure that many SIOs would distance themselves from an investigation like this and manage it from behind a desk.

'Ah, Jake,' she began as he caught her attention. 'I need you to do something for me.'

Jake glanced at Bridger. The man replied with an almost imperceptible nod. He'd saved him the embarrassment of having to explain himself and tell her why he'd had a panic attack. For that, he owed Bridger one.

'I need you to call in forensics and bomb squad. I should have done it sooner, but I didn't realise it was *this* bad.'

'Of course, guv. No prob—'

'Let me do it,' Bridger interrupted, already pulling his phone and holding it to his ear before either of them had the opportunity to object. 'It'll be quicker.'

Jake watched the sergeant disappear further up the road before he turned his attention back to the mansion. The armed officers were in the middle of approaching the vehicle, their weapons raised and eyes trained on Candice and the surrounding area.

The radio attached to Pemberton's hand bleated. 'The vehicle is clear. Approaching the property now, ma'am,' one of the armed officers said. Despite being a short distance from an unknown and potentially dangerous device, there was a high measure of calm in the firearms officer's voice.

'Understood. Approach with caution,' Pemberton replied, holding the radio against her lips.

Jake was transfixed on proceedings until a noise distracted him. A police dog – a gorgeous German Shepherd – had just jumped out the back of the dog van and was busying itself with the new scents and smells offered on the concrete, its handler standing a few feet behind. German Shepherds were Jake's favourite. His family had owned one once, when he was a child, and it had been his best friend. They were gorgeous animals, loyal, trusting, and Jake had longed to have another one ever since, but there was no way they could afford the extra expense right now.

'House is clear, ma'am. Safe to proceed,' the radio echoed, and thirty seconds later the armed officers exited the mansion, giving Candice a wide berth.

As soon as she received the order, Pemberton turned her attention to the officer holding the police dog. She called him over and waited until they came to a stop by her side, both as attentive to Pemberton as the other.

'We don't know what that thing around her neck is,' Pemberton started. 'But we need to be able to communicate with her so we can help her and find out what it's for.'

'Understood, ma'am,' the handler replied with a slight dip of the head.

Pemberton spun on her feet and looked at Jake. 'Can you find me a spare radio?'

Feeling like he finally had a part to play – albeit a minor one – Jake propelled himself from Bridger's car and raced towards the nearest police vehicle. There, he found one of the uniformed officers dawdling, caught in the middle of trying to make himself look busy. Jake asked him for a radio, and the man handed him the one from inside the car.

'Will we get it back?'

Jake shrugged. 'I hope so.'

Pemberton was grateful for the radio and told him so. She passed it to the handler, who placed the small device on the dog's back, clipping it onto his harness. During times of hostage negotiation, the animal was usually deployed to open up a two-way communication with the abductor and begin a negotiation. But this wasn't a negotiation in the traditional sense. There was no madman holding a gun to Candice's head making incredulous demands. Instead, there was an invisible enemy and an unknown device, and everything about the situation was unprecedented.

As soon as Pemberton gave the order, the officer led the police dog through the gates, across the gravelled driveway and over to the perimeter that the armed officers had set for themselves. As they arrived at the firearms team, the officer bent down and let the dog off the leash. The animal bounded towards Candice in a flash and stopped by her side. When Candice picked up the radio and held it to her face, the dog hurried back.

'Candice,' Pemberton began, seemingly as relaxed as the firearms officer she'd spoken to moments ago. 'This is DCI Nicki Pemberton from Surrey Police. We're going to need you to stay exactly where you are until we tell you otherwise. I need you to remain calm. We're here to help you.'

'Please! Please! You have to get this thing off me. I don't want to die. They said it was going to go off in a few hours if we don't stop it.'

'Who's *they*, Candice? Who did this to you?'

'The Crimsons!'

At the mention of The Crimsons' name, the quaint, empty road seemed to fall silent, and a lump swelled in Jake's throat. He thought about clenching his fist and raising it in the air in celebration, but then the severity of the situation slapped him across the face, and he remembered where he was and that he needed to demonstrate at least a modicum of decorum. A few things were certain – firstly, that he'd been right in his suspicions, but more importantly, The Crimsons had now upgraded their methods. Never in any of their previous heists had they abducted someone – let alone two people. And never had they used anything as devious and evil as a spike collar bomb.

'Are you sure it's them, Candice?' Pemberton asked.

'Yes. They told me it was. They said people were going to r-r-remember their name forever.'

'What else did they say?'

'They said it was booby-trapped. Shouldn't be tampered with.'

Pemberton nodded and stepped into the driveway. She moved gracefully across the stones, looking as though she hovered above them a few inches. When she came to a stop halfway between the gates and the ring of armed officers, she continued.

'Did they say how to defuse it, Candice? Did they give you any instructions?'

Candice nodded, the whites of her eyes shimmering in the sun. As she moved, the device bounced up and down on her chest.

58

'They left a note with some instructions on it. It's in the house. I can g-g-get it.'

Candice took a step forward, but as soon as she moved, the armed officers raised their weapons.

'No!' Pemberton shouted. 'Stay where you are. Do not move. We're setting up a perimeter, and we need you to remain perfectly still. Just wait until I tell you what to do next.'

Jake watched on in awe of everything happening around him. Feeling pleased and horrified at the same time, he wandered onto the stones, tiptoed past the gate and came to the edge of the shadow that ran along the driveway. One more step and he'd cross into the unknown. Holding his breath, he did it and stopped beside Pemberton.

She lowered her radio and spoke to him. 'Roger Heathcote's missing still. Advise uniform to look for him. He's got to be out there somewhere, and he might be able to help us track The Crimsons. Give them the witness report Mr Heathcote's wife gave us.'

Jake turned his back on her, found a police constable by the gate and relayed the instruction. When he returned, Pemberton was in the middle of ordering the armed officers to carry out a search of the outskirts of the property and the back garden.

'Make sure nobody's hiding in the bushes with any unfriendly weapons,' she told them.

At once, the armed officers headed down the right-hand side of the building into the garden. In the distance, Jake thought he saw the metal handrail of a swimming pool strutting out of the ground.

'You ever seen anything like this before, Jake?' Pemberton asked, distracting him.

Jake shook his head. 'Never.'

'That makes two of us. You think it could be The Crimsons? You know them better than anyone else.'

Jake opened his mouth to speak, but the words never made it past his teeth.

'I read your file, Jake,' she said. 'You did a good job in Oxford. That's why I brought you down here. Thought you might be best placed to offer a helping hand. Like I said, you've got more experience with them than anyone else.'

'*If* it is them, guv.'

Pemberton checked her watch. 'That's why I'm asking you, Jake. Your opinion counts just as much as everyone else's.'

Jake swallowed a catch in his throat. 'Honestly… I don't know. Earlier I thought it was, but now… They've never done anything this… merciless. But regardless of who it is, we need to find those instructions.'

'We can't enter the property until bomb squad have had a look at the device and confirmed it's safe,' Pemberton advised.

'How long could that take?'

Pemberton twisted her neck backward and watched Bridger, who was pacing from side to side at the end of the driveway. He held his phone to his ear and appeared to bark orders into the handset. 'What's taking him so long?'

A few seconds later, Pemberton had her answer.

'Ma'am,' Bridger said, returning. His hair and forehead shone under the sunlight. It wouldn't be long until they all started to carry a smell with them wherever they went. 'Forensics are on their way. ETA fifteen minutes. Bomb squad are going to take even longer.'

'Why?'

'They're having to come from Reigate. And there's backed-up traffic on the M25. RTC involving a lorry and a busload of children.'

'My goodness. Is there no one closer?'

'Sorry, ma'am,' Bridger said, pursing his lips and shaking his head.

Pemberton sighed as she returned her focus to Candice. The woman was distressed, eyes beading, and her hands still clung to the collar bomb. Jake had never seen one before, and he hoped he never would again for the rest of his career.

'What do we do now?' he asked.

Pemberton hesitated a beat before answering. 'Candice,' she said into the radio, 'a team of explosive experts are on their way down to help you.'

'You don't understand. There's a timer on it, and we still need to find the keys.'

'Keys?' Jake and Pemberton repeated simultaneously. 'What keys?'

'To unlock it. There are keys. F-Four of them.'

'Where?' Jake asked, hoping he hadn't overstepped the mark. He swallowed deeply.

'They're everywhere.' Candice pointed to the mansion. 'There's one in the house, but I… I can't find it… and then – then the rest are around Surrey. Please, we have to find the keys before this thing goes off.'

CHAPTER 17

BRIGHT IDEAS

It had taken just over five minutes for Candice to retrieve the instructions that had been given to her by The Crimsons. Pemberton had come up with the idea of sending her back into the house with the radio and a pair of gloves. The longest part of the process was making sure she moved slowly and carefully, lest any sudden and drastic movements detonate the device around her neck. Everyone in the street realised that, no matter what they did, they were playing with an innocent woman's life. One wrong move, one wrong decision, and—

Finished.

That wasn't lost on Jake, and he was grateful it was Pemberton's responsibility and not his own. So he kept his mouth shut and his suggestions to himself. Not only did he not have the clout for such a thing, he also didn't want blood on his hands.

After exiting the mansion, Candice placed the sheet of paper in the dog's bag and sent the animal hurrying towards them. When the dog arrived, Jake bent down, seized the note, photographed it and placed it in an evidence bag. As he stared at the image on his screen and read the instructions, the words filled him with fear, with a sensation that made him want to run up to Candice and begin sawing the collar bomb free from her neck. A sensation that also made him want to run away and not have to deal with what lay before him at the same time. If he thought he was in a difficult position, it was nothing compared to what Candice was going through. He couldn't be that selfish to run away; that wasn't him – he'd crossed the line into the garden and there was no going back now, no matter how much he wished otherwise. Instead he needed to remain cool and think logically, like Pemberton, if he was going to stand any chance of making today a success. She needed him as much as he needed her. Same rules applied to Bridger.

Jake lowered his arm and handed the instructions to Pemberton, who continued reading. For someone in such a prominent position, Jake was surprised to see that she was the type of reader who ran her finger along the line to help keep track of where she was on the page. She took an age to finish.

'First things first,' she said eventually, 'find out where the hell forensics and bomb squad are.'

'Yes, ma'am,' Bridger said, stepping beside her. 'I'll give them a chase now.' He strode off towards the other end of the driveway.

'Whoever's written this has got neat handwriting,' Pemberton remarked, shielding the screen from the glare of the sun.

Jake followed her arm, his eyes half-closed. The sunshine was almost blinding. 'I think they've stencilled over a Word document or something. It looks almost immaculate. No one has handwriting that precise.'

'Send the original to the office. Tell them to get it investigated by the graphologist as soon as possible. Get them to cross-reference it with any documents and signatures in Bridgewater Jewellers... in particular those employee files they all seem to have.'

Jake nodded, hurried away and instructed a uniformed officer to deliver it back to the station. After the officer nodded, Jake raced back to Pemberton's side.

'This is insane.' She sighed and rubbed the bridge of her nose with her fingers. 'How are we going to get inside the property safely?'

Jake wasn't sure if she was asking him directly or thinking aloud. Nevertheless, he felt called upon and started looking around him, taking in the minutiae of his surroundings. He froze as he glanced at the side of the mansion. 'The garden,' he said.

'Excuse me, Jake?'

'The garden. Move Candice into the garden where there's a lot of space – a *lot* more. That'll free bomb squad for when they get here, and it'll free forensics up to get inside the property without any issues.'

'Hope you keep the bright ideas coming,' Pemberton said. She stepped from side to side on the balls of her feet as if she were waiting anxiously outside the school disco for the boy that she had a crush on to tell her that he loved her. 'Add it to my decision log. We'll take Candice round to the back while you and Bridger get yourselves suited up. Let's get you guys in there.'

| PART 2 |

CHAPTER 18

PIT STOP

As the three of them headed further south on the A287 through Beacon Hill, with the sunlight breaking through the arms and leaves of the trees hanging overhead, Luke constantly glanced behind him. Searching for an entourage of blue flashing lights atop liveried police cars chasing after them, drawing closer with every passing second. Each time he found none, and it was only the paranoia in his mind playing tricks on him and making him think that the sun's reflection on the traffic was the incandescent blue and white of a police car. Even the sound of a horn from an aggrieved driver turned into a police siren. It was relentless and it grated on his sanity.

'Pull the car over,' Luke said, clutching the back of Danny's seat.

Danny ignored him.

'Pull the car over,' he reiterated.

Silence.

'Dan – we've been in this car for too long. Way longer than we usually are. We need to pull over and switch. They'll have picked up the new plates by now. And I need a piss. Pull the car over.'

'We're not stopping,' Danny said, keeping his eyes trained on the road. 'Not until we get to Portsmouth.'

'I need a piss,' Luke said. He didn't care if he sounded like an insolent child. His guilt was getting the better of him. Images flashed intermittently in his mind's eye – vivid, visceral. Images of the dead woman Danny had shot in the neck. The lifeless eyes. The way her body slumped to the floor slowly. And then they moved to images of Candice, lying on the marble with the collar bomb attached to her neck. The screams. Shouts. Cries for help and mercy.

'Piss in a bottle or something,' Danny said, grunting loudly.

Luke scanned the back seats. 'There aren't any.'

'Piss on the seats then.'

'You can't be fucking serious,' Luke said. 'I thought you said no DNA? No trace? Just like every other time we've done this. Eh? So what makes this time different? Because it's Dan's Big Finale, Dan's Big Brilliant Idea, he thinks he can sacrifice those rules for everyone other than himself?'

Danny remained silent.

'Are we going to talk about the elephant in the room?' Michael said.

'What elephant?' Danny asked, his head snapping towards Michael.

'The fact that you fucking killed someone, Dan. Where did that come from? We never agreed to killing anyone. You could have at least warned us,' Michael explained. 'And what did she do to deserve it? She wasn't getting in the way of anyone. That's cold-blooded, Dan. I never expected to see that from you.'

'I did what I had to do.'

'I saw you pointing that gun at Candice as well… You almost shot her. We need her – without her, this all goes to shit.'

A Ford Insignia pulled out from a rural road, cutting in front of them. Danny slammed on the brakes. Luke propelled forward again, his seat belt biting into his shoulder. As his brother sounded the horn, gave the driver the finger and gradually brought the car back up to normal speed, Luke placed a hand on his bladder; the sensation in his lower stomach worsened, pressing down on him every time they swerved in and out of the traffic, overtaking and undertaking at every opportunity. Luke glanced at the speedometer. It was cradled just above 80mph.

'There's only one lane of traffic,' he said, slapping Danny's headrest. 'Are you trying to kill us?'

'Don't tell me how to drive, Luke. You can't even pass your test.'

Danny slammed on the brakes again. This time Luke saw it coming and tensed his legs while extending his hand into the back of Danny's seat to avoid any pain in his shoulder from the seat belt.

'Freddy said I was a decent driver,' Luke retorted, adjusting himself on his seat and gazing out of the window, trying not to think about how close his bladder was to exploding. It felt weird for him to mention their old friend's name. In fact, he had been more than a friend. A father. The dad they never had. And he was responsible for leading them onto the path they were currently travelling.

'Freddy ain't here now, is he? So you're going to listen to me instead.' Danny smacked his hand on the steering wheel. 'Christ – if only you both knew what Freddy was like. He's not the hero you think he is.'

'What's that supposed to mean?' Michael asked.

'He taught you everything you know. He taught *us* everything we know,' Luke added.

'And look where he ended up. Locked up for the next fifteen years.'

'And we're gonna be locked up for the rest of our lives if you don't swap this car over and get into a new one.'

Danny ignored him. 'Freddy ain't worth shit.'

'What'd he do to you?' Michael placed his hand on the dashboard, twisting to face Danny. He was giving his older brother that look of disappointment – the same one they'd all seen on their father's face too many times, back when he'd been a small part of their lives.

'Nothing.' Danny dismissed Michael with a wave of his hand. 'Leave it.'

They slowed as they approached a roundabout. To their right was a slip road that led onto the A3. Danny swerved the car around the bend, up the slip road and merged into the two lanes of traffic. The sound of the engine growling filled the still and silent interior. Luke continued to stare out of the window, watching the world fly past in a mirage of green and grey.

For a long time, he had wanted out of his life as a career criminal. It was horrible – constantly turning your back on everyone you loved. Watching over your shoulder every step you took. It wasn't the life he'd imagined he'd have when he was growing up. He'd never been academically smart, but from an early age he'd wanted to be an architect. An artist. A graphic designer. Someone who could draw. Someone who could make the world a better place with his art – and the only contribution he'd made so far was creating the concept for the devil masks that were synonymous with their name. Other than that, it had been a pipe dream. Something he could never share with his brothers, especially not after they'd formed the group. How could he leave when they'd been so adamant about loyalty and trust and brotherhood? What sort of brother would he be if he turned his back on them? Neither of them would forgive him.

But now there was hope. They were finally on their way out of the country – and out of this life forever. Now his passions had the chance to become a reality in the new lives they were going to make for themselves. Soon the three of them would be able to enjoy the rest of their time on earth doing what they loved, together. At least, that was what he told himself.

A road sign for a nearby service station flashed past less than a quarter mile away.

'Pull over here, Danny. I need a piss. *Still*.'

Danny expelled a puff of discontent from his nostrils.

'I think I saw one of those speed cameras flash a few miles back.

This'll be a good place to ditch the car and get a new one.'

'OK, you can put those *skills* Freddy taught you to the test. Just don't fuck it up.' Danny's voice was replete with disdain, but Luke appreciated the poor attempt at trying to lighten the mood.

'Dan…' Michael began. 'You sure that's a good idea? We've got half the feds looking out for—'

Danny dismissed him with a wave of the hand. 'No, no. If star boy wants to prove himself, let him. It's our last time at this, so it's only fair. Then we'll see how much he knows.'

It was settled. Luke eased into the comfort of the leather seat. His hand gravitated towards his crotch and applied pressure, relieving the burning sensation in his bladder once more.

Danny moved the car across the two lanes of traffic, bringing it down to a legal speed, and pulled off into a service station. He slid in to park behind an Audi A4 and yanked the handbrake on. The service station was surprisingly quiet, save for a few cars filling up with petrol and heavy goods vehicles that were parked up behind the building, their drivers either sleeping or devouring a fast-food feast.

Luke placed his hand on the door handle.

'What are you doing?' Danny asked, twisting back in the seat.

Luke glanced at the handle. 'I thought it was obvious?'

'Not dressed in *that*, you're not.'

'Shit.'

'Get undressed. Mess your hair up. Put your hat on. Keep your head down. And try not to touch anything.'

In the back seat of Candice's GLC, Luke unzipped the front of his crimson overalls, slipped them off his body and shoved them to the side. He then reached inside the gym bag, sifted through the jewellery and found his beanie. Pulling it low on his head, he swept a few strands of hair out of his eyes and concealed the bag with his overalls before hopping out of the car.

Danny called back: 'You've got two minutes. Finish your piss and then come straight back.'

CHAPTER 19

THE SIGNS

The atmosphere inside the car was sour.

Michael watched Luke adjust his beanie and advance towards the Shell petrol station, hopping over the potholes in the ground before speaking. 'What was that all about?' he asked Danny, keeping his gaze focused on the building's revolving doors.

'What you talking about?'

'That Freddy bollocks you was spouting off to him. What ain't you telling us?'

Danny undid his seat belt buckle and folded his arms. 'Luke doesn't stop talking about that fucking prick. He worships him.'

'Can you blame him?'

'You seriously want to get into this again? The man who raised us was serving, defending our country. He was a fucking war hero. Ain't right what they did to him afterwards. But Freddy ain't nothing like that – just a jumped-up little shit who was there at the right time and turned out to be good at robbing places. Freddy's half the man Dad is.'

Michael sighed, hooked his fingers in the grab handle above his head and said, 'You can't blame Luke for being born when he was. It's not his fault Dad missed him growing up. And it's not his fault Freddy was the only role model he had.'

'What about me?' There was pain in Danny's expression. As if the stresses and turmoil he'd been through his entire life were now showing up on his exterior. The narrow lines in his forehead and sides of his eyes were beginning to deepen, the bags beneath them darkening. 'What about me, Michael? *I* tried to be a good role model for that kid. You know I did. We're his blood. Freddy isn't.

And I'll be fucked if he thinks Freddy is a better man than me. The bloke don't even know his own son.'

'I just hope you're not lying to him,' Michael said. 'Whatever you do. It'll only make things worse.'

Danny tutted, sighed and then shifted his attention to the cars pulling in and out of the petrol station. Michael knew his brother better than anyone, and he knew when Danny was hiding something from them. The only problem was working out what it was.

Out the corner of his eye, he watched Danny rub his forearm and squeeze the skin through his overalls, alleviating an uncomfortable sensation. Danny didn't even realise he was doing it, but Michael knew what it meant. He'd seen the signs before.

'Oi,' he said, slapping Danny on the leg with the back of his hand. As Danny's gaze shot towards him, he pointed at his brother's arm. 'You all right?'

'Yeah.' Danny slid the sleeve further over his hand and placed his hands in his lap.

'Don't lie to me either, Dan.'

'It's nothing.'

'Did L—'

At that moment, the rear passenger door burst open, and Luke fumbled in, a relieved smile beaming across his face.

CHAPTER 20

HIJACK

'What took you so long?' Danny jibed as he entered the car.

'I told you – I *really* needed that piss.' And he had. He had stood there for what felt like an eternity, waiting for the tanks in his body to empty. But now that it was out of him, he felt as though he could run a mile.

'Come on. Get your gear back on,' Danny ordered. 'This Audi's been sat here for a while. Ain't seen anyone coming anywhere near it.'

Luke slipped back into his overalls, zipped the top up to his neck and pulled the hood over his head.

'Masks?' Michael asked from the front.

Luke reached across the seat and grabbed their red devil masks. Despite his misgivings about this life, he couldn't deny he felt powerful every time he wore one. He could be anyone he wanted beneath it. He could don a new persona, a new way of life, a new outlook on everything. Luke pulled the strap tightly over the back of his head, tucked small tufts of hair in the sides of the mask and grabbed the gym bag next to him.

'Guns?' Luke asked, turning round to search the boot of the car.

'With me,' Michael said, before reaching into the footwell and producing Luke's Mini-Uzi.

Luke took it from his brother and bounced the weight of the weapon in his hands. It felt as light as a tennis ball, and as he tightened his grip around the handle, adrenaline surged through his body again. All notion of what had taken place in the past two hours flew out of his mind. They were too far gone now. It was time for a blank slate. As a result, his breathing quickened and he clenched his jaw, grinding his teeth together. It made him feel alive.

'Ready?' Danny asked. 'Is that everything? Luke – give Micky the bag. You're gonna need your hands free if you're gonna break into this car.'

'Does that mean I'm driving?'

Danny hesitated for a moment. He looked at Michael, back to Luke, then Michael and back to Luke again. He shrugged. 'So long as you don't kill us.'

'Are you sure this is a good idea, Dan? It looks too open to me,' Michael asked, placing a hand on Danny's back. 'Freddy always said to never—'

'Shut it. He's not here. The bigger the risks we take, the bigger the reward, trust me. Now get on with it – somebody's coming.'

In the distance, a stocky man wearing a light blue Ralph Lauren jumper, pink shorts and brown boat shoes started towards them. Luke didn't know him, but he already thought the guy was a flash prick. Audi, Ralph Lauren, boat shoes – he fitted the stereotype well.

Wasting no time at all, Luke hopped out of the car, hurried to the driver's-side of the Audi and yanked the handle. Locked. Surprise. He reached inside his overalls and produced a long, thin piece of metal similar in shape and size to a ruler. As he slid the slim jim between the window and the door, Danny and Micky raced towards the Audi's passenger doors.

'Fuck it!' Luke grabbed for his gun, gripped it in his hands and smashed the butt against the car window. The glass shattered and scattered inside the car and over Luke's feet, but he didn't care. The adrenaline had clouded his mind. He reached for the inside handle and swung the door open. Then he threw himself into the car and kicked open the plastic housing beneath the steering wheel.

Time was running out, and to make matters worse, the man in the ridiculous outfit started shouting at them. 'Hey! What the fuck do you think you're doing?'

Before Luke was able to react, erupting from behind the back of the car came Danny, approaching the man with his arm raised. At the sight of the weapon, screams and cries erupted from around the forecourt, car doors slammed and tyres squealed as they searched for grip on the tarmac.

'Give us the keys!' Danny screamed at the man.

There was no response.

'Give us the keys!'

Still nothing. The man froze with his arms in the air.

Realising they couldn't afford to waste any more time, Luke leapt out of the vehicle and rushed over to the man. As he reached for the car owner's pockets, something inside the owner changed. Fighting instinct had come to the fore, but Luke was first to react. Determined to prove himself, he wasn't going to let this guy best him. And he wasn't about to have his reputation tarnished any more in Danny's mind than it already was.

Luke leant into the man, jabbed him in the stomach and unleashed a left hook. With one clean hit, the man fell to the ground. While he rolled on the floor, holding his face, groaning, moaning, begging not to be shot, Luke fumbled for the keys inside his shorts' pockets. The man made a poor attempt at defending himself, but it was immediately stifled as soon as Luke flexed the Mini-Uzi. As he hurried back to the car, Luke barked at Michael to change the Audi's number plates.

Luke dived into the vehicle and threw the keys in the ignition, slamming his foot down on the accelerator as it sprung to life. A few seconds later, Danny leapt in, and then Michael. The plates were changed. They were all together. And they were ready to go.

Cheers erupted and Luke slammed his hands on the wheel and dashboard as he merged back onto the A3.

'Fucking excellent, Lukey Boy!' Danny said, slapping him on the back.

'Job well done, son,' Michael echoed.

'For a moment then, I didn't think you'd pull it off,' Danny added. 'But you did good, kid. You did good.'

CHAPTER 21

SEARCH

A row of elm trees bordered either side of the property and ran down the length of the garden, where they met with another row of cedar trees, interspersed across the grass, giving the other room to breathe and grow. Each tree was unique, vibrant, and full of history. Jake wondered what secrets they held.

Immediately in front of the house was, as Jake suspected, a rectangular swimming pool, with a diving board attached to one end. To the left of the garden was a small wooden structure, and inside sat two lounge chairs, soaking up the summer sun. Beyond, further down the garden, running down the middle was a small path, constructed of the same stones found on the driveway, dissecting Candice's attempt at an RHS showstopper. A soup of colours sparkled in the light – purple and white from the beardtongue, furious red from the dahlia, golden yellow from the primrose. Several butterflies and various other insects floated through the air, jumping from plant to plant, unsure what to feast on next. Finally, at the bottom of the garden, far off in the distance, was an enormous summer house that was almost the same size as the mansion. Connected to it at the front was a glass greenhouse. Jake was curious how Candice was able to keep it all in such perfect condition with a full-time job and a business. If the garden was anything to go by, then he knew that as soon as he set foot inside the mansion himself, he was in for a treat.

'That's it. Right there. Keep your arms high in the air for me, Candice. Don't move any further.' Pemberton gave the final command for Candice to come to a stop in the space between the pool and the flower arrangement, while Pemberton and the rest of the team stood on the other side of the swimming pool, separated by fifty feet of luxury. 'My colleague, DC Tanner, is going to see if he can find the key for you. Is there anything you haven't told us that he might need to know before he goes in?'

Candice frantically shook her head.

'Jake,' Pemberton said to him, keeping her voice low, 'get inside there now. I'll stay here and send Bridger in when he gets back from whatever he seems to be doing.'

At that, as if on cue, Bridger returned, breathless and exasperated.

'Sorry, guv,' he began, his voice raspy. 'I couldn't find you.'

'It's not like we disappeared off to the Isle of fucking Wight, Elliot!' Pemberton snapped.

If he was offended or upset by the reaction, he didn't show it. 'Forensics are less than five minutes away. EOD ten.'

'You'd both better hurry then. The key won't find itself.'

Bridger elected himself to go first and hurried to Pemberton's car at the end of the driveway. Jake followed. There, he dressed himself in his second full forensic suit of the day. The texture felt soft over his skin, but he knew that in a few minutes his body would be slick with sweat. As he pulled the overshoes over his feet, Bridger held out a set of body cams to him.

'We should wear these as well,' he said.

Jake took one from his senior and strapped himself in. Once they were ready, they moved across the gravel carefully, keeping a wide berth from the Transit, and entered through the front door. The splendour of the mansion took Jake by surprise and forced him to stop. He'd never set foot in a house as magnificent as this. The closest he'd come was seeing photos of them online when he and Elizabeth played House Roulette, a fun game they'd created when they were bored one afternoon to see who could find the nicest house on Zoopla or Rightmove in their local area – but there was only so much that online images could convey.

A glass chandelier dangled from the ceiling only inches from his head. To his left was a door that led into a living room; to his right, the dining room. Ahead lay the kitchen. The marble surface looked like something from a sci-fi film – even with the pile of vomit splashed across it. Great wooden beams ran up the length of the walls, and the staircase to his left spiralled to the first floor.

Jake snapped himself back to the present. There was no time to stand and admire the property. They had a life to save.

'Come on,' Bridger called, pointing at the stairs. 'This way!'

Bridger leapt up the steps two at a time, rapidly increasing the gap between them. At the top, they entered a vast landing that looked out around the rest of the house. Jake counted seven doors: one behind his right shoulder, three on his right, one to his left, and two more behind his left shoulder. Fortunately, they didn't have to look too far; the master bedroom was immediately in front of them.

Jake followed Bridger inside and stopped as he crossed the threshold. It was a mess; clothes, hangers, shoe boxes filled with old photographs and footwear littered the floor. If they'd had any chance of finding the key quickly, they were now greatly hindered.

'I'll take the wardrobe, you take the bed,' Bridger instructed.

Jake wasted no time in his search. He moved towards the bedside table, knelt beside it, yanked the door open and rummaged inside. There he found a small notebook, a Kindle, a jewellery box containing a watch and a chequebook. Disappointed not to find the key on the first attempt, Jake moved to the drawer beneath. Empty. He then moved to the other side of the bed, running his fingers underneath the mattress and duvet, feeling for anything hard and rigid against his skin. Meanwhile, out the corner of his eye, Jake glimpsed Bridger rummaging through the walk-in wardrobe, flinging the remaining clothes and shoes onto the carpet, demonstrating a surprising lack of care towards protecting forensic evidence.

Jake reached the other bedside table and sifted through the contents like a fox searching a rubbish bin. It was empty as well. He clenched his fist and scratched his cheek. What if the key wasn't in the bedroom at all? The note had said where clothes hang to *dry* after all, and the bedroom didn't quite fit that description. Then again, what if it was all a ruse? What if they had strapped the collar bomb to her neck knowing that she was doomed to die? What if there was no way they could save her, and they were wasting their time?

Jake dismissed the thought and occupied his mind with something else: the en suite on his immediate right.

He wandered through. In front of him was the bathroom sink and above it a mirror. The sight of his reflection caught him by surprise and made him jump. His body turned tense and his muscles tightened. He wasn't sure whether he let out a little gasp, but if so, he hoped that Bridger had been unable to hear it. The less reason he gave his senior to think he wasn't up to the task, the better.

To the right of the sink was the toilet, and beyond that the shower. Everything sparkled and shone in the incandescent light overhead. The bathroom shower was pristine, devoid of any streak marks and limescale residue, as though it hadn't been used in years, and the toothbrush holder looked almost brand new. There was a small cabinet hanging on the wall beside a towel rack to the left of the sink, and the faint smell of cleaning chemicals lingered in the air. Everything was clean. Too clean. The rest of the bedroom's cleanliness didn't match the bathroom's. There was a disconnect, almost as if The Crimsons – or Candice – had cleaned the bathroom before leaving it.

Jake approached the cabinet on the wall and held his fingers underneath the handle. His breath steadied, and he inhaled through his nose and out through his mouth.

In. Out. Preparing himself for what lay behind the door. Like Alice. Except this was no wonderland.

Jake pulled.

The cabinet was completely empty, save for two items resting on the middle shelf. A key – the size of his thumb, darkened and rusty. And, lying beneath it, a note.

Jake felt his entire body relax. He'd found it. And he'd done it without Bridger's help. Jake grabbed the key, along with the note, and read silently to himself before calling out to Bridger.

> THERE ARE EIGHTEEN HOLES. EACH MORE CHALLENGING THAN THE LAST. ROLL THE DICE AND FIND WHICH ONE, OR THREE, WILL BE THE WINNER.

Jake read through the note a second time, assimilating the information, then paused, his attention gradually pulling away from the paper. Silence echoed around the house, and through the bathroom window, he heard distant chatter coming from the garden, carried on the breeze. Then he heard softened footsteps approaching him.

A second later, Bridger appeared at the door. At the sight of the key in Jake's hand, he stepped into the bathroom and took it from him. 'You found it. Well done.' He took the note from Jake and read it.

'Any ideas?' Jake asked.

'Doesn't seem too difficult,' Bridger said, his Adam's apple convulsing as he swallowed deeply. 'Can't imagine these robbers are the brightest bunch.'

CHAPTER 22

CONFUSING CONVERSATIONS

'Guv!' Bridger called, bounding across the garden towards Pemberton. He slowed to a halt by her side and passed her the note.

'Oh my God! You found it!' Candice interrupted. At the sight of the key in Bridger's hand, she rushed towards the three of them. Her breathing shook with excitement. 'You found it. You found it. You found the first key.'

Pemberton twisted and held her hands in the air, keeping Candice at bay. In the short time that they'd been gone, she'd put her hair in a ponytail, presumably to let the back of her neck breathe. Jake thought it made her look a few years younger.

'Stay back Candice. It's for your own safety. I don't want to have to ask you again. We'll give you this key, but not until the bomb disposal team arrive.'

'No! You have to give it to me now! Please. We need to find the other ones.' Candice's voice was hoarse, the effects of screaming and vomiting finally beginning to take their toll on her.

'And that's what we're going to do. You just have to be patient. We're not going to make any progress if you keep interrupting us every time we try to do something. Understood?'

Like a chastised dog, Candice retreated a few paces.

Pemberton swivelled on the spot and faced Bridger. 'Get some extra uniform down here. We're going to need all the help we can get. Especially if she gets carried away with herself.'

'Yes, guv.' Bridger nodded and then left.

Pemberton returned her focus to Candice. 'Candice, I promise you, we *will* get these keys for you. But we don't know what condition your collar bomb is in. The instructions say it's trip-wired – for all we know, as soon as we fit the key inside, it may detonate.'

Candice let out a whimper. It was so visceral and raw it made the hairs on the back of Jake's neck stand on end as he lingered on the outskirts of the conversation. He hated this. What this woman was going through. The nightmare she was facing. And now that Pemberton had just landed a truth bomb on her, he sensed it wouldn't be the last. If she survived, the horrors of the day would follow her everywhere she went, lingering, looming, waiting to pounce on her when she least expected it: when she slept, when she was sitting in front of the television, when she was driving towards work or the supermarket. The mind was a puppetmaster with the power to flick a finger and incite chaos. Jake knew all too well about how it needed to be tamed.

'Where are the explosive experts? We've been waiting ages!' As she spoke, tears streamed down her face, and Candice's poorly administered make-up made her look like a budget version of the Joker. Obviously she hadn't learnt anything from the make-up artists she'd worked with as an actress, Jake thought.

'They're coming. They'll be here any minute now.' Pemberton held her hands in the air. But her attempt to allay Candice's fears was having little effect.

'Do you know anything about golf?' Jake asked openly.

Candice hesitated before responding. 'Only that there are eighteen holes in each game.'

'Then at least you and I are on the same page. Is there a golf club nearby?'

Candice nodded and pointed towards the sun. 'That way. About five minutes away. Farnham Golf Club. You can't miss it. My husband knew the owner back in the day.'

'Thank you,' Jake said.

At that moment, Bridger returned, holding his phone in his hand. By now he'd removed his latex gloves and had stripped down to his shirt and tie. Behind him was an entourage of scenes of crime officers clad in white scrubs, their heads concealed by hoods and protective goggles. Jake didn't envy them wearing that in this heat. It was bad enough that he'd worn it for ten minutes; he could only imagine how long they were about to spend sifting through the entirety of the property.

'Finally!' Pemberton exclaimed before marching towards the SOCOs. She made it a few steps before turning and heading back to Jake. She stopped in front of him and placed a hand on his shoulder, then leant closer to his face and brought her voice down to a whisper. 'I need you to stay here with Candice. Make her feel more comfortable, at ease. Get her talking. But don't tell her anything she doesn't need to know. I'll be back in a minute.'

Before Jake was able to respond, she and Bridger had left him alone with Candice, and he watched them disappear round the other side of the house with the forensic team. For a long moment, Jake just stood there, staring at the building, as though he were a child pining after its parents, patiently waiting for them to return. He swallowed before adjusting his attention to the garden. Without Pemberton or Bridger, the atmosphere was quiet, eerie – the sounds of the driveway muted as if they were coming from miles away – and all he could hear was the rustle of leaves in the soft breeze that flittered in and around him. Pivoting on the balls of his feet, he faced Candice, his gaze falling on the device on her chest.

'How old are you?' Candice asked, her voice calm, neutral, almost as if she'd suddenly come to terms with her fate.

Her question took him by surprise.

He hesitated, stammered. 'Twenty-f-four. How old… how old do I look?'

'You're young. I didn't think they'd send someone your age into a job like this.'

'Sorry?' Jake lifted his right arm and scratched the side of his cheek.

As he did it, Candice's eyes widened. 'My son has that watch,' she said.

'Excuse me?' Jake held his arm in front of his face. On his wrist was the watch Elizabeth had bought him for his birthday last year. It had come at great expense given the little finances they had, and he'd begrudged her for feeling obligated to buy him something so nice for something that was over so soon, but he was appreciative nonetheless. It was a G-Shock GLX-5600-1JF. And it was one of his most prized possessions.

'Your watch,' Candice repeated. 'My son has that watch. You wear it on the same arm as him. The right. Few people do. Are you left-handed?'

Jake lowered his arm to his side slowly. *What is she talking about?*

'I'm right-handed,' he corrected. 'I'm just awkward. I like to wear it on the right side. Always have done.'

'You look like him.'

Jake held his breath. 'Like who?'

'My son.'

'How old is he?'

'Similar age to you, in fact,' Candice said. 'He was taken from me when he was very young. Social services.'

Jake didn't know what to say. In the end, he settled on the only thing his instinct would allow. 'I'm sorry to hear that.'

'You're going to get me out of this, aren't you, Detective?'

'I'm going to try.'

'You know what you have to do, otherwise you know what will happen if you don't.' Her finger pointed at the collar bomb.

Jake took a step back.

'If you need help, you know who to go to, right?'

Jake said nothing.

'I heard on the news that there's one of them in jail, isn't there? One of The Crimsons. If you need help with what they're planning next, I'm sure… I'm sure he'll be able to help.'

'Freddy?' Jake whispered to himself, his attention moving away from the conversation.

Before he could say anything loud enough for her to hear, the sound of gravel moving underfoot distracted him. It was Pemberton. Running back with Bridger in tow.

'SOCOs are in the building now, conducting a full sweep of the house,' she said. 'Nobody else is allowed in or out until they've finished their investigations. Now, I want you both to go to the golf course. We've got to find this other key before EOD get here.'

Jake and Bridger sprinted over to Bridger's car.

'You're the directions boy,' Bridger said as he slipped the gearstick into reverse and pulled out of the driveway.

'Shouldn't be too hard considering it's only round the corner.'

CHAPTER 23

HEATHCOTE & SONS

Roger Heathcote had been found outside the Dawson Veterinary Clinic. He'd made it less than a mile from Candice Strachan's house before sprawling across the pavement and passing out while the blistering sun burnt seven shades of tan into his skin. He'd been found by a visiting customer, who'd hoped to get their dog's testicles removed rather than find an unconscious man on the concrete. After a quick check from paramedics he was brought in to Mount Browne for questioning.

'It's nothing to worry about,' Danika told him. 'Just routine. We need to know what you know.'

She was sitting in Interview Room 4 with Roger opposite her, in a relaxed setting, a standing fan circulating cold air around the room. Roger's face was tomato red, and Danika didn't know whether it was from the heat or whether it had anything to do with the physical movement he'd exerted in running for his life. Probably both. He reached for his cup of water and downed it. His fourth in as many minutes.

'I'll get you another.' Danika left, hurried to the water filter and returned with another cup. If he had any more, he'd soon be able to finish the tower he was creating. After she'd given it to him, she opened the MG11 witness statement form and clicked the end of her pen. 'I just want to gather a few things about you first, if that's all right? The preliminary stuff.'

'Yes… of course, anything. I understand what you need to do.' He grabbed the water and polished it off in one.

Danika decided that this was his last one for now. There was a job to do, and information to pry, so she spent the next ten minutes ascertaining everything about him: name, date of birth, address, next of kin, place of work.

'I work for a solicitors. Well, I'm actually one of the firm's owners.' He reached into his pocket and produced a business card from his wallet.

Danika inspected it. The small piece of card was flash, much more highbrow than hers. The card was cream, textured, and the lettering was embossed gold, reflecting the light as she wiggled it in her fingers. In the centre was Roger's name; beneath it his contact details as well as the office's address. At the top was the business's logo:

'I run it with my sons,' Roger said. 'Family business.'

'Lovely.' Danika had no interest in it; now it was time to move the conversation along. 'Can you explain to me what happened this morning? As much detail as you can remember?'

'Certainly, of course.' Roger shuffled further to the edge of the seat and knitted his fingers together, and for a moment Danika felt like she was the one about to be questioned regarding her connection with a murder and armed robbery and abduction.

'Where to start… where to start? I was with my wife. We'd gone out for a morning walk at about 8 o'clock – something we've done for years to get the legs working, keep ourselves healthy. She and I are partners in the firm, so we usually discuss the latest cases we're involved in – domestic law mostly, before you ask. Sadly, lots of cases involved, always sad to see couples going through what they do.'

Fancy giving me a freebie in exchange for this?

'We'd left our house at about eight, as we usually do every morning like I said, walked into town and grabbed ourselves a coffee from The Coffee Company. It's our favourite place to go, and we're always happy to support local businesses. We were on the way down to the coffee shop when I noticed a black van roaring up the high street. I thought it was a bit strange—'

'Why?'

'Because the driver's expression was sullen, furious, like he was ready to just hurt whoever laid eyes on him. And… they were all wearing these weird overall things. I thought they'd all just broken out of prison.'

'Then what happened?' Danika's wrist was beginning to ache from the speed at which she was writing; Roger's lips were too fast for her.

'On the way back from The Coffee Company, I noticed the van was parked up outside the jeweller's. And then I heard all this screaming and shouting, followed by a gunshot. The whole street panicked, and people started acting weirdly. Then the robbers came out, three of them. One was carrying a woman. They had guns and they were dressed in the red overalls, but they had masks on that made them look like the devil. As soon as I saw what they were about to do to that woman, I dropped the coffee and tried to help her.'

'Why?' Danika lifted her gaze from the paper.

'Why? Why did I stop something happening to this woman? Why do you think?'

'You said that everyone else ran away. Why didn't you?'

Roger tilted his head to the side like a dog trying to understand a new phrase, then leant back in his chair and folded his arms. 'That response is indicative of what's wrong with this country. No one cares about anyone else. They're only worried about what happens to themselves – they'd rather see others get hurt and stand on the sidelines than do something about it.'

And you'd rather make money out of people's misery than do anything about it.

'That's not what I'm suggesting at all,' Danika said. She set her pencil down. 'Why don't I get you another drink?'

She stepped out of the chair and returned a few seconds later with another cup in hand, hoping that the brief interlude had been enough to settle Roger's temper. Fortunately, it had.

'What happened after you'd tried to help?' she asked.

'They threw me into the back of the van.'

'Then what?'

'They closed the doors and pulled away.'

Danika chewed the end of the pen. 'Explain to me what you heard, what you felt, smelt, saw, stuff like that.'

Roger hesitated for a moment. His brow creased and he closed his eyes as he transported himself back to that time. He kept them shut while he spoke. 'It… it was dark. Very dark. And cold, despite the heat outside. I was on my back against the floor of the van, and things were digging into me. There was one of them in the back of the van with us, and he kept shouting at us, telling us to be quiet, and that he would shoot us if we didn't.' Roger opened his eyes and sniffed heavily, as if sucking in his emotions. 'Naturally, I did whatever they told me. I'd heard the gunshot from the shop and didn't think they'd hesitate pulling the trigger again.'

'Did you hear anything from the other robbers?'

Roger shook his head. 'Their voices were drowned out from the sound of the exhaust and the other one shouting at us.'

'What about the woman who was taken with you?'

'Hysterical. Crying. Begging them not to hurt her. She was becoming a liability.'

Danika looked up again. 'How so?'

'Because…' Roger bit his lip. 'I hate to say it, but I thought… if she didn't shut up, they were going to kill us. I was sure of it.'

'Is that why you left her in the mansion alone?'

'Excuse me?'

Regret washed over her. She'd spoken too soon and out of turn. Grateful that no one else was with her, she backtracked, apologised and continued, even though it did strike her as hypocritical that he would leave a woman defenceless after claiming that that was the very thing wrong with society in the first place.

'What happened when they stopped driving?' Danika asked, hoping her apology was enough to placate Roger for the time being.

'They got us out, took us inside this mansion and threw us on the floor.'

'Then what?'

'They pulled out this… this *thing*. I don't even know what it was.'

'Did they not say?'

Roger shook his head. 'Maybe. I don't remember. But they put it around the woman's head. One of the robbers disappeared upstairs for a brief bit and then they left.'

'Just like that?'

'Just – like – that.' Roger slowly dipped his head.

Danika finished writing the last of the explanations and, after rotating her wrist a few times to get the movement back into it, set the pen down. There was no doubt that Roger Heathcote had been through a terrible ordeal – abduction, held at gunpoint, disorientation, outright fear and panic – but there was also a seed of doubt beginning to creep through the recesses of Danika's mind, weeding its way through her thoughts.

'Just a few more questions for you,' she began.

'Go ahead.'

'Does the name The Crimsons mean anything to you?'

Roger pursed his lips and shook his head. 'Should it?'

'Does the name Candice Strachan mean anything to you?'

Roger shook his head again. 'Anything else?'

Danika tidied her documents up – including Roger's business card – and grabbed her pen. 'No, that's everything for now.'

'Great.' Roger leapt out of his chair. 'I can't wait to see my wife.'

As soon as she returned to the Incident Room, DI Mark Murphy pulled her aside.

'How was it?'

'Interesting,' she replied. Her mind was still trying to process everything Roger had told her, and she wasn't sure she was ready to share any of it.

'What were the main takeaways?'

Danika hesitated. 'I mean… his version of events coincides with the witness statements taken from the employee and the customer. But…'

'But?' His voice sounded forceful, like there was something he wanted to hear.

'He was giving me this speech about nobody rushing to Candice's aid, but then as soon as they were left alone together, he deserted her.'

'Right. Totally. Anything else?'

'I don't know,' she said. 'There was just something *off* about him. When I asked him if he knew anything about Candice Strachan, he seemed to hesitate almost.'

'Really?'

Danika nodded, even though she wasn't sure herself. She thought she'd noticed the slight discrepancy, the slight hesitance in Roger's response to the million-dollar question.

'I thought maybe he'd known her through work. He's a partner in his own solicitor's firm.'

'Which one? I'll get one of the guys to check it out.'

Danika opened the folder of documents. Roger Heathcote's business card was sitting in the crease. She handed it to him, and Murphy inspected it, his thumb running over the grooves of the lettering. His impression of the card was evident: flash prick. Danika had felt the same.

'Hold on a second…' Murphy said and instantly turned his back on her before she could reply.

While she stood there, she felt a yawn coming. She stifled it, and by the time it was gone, Murphy returned, document in hand. He shoved it under Danika's nose.

'This is the letter of instructions given to Candice Strachan.' Murphy pointed at the top of the document. 'H&S. I wondered where it was from.'

Danika held the document close to her eyes. At the top of the page was the H&S logo of Roger's firm with the relevant contact details beside it. The only problem was it was faint, barely discernible.

'Is this the original?'

'A copy. The original's with the graphologist. She reckons it's been printed from a Word document. The letterhead suggests the logo and everything is on the other side – that's why it's so faint.'

Danika lowered the paper as the insinuation settled on her like lead falling to the ground. 'You think Roger Heathcote may have been involved with this?'

'I didn't until you just told me this. Good work, Danika.'

CHAPTER 24

CHARACTERS

The bedroom was a mess, that much was apparent to Charlotte Gibson, the first of the three SOCOs that had been positioned in the focal points of the mansion: the entrance, the bedroom and the black van stationed outside the house.

Charlotte had been in the job for seven years, and never in her experience had she encountered a critical incident as jaw-dropping as this. The device wrapped around Candice's neck was unfathomable. But she had accepted the call to say that she would attend – it might have been the most diabolical case she'd worked on, but it was also the most interesting, the one that would put her name in infamy. This case – if she could prove herself during it – would skyrocket her career. Call it narcissism, call it vanity, call it whatever you want. She didn't care. And if she helped solve it, then no one else would either. She had dreams of achieving stardom with a slight hint of celebrity. How? The logistics of it needed ironing out, but there was a process, and with each opportunity she had to shine, she could climb further up the ladder. She could maybe even write a book about it one day. Something that would put her name out there in the public domain, and then she could pursue what she *really* wanted to be doing.

Standing in the door frame of the master bedroom, she gazed about the vast expanse of space, lost for ideas of where to begin. There was too much choice, and the overflowing wardrobe to her left looked like the least appealing option. *Work smarter, not harder*, she told herself. In her hand, she held her camera, and dangling by her leg was her side bag full of everything she needed. Spare pair of gloves. Tweezers. Evidence bags. Brush. Powder.

Tucking the final few strands of her hair beneath the hood, and pinching the mask over the top of her nose, she stepped into the room. When she stopped at the foot of the bed, she noticed the en suite to the right. Perfect. Smaller and a much more manageable task than the rest of the room.

Upon entering, she surveyed the walls and furniture, and noticed it was clean. Too clean. As though it had been industrially cleaned only a few hours ago. Already her mind was beginning to imagine the last tenant, cleaning after themselves, moving about the bathroom, making sure nobody would find out what they'd touched and where exactly they'd touched it. Her old mentor had once told her that evidence was like true love. Time and care had to be dedicated to it when uncovering it, and once discovered, it needed to be protected at all costs.

Charlotte reached inside the bag, found her zephyr brush and flake powder, and set to work. First, she started with the sink, rubbing the fine animal hairs on the aluminium powder before transferring it onto the surface. A thin dust billowed into the air as it made contact with the porcelain, and she carried on regardless, methodically moving her way around the basin until its entire surface was covered. Then she moved to the cabinet, wiping an extra load of powder on the bottom-left corner and on the shelves, the prominent touch points.

Within a few seconds, she had something. A thumbprint. Followed by another. And then another.

Charlotte leant closer and inspected the minutiae of the three prints. The bifurcation. The core. The delta. The pore. The beauty of it. She wondered who they might belong to, trying to conceive of their appearance, their mannerisms, their final few moments before leaving a perfect stain. They'd make fantastic characters in her book.

Smiling, she delicately set the brush aside on the bathroom sink, removed a piece of adhesive tape from her bag and set it on the first of the three prints. Then she peeled the tape free from the surface and smoothed it down onto a piece of Cobex – a thin plastic sheet. She scored the ends of the tape, signed and sealed the evidence in a plastic bag, and then repeated the process for the remaining two.

'Bye-bye, little beauties,' she whispered playfully. 'Let's see what details you can tell us.'

She pocketed her findings and headed downstairs. She was under strict instructions to notify the crime scene manager as soon as she'd found something of interest.

'Guv,' she said, holding the evidence bags in front of his face. His features were concealed behind the white mask, yet his dark eyes growled at her. 'I found this. Fingerprints. From the en suite upstairs.'

'What's special about them?' he replied, deadpan.

'They're fresh from the cabinet on the wall. One on the door and two on the shelves. The entire bathroom looks like it's been cleaned; there's not a single print on the rest of the surfaces. Nothing on the taps, toilet seat, shower head. Nothing.'

'Interesting. Now upload them to Ident1,' he ordered and turned his back on her.

As she started off, he pulled her back by the arm gently. 'Oh,' he began, 'erm… good… excellent work.'

Charlotte said nothing as she headed out of the house. The attempt at making her feel better was acknowledged but not accepted. It was just a shame she couldn't tell him what she really thought about him. If she could, she was sure she would have lost her job months ago, before everything else between them began. If she ever needed a disgruntled, backstabbing dictator for one of her books, then he was the perfect man for the job.

CHAPTER 25

HOLE 13

Jake and Bridger's abrupt presence alerted everyone in the vicinity of Farnham Golf Club's car park. Heads snapped towards them like meerkats on guard, and some of the would-be golfers retreated a few steps; more to protect their expensive gear from getting hit by the car and kicked-up gravel than themselves. Jake had never golfed before, but he'd been around several golfers at university, and he knew that they often treated their equipment with more care and attention than anything else.

Jumping out of the car, Jake slammed the door behind him and jogged over to the club's entrance, slipping into the building after Bridger. They were standing in the middle of what looked like an upmarket version of Sports Direct. Golf clubs dangled from the walls, trollies were placed neatly in a row beneath and there were racks of clothes, shirts, gloves and trousers in the centre of the space. At the other end of the building was a reception desk. A sign that said 'Restaurant This Way' hung above, pointing to another door in the far-left corner of the room.

'Can I help, gentlemen?' a concerned voice came from behind the counter.

'Are you the owner?' Bridger asked, reaching into his trouser pocket.

'Yes. James Atwood. This is my establishment. Is something wrong?'

Bridger flashed his warrant card. 'We're investigating a murder and a robbery in Guildford High Street. Have you seen – or has anyone handed in – a set of keys today? Or anything mysterious that may have been found on the course?'

James Atwood's brow furrowed as the obvious question crossed his face: what the hell did a set of keys have to do with a robbery and murder?

'We've only been open about an hour,' he said. 'I doubt anyone's made it all the way round yet.'

'Is there… is there anybody who will know for certain?' Jake asked, trying not to sound too condescending. He took a step back to allow Bridger to take control.

James's face contorted.

'It's urgent,' Bridger said, feigning a sincere smile.

James arched his back away from them and twisted his head to look down a small corridor to the right. 'Denise, love – has anyone handed in any keys?'

A second later, a distant voice cried back, 'Yeah. About half an hour ago. Think I put them in the safe.'

James grunted and then ducked beneath the cash desk. The noise of a six-digit pin being entered into the safe sounded, and within a moment, he reappeared.

'Is this it?' he asked. In his hand he held a small key, as brown and rusty as the one Jake had found in Candice's bathroom.

'Excellent. Yes. That's the one.' Bridger snatched it from James. 'May we speak with Denise for a moment?'

'I… I don't see why not.' James shrugged and called Denise again. She arrived a few seconds later, drying a dinner plate with a tea towel. Dressed in a thin white blouse that was cut low, hair tied up, she looked out of place, as though she'd be better suited behind a bar somewhere rather than a high-end golf club.

'Would you be able to describe the person who gave you this key?' Bridger asked.

'It was a woman. Young. Maybe in her mid-twenties. Said she found it in the car park.'

'Was she alone?'

Denise nodded.

'What did she look like? Do you have any CCTV footage?'

'Yeah.'

Bingo.

'Do you mind if we take a look?'

'Certainly. Please follow me.'

Holding the plate in one hand and flinging the tea towel over her shoulder, Denise turned her back on them and headed down the corridor she'd just come from. She led them into a cramped office that was barely large enough for the three of them. Lever-arch files rested perilously on the shelf's edge, bowing it in the middle. And beneath them was a computer monitor, showing the live feed from the CCTV cameras posted around the clubhouse and car park.

'Would you be able to go back to when the person entered the shop please?' Bridger asked.

Jake removed his pocketbook in preparation and Denise did as instructed. As soon as she'd finished, she prodded the return key with an oversized finger and played the footage. Jake crouched so that the screen was at eye level and rested his elbow on the desk, watching, waiting for the woman to enter.

And then she did.

Pen pressed to paper, Jake made a note of the timestamp – 09:55:32. Nearly an hour after the heist. The woman entered the shop, sauntered up to the cash desk, handed over the key and then left, heading back to her car. Her face was hidden behind a baseball cap, and she was dressed in a short white skirt, a black-and-white-striped shirt and held a golf club in her hand. At the back of her head, poking through the baseball cap, was a brunette ponytail.

Jake continued to watch the woman's movements. After she was finished with her car, she grabbed a trolley and wheeled it away, disappearing onto the golf green.

'Can you go back a few minutes please?' Jake asked.

Denise rewound the video, and Jake told her when to pause it. He leant closer, removed his phone and photographed the still, heavily pixelated image of the woman's face. He wasn't sure whether she was a suspect, or whether she was a Good Samaritan, but he was going to make sure he found out.

'Would you be able to zoom in on the car park?' Jake said as he adjusted his positioning to ease the aching in his joints. He was only twenty-four but the grief his knees and back gave him made him feel forty years older.

'I can try,' Denise replied. 'The image isn't very good though.'

'I'm sure we can work with it.' Jake glanced up at Bridger for an approving look and then returned his attention back to the screen when it came.

Once Denise had gone back to the image of the car park, he took another photo. This time of the number plate. He zoomed in on the photograph he'd taken. It was illegible.

'Do you mind if my colleagues seize this as evidence?' Bridger asked. 'I can get someone down here soon. We're working on a murder investigation.'

At the mention of those final two words, Denise's eyes bulged. Jake sensed that it was more out of curiosity and excitement than fear that a killer may have set foot on her golf course. Something to spice up the mundanity of swinging a ball and wandering around a field all day to find it, Jake supposed.

'Anything we can do to help,' she said, nodding excitably.

As they returned to the cash desk, Bridger thanked both James and Denise for their time, and then the two of them exited the premises. A wall of dense, stifling heat punched the air from Jake's lungs as he breached into the open. Moving across the car park, he inspected the cars' number plates. From the footage, he'd been able to discern the make and model of what he was looking for: a silver

Audi A3. And, in front of him right now, he was faced with a row of black Range Rovers and Volvos.

'She's gone,' Jake said, thinking aloud as Bridger unlocked the car.

'Maybe she finished early. Maybe there was an emergency. We've got what we came for.'

'Hmm.' Jake was dubious. Something wasn't sitting right with him – something that was niggling at the back of his mind like the letter that was still on the table back home from HMRC telling him that he owed them a substantial amount of money that he didn't have. 'I think there are more keys out there.'

'What makes you think that?' Bridger shut the door gently.

'The note. It said "roll the dice and find out which one, or *three*, will be the winner". I don't think we should go back to the house only to realise we've got the wrong one – that we've missed some.'

Bridger fell silent and looked out at the gorgeous stretch of green in front of him, pockmarked by small holes of yellow. 'Nice thinking. But we'll have to be quick – we've got the other clues to find and I'm conscious of the time.'

Jake didn't need reminding. The ticking was silently reverberating around his skull with every passing second, counting down until those spikes impaled themselves in Candice's flesh.

Bridger locked the car again, pocketed the keys and rounded the bonnet. 'I'll start at the first hole; you start at the last. Then we'll meet in the middle, yeah?'

Jake nodded his assent and headed right, towards the eighteenth hole. The course was mapped out in a circle, and it didn't take long for Jake to lose sight of his partner. He sprinted to every hole, checking inside the flag and the surrounding area, but found nothing in the first three.

Jake jogged up and down the undulating surfaces, his legs quickly fatiguing as he covered the massive distances between each hole. Despair quickly sank in. He was approaching the fourteenth hole and he still hadn't found anything. But he was determined not to give up. Breathless, he slowed his pace to a jog that was more like a walk than a run.

On the fourteenth hole, Jake stopped by the course's sandbank. He scanned the surroundings, made sure he was alone and that there was no one else in the vicinity, then removed his phone.

'Danika?' he said, holding the device close to his ear as he walked towards the next hole.

'Jake – are you all right?'

'I'm fine. What's going on your end?'

'It's busy. Non-stop. Everyone seems to have disappeared to the crime scene, but I'm pulling some research together for the team now. Oh! And uniformed officers found Roger Heathcote in the middle of the road, collapsed.'

'Is he OK?'

'They found him passed out from exhaustion. He was checked over by paramedics then they brought him here. Turns out he's a family lawyer, owns his own company with his wife.' Danika hesitated. 'What's it like down where you are?'

'It's worse than we thought,' Jake replied, filing away what Danika had told him to examine later. He was grateful that he'd now caught his breath. Too many snacks, sugary drinks and long moments of inactivity. Not to mention the gluttonous portions Elizabeth placed on his plate every night because she was afraid he was starving during work. 'We found Candice Strachan, but she's got a collar bomb strapped to her neck. The only way to disarm it is by finding four sets of keys. We're in the middle of sourcing them now.'

'*Jézus*.' Danika's voice was swamped with deep concern. 'What about The Crimsons? You were right about that, eh.'

'I wish I wasn't.'

'Do you know where they are?'

'I was hoping you'd be able to tell me. Have there been any sightings of them?'

'Not that I've heard.'

'OK.' Jake hesitated and looked around him one last time, searching for anyone listening nearby. When he realised he was alone, he swallowed and kept his voice low.

'Danika – I need to ask you for a couple of favours.'

'OK…'

'Can you keep me in the loop? Anything that comes into the office relating to The Crimsons, I'd like to know about it. Something about this entire thing is throwing me off. I'd just like to be prepared, look like I'm on the ball, that kind of thing. Any information you can give me will go a long way, especially if we're on the road.'

On the phone, Jake heard someone in the office approach Danika and stop by her side. They asked her a question and she replied, quickly getting rid of them.

'Who was that?' Jake asked as he listened to the footsteps disappear.

'Just someone I spoke to earlier. Nothing you need to worry about.'

'OK. Fine. There's one more thing.' Jake was expecting a response from Danika, but when one didn't come, he continued, 'You're in charge of research, right? Good. I want you to find out *everything* you can about Candice Strachan.'

'What do you mean?'

'Something doesn't seem right. She started talking to me about my watch and the fact that I look like her son, and it just… it seemed odd. I just think it'll be worth investigating her, so we know she's kosher.'

'Does Pemberton know you're asking me to do this?'

'No… not yet. I don't want to distract her. She's snowed under at the moment and her thoughts must be going a hundred plus. If I'm going to say anything, I want to be armed with the facts.'

'I'll do what I can.'

'Thank you. I have every faith you won't fuck it up,' Jake said playfully.

'You really are a prick sometimes, Jake Tanner,' Danika said and hung up. Jake felt a little lighter.

The thirteenth hole was in sight. He jogged the remaining twenty feet and peered into it. An object glimmered in the sunlight. Jake reached inside and retrieved the key. It was almost identical to the one James Atwood had given them. The same size. The same colour. The same texture. And, beneath it, was another note.

Jake was too excited to read it. Instead, he pocketed it, along with the key, and hurried round the rest of the course where he eventually met up with Bridger at the ninth hole.

'You got one as well?' Bridger asked, holding another key in his hands. 'You've come a long way from making coffees in the office.'

Jake smirked. 'Not just a pretty face, am I?'

'No one's ever said that. Except maybe your mum.'

'Hers is the only opinion that matters. Now, stop wasting time and let's get back to Pemberton.'

CHAPTER 26

DIRECT MATCH

Bridger manoeuvred the car into the same spot they'd picked it up from. By now, the forensic team had set up a perimeter around The Crimsons' van, cordoned off by tape, and small markers were dispersed around the vehicle, signalling points of evidence that were not to be touched. A group of three SOCOs clad in their white oversuits were inside the back of the vehicle. Flashes sparked from inside as they snapped photographs of new pieces of evidence.

Jake was first out of the car and made his way to the garden. He came to a stop as soon as he realised it was no longer just Pemberton and Candice situated in the centre of the grass. In the time they'd been gone, four members of the bomb disposal unit had arrived and replaced the armed officers from before. The bomb squad looked like characters from a video game dressed in dark grey bomb suits – heavy-duty outfits designed to protect them from the threat of potential detonation – and helmets of the same colour.

'I'm glad to see you both,' Pemberton said as she approached them. It was clear she was no longer in control of the situation; that baton had been passed to the man currently standing inches away from Candice's chest, his hands fumbling around the device on her neck.

'What have we missed?' Bridger asked.

'Right now, EOD are looking over the device to see whether we can remove it without blowing her face off.'

'And?'

'No luck yet. Did you find the key?'

Jake held his triumphantly in the air. Bridger did the same with the other two.

'Three of them?' Pemberton asked.

'That's what the riddle said. But only one of them works. Where's the one I found earlier?'

'It's with the guys over there. They're going to try it when they know more about the device,' Pemberton explained.

The three of them watched the bomb expert set a metal detector on the ground and remove a pair of wire cutters from his pocket. Jake opened his mouth to speak but was too afraid to voice the question, too afraid to hear the answer he already knew.

'What happens if we can't use the keys?' Bridger asked for him, as if he were able to tap into Jake's thoughts.

'With any luck we won't need them. But if they're useless, we'll just have to find another way to defuse it. Any word on The Crimsons' location?'

Both men shook their head. 'None yet, ma'am,' Bridger responded. 'HQ are running reports on Candice's stolen Mercedes. We're still waiting on ANPR and CCTV hits. But it's very possible they've changed plates, so it could be a while until we find anything concrete.'

'Right. As soon as we hear something, I want you both to go after them.'

Jake's ears perked up. 'What about the keys?'

'You can leave that to us. There are enough uniforms here to go to the locations. But I want you both to follow and get after these guys. I've got a feeling we're not going to be out of this place for quite some time.'

Jake nodded. And then an idea popped into his head. Something he'd thought about on the way down to the golf course and on the way back. 'Ma'am,' he said tentatively. 'Might I make a suggestion?'

'What?'

'Their old leader. Freddy. He's in Winchester Prison – it's just a few miles down the road. He might be able to tell us a thing or two. Do I have permission to speak with him?'

'What? No. I—'

'Ma'am, please. I've had dealings with Freddy in the past. I'm the reason he's locked up. And I'm worried that this is all an elaborate plan for something else.'

'You think they're going to try and break Miller out of prison?'

Jake looked at her blankly. He shrugged.

Pemberton dropped her gaze to the ground in a deep state of reflection. 'If you think you can muscle any information out of him, then yes. But I want a full update once you're done,' she said, staring deeply into his eyes. Her gaze filled him with a determination to succeed.

So far he was making two for two on the brilliant ideas front. He hoped he'd be able to bag himself a hat-trick.

'Bridger, I want you to go with him. DC Tanner has a unique

connection to this case, and these are extenuating circumstances. I need you to get in touch with the prison and find out what you can do. I want you there to make sure there's nothing else going on.'

Something moved in the corner of Jake's eye and distracted him. It was the explosives officer. He'd stepped back from Candice's stiff, frozen body and started towards them.

'Ma'am,' he said as he neared, his voice barely audible through the thick helmet. 'I've X-rayed the device. There's a small charge in there that's connected to the spikes. When the charge goes off, it'll shoot them into her neck. But other than that, there's no explosive. So it's safe to get close to her.'

'What about the keys?' Pemberton asked.

'I think we're ready to try, from what I can tell,' the expert said. 'There's nothing to suggest the keys will initiate the device.'

'How certain are you?'

A pause. 'Seventy-five per cent.'

'We don't like those sorts of numbers, Officer,' Pemberton replied. None of them did. They were far too low – far too low to be gambling with an innocent life.

'I'm afraid it's all I can give you at the moment, ma'am. If I had a little more time, I could be more confident.'

Pemberton glanced at her watch. Jake looked over her shoulder and saw it was 11:02 a.m.

'You have three extra minutes,' Pemberton said. 'Discover what you can, and then unlock it with the key.'

'The machinations in here are incredibly sophisticated. Whoever built it certainly knew what they were doing.'

'Yes, thank you for that,' Pemberton snapped. 'We just need to know how to stop it.'

The explosives expert fiddled with the device for the next couple of minutes before he took another step back and turned his focus to Pemberton, Jake and Bridger.

'It looks good to me,' he said finally.

Paralysis gripped Jake as he watched the officer fumble for grip with his oversized flame-retardant glove. Eventually, he found purchase on the small key, steadied it against the lock and inserted it. Jake's palms dampened with sweat, the stress and paranoia finally beginning to take hold of his body.

The officer switched the lock. The sound was deafening, muting all other noise around them. And then everything seemed to stay still. Nobody moved. The breeze stopped. Jake's breathing stopped. Even the trees and small blades of grass stopped swaying. It felt like an eternity before someone said or did anything.

And then when nothing happened, they had their answer.

'It worked?' Jake asked hesitantly. He kept his voice low, lest he disturb the device and cause it to detonate.

'I think so,' the explosives officer said, taking a step closer to Candice.

As soon as he placed a hand on the device, everything changed.

An aggressive beeping sound emanated from the collar, shouting at them, enraged.

Beep-beep-beep-beep-beep-beep-beep-beep.

'What's happening?' Candice asked, panicking. Her hands lashed at the top of the device and she strained her neck to peer over the top at the source of the noise.

Nobody responded.

Beep-beep-beep-beep-beep-beep-beep-beep.

'What's going on? Somebody tell me what's going on!' Candice's screech pierced Jake's eardrums. He felt useless. All he could do was stand there and watch.

'I don't know,' the officer said, struggling to keep the device still amidst Candice's thrashing. 'Hold on! Stay still!'

Eventually, he steadied the machine and inspected it. 'The timer's gone down. It says we've got ten minutes left before detonation.'

Beep-beep-beep-beep-beep-beep-beep-beep.

'What?' Candice screamed.

'How can that be?' Pemberton whispered.

'Jesus Christ,' Bridger groaned, throwing his hands into his hair.

Jake tried to say something, but words failed him.

'Give me the keys,' the officer said. 'Let me try the other keys, for crying out loud! Hurry, before this thing goes off!'

Beep-beep-beep-beep-beep-beep-beep-beep.

Pemberton panicked. She mishandled the keys and dropped them to the ground. Cursing herself, she bent down. Jake knelt beside her and grabbed two by her left foot. He took the other one from her hand, hurried over to the expert and passed them to him, ignoring Pemberton's calls for him to retreat to a safe distance.

Jake watched the officer scramble for the lock and insert the keys one by one. By now, the sweat on his body had multiplied, and layers of salty liquid coated his skin.

The first attempt failed. As did the second. As Jake watched the officer insert the final key – the one that he had found – he prayed, for the first time in a long time, that it would work. He didn't want to see Candice's head strewn all over the grass.

Beep-beep-beep-beep-beep-beep-beep-beep.

The officer inserted the key. Twisted. And then an eerie silence filled the air again.

Jake exhaled heavily. 'Did it work?'

'Yes,' the officer said hesitantly. 'It's gone back to the normal time.'

Candice let out a loud moan of relief, and then her legs buckled as she blacked out. The officer beside her caught her and eased her to the safety of the grass.

'Jesus,' Jake said. 'Is she going to be OK?'

'She'll come round soon enough,' the officer said.

'What happened just then?' Bridger asked.

'There must have been a setting in the countdown. As soon as we entered the first key, it required the second—'

'Which means we're going to need the third and fourth at the same time before we can do anything else…'

The officer nodded.

Two down. Two to go.

Saying nothing, Pemberton turned and started towards the house. 'You two – with me.'

Jake and Bridger looked at one another before following behind her.

'What's the matter, guv?' Bridger asked.

Pemberton stopped abruptly and pointed at them. 'We need to move faster. Hurry yourselves and get to the prison. Speak with Freddy and see what he knows, if anything, about this robbery and —'

Pemberton was cut off by her mobile ringing. She held a finger in the air to pause the conversation and answer the call. 'Yes… OK… Thank you… Understood… No. I'll be in touch if I need anything else… You've been a great help. Stand by for further instructions.'

She shut the phone off. 'Forensics found a series of fingerprints in the bathroom upstairs. They've just run them through Ident1, and we've got some hits. All of them came up with a direct match. A Mr Luke Cipriano.'

CHAPTER 27

AN ARRANGEMENT

After what felt like an age – with precious time lost between convincing the relevant persons to allow them access and then funnelling themselves through the various security checks and checkpoints and X-ray machines – Bridger and Jake were finally able to sit in a room opposite one of Britain's most dangerous and prolific criminals, Freddy Miller. Except, after hearing who he was meeting, Freddy had requested only Jake, which meant Bridger was forced to wait outside until their conversation had finished.

'I was wondering when you'd visit,' Freddy said, pulling the chair opposite from beneath the table. 'I hear you bat for the other team now.'

Jake dipped his head slightly, glancing down at his suit. He straightened his tie and adjusted the metal clip. 'I've got a lot to thank you for.'

Freddy bent forward on the table, his face shining under the light. The man Jake had encountered during The Crimsons' last hit was completely different to the one in front of him now. Despite his size and domineering presence, there was no energy left in his face. No life. No vigour. The colour had gone from every aspect: his cheeks, his eyes, even his lips. His facial hair was messy and unkempt, and he looked as though he'd only just woken up. And he'd lost a lot of weight too. So much so, in fact, that the prison-issue tracksuit drowned him, hanging from his shoulders and revealing half his chest hair. Jake reckoned he wouldn't have recognised Freddy if he'd passed him on the street.

'Have you really come all this way just to thank me. Or are you asking for help?' Freddy asked.

'Can it be both?'

A smirk grew on Freddy's face. 'I know what this is about. They've done it again, and they've got you right where they want you, haven't they?'

'You've heard what's happened?' Jake asked. He had to be careful how to play it – give away too much and he would risk losing his hand to Freddy who, in fact, had Jake right where he wanted him: begging on his knees.

Freddy shrugged. 'I've heard things.'

'Where from?'

'The walls. You spend a lot of time in this place, they start speaking. Gets quite scary after a while.'

'Perhaps you should see a doctor?'

'Shrinks aren't my friends.'

'I'm sure I could do an evaluation – I've got a degree in psychology.'

'You clever boy. I'm sure your parents were very proud.'

'My mum was.'

'And your dad?'

'Dead.'

Freddy leant back in the chair, folding his arms. He bounced on the plastic then placed his entire weight on it. He commanded Jake's attention in one move. 'How's that girlfriend of yours? What was her name?' Freddy touched his temples with his index and middle finger. 'Alice? Alicia? Eliza? Elizabeth! That's it. How's she doing? She still stuck around with a little shitbag like you?'

To Jake's surprise, he found himself chuckling at the remark. 'Yes. She's still with me, by some miracle. We've even got a beautiful little daughter together.'

Freddy clapped. 'You don't hang about, do you? Did you conceive her on the night we had our little foray? Testosterone levels running high. Ego through the roof. You really had a lot going for you that night, didn't you?'

'If only that were the case,' Jake said.

'Is the baby healthy?'

'Fine,' he lied. The less Freddy knew about his family life, the better.

'I'm pleased for you.'

Jake shifted the dynamic of the conversation away from him to focus it more on Freddy. 'What about your little boy? Have you spoken to him?'

'Don't be fucking ridiculous. He's not allowed anywhere near here. I've written letter after letter, sent it to his mum's last known address, but have I heard anything? Fuck no.' Freddy made a *zero* gesture with his fingers. 'His mum wants nothing to do with me, so by default that means Sammy doesn't want anything to do with me neither.'

Now that he was a father, Jake could think of nothing worse

than having Maisie ripped from him. Not seeing her every day, holding her, stroking her hair, kissing her goodnight at bedtime or when he got in late and she was already asleep. She was his everything – his entire world. And he would permit nothing to hurt her. Especially after he and Elizabeth had been told they wouldn't be able to become parents by a multitude of professionals in the first place.

He allowed himself to think about Maisie properly then. Since he'd arrived at work, he'd forced himself to push her to the recesses of his mind for the most part, yet still within arm's reach, because he knew that the more he thought about her suffering, the less focused he'd be. The coughing had started a few days ago, and within the space of a day had gradually worsened until eventually, Jake and Elizabeth had made the decision to take her to the doctor. He was still waiting to hear back from Elizabeth.

'I'm sorry to hear about your son,' Jake said eventually, finding the courage to say the words.

'You should be.' Freddy paused a beat. 'You're the reason I'm in here. At least before I was able to watch my son grow up from the outskirts of his life. Now I have nothing, and no way of contacting him. He'll never know I existed, and there's fuck all I can do about it.'

There was an emotion in Freddy's voice that Jake hadn't heard before. When they'd first met, Freddy had told him about his son, but he hadn't expressed as much passion and adoration as he had just now. Jake was sure he saw the corners of the man's eyes glisten in the light.

'I don't know anything about what they've done,' Freddy said. 'This is all on them. *Their* heist. *Their* job.'

'I'm not here to ask you whether you know anything about this one.'

'What do you need from me then?' There was no expression on his face and no energy left in Freddy's tone, as if their previous topic of conversation had vacuumed it out of him.

'I need to know everything about the brothers. Their past. Their present. Their future. This job's different, Fred. This one's more… *evil*.'

Freddy stroked his stubble and smiled. It was clear who had all the power; Jake would have to change that.

'You don't ask for a lot, do you? And what do I get out of this little arrangement?'

Jake swallowed before replying. This was it. His ace card.

'I can get you to see your son. I'll just need some time.'

CHAPTER 28

GOOD EGG

Dumf-dumf. Dumf-dumf. Dumf-dumf. Danika's beating heart thumped in her ears and drowned out the sounds of furious typing and chatter and discussion amongst the office. The investigation was gearing up a notch. News and updates from Candice Strachan's mansion had begun to filter through the team – that the device connected to her neck was live and required a set of keys to defuse it; that DS Bridger and DC Tanner had already found two keys; that there were still a couple more, and that this was the most ingenious and difficult device for the explosives team to encounter.

Danika propelled herself away from her desk, hurried to the printer and grabbed her documents. They were still warm. She paced across the room and stopped beside Murphy. Steam from his freshly brewed cup of tea floated in the air.

'Excuse me, Mark,' she said hesitantly. The smell of tobacco still lingered on his clothes.

He peered up at her. 'Ah, Danika, what can I do you for?'

'I… I have the suspectology report on Luke Cipriano you asked for.' She handed him the pages she'd just printed out. After the identity of one of the individuals behind the mask had been discovered, Danika had been forced to stop what she was doing and rearrange her priorities.

Murphy took the documents from her, and as he began to leaf his way through, Danika gave him the condensed version. 'Luke Cipriano, born nineteenth October 1985 in Newcastle. During his teens he was arrested several times for theft and one incident of assault concerning a vehicle owner, so we were able to find his fingerprints on Ident1. He also has two brothers – Danny and

Michael – and they too were arrested for anti-social behaviour when they were younger. They were abandoned as children and, from what I could see, they jumped from foster home to foster home.'

A smirk grew on Murphy's face. 'Excellent. Stellar work, Danika.'

His words filled her with pride. It wasn't often she was appreciated, either at home or in the job – policing was a thankless occupation at the best of times – but whenever she was, she always stood there awkwardly, uncertain how to accept it.

In the end, she settled on, 'Thank you, sir.'

Murphy turned his back on her momentarily, handed the documents to a female officer beside him and instructed her to write the information on one of the whiteboards in the Horseshoe. Returning his attention to Danika, he said, 'I'm impressed. We'll make a good copper out of you yet. What else have you found?'

'Nothing at the moment, sir.' She hesitated, glancing back at her desk. 'DC Tanner mentioned that there was some CCTV footage coming in from Farnham Golf Club? He believes a suspect may have handed in a key there.'

Murphy's face illuminated. 'Is that so? First I've heard of it. Thanks for the heads-up. When it comes in I'll make sure somebody gets on it immediately.'

'Of course, sir. Is there anything else you need me to do?'

'No, that's everything for now.'

Danika nodded and thanked him once again. As she started away, Murphy called her name and waved her back.

'Actually,' he began, keeping his voice low. 'There is something. It's about Tanner... if he's not following the chain of command, I want to know about it. Information should be coming through either myself or DCI Pemberton. I want you to keep me up to date with everything he's telling you.'

'Of course, sir. No problem.'

There was a pause. Murphy glanced down at her feet and then back into her eyes. 'Is he asking you to do anything else for him?'

Danika opened her mouth, but nothing came out. Her mind had turned completely blank. Then she stuttered, 'He... yes... he wanted me to... to... to develop a victimology report on Candice.'

'What about her?'

'He said that she was acting strangely – that there was something a bit *off* about her.'

Murphy nodded approvingly. 'Right. Make that your next project. Anything you find, I want you to tell me about it, all right? I'll need to sign off on any information you choose to share. Can you do that for me?'

'Of course, sir.'

'Great. Thanks, Danika. You're a good egg.'

CHAPTER 29

SPORTS DAY

In all the years that Carl Jenkins had been a detective constable with Surrey Police, he'd never experienced as much excitement as he had today. Murders, rapes and other forms of serious crime were only able to offer a certain amount of exhilaration. They were the norm, the mundane tasks required to complete the day so it could roll over to the next. But this… this was like sports day in the yearly school calendar. The day everyone looked forward to, that gave them a renewed sense of enjoyment for sticking out the rest of the school year. It gave him a sense of purpose. And now he was in the thick of it, helping DCI Pemberton to save the life of a middle-aged woman who'd found herself in a predicament, trying to find the third and fourth keys that would, with any luck, remove the device from around her neck. *There's hoping. Or not.* The collar device was the hundred-metre sprint, the event everyone crowded behind the thin white tape to see. Where the fastest – and most often coolest – kids got to show off their skills in front of the entire school. Notoriety was either gained or lost in such a small distance, and part of Carl almost wanted to see how it ended at the finish line.

He was headed towards the location of the third key. With a little help from the team in the office, they'd been able to solve the clue:

> MONASTERY, O MONASTERY, WHERE FOR ART THOU, O MONASTERY? HIDING IN THE THREE WINDOWS OF YOUR MIND.

If the device was a hundred-metre sprint, then the clues were the four-hundred-metre relay, the second most popular sporting event. Carl had never been much of a runner, but now he was just happy to be a participant.

'Pull a left after this bend,' Smithers said beside him. The young, fresh-out-of-school constable had been sent with him by Pemberton and it was Carl's job to babysit and make sure he followed instructions.

From the little time Carl had spent with the man, he'd realised Smithers had a youthful set of legs and keen eyes. He was full of life and excitement. Eager. Like Carl had once been before the stresses and inane politics of the job had withered him down to nothing but the miserable bastard he was. But, more so, there was a fire to Smithers that he appreciated. The only problem was that Smithers wasn't afraid to speak his mind, and if he didn't agree with something – like the original answer Carl had given for the third clue, or the route to get there – then he had no qualms about voicing it. That irked Carl some. On the journey down, Carl had already told Smithers to watch himself, and that any more out of place chat would result in the termination of their journey together.

At the edge of the bend, Carl turned off the road and parked up beside a sign pointing towards the location of the third clue: Waverley Abbey, the ruins of a twelfth-century Cistercian monastery, situated a few miles north of Candice Strachan's mansion. Home to monks and lay brothers, the abbey had been a celebrated community of worship before it had been suppressed by Henry VIII in 1536 following the dissolution of the monarchies. Now a protected heritage site, the abbey attracted hundreds of visitors a year.

Carl parked beside a wooden fence and alighted the vehicle, the torrential sound of the River Wey gushing over rocks and discarded branches coming from behind them. They followed the signs to the abbey, through a gate, and then along an unmade path littered with mud and rabbit holes. A small lake ran to their right, home to a handful of ducks and geese, gently gliding across the water. Beyond the lake was Waverley Abbey House, a Grade II-listed Georgian mansion that looked out across the fields and abbey.

After reaching the end of the path, they arrived at a turnstile, then continued through a minefield of dog and horse manure until they came to another gate. The English Heritage emblem and information on the site was proudly displayed in front of them. On a good day, Carl would have liked to visit, but now there was no time for him to appreciate the magnificence of the site. That didn't stop him admiring the view, however.

Over a hundred yards away to his left was a yew tree, its leaves and branches blossoming into a perfect mushroom over the grass. Beneath it was a piece of ruin, rivers of petrified and exposed bark weaving its way through the stones, gradually claiming it as its victim. To its right were the well-preserved north and south transepts of the abbey. Within the transepts were the remains of three lancet windows, the lower stages of which had been intricately built to allow for the cloister on the other side. Beyond it, at the back of the abbey, knots of tourists and families ambled the grounds, marvelling at the magnificence of the site, cooling themselves off with makeshift fans constructed of newspapers and hats.

For a moment, Carl contemplated evacuating the site entirely but decided against it; it was unlikely that anyone would have found the key already and taken it for themselves. It wasn't in the nature of the type of people who visited these sorts of sites; he always found they were more a 'look but don't touch' type of community.

He and Smithers arrived at the centre pieces of the abbey, the most well-preserved parts of the remains: the undercroft to the right and the monk's dormitory to the left.

Monastery, O monastery, where for art thou, O monastery? Hiding in the three windows of your mind.

Three windows.

Carl started with the vaulted undercroft first. A portion of the rectangular building on the left-hand side was missing, and the roof was held in place by two pillars, gorgeous archways spreading out across the ceiling like the underside of an umbrella. The ground was dry and course, and small stones – remnants from the walls – had fallen onto the floor. The lower half of the brickwork was darkened a shade of black and covered in moss, evidence of the floods that the abbey had suffered over the centuries thanks to its proximity to the river. Where there wasn't evidence of decay, there was evidence of graffiti – brickwork and stones defaced by those ignorant enough to destroy such wondrous feats of history. Those were the real criminals, Carl thought as he reached the back of the undercroft and came to a stop by two windows that looked out onto a row of trees. Somewhere amongst the undergrowth was the river, which snaked its way round the abbey.

Two windows. Not three.

'I want you to stay here,' Carl told Smithers, his voice echoing beneath the ceiling. 'Have a look around and see if you can find something. Also make sure nobody comes in. I'm not expecting it to be heaving with people in the next thirty seconds, but if anyone gives you any lip, get them out of here. They start launching verbal assaults on you, come and let me know. I'll take care of it.'

'Absolutely! No problem,' Smithers said, far too jubilantly for Carl's liking.

Carl left the young man alone and headed towards the monk's dormitory. As he entered, he slowed to a halt and absorbed the surrounding atmosphere. It seemed as if the ghosts of everyone who had ever set foot in there were alongside him now, gazing at the wall at the back of the dormitory. The structure was bare, save the skeletons of three windows, nearly twenty metres tall, splitting the wall.

Hiding in the three windows.

Perfect.

Carl carefully edged forward, looking down at the ground beneath his feet, wanting to savour every moment as the rocks and grass squashed under his weight. As he approached the wall, Carl pulled on a new pair of latex gloves. He studied the windows for a moment, wondering if he could uncover the secrets of what had taken place there.

He reached for the centre window and moved a piece of rock he'd noticed nestled at the bottom of the window frame, placing it delicately on the ground before returning his attention to the window. There, hidden beneath the rock, was the key, wrapped tightly in another strip of paper. At the sight of it, Carl let out a small celebratory fist pump.

He was one step closer. Three hundred metres down, another hundred to go.

Now all he needed to do was keep the key safe.

Carl pocketed the small piece of metal against his breast and unravelled the fourth note.

> RUNAWAY, RUNWAY, RUNAWAY – YOU ARE NOT WANTED HERE. SEVENTEEN MILES OF TARMAC FROM TAKE-OFF SEPARATES YOU FROM TOUCHING DOWN SAFELY BACK ON EARTH.

CHAPTER 30

MINEFIELD

'I thought you were looking after the kids tonight?' Pemberton snarled into the phone. She kept her voice low and shifted from one foot to another, struggling to find a comfortable standing position.

'I know,' her husband replied. 'But something's come up with work. They need me to come in.'

'Can't it wait?' She nestled the phone in the crook of her neck and rolled back her sleeve to check the time. She had only been on the phone for a minute, but it was already beginning to feel like ten.

'Leakages tend not to wait, love,' he said, his voice deadpan. 'Especially if they're your biggest client.'

'And no one else is available to do it?'

'No. I've tried.'

Pemberton sighed in despair and ambled away from the crime scene through the beds of flowers to the conservatory at the end of the garden, lest she draw any unwanted attention to herself.

'When will you be gone?' she asked.

'Soon. I'll need to come back to pick up the boys from school, but then they'll need someone to look after them afterwards.'

'Well, I'm sure as anything not going to be able to leave on time. Nowhere near it. I could be here all day.'

'So you've already had to cancel with the girls, no?'

'I'm definitely going to need a drink after the day I'm having,' she said, folding her free arm across her chest and planting her hand under her armpit, 'regardless of what time it is. They'll wait for me. Even if I only get to see them for five minutes.'

'Then what do you suggest we do?'

'You need me to tell you?'

111

'I—'

'Book a sitter.'

'No.'

'Come on. Someone we trust.'

'No.'

'William – stop being ridiculous. How many times do I have to say it? Not everyone we hire to look after our kids is going to turn out to be a predator. That was one time—'

'Which was your fault. You convinced me to let him into our home.'

'I'm not getting into this with you again – I haven't got time right now. I'm stressed to the max, and the last thing I need is to get into an argument with you over something so trivial and something we've both discussed a thousand times already.'

Pemberton paused. There was silence in her ear, save for the sound of her husband's wheezy breathing. She had won... at long last. But it was bittersweet.

'Like I've told you before, if anything happens to our children under the watchful eye of a babysitter, I will not stop until I find them and hurt them. Just like last time. Surely there's someone we know who we can ask?'

'I'll find out,' he said and hung up on her.

Immediately after the call disconnected, she scrolled through her address book, searching for another number to dial. It was a phone call she wasn't looking forward to making. She was going to have to cancel the plans she'd been looking forward to for weeks; it was a nightmare trying to organise anything anyway, let alone an evening for them both to be together without the risk of children and husbands interrupting.

Pemberton found the mobile number in her address book and dialled. The phone rang and rang. Rang and rang. Until it clicked through to voicemail. She sighed and tried again. On the second time, the person on the other line answered.

'Ma'am?' he said tentatively, as if he were uncertain it was her on the other end.

'Mark – where are those files I requested? It's been a couple of hours now,' she said, cupping the microphone on the device with her hand, even though the nearest person was a little over a hundred feet away.

There was a brief pause as Murphy registered what she'd said. 'Sorry, ma'am,' he replied. 'I've been swamped. I'll have them over to you ASAP.'

Pemberton moved towards the patio doors of the conservatory. She peered in, trying to focus on the inside of the building and not the reflection of the garden behind her. From what she could see, there were four chairs positioned around the edge of the structure, facing the centre. In the middle was a small fireplace, its chimney protruding from the top of the conservatory.

'Ma'am?' Murphy insisted. 'I said I've been swamped. I'll have them back to you as soon as.'

Pemberton snapped to reality. She shook her head and focused. 'Something's come up.'

'What?'

'I have to cancel tonight. William's been called into work and I might have to look after the kids.'

'You're shitting me?'

'I wish I was. I tried to argue against it, but he doesn't want to get a babysitter.'

'Fucking idiot. The guy's a tool. You need to break it off with him.'

'It's not that easy. You know I'm trying. Slowly.'

'He's such a flannel.'

Pemberton shuffled her feet from side to side. She hated letting Mark down like this. It had happened on too many occasions, and she was beginning to think that she might have to fake her own death to even get a chance to speak with him in a non-professional capacity. They had even tried romancing their time together at work after hours, but even that had been interrupted by late-night staff and the cleaning crew. And there were only so many training weekends she could fabricate as an excuse to get away from her husband and kids.

'What have I said before, Mark?' she continued. 'William's a good guy. And I have my reasons for doing what I'm doing, but you don't need to make sarcastic comments like that, OK?'

'Sorry, Nic. I was just really looking forward to seeing you.'

'And so was I. I know we've had tonight organised for weeks.'

'It is what it is,' Murphy said, his voice rigid.

'Don't be like that,' Pemberton replied, casting a glance over her shoulder. 'It's going to be tough, but I'll make it worth your while when I do eventually get to see you. Maybe we'll just have to find a nice quiet place in the toilets tomorrow night after work – after everyone's gone home. Not the most luxurious place, I know, but we'll have to make sure we don't have a repeat of last time.'

'Depends on whether your arsehole husband decides to throw a fit again.'

'It'll be all we can afford to risk at the moment. Listen – I'll speak to him tonight whenever he gets back from work, and we'll reorganise something soon, OK?'

'I won't hold my breath.'

Pemberton sighed and pinched the bridge of her nose with her fingers. 'Don't be like this – please. I do want to see you. I really do.'

'You sure? Because so far, it doesn't seem that way to me. I'm always second best.'

'I have a family – a husband and kids to think about.'

'A husband you no longer care for and kids you hardly see?

113

Yeah,' Murphy said. 'That's what I thought. Sounds like a *real* happy family to me.'

He rang off, leaving Pemberton to stand there blankly, staring into her reflection in the window. She closed her eyes, swallowed and exhaled.

She had hoped he wouldn't say that. She loved her family – her husband, Damian, Jules – but things hadn't been the same for a long time, especially with William. The arguments. The late nights. The black hole that her libido had fallen into. The revulsion she felt every time he tried to touch her. But there had been a light at the end of it. Mark had made her feel things she'd forgotten existed. Made her feel things she wanted to feel every day. Her marriage had stagnated, and the only thing keeping her from being with him was the crippling guilt she felt every time they met up. The situation itself was a minefield: she was his senior, and if word spread, she could lose her job, and everything she'd ever cared for.

A voice behind distracted her.

'Ma'am.' It was the explosives expert, carrying his helmet under his arm. His short black hair was damp, and thin beads of sweat bubbled on the pores of his nose.

'Yes?' she said, forcing the debilitating thoughts of the future from her mind. She needed to be present at the crime scene; she needed to save Candice Strachan. 'What's the latest?'

'I need to have a word. I don't think she's going to make it.'

CHAPTER 31

CALL

One thought occupied Danny's mind as he stared out of the window. The woman waiting for him at the port in – he checked his watch – two hours' time. She had agreed to travel abroad with him, to another country with him, to another way of life with him. She was happy to do all that with him, and he couldn't wait. They had been dreaming of this day for months, ever since they'd first met. *Louise.* Even the thought of her name sent shivers running up and down his spine, round his pelvis and into his crotch. He was besotted with her, and she had a hold over him like no other woman had been able to maintain. He counted down the minutes until he would be with her.

In the front of the stolen Audi, Luke blasted the radio. He drummed along to the beat of the song, tapping his fingers on the steering wheel. Luke was driving conservatively. Perhaps a little too conservatively for Danny's liking, but his brother was in control, and he was doing a good job of it, so he wasn't going to interfere. There was still a long way to go unnoticed, and he was right – the less attention they drew to themselves, the better.

'You feeling all right, Lukey?' Danny asked. He placed his palm on the back of Luke's headrest.

'I got this.'

'That's not what I asked,' Danny said.

'Have we crashed yet?'

'Don't tempt fate, mate.' Danny returned his attention to the outside word – outside the confines of these four walls of glass – and considered his future life. 'Any news on the boat?'

'Last I checked it was fine. Still scheduled to leave on time,'

Michael said, unlocking the brand-new iPhone that someone else's hard-earned money had given him.

'Assuming the police aren't waiting for us down there.' Luke glanced at Danny in the rearview mirror.

'Why you always got to put a downer on everything?' Danny said. 'It'll be fine. Trust me. Nobody saw our faces. Nobody left any DNA. Nobody knows who we are. Who said we needed Freddy anyway?'

'You fucking shot someone, Dan. There'll be gunshot residue all over that place.'

'I thought I told you boys there's nothing to worry about. I'm in charge. Besides, if you're really that worried about it, we've got our help, remember?'

'Yeah. And you know how successful the last little piggy was,' Michael said, tutting.

'That was an anomaly. That fucking prick Tanner got in the way last time. It won't be happening again.'

'And what about the rest of the stuff?' Michael asked, rotating in his seat and peering back at Danny. 'Has that all been picked up?'

'Yes, Micky. It's all under control.' Danny checked his watch again. 'My contact should be picking it up right about now, in fact. Relax.'

'You gonna tell us who this contact of yours is?'

Danny flashed a smile. 'Now where's the fun in that?'

Michael twisted back in his seat, and for a while nobody talked. In the driver's seat, Luke shuffled. His eyes flicked repeatedly to Danny in the rearview mirror.

Eventually, Luke cleared his throat. 'You sure this is going to work, Dan?' It was evident to see he was sceptical. In fact, it was clear he'd been sceptical since the beginning, and it was Danny's job to change that.

'When have I ever let you down before?'

'You really want him to answer that?' Michael glanced back at Danny, facing him but not looking directly at him.

Danny hesitated a moment before continuing. He swirled his phone in his fingers like a toy and then dangled it between the two front seats so they could see it.

'I think it's time to give them a call,' he said.

'Who?' Luke asked.

'Luke Skywalker and the Rebellion... who fucking else, dickhead?'

The A3 widened into four lanes as it gradually turned into a motorway. They were just on the outskirts of Portsmouth, and Danny estimated they had less than twenty minutes until they arrived at their next destination.

'I don't approve of this,' Luke said.

'I don't know why you think this is a good idea,' Michael

added. 'You're just shooting us in the foot.'

I don't care, he thought. This was his job. He was in charge. This was going to be his biggest achievement yet. One that everyone would remember him for. They – his inferiors, those who had doubted him and those chasing after him – would think about him every waking moment of the day. He would haunt them. The one that got away with one of the UK's largest heists.

And now it was his time to speak with them directly.

He unlocked the phone and dialled.

'999, what's your emergency?' came the operator's voice moments later.

'Yes. This is The Crimsons.'

Pemberton's heart caught in her mouth, and for a moment, she wasn't sure whether she'd vomited or not. She swallowed it down, and then, for a long while, stared blankly into the officer's face.

'What's your name?' she asked.

'Armitage, ma'am.'

'And you're sure? There's nothing we can do to save her?'

Armitage glanced behind his shoulder before turning his attention back to Pemberton. 'The device is intricately manufactured. The locks are all connected to different wires. When we used the first two keys, it severed the cables. I followed where they led to… nowhere. We just cut open two pieces of copper wrapped in plastic. That was it. There also seems to be a tripwire on the edges of the device, so if we try to open the seal, whatever's inside will detonate for sure. But I also found something else…'

'What?' Pemberton asked, her mouth dry.

'A phone.'

'A phone?' Pemberton asked.

'A phone.' Armitage nodded as he said it.

Pemberton's skin went cold. 'Why wasn't this picked up when you inspected the device?'

'It was hidden, ma'am, behind a solid piece of metal. I just thought it was a part of the design. But since we introduced the keys to the device, it opened – almost as if it were some sort of treasure that we unlocked.'

'What does it mean for the device?' Pemberton asked, even though she already knew the answer.

'It means that potentially it can be remotely detonated?'

'What are the keys for then? Why go to all that trouble if they're going to remotely detonate it anyway?'

'I don't know. Maybe they're a decoy. Something to keep us occupied. I wish I had better news for you.'

'No,' Pemberton said, stunned. She found herself struggling for the words that would have usually come so easy to her. 'You're doing a fantastic job. Keep up the good work.'

The telephones in the office bleated. Each device played together in a symphony of noise across the room. Danika lunged forward and grabbed the phone. It was an instinctive reaction, one that had been ingrained in her from her time as a receptionist back in Slovenia. But as she held the phone in her hands, she regretted the decision to pick it up. She was new, untrained and knew nothing about any of the procedures or protocols in place.

'DC Oblak,' she said carefully, making sure not to pronounce her name wrong.

'Is this Surrey MCT? Have I come through to the right department?'

'Yes. Who's calling please?'

'Forgive me, I'm calling from Surrey control. We've just received a suspicious call from someone claiming to be a member of the organised crime group called The Crimsons… I understand you're dealing with the robbery in Guildford?'

Danika's attention narrowed in on the microphone pressed against her ear; she drowned out all the ambient noise and listened intently to the woman's voice.

'Our officers are dealing with the case right now.'

'They said they needed to speak with the SIO. Someone's going to die if they don't.'

Sránje. Sránje sránje sránje. Her heart beat fast and her mind fogged. *Miren. Inhalirati. Odviti. Calm. Breathe. Relax.* She inhaled and exhaled slowly through her nose and mouth.

'Thank you for letting us know,' she said. 'I'll find the right person for you to speak with. One moment please.'

Danika looked at the phone console, searching for the mute button. She found it a second later then, holding the phone in her hand still, she leapt up and scanned the office for someone to help. Those nearest to her were either on the phone already or walking away from her.

She looked for Murphy.

As soon as she spun around, he appeared.

'You look frightened,' he said, bearing a big grin. 'What's up?'

Danika explained.

'You're joking?' he asked, his brow creased.

She shook her head.

'I'll call Pemberton.' He dialled her number and held it to his ears. Within seconds she answered.

'Boss? Hello? It's me. We've got an issue. One of the Cipriano brothers has just called 999 and is asking to speak with you directly… Yes?… I don't know. You're right. OK… That'll take a moment to set up, but we can do it.'

Murphy hung up and disappeared towards the other end of the room. Danika watched him bark orders to other members of the team, and a clutch of them came rushing over to her desk.

'What are you doing?' she asked.

'Tracing the number. If we can get that, we can trace the call and find them.' He gestured for the phone in Danika's hand. Reluctantly, she ceded control.

'This is DI Murphy, deputy SIO,' he said into the receiver once the wiretap was set up. 'What's the mobile number and the IMEI that the civilian is calling from?' He made a note of the number and flagged it to everyone else around them. 'Please hold a moment while I put you through to the right person.'

CHAPTER 32

AN EYE FOR AN EYE

'This is DCI Pemberton.'

The words sounded like a song in Danny's ear, laced with euphoria. It had taken five minutes of patiently waiting, but he was finally through to the person in charge, his number one opposition, the one whose job it was to ensure they were caught.

Unfortunately, Danny was going to disappoint them.

'Good afternoon, DCI Pemberton,' he said, keeping his voice monotonous and deep.

'Who am I speaking with?'

'Names aren't important.'

'I've given you mine.'

'Quid pro quo? Is that how you want to play it? Like Hannibal Lecter and Clarice Starling?' There was no response. 'Do you need me to silence the lambs, DCI Pemberton?'

Still no response.

Danny was testing how far he could take Pemberton's temperament. Dipping his toe in the waters of sarcasm and belligerence. And he was revelling in the excitement of it.

'You still there, Officer?'

'I don't think the line's very good. You must be in a bad signal area.'

'Nope. Don't think so.'

'Where are you?'

'Somewhere we won't be for too long.'

'You still haven't told me your name. If we're going to give a tit for tat, I need to know you're fully on board.'

'Danny.'

'And what do you want, Danny?'

Danny smirked. 'What do you think of the collar? Spectacular, isn't it?'

'Depraved is what it is.'

'I'm disappointed you don't appreciate it. A lot of time and effort went into making that. Aren't you lot supposed to take an objective look at things?'

The car slowed to a gradual halt and the number of vehicles either side of them increased. Danny leant into the centre of the car and peered through the windscreen. Traffic stretched in front of him for as far as he could see, and more cars were beginning to pile up behind them as well.

A car horn sounded beside them.

'What's that noise?' Pemberton asked. 'Are you in a spot of traffic. Let's hope we don't catch up with you.'

'You won't.'

'You sure of that?'

'You like wasting questions, don't you? Would you have wasted them if I'd told you that you only had three to begin with?'

'What are you—'

'Are you sure you want to use that as your final one, Detective?'

There was a long pause. Danny waited, but he soon became bored. 'How far behind us are you? With the keys, I mean. Find any?'

'We've only found the one.'

Danny pulled the phone away from his ear, placed DCI Pemberton on loudspeaker and opened his text messages. He opened the chat at the top of the screen and scrolled through the latest text.

'Danny? You still with me?'

Danny snapped to. 'You say you've found one key?'

'Yes,' she replied.

Liar. Evidence suggests otherwise, love.

'Which one did you find? The one inside the house?' Before Pemberton had a chance to respond, he continued. 'We wanted to make it nice and easy for you.'

'We've got a lot to thank you for.'

'You're sounding unappreciative again.'

'That's a habit of mine. My husband tells me it's something I need to work on.'

'You been together long?' Danny probed.

'I'll tell you that when you answer my question: what's going to happen to Candice? We know about the mobile… the remote detonation.'

Well, shit. Danny hadn't expected them to discover the mobile so soon. He'd tried his hardest to bury it deep within the complex inner workings of the bomb. His hand moved to his overall pocket. Inside was a small key. It was metallic and cold to the touch. His

121

thoughts turned to Candice, crying on the floor, squirming, begging for her life in front of Michael and Luke and the Good Samaritan. He squeezed the key in his hand until it dug into his skin, drawing the pain away from the rest of his body.

Danny exhaled deeply. The traffic hadn't moved while they'd been talking, and the idle sound of the engine purring underneath reminded him they were still a long way away.

'If you didn't appreciate the collar at first, then hopefully by the end of it all you will,' he said softly.

'What do you mean?'

'There are three layers to it. The keys. The timer. The phone. If you get all the keys, you disarm the charge. If you do it before the deadline, you disarm the charge. And if you find the phone that detonates it remotely, you'll disarm the charge.'

'How do we find the phone?'

'I have it. I'm calling you now on it. The only way you'll get that is by arresting me.'

'Nothing would give me greater satisfaction,' Pemberton said. 'But how do I know you won't just detonate it now?'

'I like to play fairly. I'll give you some time. My recommendation would be to find the keys instead. You've got three more to go and not long left on the countdown.' He rubbed the key in his fingers. 'Although, I have a sneaky suspicion you'll struggle with the final one. I made it *extra* difficult to find.' He whispered so that his voice was inaudible to Luke and Michael over the softened sound of the radio. 'Especially if I've got it in my pocket,' he said. Returning his voice back to normal, he continued, 'If you're not quick enough, Detective, Candice is going to die today. Soon she'll be nothing more than a lifeless body without a head. And her blood will be on your hands. Goodbye.'

Danny hung up the phone, removed the SIM card and snapped it in half. He rolled down the window and threw it onto the motorway. There was no way the police would be able to track them now.

CHAPTER 33

THE CONSPIRACY

'Luke, Danny and Michael Cipriano – they're who you're looking for,' Freddy said, a cup of water dwarfed in his sinewy hands. 'Danny's the eldest, Luke the youngest. Five years separates them. With Michael in the middle. And there's not a hint of Italian in any of them, other than their surname and a strong family bond.'

'What about their parents?' Jake asked. He sat with his elbows resting against the edge of the table and his hands knitted together. He had a pen and paper in front of him, but he was making little use of it. The most important information would be stored in his brain.

'Both English.'

'That's not what I meant… What did they do?'

Freddy eased deeper into his chair and rolled his left sleeve back, revealing a wrist so skinny Jake saw the tendons and river of veins disappearing into the material. 'The dad was in the military. And the mum ditched them and did a runner on them when they were really young, when Luke was about three. She had a string of problems – drugs, attention, drink – but then she finally ran off with some other fella who had money and, I can only assume, a smaller cock. It had to compensate for something, I guess.'

'What happened when the dad was in the military?'

'He looked after them for a bit, but between touring and suffering the consequences of being shot at in the middle of a desert, he gave them up to a foster home. Danny will tell you that it was because he was too focused on serving the Queen's horses and all her men – which is something he strangely seems to be proud of – but if you asked Michael, he'd tell you that their dad put them in there because he struggled with managing the PTSD. I don't know which one's right. That's up to you to decide. Luke was just caught in the middle of it, too young to know anything.'

'Where did the dad serve?'

'Afghanistan. I don't know which regiment exactly, but I know he dealt with explosives of some description.'

Jake nodded. 'That explains where the collar came from.'

'That thing Danny created is a technically difficult device to conceive of, let alone make. I'm surprised he managed it.'

'You and I have got very different philosophies on praising people. How do you know it was him that made it?'

Freddy rolled his eyes. 'He never shut the fuck up about it when we were working together. All the time. How he wanted to build something – *do* something – that would make him one of the most notorious armed robbers in existence.'

'Where did he get the idea from?'

'Not me, if that's what you're insinuating. I wanted nothing to do with it. Besides, I haven't seen them boys in years. Not even a letter or anything.'

'I'm sure they've got their reasons. Least of all trying to lay low. As soon as they come to visit you, the first thing someone's going to do is arrest them.'

'But not even a letter?' Freddy rolled his right sleeve higher up his wrist. 'They could have done it anonymously. I kept them safe while I've been in here. Protected them. When I was interrogated, they offered me a shorter sentence in exchange for information. But I didn't give it. I gave my life for those kids. I kept quiet. And now look at the thanks I get.'

'Don't worry,' Jake said. 'We'll catch them.'

'I'm not worried about you catching them. I'm more worried about them doing something stupid. Before, we liked to keep things simple. Rush in, get what we needed, and then get back out again. But this time's different. This is the first time Danny's been in charge of a raid, and it follows none of the patterns from our previous ones. He's gone rogue. I mean, they've fired shots, they've spent cases, something we never did when I was in charge – you can vouch for that.'

Jake nodded. He could. He recalled the time he and Freddy had been locked inside the HSBC bank in Oxford, Freddy holding a shotgun to a door and explaining why he'd needed to pull the trigger for the first time in his life. Up until today, the only thing The Crimsons had shot was an unsuspecting inanimate object.

'Danny's gone more sadistic,' Freddy continued. 'And I doubt they're following the post-heist protocol either.'

'Which was?'

Freddy leant forward in his chair. Two feet separated them now. Face to face. The smell of warm stale breath assaulted Jake's senses.

'Have you got a map?' Freddy asked.

Jake looked at him, perplexed. When he and Bridger had arrived at the prison, they'd been forced to hand in all their possessions – including phones and wallets. 'I don't have my AA map with me unfortunately.'

'Well, you're going to need one,' Freddy said.

Exhaling deeply, Jake lifted himself out of his chair, hurried over to the door and spoke with the prison officers standing guard outside. He ordered them to bring him a map, and within minutes, they returned. As Jake scurried back to the desk, he was already unravelling the pages. He set the map of England down on the table and placed his hands on the corners to stop it from folding over itself.

'Our first hit was here.' Freddy pointed to Newcastle. 'And then we moved down to Leeds, Leicester, Oxford and now Guildford.' Freddy pointed to each corresponding location as he went through the list. 'For each hit, we had designated extraction points, and a series of cars to get us there – a trail of automotive breadcrumbs, if you will. We'd leave cars all over the place so that we could chop and change. None of the reg numbers were legit, and we always had several changes of clothes. Then, once it had all died down, we'd just slip out of the city and move to the next, staying in hostels and hotels and rented places. You'd be surprised how many people are willing to turn a blind eye to criminals staying in their property when it comes to a large chunk of cash.'

'Sounds like you had a solid plan.'

'We were meticulous. *I* was meticulous. But if that didn't work then we always had extra help.'

Jake's ears perked up. The air temperature seemed to drop suddenly. 'Extra help?'

Freddy slid the map back to Jake and made a pig noise. The sound reverberated around the walls.

Jake said nothing; his face fell flat, bemused.

'Come on, Jake,' Freddy began, 'you didn't seriously think we could get away with it *all* on our own? All those years. All those robberies. Never a single arrest.'

'I…'

'We had help from the inside every single time. Someone working against you. But when it came to Oxford… well, we could never account for *you*. There was a cock-up with our contact. He got delayed and then you decided to be a hero and get in the way. He didn't know how to handle it in time. Never found out what happened to him.'

'What about now?' Jake asked. 'Have Danny, Michael and Luke got someone helping them?'

A smile grew on Freddy's face. He snorted and wiped his nose with the back of his hand, leaving a green trail of snot behind. 'I don't know. This hit was organised *after* I got sent down. Chances are, yes. Someone in your band of little merry men is working against you, helping them escape. Couldn't tell you how, couldn't tell you who – it changes every time.'

Jake felt the knot in his stomach return, and this time it wasn't like the first day nerves that had wracked his body earlier; it was something more malicious, more volatile. The fear of someone betraying himself and the rest of the team. That someone was helping Danny, Michael and Luke evade capture, evade justice, evade the murder of an innocent person. Jake felt like he needed a moment to comprehend what Freddy had told him, but time was a commodity he couldn't afford to waste, and there was a treasure trove of answers he needed to unearth.

Jake lowered his gaze to the table, turned his attention to the map and ran his finger down the country. As his finger fell over Oxford, an idea popped into his head. He glanced up at Freddy.

'All of your heists… each one got further and further south.'

'Exactly. Why do you think that is?'

Jake shrugged. He didn't appreciate the belittling, being treated like he was a schoolchild, but he was under Freddy's power at the moment, so there was nothing he could do save suck it up. 'Because there's more money down south?'

Freddy brandished his middle finger and aimed it at Jake. 'Think bigger. Think differently. You're an intelligent guy – I'm sure you can work it out.'

Jake looked at the map again. His eyes ran along the south coast of England from right to left. Brighton. Portsmouth. Southampton. Bournemouth. Back to Portsmouth. Dozens of thin blue lines ejected from the city in a spider's web that stretched across the Channel.

'Port,' Jake said slowly, the cogs in his brain beginning to whir. 'They're heading to a port. Portsmouth Harbour?'

'Distinction. Top of the class. Well done. When we started, we made a pact. We decided that we would head down the country, taking more and more money with us, taking bigger and bigger risks, and then we'd get the fuck out of here like a whore in the night. Your boys, if there's nothing else they've made good on, won't be staying still. They'll be on the move. They'll be heading towards a boat that'll ship them out of the country as soon as possible. And then you'll never see them again. How much did they take in Guildford?'

'I don't know. Couple hundred thousand? Half a mil? Maybe more. I have no idea. It was a jewellery store.'

Nodding, Freddy said, 'Add that to what we took in our previous hits and they're going to be smuggling over two million out of the country. Easy.'

'How? How are they going to smuggle that much?'

Freddy smirked. 'You're so naïve, Jake. You've got a lot to learn. I can tell the past couple of years have taught you nothing.'

'Just tell me how, Freddy.'

'A few ways: the friends in high places, the friends in low places and the friends in middle places. They'll have contacts who can facilitate the expatriation of all that money. They'll be looking to export a lot of bags out of this country.'

'Where are they going?' Jake asked.

'I don't know.'

'Bullshit.'

'It's true.'

'Come on, Freddy. You expect me to believe that you never discussed where you would end up after all this was done?'

Freddy started picking at his nails, unearthing the dirt and grime from beneath them and wiping it on his trousers. 'We discussed it, yes. But we never settled on anything – or anywhere – concrete. They could be going to Australia for all I know.'

'Would they have booked the tickets under their own name?'

Freddy shook his head. 'Unlikely. We all had fake passports – purchased them from a guy called Mick the Mandate – just in case you guys did manage to identify us.'

'What were your aliases?'

'They've changed by now. You've got to give them some credit. We had a rule that if one of us was caught or anything happened to us, we would change everything like that' – he snapped his fingers – 'in an instant, just in case someone grassed to the police.'

Jake hung his head low.

'I know it's not the breakthrough you were looking for, but it's all I can give you.' Freddy twisted his head left and right, clicking the joints in his neck. 'But there is one silver lining…'

Freddy let the comment hang in the air.

'Go on…'

Freddy cleared his throat before continuing. 'If there's one name they would've changed it to – at least *one* of the brothers – it would be their mother's maiden name.'

'Which is…?'

'Harrington.'

CHAPTER 34

OVERACTIVE IMAGINATION

The muscles in Carl's body clenched, his hand wrapped around the steering wheel as he tore through the seventeen miles of Surrey countryside that separated Waverley Abbey from their next destination: Dunsfold Aerodrome, the home to one of television's most popular series, *Top Gear*. The clue had taken some time to decipher, but with a little help from the internet and Smithers – who'd been looking out of the window the whole journey as though he'd never seen grass before – Carl had managed to crack it.

He pulled off the main road and into the runway's entrance, a narrow, unmade path barely wide enough for a single car, framed by an archway of brambles. Carl slowed the car to a stop, rested his chest against the steering wheel and gawped at the hangar in front of him. Aviation had always been a hobby of his, a second love – behind the job and before the wife – but he'd never possessed the ability to become a pilot, thanks to an eyesight problem that rendered him almost blind at the age of nineteen. Now, with the help of modern technology, he was able to see, but his flying days were behind him. As he gazed out at the hangar, he revelled in the history of it, at the aircraft, the lives of the individuals that had flown inside it, the engineers that had worked on it, the care and attention to detail that had been executed on the magnificent feat of machinery that it was.

'Are we going?' Smithers asked.

Carl didn't appreciate the intonation in the young man's voice, but he was too excited to reprimand him for it.

He slipped the car into gear and followed the signs towards the car park. Rolling down the path, a thin row of bushes began to thaw out, gradually revealing the vast expanse of runway tarmac, and Carl was immediately hit with the stark reality of the task in front of them. Dunsfold wasn't on par with Heathrow or Gatwick certainly, but if their search was for a key the size of a thumbnail, they would be there for days – and there was just the two of them. It would take a small army to sift through the cracks in the tarmac and patches of weed-covered concrete.

Twenty yards ahead, at the end of the road, was a booth. Inside sat a man dressed in black with a radio attached to his hip. *Poor sod*, thought Carl. *Bet he's sweating his bollocks off.*

After seeing the car rolling towards him, the security guard slipped out of the booth and sauntered towards them, like he wasn't in any rush.

'Good thing there isn't a murder and robbery investigation going on,' Carl whispered to Smithers. 'Oh… wait.'

The security guard, thumbs hooked into the belt straps around his waistline, stopped by Carl's window. Carl unwound it.

'Sorry,' the guard said, 'no visitors.'

'We're not visitors,' Carl replied.

'Do you have crew passes?'

'No, but—'

'Then in my book you're visitors. You'll have to reverse your way out.'

Without looking, Carl grabbed Smithers by the shoulder and yanked him over into his lap, bringing him into view. 'Does *he* look like a visitor?'

At the sight of Smithers' fluorescent clothes, the guard's eyes widened.

'Is there an issue, officers?'

'We need to gain access to the runway. We're searching for a key that may have been left here this morning.'

'I'm sorry, but nobody's been here this morning. The premises are closed for the week.'

'Are you sure?'

The guard nodded. 'I've been here overnight and all morning. My shifts ends at four.'

'Is that legal?' asked Smithers.

Carl realised the young officer was still in his lap and thrust him back into his seat with a force that almost strained his ageing shoulder muscles.

'It's a slog but someone's got to do it,' the guard replied.

Carl had to intervene before the conversation descended fully into unnecessary chit-chat.

'Are there any other access points to the runway?' he asked.

'None. It's all surrounded by ten-foot barbed wire and a line of trees. Plus, we've got CCTV all over the place, so if someone set foot in here, I'd know about it.'

Carl considered for a moment. He surveyed the guard – the

minutiae of the man's face – and then told him to wait back by his booth. He pulled his phone from his back pocket and dialled Pemberton's number.

'DCI Pemberton…'

'Boss, I—'

'What do you want, Carl? We've just had direct contact from The Crimsons.'

'What did they say?' He sensed the urgency and dread in her voice. Even though he'd been in the job a lot longer, he respected her seniority and rank.

'Where are you?'

'Dunsfold, ma'am,' he said. 'With Smithers. We've spoken to the security guard posted by the entrance and he said nobody's been in or out all morning.'

'You won't find anything,' Pemberton added. Her voice went hoarse as she said it. 'I have reason to believe the final key isn't where the instructions say it is. I believe Danny Cipriano has it.'

'What makes you believe that?'

'The fact that he told me over the phone… Bomb squad found a mobile inside the collar device which means it can be detonated remotely. Danny has both the phone and the key. The Crimsons never intended for us to save her.'

'It was all a distraction?'

'Yes.' Pemberton's voice sounded weak.

'Where are they? Did they tell you where they're headed?'

'We set up a trace on the call, but we lost it as soon as the call ended. The number disappeared – he must have switched the phone off. I'm told the last ping from the cell tower was somewhere near Portsmouth.'

'Maybe they're trying to smuggle themselves out of the country, ma'am.'

Pemberton had barely put her phone inside her blazer pocket before it rang again. *If that's you, Carl, I swear to God, I'm going to—*

'Hello?' she answered with her telephone voice, the one that she found almost everyone had – the higher pitch, the joviality, the sense that she was happy to be interrupted in such a way.

'Guv,' the voice on the other end replied. 'I think there's something we should be worried about.'

Something caught Pemberton's eye. 'Oh yeah?'

'I think we need to be careful around Jake.'

'What do you mean?'

'How do we know he's not in with *them*? I mean, think about it. The first time he comes across them is on their last robbery in Oxford, and he sets one of them up to take the fall. I read the paperwork on the case after it happened, and in the report he never explained what really happened inside that bank. How do we know they didn't plan something together? Freddy took the rap so Jake could get out free and become the new leader of the gang. It worked out perfectly. Now Jake's getting cosy with us while working on the side with The Crimsons for today's hit.'

'You have an overactive imagination.'

'Think about it, Nic – he rocks up today on his first day with us. And, on the same day, The Crimsons strike. Seems like too much of a coincidence to me.

A long silence followed. Pemberton sucked breath through her nostrils, held it there, and then let it fall slowly back out again.

'What do we do?' she asked.

'I say we keep an eye on him. Keep him close. He knows something he's not telling us.'

'I… I just can't see it happening.'

'It's the people you least expect to hurt us that do.'

'And if you're wrong?' she asked.

There was a brief pause and the sound of the phone passing from one ear to the other.

'We'd better hope I am.'

The pounding in Jake's head was malicious – it had a devilish intent behind it, and it was beginning to make him nauseous. It wasn't the onset of a panic attack – he'd had enough to know the symptoms by now – but that didn't stop it feeling like one. As he closed the door behind him, the reality began to settle in like a snowflake melting into the ground. Someone within the team was corrupt, working against him and everyone else to help The Crimsons.

He was finally understanding why, sometimes, reality was a bitter pill to swallow. Throughout his career – and the early stages of his life – he'd grown up with this ideal that all police officers were good, that they were there to help people, that the harsh depictions of them he saw in the movies were just that – fabrications, fiction. Now it was making him question everything he knew about the job, and everyone he'd ever worked with. The team back at Croydon CID; the constables and sergeants and inspectors and the rest of the uniform team. And, worse, he was now questioning his new team, the new faces, the new names. He hardly knew any of them, so it was impossible for him to guess, which only made it harder. The pool of detectives was too big.

But then he took a mental step back and considered. It would have to be someone high up. Someone senior within the team, someone in control of what was happening, so they were able to manipulate the investigation to suit their needs. Only two names came to mind.

Jake rested his head against the wall and exhaled. Bridger was coming to meet him from the other end of the hallway.

Bridger.

'Everything all right, kid?' Bridger had removed his tie and undone his top button. Both of them were gradually undressing as the day wore on.

'Perfect,' Jake lied. He pushed himself off the wall, threw his hands in his pockets and started down the corridor.

Chasing after him, Bridger asked, 'What did he say? What's the latest?'

'I'll tell you in the car. But first I need to make a call.'

CHAPTER 35

HARRINGTON

Danika had been sitting at her desk for hours and her lower back was beginning to flare up. It was an annoying sensation, deeply rooted in her spine – as if someone was constantly prodding and poking it – and no matter what angle she positioned herself in, the tiniest movement set it off and sent a shockwave of agony up and down her body. She winced, clenched her fist and allowed her palm to absorb the brunt of the pain. On a few occasions, she had drawn blood, but it was nothing a quick wipe on her trouser leg wouldn't sort out.

Less than ten minutes had passed since the surprise call from one of The Crimsons. Since then, the office had been sent into a furore of activity. A trace had been placed on the number and emergency responders were being sent to the location rapidly from the local Hampshire police force. Information was being dug out on Danny's, Michael's and Luke's lives, but Danika had paid little attention to the goings-on in the office. She had instead doubled down on her own investigation, focusing her efforts on the life and times of Candice Strachan.

As she reached across the desk for a highlighter, an email popped into her inbox. It was one of the information requests she'd submitted less than an hour ago. She opened the email and read through the report, her eyes widening as her mind absorbed the text.

She had something! Finally. Something of further use to the investigation. But where was Murphy? She craned her head over the desk, searching for him, but he was nowhere to be seen. In fact, she hadn't seen him since the phone call had ended.

Before she could do anything, her phone vibrated. She answered it without checking the caller ID.

'Can you talk?' the voice asked. It was Jake. His voice sounded hoarse and dry, as if he'd been talking for hours without a break.

'This is a bad—'

'The Crimsons are heading south,' he interrupted. 'I've just got out of a discussion with Freddy Miller, and he confirmed they were trying to get out of the country.'

'We've just had a call from one of the brothers. Danny—'

'Cipriano,' Jake said, finishing her sentence for her. 'What did he want? What did he say?'

'He spoke with DCI Pemberton. He told her that there are several ways to detonate the collar, and that he's got the final key. After the call we traced the number to the outskirts of Portsmouth. But that's not everything,' Danika said. She was getting excited now. All thought of Murphy had flown out of her mind. She was getting a kick out of sharing her findings – her ego needed massaging just as much as anyone's. More so when Tony couldn't care less about it. 'I've got some of the information you requested on Candice. Turns out her recent movements have been incredibly suspicious. In fact, everything about her has…'

'I'm listening.'

'SOCO found a ton of bank statements and financial records of hers in her house – both personal and business. According to them, she loved shopping. A lot. But I'm not just talking about any old shopping sprees; I'm talking thousands of pounds' worth of transactions, luscious trips abroad, expensive restaurants—'

'None of this sounds incredibly surprising, Danika.'

'Wait. Let me get to the point and stop interrupting. All of that *normal* behaviour was used to mask something else.' She ran her finger down the page. 'On the twentieth and twenty-fifth of last month, she made a trip to the local bank and B&Q store.'

'Right?'

'This woman has never been to a B&Q in her life as far back as her bank records go. And, to make it worse, her debit card registered the payments in Oxford.'

'Do you know what she purchased?'

'I've spoken with the company, and they confirmed that, in accordance with their records, she purchased a set of four separate locks.'

'You're shitting me.'

'I wish I was. But that's not everything.'

'What?'

'I've looked into her records a little further, and I've noticed that, for the past year Candice has been renting a storage unit in Southampton. It's all in her name.'

There was a long pause.

'Freddy Miller just told me that the brothers are going to be smuggling their money out of the country. They're using Candice's storage units to do it,' Jake said.

'You're not suggesting what I think you're suggesting, are you?'

'Did you ever follow up with that CCTV request from the golf club?'

The change in conversation stunted her. 'Yes… I, er, I passed it to DI Murphy.'

'And you've not heard anything back?'

'No. I—'

'Danika,' Jake began, 'who else knows about the storage units?'

At that moment, her thoughts turned to Murphy, and then she remembered that he'd instructed her to run all information by him first before sharing it with Jake.

'You're the only one who knows about this.'

'Keep it that way. When I spoke with Freddy, he told me that they always used to have inside help. I think you need to be very careful about who you can trust.'

Danika lowered herself into her seat, wincing as bolts of pain shot across her lower back. She surveyed the room, observing those around her, scrutinising their every move.

'I need you to find out something else for me too,' Jake said. 'I need to know Candice Strachan's maiden name.'

Danika leafed frantically through her notes. She knew she'd scribbled it down somewhere – it was just a case of finding it. Even though he didn't say anything to her, she sensed his patience dwindling.

'Yes!' she screamed, brandishing the small Post-It note she'd scribbled on. 'I found it earlier.'

'What is it?'

'Harrington.'

CHAPTER 36

SHOULDER

Danny fidgeted in his seat and scratched the back of his neck. Mercifully, the traffic had eased, and they were finally able to open up the full power of the Audi engine as they reached the end of the A3 and merged onto the A3(M). The call with the woman named Pemberton had been a success, but he'd found it difficult to relax in the back seat. Time was running out, and they were still over twenty miles out from Portsmouth. And that was twenty miles of potential error and mistake. Nothing could go wrong. And that allowed the paranoia in his mind to wander and fester like an infection in an open wound.

They were driving in the fast lane, Luke cradling the speedometer a few miles per hour over seventy. Discretion and remaining as under the radar as possible was paramount. So far, Luke had impressed Danny. The youngest brother had shown his ability in keeping to the stringent restrictions of the Highway Code. But it was bittersweet, because it meant that Freddy had taught him something worthwhile.

In a world where they didn't have a dad, Freddy was the closest thing to a figure that Luke could look up to. There were times when Luke and Freddy would venture to the shops together, chill together in the living room, play video games and smoke cigarettes while Danny worked tirelessly in a supermarket to put food on the table. It was unfair, and a piece of Danny had died every time he'd realised how close they were – every time he'd come home and found Freddy poorly helping Luke with some of his homework or teaching him how to roll his own joints. It was more than just a slap in the face; it was a punch in the stomach, a kick in the balls and a knife in the back. But without Freddy, The Crimsons wouldn't have existed, which was something he was painfully aware of.

'Uh-oh,' Luke said, his eyes jumping up and down in the rearview mirror.

'What is it?' Danny didn't like the sound of that. Not good. Not good. He tilted forward and clung to Luke's headrest. At first he thought it was an engine issue, a puncture, or maybe they'd bizarrely run out of petrol. But then, when the sirens sounded behind him, everything seemed to slow down. Feeling like he was moving in slow motion, Danny twisted in his seat and peered out of the back window.

Over a hundred yards behind them, gaining rapidly on the right-hand line, blue and white lights flashing vehemently, was a police car.

'Shit!' Danny spun round and shifted himself into the middle of the back seat. Luke's eyes were moving left and right furiously, his chest heaving and his knuckles as pale as the rest of him. 'Just keep it steady, all right. Don't do anything stupid. Pull into the middle lane and let them pass. We don't know whether they're looking for us or whether it's—'

Luke swerved the Audi into the middle lane of traffic with a movement so drastic Danny was propelled into the door and smashed his head against the window. The sound of cars blasting their horns told him that they'd cut up a handful of drivers. Lying on the leather upholstery, beneath the window, he felt his body begin to move and rotate, like he was experiencing weightlessness for the first time.

Screams of profanity erupted from the front and Luke's limbs flailed ferociously as he fought for control of the vehicle. The car skidded to the left and then the right, snaking dangerously across the tarmac. Before Danny was able to regain control, the door frame by his head imploded and a shower of splintered glass rained down on him. He protected his face with his arms, but it didn't stop small pieces sprinkling his skin.

After a very long second, the car came to a stop and the engine stalled. Danny was dazed. Covered in glass popcorn, he lifted himself to his elbow, keeping his hands away from the jagged edges. As the broken window came into view, he realised what had happened.

Somehow, in Luke's efforts to merge into the other lane of traffic, he'd lost control of the back end. Now Danny was staring directly at the logo of a Peugeot 2008, while the driver massaged his neck and checked on his wife beside him. What a shitshow. It was difficult not to feel slightly smug that Freddy had failed Luke in teaching him how to remain calm in situations like that, but it dawned on Danny that he was going to fail Luke even harder if he didn't get them out of there soon.

Danny snapped his head back and forth, left and right, his eyes searching for signs of the police vehicle. The mile upon mile of tarmac in front of them was empty, the cars ahead of them disappearing over the wavy horizon. All except one. The police car, angled across two lanes of traffic.

'Grab everything!' Danny bellowed.

'What?' Luke was immobile, frozen into the seat, paralysed by fear.

Danny reached for Luke's belt buckle, unclipped it and punched him in the arm. The movement was enough to stir some action in his youngest brother, but there was still a long way to go. By now, the police officer was out of the car and hurrying towards them. Surrounding them from the left was a row of traffic. Drivers and passengers were beginning to disembark their vehicles and help in any way they could. It was an ambush, and Danny was grateful they hadn't rolled over or flipped; otherwise they would have been heading towards Destination Jail Cell for certain.

Grabbing his gym bag and Mini-Uzi from the footwell, Danny kicked open the other door and slid out, brandishing the weapon in the air, swinging the gym bag over his shoulder simultaneously.

'Everyone get back and stay where you are!' he screamed, small bits of spittle and phlegm expelling from his mouth and landing on his arm.

He trained the weapon on the police officer, who slipped on the ground in panic then corrected himself, hands held high in the air.

'Nobody do anything stupid otherwise I *will* shoot.'

Danny stole a glance at Michael. The heavy man was in the middle of shimmying himself out of the car, bag and gun in hand. Meanwhile, Luke was doing the same, just slower. *Good lad. Come on.*

'Get a car,' Danny hissed to Michael. 'Anything. The nearest thing.'

The sign for Portsmouth, indicating that the small city was only ten miles away, dangled in the middle of the motorway a hundred yards ahead. Nearly there. They were so close. Danny was determined to see it through to the end. They'd come this far.

A series of screams and shouts – male, female, juvenile – erupted from behind him. Michael and Luke were raiding the car at the front of the traffic, a 2004 five-door Saab, missing an alloy and with a dent in the bonnet that looked as though it had been caused by a body being impaled on the front as the driver attempted to run someone down. Hardly the most inconspicuous vehicle, but right now they didn't have the luxury of choice.

Michael grabbed the driver by the neck and threw him onto the ground, while Luke took care of the passenger. In the back seat, strapped into a car seat, was a toddler, screaming, bawling its eyes out. Letting the gun drop to his hip, Luke yanked the child and seat out of the car and handed it to the woman. They were in. Two down. One to go.

As Danny turned his attention back to the police officer, he noticed the constable was charging towards him, a few steps away from signing his own death wish. Danny refocused his aim and fired a few warning shots, burying a series of bullets in the tarmac. The officer paid it little heed, his momentum too strong. Danny didn't want to kill him – not a police officer. If he did, he knew everyone the police had at their disposal would come after them. Killing one of their own was an ill-fated decision, the biggest sin of them all.

He turned away from the officer and hurried to the back of the Saab, bumping into the woman as he went. It was Michael's turn to drive, and Luke was sitting shotgun in the passenger seat. Throwing the door open, Danny chucked the gym bag into the back and hopped in. As he leapt into the vehicle, his finger caught on the trigger and sent a projectile barrelling through the air.

Michael floored the accelerator and propelled Danny into the back of his seat, the door dragging closed by itself from the momentum of the vehicle. After regaining himself and dropping the weapon by his feet, Danny turned to see the devastation he'd caused.

The bullet had collided with the police officer. The man in uniform was down, clutching his shoulder while strangers jumped out of their cars to tend to him. The last thing Danny saw before they drove out of sight was the officer reaching for the radio strapped to his shoulder.

CHAPTER 37

CRY FOR HELP

'I don't believe you,' Pemberton said to Jake on the phone, running her fingers through the back of her hair and massaging her scalp. Third phone call in the space of three minutes, and it was the worst one yet. She didn't want to believe it. Couldn't. Like the time her sister-in-law had been diagnosed with Parkinson's disease. It wasn't fair, and neither was this.

'I wish it wasn't true, ma'am,' Jake said loudly in her ear.

'I need hard facts though, Jake. I can't just go in there and accuse her of being involved with all of this without anything to back it up. I don't want to be standing there with my pants down by my ankles in an uncompromising position.'

'I've asked Danika to check them over multiple times,' Jake replied. 'They're solid.'

Pemberton was standing on the driveway, outside the front door of Candice's mansion. She'd left Candice alone with Armitage and the rest of the explosives experts. She needed breathing space. Meanwhile, the SOCOs continued to remove dozens of bags of evidence they'd found in the house and surrounding area to be sent back to the station.

'This is not the sort of situation I want to be in, Jake.'

'Is there a way we could get her to confess?'

'What are you talking about?'

'If she's in on this, then she'll know the spikes in the collar are fake. She'll know the charge inside it isn't live. The whole point of chaining that thing to her neck has been to distract us this whole time while they escape. All you need to do is try and take it off. Gauge her reaction. Even if for a second she believes that there's an issue with the keys or the device itself – we've already seen the little twist he's thrown in there with requiring both keys at the same time – then she'll panic. She'll know that she's been betrayed.'

Pemberton nodded as she listened to Jake. 'Leave it up to me,' she said, shuffling her feet in the gravel until her foot disappeared underneath the stones. 'I'll deal with it my own way.'

His hands trembled as he pulled the Nokia mobile from his back pocket. Things were rapidly beginning to take a nosedive, and he didn't know how much more control he had over things, if any. It was supposed to be a simple run. The Crimsons – the only name he knew them by – were going to rob the jewellery store, and all he had to do was make sure nobody found out who'd done it. But they'd said nothing about murdering someone, taking a hostage and wrapping a spiked collar round their neck.

The Cabal had told him it would be simple. A morning's work, at most.

Now look where he was: beginning to feel like soon he'd be without a paddle.

He opened the address book, found the mobile number and typed out a message.

Not going well. Struggling. Need assistance.

A cry for help – he never thought he'd have to do that. What sort of impression would that leave The Cabal with? He stood to make a lot of money from this little act of corruption, and if he couldn't make it a success, then there was no brand-new car, no extension to the house. There was nothing.

If he was going to make it a success, then he needed to pull his finger out and play dirty.

CHAPTER 38

CONFRONTATION

Pemberton stormed round the side of the house and over to Candice, parting the sea of officers either side of her. The helpless woman now sat on a garden chair that one of the explosives officers had brought across for her. She had her arms folded on her lap, and her expression remained still. Nothing had changed in the few minutes Pemberton had been gone.

'Is everything OK, Detective?' Candice asked hopefully.

Pemberton paused a beat before responding. How much did she want to let on? Should she trust Jake and follow his suggestions? Or should she deal with it her own way? She had too many voices inside her head clouding her judgement.

'No, Candice,' she said eventually. 'You and I both know it's not OK.'

Candice's head frantically darted between Pemberton and both the explosives officers beside her. 'You're scaring me. What's happening?'

'Tell me about your acting career, Candice,' Pemberton said plainly.

Candice's eyes widened in horror. 'What— I... er... what do you mean?'

'You know, your acting career. The one you had when you left school. The one when you were in your twenties.'

'I... How did you...?' Candice swallowed, and her throat convulsed. 'It didn't last long. I had a couple of auditions for plays. Had a few minor parts, nothing major. I had to leave the industry.'

'Why?' Pemberton asked without giving Candice an instant to carry on.

'Because…' Candice swallowed again, this time lowering her head onto the metal plate of the collar bomb. She sniffed hard and her chest started to heave. 'Because the director… I was starring in this Hollywood production. It was a small thing. Nothing… nothing major. Nothing like on the big screen. But it was *my* big break. And then… then the director called me to his dressing room one time after we'd just finished shooting for the day. He said I'd done really well. Said I was a real talent. Had a real career in acting ahead of me.'

'Bet that was nice to hear.'

Candice glanced up at Pemberton and scowled. 'It was. But he took it one step too far. He raped me. And I got pregnant.'

'What happened then?'

'I… I kept it.'

'And what did your husband have to say about it?'

Now the tears came, but when Pemberton gave her no sympathy, she stopped. 'I never told him it wasn't his.'

Pemberton thought for a second. About the conversation she'd had a few moments ago with Miriam, one of the people in the office she'd considered her closest friends, one of the people she trusted most, one of the only people in the office to know about her affair. After Miriam had called to update her on Luke Cipriano's identity, she'd uncovered the names of his brothers, Danny and Michael, and told her how all three shared the same father. Which, in Pemberton's mind, meant it would be impossible for what Candice was saying to be true. There was no rape, there was no pregnancy, there was no birth.

Candice was lying.

Pemberton bent down on her knees, taking care not to split her trousers in two. She placed a finger on the grass for extra balance. 'You know what they say about actors, don't you? They make very good liars. After all, that's what you're doing, isn't it? Lying. Pretending to be someone you're not. And getting paid to do it as well. I think the director was right – you are a good one, and you probably did have a great career in front of you.'

Pemberton let the statement hang in the air in front of Candice's face.

'Please,' Candice implored. She reached out and clawed at Pemberton, who threw the woman's arms away. 'You have to get this thing off me. You have to find the key. You have to save me.'

'There is no key, Candice. We know what's going on.'

The whites of Candice's eyes brightened, her pupils darkening and dilating into small marbles.

'Wh-Wha-What do you mean there's no key?'

'Your eldest son, Danny – he told us as much.'

At the mention of Danny's name, Candice's face dropped. It was a picture: the colour that rushed from her cheeks, the muscles in her face that contorted into a frown, her bottom lip quivering.

Never before had Pemberton seen fear strike someone so coldly; she just wished she had a camera with her so she could relive the moment again and again. She took a mental image instead.

Candice shook her head frantically. 'No. No. No, no, no, no. I don't understand. *You* don't understand.'

'You can stop the act now,' Pemberton said, standing. 'The play's over.'

'No – you don't understand.' Candice scratched her scalp with her fingers and rubbed her eyes with the other. 'You *need* to find the keys. Please.'

'I told you, there are no keys.'

'Find the fucking keys, you bitch!' Candice's voice carried across to the other end of the garden, rousing the attention of the officers in the vicinity. 'Can't you realise I'm going to die if you don't get this thing off me?'

'What are you talking about?' Pemberton asked. 'There are no spikes in there. There's no detonator inside. You know it.'

'There is. There are. For Christ's sake there are!'

Pemberton retreated slightly. 'Explain yourself.'

'I lied. About the rape, about the pregnancy. The-They're my sons. All of them. The Crimsons. Danny. Micky. Lukey. I gave birth to them at a bad time in my life and I hadn't seen them for years. But after my husband died, they made contact, and I was ready to accept them for what they were. And then we staged today. But I had no idea that Danny was going to shoot Rachel. I had no idea. Each of them were in charge of different keys. Luke did the first one, but he hid it in a different place in the house – it wasn't where we'd agreed. Micky was responsible for the golf course and Waverley Abbey ones. Danny should have left his key on one of the Dunsfold runways. He promised he'd leave it in plain sight,' Candice said. Something caught in her throat and tears began to well in her eyes.

'But he hasn't, has he?' Pemberton asked. 'What's he done with it?'

'He's kept it. Or put it somewhere else.'

Candice choked. Her chest heaved rapidly. She grabbed the collar and began to shake the device free from her neck, alerting the explosives officers. They rushed to her side and pinned her arms behind her back.

'What happens now, Candice? Stop resisting!' Pemberton whistled two nearby police constables to rush to their side. They straddled Candice's legs and placed handcuffs around her wrists behind her back. 'What happens now, Candice? We're trying to help you.'

'Get this thing off me!'

'Tell me about the device. What will it do?'

Panting heavily, Candice said, 'I don't know. Danny built it. He told me the keys would defuse it.'

'But how do you know there's a charge in there? Why would he build it to be live? Why would he want it to activate those spikes?'

'I-I-I don't know. We agreed that the keys would disarm it, but when I heard you talking about remote detonation, that was when I knew that he wanted to kill me. I should have seen it coming when we were in the jewellery store. He held that gun in my face for too long. He had the opportunity to shoot me dead there and then, but he didn't take it.'

'Why would he want to kill you, Candice?'

'For the years he's been alone. For the years they've all been alone. I thought this was a way for me to rebuild their trust. A way for me to come back into their lives. After my husband died, I had nothing, no one. But when they made contact with me, I thought we were going to be a family again. We were all going to leave the country and never look back.'

'Leave the country?' Pemberton repeated, her voice turning shrill.

'That's what we agreed. To get on a boat out of here.'

I don't believe it.

'Where?'

Candice shook her head. 'Please. You have to get this thing off me. I'll help you find them. I promise I will. Whatever it takes. I don't want to die. I'll help you – but I need you to promise me something first.'

'What?' Pemberton asked. Her mind wasn't with it. She was in disbelief. Jake Tanner had been right about everything. There was no possible way he could be working against them.

'I want you to promise that nothing will happen to Luke or Micky if they're caught. Danny's the one who should be done for all of this.'

'And if we refuse that?'

'Then I won't tell you where they are or where they're going to be.'

'And you won't be alive to see their trial.'

CHAPTER 39

DAD

Jake's body tingled as he felt the stress and tension slowly dissipate in his shoulders the way a drop of blood spreads through water. He'd just finished explaining to Bridger what Freddy had told him – about where the Cipriano brothers were headed, and that there was an internal force opposing them – and the brief information Danika had relayed about Roger Heathcote.

'You have to be careful believing everything you hear,' Bridger told him, his wise words warming Jake. 'Freddy might have been telling you that just to confuse you. He's still a criminal, don't forget.'

The smell of the strawberry Jelly Bean car freshener dangling from the rearview mirror reminded Jake of his own one, but it was tinged with a slight chemical smell – from somewhere in the car or outside world, the smell of bleach seeped through the fabric and reached his nostrils. Disregarding it, Jake shuffled deeper into Bridger's leather seats and contemplated, casting his mind back to 2006, when he and Elizabeth had been planning to buy their very first car. To the trip to the bank that had been cut short by The Crimsons and their raid on the Oxford branch of HSBC. He tried to think of the experience he'd had afterwards, dealing with the police and the subsequent investigation. Whether it was possible that someone had been working to help them even then. But there was nothing. He even tried to think of the plethora of case files and notes he'd memorised from their previous three heists before Oxford, whether there were any anomalies in there.

And then it dawned on him.

The Crimsons' first heist in Newcastle. There'd been an issue – a flawed escape, and a subsequent high-speed pursuit. But one of the police officers involved in the pursuit had cut up another police vehicle, and The Crimsons had been able to flee the city. It had been investigated but it had been put down to an accident, no serious foul play. Was that enough to convince Jake that everything Freddy had said was true?

Jake explained his theory to Bridger.

The man's face remained the same as he listened, his eyes focused on the road ahead, silent, nodding his understanding every now and then. Eventually, after Jake had finished, he scratched the underside of his chin, tickled the top of his Adam's apple, and said, 'Some people just want to watch the world burn, don't they?' He glanced at Jake. 'Don't go overthinking it, but I suggest you and I be extra cautious of everyone and anyone now. I never thought I'd say this, but I think you might be right.'

'Do you have any idea who it could be?'

Bridger shook his head. 'Wouldn't want to guess. I *know* these people – I don't want to accuse them of anything until I know more.'

'How do we do that?'

'We wait and see how things progress. If anyone makes any obvious attempts to throw the investigation, then we'll have our answer.' Bridger paused, chewed the inside of his cheek. 'But if I had to guess… and this is just my gut instinct…'

'Yes?'

'You're not going to like it.'

'I don't like it either way.'

'I think you should be careful of Danika.'

Jake felt like he'd been slapped round the face twice, on both cheeks, extra hard. Danika? No, surely not. It was unfathomable, it was—

'Why?'

Bridger massaged the steering wheel as he prepared himself to speak. 'Before you guys started,' he began, 'Pemberton sat me down and told me I'd be supervising you both. She gave me a handful of reports – your personal files – and suggested I read them. So I did. Spent the entire evening on it, truth be told. And, well… Danika's made for interesting reading. Her and her husband, in particular. They're both going through external counselling, and Danika's going through personal therapy through the service.'

Bridger took a moment to pause, and Jake joined him. This was all new to him – he felt like he didn't truly know his friend at all.

Bridger continued: 'Anyway, after you told me about Roger Heathcote and his background, I just… well, I put two and two together. Woman seeking divorce meets wealthy family lawyer meets organised crime group meets happy ending. Danika helps them escape, Heathcote gets his five minutes of fame, they each

147

take a share of proceedings and they're all happy. After, Danika can pay for a divorce, or run away with the kids and, well…'

In the time that Bridger had been speaking, Jake had zoned out, only half aware of what was being said. His mind was in a brief state of shock, a blank canvas, devoid of any thought.

'Sorry,' Bridger said, luring Jake back to the present. 'Sorry. I shouldn't have said anything.'

'No.' Jake held a hand in the air to no one. 'You… you were right. Some people just want to watch the world burn.'

Jake lifted his head and looked out of the window. According to the satnav, they were fifteen miles away from Portsmouth, on the M27 heading south with mile upon mile of open road in front of them. As they passed over the River Hamble, Jake's mobile rang, offering him a chance to forget about what he'd just heard.

'Jake?' It was Elizabeth.

'Liz? What's wrong? Is everything OK?' At once all thoughts of Danika evaporated and made way for an eruption of a different kind of paranoia.

'Can you talk?' she asked slowly. He sensed, from the reticence in her voice, that she was hiding something.

'Of course I can. What's happened? Have you heard?'

'Yes. She's fine. She's going to be all right.'

Jake breathed a monumental sigh of relief.

'The doctor said she's just got a severe cough and should be kept in bed for the next couple of days.'

'Thank God,' he said and meant it. 'Where are you now?'

'Coming home.'

'Good. Don't tell your mum – I don't want her near Maisie when she's like this. On the other hand, maybe you should invite her, that way she might get sick.'

'Leave it, Jake. Our daughter is more important than your issues with my mum,' Elizabeth said as Bridger slowed behind the car in front of him. 'When can you come home?'

She'd learnt very early not to ask when he was coming home, but when he could come home. The questions were completely different, but in most instances, the answer was always the same: late.

Jake hesitated before responding. 'I don't know, Nelly. I'm sorry. Something big's come up.'

Nelly was his nickname for her. After she'd told him that her favourite animal was the narwhal, it was the first thing that had come to mind. Nelly the Narwhal.

'Where are you?' Elizabeth asked.

'Portsmouth.'

'God. Please be careful, Jake. I don't want something to happen to both of you. Not in the same day.'

'Everything's going to be fine. I'd love to come back and help – it's killing me that I can't. But there are things I've got to take

148

control of first. It's my first day and I'm dealing with some old friends.'

'Old friends?'

Jake paused a moment before continuing. 'The Crimsons. They're back. And this time they've killed someone and taken a hostage.'

'Please be careful… don't put yourself in any unnecessary danger. I want you home in one piece.'

'I'll be safe, I promise. I'm going to end this once and for all.'

He hung up and returned his attention to a still atmosphere, save for the sound of the engine purring beneath them. Bridger was silent, patient, pretending as though he hadn't been listening to every word, even though his very stiff reaction said otherwise. Jake could hardly blame him; it was human nature to be inquisitive and curious.

'Everything all right?' Bridger asked politely.

'Getting there. My daughter's sick. My wife's taking care of her.'

Bridger slipped the gear down to fourth as he overtook a car. 'How old is she?'

'Two.'

'Lovely. You sound like a wonderful father.'

Jake scratched his jaw. 'You got any?'

'None. Never been married either. Single pringle is the phrase, I believe. But the old body clock's running down on me.'

'Never say die,' Jake said. More and more Bridger reminded him of his dad.

He must have voiced part of this thought aloud, because Bridger said, 'I remind you of who?' his voice laced with surprised.

'My dad,' Jake replied sheepishly, feeling a wave of embarrassment roll over him.

'I suppose that's a good thing. I've always been under the impression that dads are like arseholes.'

'Erm…'

'Everyone's got one, and also they're arseholes.'

'You didn't get on with yours I take it?'

'Not from the little I saw of him. Left me and my brother when we were young. But I guess I turned out all right. How about yours?'

'Dead.'

Jake found the monosyllabic response to that question always shocked people, as though it was taboo to speak it so frankly and abruptly. They always looked at him with an expression on their face that asked whether he was all right mentally. Everyone except for Freddy and Bridger. Jake supposed it was because, in both men's eyes, dead was probably the same word they would have used to describe their relationship with their own fathers.

'What happened to him?' Bridger asked.

149

'Car accident on the way to picking me up from a football match. I was fifteen. Never kicked a ball since.'

'Shit, man, that's heavy. I'm sure he was a wonderful bloke.'

Jake turned his gaze from Bridger and looked into his lap. He inhaled and exhaled slowly, deeply, smoothly. 'He was. The best.'

'You miss him?'

'Everyday.'

'It gets easier. Trust me.'

Jake grunted. If there was anything he could do to have his dad back with him, he'd do it and not throw the relationship away. Jake thought Bridger's attitude was somewhat blasé, but who was he to judge? He didn't know the ins and outs of Bridger's relationship with his dad, so he decided to keep his mouth shut.

'I think maybe after all of this is done,' he said in the end, 'we should get a beer somewhere.'

CHAPTER 40

DECISION

Never before in her illustrious career had DCI Pemberton been forced to make as tough a decision as the one in front of her now. Candice Strachan had just confessed to being the fourth member of The Crimsons, to having a role in the robbery and kidnapping, to helping them smuggle themselves out of the country, to aiding and abetting their crimes. And Pemberton hated her for it.

But now Candice *was* the victim. She *was* going to die. The collar would detonate if the final key wasn't found. There wasn't enough time on the countdown for Jake or Bridger to retrieve the key from Danny and return to Farnham. There wasn't enough time to find Danny and the rest of the brothers, arrest them and then bring them back to the garden. Whichever way she looked at it, she was faced with an impenetrable brick wall of indecision from every angle. If she remained inactive, Candice's blood would be on her hands.

'PC Mooney,' she called to one of the uniformed officers who'd been standing on the outskirts of the garden; he came rushing over.

'Yes, ma'am.' His face beamed and his cheeks shimmered with a thin layer of sweat.

'I need a vehicle. A police escort vehicle. Something big. Something that's going to be able to transport Ms Strachan over there.' Pemberton nodded in Candice's direction.

'Are… are you sure, ma'am? Would we not be able to use the OED's van?'

Pemberton shook her head. 'It's not the right kind of vehicle. That's just a Transit. We need something that we can isolate Candice in. The same thing we use to transfer criminals from prison

151

to prison. You know what I mean?'

Words weren't making sense to her. It was like the events of the past few hours had destroyed the synapses in her brain that controlled all thought processes and communication. All her training and use of police jargon had flown out of her head.

'I think so…' Mooney said, nodding, uncertain of himself. 'Leave it with me. I'll sort it out. When do you need it?'

'Ten minutes ago.'

Mooney started off, speaking into the radio pack on his shoulder. He was authoritative and calm and, to Pemberton's surprise, able to concisely tell the person on the other end what they needed. A prison transport vehicle. *Of course it was, idiot.*

Pemberton wandered back to Candice, who was still sobbing and pleading on her knees.

'Pl-Ple—' she began but was cut off by Pemberton's hand.

'Stop. Just stop. We're doing everything we can for you. God knows you don't deserve it,' Pemberton added. She had lost all prudence in her voice; it was now filled with disdain. She no longer cared for the spite in her words. 'I've had an idea that's going to get you out of that thing.'

Candice looked up at her, eyes beady and bloodshot. 'What is it?'

'We've received reports that your sons have stolen a vehicle, been involved in a road traffic collision, shot at a police officer, and —'

'Oh my God,' Candice whispered, her voice trembling as it turned into a whimper. She tried to move her hands, but they were still wrapped behind her back.

'You know what their next moves are,' Pemberton continued, 'because you're a part of this. Which boat are they getting on, Candice?'

'I can't remember.'

Liar.

'Do you remember when I told you that I had an idea?'

Candice nodded.

'Your survival hinges on your next choice. Do you understand?'

Candice nodded again, but this time she pulled her gaze away from Pemberton.

'We have a special vehicle we can transport you in. Now, we would usually move you to the station, but these are extenuating circumstances. And I'm the person in charge of making the decisions for said extenuating circumstances. How lucky you are.' Pemberton was enjoying the delicacy of this revenge, and she was savouring every moment of it. 'This vehicle… it's safe, robust and will keep you isolated. It's got a lot of petrol inside it, and it's fast. Do you know what that means, Candice?'

Candice didn't reply. Pemberton eyed her for a moment before continuing. A part of her wanted to leave Candice there, stranded, helpless. To use it as a form of punishment. It was what she deserved. It was her own fault for becoming an accomplice in such a heinous crime in the first place, regardless of her motives. But then the prospect of disciplinary hearings and potential dismissal if anything happened to Candice were enough to convince her otherwise.

'It means that we can transport you to wherever your sons are. You might want to protect them, but remember who put you in this situation. They did. So it's in your best interest to tell us where they might be, because if we can find them, we can find the key, and if we can find the key, we can get you out of this – and then you'll be able to live longer than the countdown timer indicates. How does that sound?'

Candice opened her mouth and voiced something, but it was weak, inaudible.

'Excuse me?'

'Yes.'

'Yes what?'

'Do it!' Candice screamed, thrashing her body left and right. 'They were talking about boarding a boat in Portsmouth sometime in the afternoon. They needed to give themselves time to get there.'

'And were you supposed to be joining them?' Pemberton toyed between placing her hands on her hips or folding her arms. In the end, she went with the former.

'Yes. I'm s-s… I'm sorry.'

'It's a little late for that now.'

Mooney arrived behind her.

'Ma'am,' he said, hovering a few feet away. 'I've just spoken to HQ. The vehicle you requested is on its way. ETA five minutes.'

CHAPTER 41

FINAL GOODBYES

The Crimsons reached the end of the arterial road's tail and were on Queen Street, right in the epicentre of Portsea. Directly ahead of them, half a mile away, was a tower block that jutted out of the flat skyline like a pimple on a teenager's face. To their right was HMS *Nelson*, Portsmouth's home to the Royal Navy. Danny glanced out of the window and glimpsed a short view of the base's gate. A sense of elation washed over him. The finishing line was in sight. But it wasn't without its risks. Only moments ago their endeavours had almost been cut short, and any one of them could have been knocking on death's door.

After the incident, Danny had closed his eyes and, for the first time in his life, prayed to God. Whether the big man upstairs had heard him, he didn't know, but he felt like there was a spiritual awakening beginning to bubble in the bottom of his stomach. Somebody was testing them – testing *him*. Throwing obstacles in his way, making him a better criminal for it. But, at the same time, somebody was watching out for him, guiding him through those obstacles. Danny liked to think it was their dad, the man who'd taught him everything he knew about explosives and engineering. For all his faults as a father – the abandonment, the drinking, the abuse – he'd taught Danny the most important life lesson he could've learnt.

'Never give up no matter what stands in your way,' his dad had said as he rolled a cold tin of Stella in one hand, cigarette in the other. 'Life's full of shit, but you just gotta wade through it.'

As they sped down the road, nearing the end of Queen Street and the towering block of flats, Danny realised they were wading through a different type of shit: students, families, groups of teenagers, boys, girls, men, women, children, all enjoying the sun and stifling temperatures in their T-shirts and shorts and skirts, ice creams in hand along with bottles of water and buckets and spades, preparing for a day of luxury, freezing water, sand, and the delight of spending a nice afternoon in the company of everyone else from the town in close proximity with one another on Southsea beach. Danny couldn't think of anything worse.

He stretched forward and pointed to a junction a few hundred yards away. 'Swing a left up here.'

'I thought we needed to go straight,' Michael began.

Before he knew it, they were at the junction, and Michael showed no sign of following his instruction. Danny lunged forward between the seats and yanked on the steering wheel. The car swerved to the left, and the two brothers fought over control.

'I said turn left,' Danny hissed. 'There's been a change of plan.'

'What do you mean, change of plan?' asked Luke, twisting in the seat. 'Since when?'

Danny ignored his brother and pointed to another sign ahead, barely visible behind the arms of a tree. 'There's a car park up there. Follow the signs for it.'

'Danny – what's going on? Where are you taking us?' Michael asked.

'Shut up and wait,' Danny snapped.

A few seconds later, Michael pulled into the car park. It was old, disused and riddled with potholes. At the back of the car park was the rear fascia of a car wash – the sun danced on the great plumes of spray and water vapour and created several rainbows that glided across the surface. Michael found a free space in the centre of the park and eased the car to a stop, then cut off the engine and waited. The air around them fell silent, save for the repetitive, monotonous din coming from the jet power washers on the other side of a brick wall which drowned out the sound of sirens and helicopter blades in the distance – the sound of the Queen's constabulary hunting them down.

'You've got some explaining to do,' Michael remarked.

'We're not getting the ship here,' Danny said plainly.

Both brothers looked back at him, eyes wide. Michael opened his mouth, ready to unleash an expletive, but Danny allayed him with a wave of the hand.

'Let me explain, before you start kicking off. The police aren't thick – they'll have worked out where we're going by now. Even with our help from the inside. It's not long until this place will be on complete lockdown – they're already above us. So we need another way out of the country. And I took the liberty of booking another set of tickets for us.'

'Where?'

'Southampton.'

'*Southampton*?' both brothers repeated.

'All we need to do is get out of this shit heap, change our clothes, hop on a bus and get on the boat. Perfect escape. The police will find this thing, immediately search it and the rest of Portsmouth Harbour for us, and then look on the ship. By the time they've done all that, we'll be long gone,' Danny explained. He felt the smile on his face growing larger. But he was the only one smiling. He was the only one who appreciated his brilliance, his genius and his forethought.

'You lied to us, Dan. When were you going to tell us?' Michael said.

'I just did.'

'Yeah, right at the last fucking minute. What else aren't you telling us?'

Danny's fingers ran over the key in his pocket.

'What about Mum?' Luke asked, his voice weak, almost childlike.

Danny clipped him round the back of the head with his free hand. 'Don't call her that. That woman has never been a mum to us. Just because she thought she could redeem herself by helping us with this don't mean she gets that privilege.'

Michael twisted in the seat and glared at Danny, his nostrils flaring. 'Answer the question, Danny. What about Candice?'

Danny broke away from Michael's gaze and stared into his own lap. 'She was the one who came up with the idea,' he lied. 'Well, both of us did. She knew about it all along. I told her not to mention it to either of you.'

'Unbelievable.' Michael rolled his eyes. 'So you trusted her more than you did us? When's the boat leave?'

'At three. It's a cruise to the Canaries.'

Michael checked his watch. 'Just under two hours. What are we going to do in the meantime?'

'We've got to get there,' Danny said. 'The bus'll take fucking ages.'

'What about Mum?' Luke repeated. Danny suppressed the urge to clip him round the head again. 'Will she make it in time?'

'Of course she will, mate. If all's gone to plan, they'll have found the keys by now, removed the collar, started interviewing her to make sure she's not involved with anything, maybe even given her a once-over by the medic or ambulance staff, and then they'll send her on her way. Then she can make her own way down. And if there are any issues, our man in office will help expedite her experience.'

For a split second, Danny believed his own lie.

'How do you know? What if they don't find the keys in time?'

Danny placed his hand on Luke's shoulder and squeezed. Lying to his youngest brother hurt the most – Luke was the most gullible, the most naïve – yet it had to be done if they were going to start new lives for themselves. 'I know you're worried about her, kid. But give the police some credit – the keys are piss-easy to find. I mean, Grandma Paula could find them, and she was almost as blind as a fucking bat,' Danny said with a smile. 'Remember when she'd try and make us a roast? Absolute fucking carnage, but she still knew where everything was, eh?'

Luke chuckled, bearing his white teeth. 'Yeah, I guess…'

One brother down, one more to go.

Danny turned his attention to the last one that needed convincing. 'Micky? You coming?'

Michael sighed. 'Not got much choice, have I? I'm having my fair share of this money regardless of where we end up.'

'And you'll get it. Down to the last penny.'

Split four ways, as agreed.

Danny waited until his brothers had started to undress themselves before he began. He unzipped the front of his overalls and rolled the top half over his shoulders. As his hands ran down his arm, he massaged the tender brown and yellow bruises on his skin, grimacing slightly in the pain. Then he pulled the overalls down his waist in the small confines of the back of the Saab and stuffed them into the footwell. Beneath his overalls he'd been wearing a pair of jeans and a hoodie. He reached into the pocket of his jumpsuit, removed the final collar key and slid it into his pocket. It rubbed against his skin, pinned next to his wallet.

'What are we doing with those?' Michael asked, pointing to the machine guns by Danny's lap.

'Those? Keep them here. Leave everything except for the bags.'

Danny opened the car door and slung the bags containing the jewellery over his shoulder. As he was about to close the door, he gave one last look at the red devil mask. It had been with him from their first heist to now. And it had served him well. He'd enjoyed witnessing the horror on the faces of those he was robbing. He'd been born into nothing, and he adored the anonymity that it invoked, like a backward version of Batman – and now he was going to spend the rest of his life overseas, hidden further beneath that cloak of anonymity, soon to be sipping on tequila sunrises on the beach.

Michael, slamming the driver's door shut, brought him back to reality. He felt a hand on his shoulder. Then on his other.

'Time to leave this world behind us, mate,' Michael said. 'For good.'

'We've got another one waiting on the other side of the Atlantic,' Luke added.

Danny turned to him, perplexed, and then broke into a fit of laughter, bent double with his hands placed on his knees, gasping for breath. 'The Canary Islands are on the same side of the Atlantic as us, dickhead!' Danny let out another howl of laughter, and he was surprised to find Michael joining him. Soon after, Luke saw the funny side of it and together the three of them laughed. Danny couldn't remember the last time they'd all done that – briefly forgotten about everything going on, focusing on just the three of them and their bond. It filled him with pride.

After the laughter died down and they suddenly remembered where they were, Danny said his final goodbyes to the mask and started off towards the Hard Interchange, a bus depot situated on the water's edge. Danny had done his research beforehand. The X4 bus from Portsmouth to Southampton ran every half an hour.

CHAPTER 42

LIMA GOLF

'As of fifteen minutes ago,' Pemberton began, her voice coming from the loudspeaker on Bridger's phone, 'there were several reported sightings of Danny, Michael and Luke Cipriano on the A3. They were involved in an RTC, fired at a police officer and stole a Saab 2004, number plate LT04 6JB.'

Jake and Bridger looked at one another in a mild state of disbelief.

'Sorry, ma'am,' Bridger said, 'but did you say they shot a police officer?'

'Yes, a constable. He was attending another call when the incident happened. When he tried to stop The Crimsons, they opened fire on him.'

The disbelief turned into shock.

'Is he going to be OK?' Jake asked.

'He's being treated on the scene. But the A3 is backed up, traffic for miles. I'm having to find a way through the back roads.'

'You're coming to Portsmouth?'

An engine growled, almost as if answering Jake's question. 'I'm bringing Candice with me. She's quarantined in the back. If Danny Cipriano holds the final key to that device, then there simply isn't enough time to get it back to her. She has to be wherever Danny is.'

'And if he doesn't have the key at all?'

There was a pause. A lengthy one.

'Then that doesn't bear thinking about.'

Bridger pulled off the M275 and brought the car to a stop beside Victoria Park, one of Portsmouth's breathing lungs. Opposite was the majestic St John's Cathedral. The gothic building was a clay-red construction made entirely of brick, and from the brief glance he stole, the two spires at the head of the cathedral reminded Jake of a meat fork used for barbecues. Jake wasn't one for religion – he was a believer in natural selection and the Big Bang – but he always managed to appreciate the architectural prowess of religious buildings. The most overwhelming one he'd ever visited was St Peter's Basilica in the Vatican, closely followed by St Paul's in London. Other than that, he was resigned to looking at them on the internet and social media whenever they appeared in his news feed.

While the engine continued to tick over on the side of the road, the car fell silent. Pemberton was still on loudspeaker, but nobody spoke. Jake could see from Bridger's face that he was worried, that he had something on his mind. Jake felt the same way. He summoned the courage to voice it, licking his lips before he did so.

'What about the rest of the team, guv? What's the latest with them?'

'What do you mean, Jake?'

Another glance at Bridger.

Burdened with knowing what he did, Jake was beginning to piece together who might be working against them, and with the unspoken support of the person sitting next to him, he asked: 'Danika, DI Murphy, DC Jenkins – what are they all doing to aid the investigation?' All the other names of the team he'd met this morning had vanished from his mind.

'Are you suggesting they're not pulling their weight, Jake?'

Pemberton's scathing response took him by surprise. It was the first time he'd posed a question to her, and she'd instantly shot him down.

'That's not… that's not what I'm suggesting at all,' he replied.

'Then *what* are you suggesting, Jake?'

Jake opened his mouth but tripped. Bridger moved his hand to the gearstick and caught Jake's attention.

'I think what Jake's trying to say is that it'll be good to know what the rest of the team are up to so we know who to go to for information.'

'Me, Elliot. You come to me. And if I don't know, then you go to Mark. The hierarchy's there for a reason. I'll see you in Portsmouth Harbour.'

The line went dead, and Bridger and Jake were left with a tangible air of awkwardness, the same one he'd felt the first time he'd ever faced rejection – when he'd asked Mary Cunningham to be his girlfriend in Year 9. She'd just looked at him, laughed and then ran away.

'Why didn't you say anything?' Jake asked.

Bridger played with the steering wheel. 'Because I think we need to be careful with who we disclose that information to. If we start telling everyone that there's a bent copper in the team, then we'll never find out who it is.'

'But we didn't even get an answer.'

'Exactly. She cut you off as soon as you insinuated something.'

Jake turned his attention to the outside world. A young woman with a cigarette in her hand and stroller in the other wandered past, with a small toddler lazily catching up behind.

'Where to now then?' he asked.

Before Bridger had a chance to respond, the radio clipped onto the dashboard sounded.

'Echo Bravo Four-Five, Echo Bravo Four-Five from Lima Golf, over.'

Bridger reached for the radio and held it against his lips. 'Lima Golf, Lima Golf, this is Echo Bravo Four-Five. Go ahead, over.'

'Echo Bravo, we've got a positive ANPR hit on the registration for the stolen Saab. Last ping was less than three minutes ago. The car was last seen situated in the Harbour Car Park, Havant Street, postcode Papa-Oscar-One, Three-Echo-Alpha. Are you able to attend with armed support? Over,' said the robotic-sounding individual on the other end of the line.

'Lima Golf, we're on the way. Will report back when we arrive, over.'

'Echo Bravo, received, thank you, over.'

CHAPTER 43

SWEET TASTE

Danika was craving another cigarette. Or a drink. Or both. Perhaps even something stronger. The sweet, delectable taste of tar and vanilla Absolut vodka on her teeth and tongue and throat. Something to help ease the stress of everything going on around her.

Tony, her husband, the man she'd agreed to spend the rest of her life with – a decision she now regretted – had messaged her. Apparently he was taking the boys to his mum's where they'd be spending the next couple of days. Without warning, without consultation. He was taking them away from her, and right now there was nothing she could do about it. Sometimes the answers were at the bottom of a bottle, she found – especially with the added confidence it instilled. Without the alcohol flowing through her system, controlling her entire body the same way an adolescent controls a video game, she wouldn't have the courage to tell him what she really thought about him, what she really wanted to happen between them, what she really hoped would happen to him. Instead those thoughts would stay locked inside her head until she either snapped or found another outlet for her misery.

She tried to force herself not to think about Tony; there were other distractions in the office. Mark Murphy was one of them, but he was too busy at the moment to pay her any sort of attention. In the past hour alone, the Incident Room had been bombarded with a barrage of information. Inquests ordered by Murphy into the possible links between Roger Heathcote and The Crimsons had come up short and had been placed on the back-burner. News of the road traffic collision had flooded into the office, and a handful of officers had been sent down to the crime scene to examine the forensics and question some of the key witnesses. So far, it seemed, The Crimsons were leaving a very messy – and long – trail of paperwork and devastation behind them.

But the most important news that had come into the office was that the Cipriano brothers were heading towards Portsmouth Harbour, readying themselves to board a ship and skip the country. Danika and some others in the team had been tasked with speaking with the port and cruise company and locating the boat they were due to be on.

'Under no circumstance,' Murphy had said, 'are we to cancel the boat or tell them to stay put. You're conducting a fact-finding mission. I just need you to tell me what boat they're due to be on, and I'll take it from there.'

And that was exactly what Danika had done. In record time too, it seemed, beating the others that had been put to the task. She'd always been secretly proud of her ability to find holes in information, find the necessary details, separate the good from the bad, the intelligence from the misinformation. Shame that ability didn't extend to finding the right man.

Danika pushed herself away from the desk and hurried to the kitchen, feeling as though, if she didn't move quickly or with a renewed sense of urgency, she wasn't doing her job properly. Like she was policing her own attitude in the workplace. In the middle of the kitchen was Miriam, the only other international individual Danika had found in the team. They'd bumped into one another in the bathroom and, as some girls were wont to do, started chatting. Born in Germany, she'd moved across to England when she was fifteen and had stayed ever since. Her hair was blonde and her accent was still thick, denser than Danika's.

Danika gave her a brief smile. 'Hey,' she said.

Miriam depressed the kettle switch. 'You having a coffee?'

'Please.'

'Let me fill her up.' Miriam removed the kettle from the plate and added more water, dribbling some down the side. As she set it back on the plate, she took Danika's mug and opened one of her own Nescafé sachets and decanted the contents into the cup. While they waited for the kettle to boil, Miriam glanced over her shoulders and shuffled closer towards Danika.

'Can I ask you something?'

'Sure.'

'I want your opinion. I want to release the mugshots of Danny, Michael and Luke from a few years ago, but Murphy doesn't think it's a good idea. What do you think?'

Danika wasn't too keen on getting roped into office politics so soon in her career. But a part of her was flattered Miriam felt confident in asking her.

I think you should do as you're told and follow the rank. It's there for a reason.

'Did he tell you why he doesn't want to do it?'

'Little to be gained. By the time it gets out, this'll all be over.'

Danika shrugged ambivalently. 'It's not my position to say. I think he knows what he's doing, and who's to say the instruction hasn't come from Pemberton? For all you know she might have told him to keep it within this building.'

To that, she had no apparent answer.

The kettle finished its boil, Miriam made the coffee and left, leaving Danika's cup on the surface. Danika took a sip of the coffee, realised it needed a spoon of sugar – and possibly a hint of Irish – and as she returned to her desk, all she could think about was that sweet, sweet taste in her mouth later on.

CHAPTER 44

X4

The bus pulled in front of them sharply, pistons hissing, brakes shrieking. The momentum caused by the sudden halt propelled the other passengers forward in their seats like they were crash test dummies. Danny, Luke and Michael stood in a line waiting for the X4 from Portsmouth Harbour to Southampton Port via Fareham. They were at the back of the queue, allowing the elderly couples and young families to board first. The less attention they could draw to themselves in this pivotal final stage of their operation, the better. Danny didn't like to think what a life behind bars would look like. Freddy had told him as much in the letters he'd received, which always managed to find themselves in the bin before anyone else could find them. Ever since the beginning, Danny and Freddy, as the eldest members of the group, as the figureheads, had decided that if either of them found themselves in prison, they would write and make contact using a series of aliases and prearranged addresses they'd sorted up and down the country. From the letters Danny saw the pain and hurt and suffering that Freddy had endured. But he had no sympathy for the man, no guilt; he was exactly where he deserved to be. And he never had any intention of sharing the letters with either Michael or Luke.

It was Danny's turn to board the bus, and as he stepped up onto the vehicle, he felt as though all eyes were on him. It suddenly made him very conscious of his surroundings, as though everyone inside the bus was an undercover police officer, and they were all just chomping at the bit to apprehend him. Danny dismissed the thought and joined his brothers on the seats towards the back of the bus, the spot designated for the cool kids. As he wandered up the aisle, his bag jostled against the sides of the chairs and other passengers' shoulders. Panic struck him as the jingles of the diamonds and other pieces of jewellery inside the bag turned a few heads his way. But then he remembered that no one knew who they were, nobody knew their faces, nobody had seen them before. Danny rushed to the seat and sat beside Luke, with Michael on the other side of the aisle.

As soon as the bus pulled off, Danny's shoulders relaxed. He knew the bus timetable off by heart; as part of their preparations, he'd tested the running time of the journey: ninety minutes. Which left them with just half an hour to get their things together and board the boat before it set off. It was cutting it fine, but everything had been calculated to the final moment. They couldn't afford any more mistakes.

As Danny sat staring wistfully at the yellow metal pole in front of him, his thoughts turned to Candice, and how every part of him was grateful that she wasn't there. For all he cared, she could be several thousand miles away and he wouldn't lose any sleep over it. Or, even better, she could be six feet under... where she deserved to be.

In the first quarter of an hour, the majority of the passengers on board disembarked before they'd left Portsmouth, and as they merged onto the wider lanes heading out of the city, as the driver began to open up the throttle, Danny felt more at ease. They were inconspicuous, just a group of lads hitching a bus ride. Nothing to look at or pay attention to.

Except something concerned him.

Luke.

His brother's attention was focused on the window and had been ever since they'd set off. His face was ashen and pensive.

Danny nudged him earnestly.

'You good?' he whispered.

Keeping his gaze fixed on the window, Luke replied, 'I'm worried about her.' His voice was so low that it was almost inaudible.

'I told you she'd be fine. With any luck, mate, she'll probably be waiting for us by the time we arrive, yeah?'

Luke said nothing and Danny took the moment to observe his brother and marvel at how much he had grown – physically, mentally and emotionally. At how much he had become an adult within the space of a few years. And at how much he loved him. The man beside him had, in recent months, become exactly that. A man. He had matured and begun to show some independence, something he'd never been able to do when Freddy was in control of them. There were times when Danny didn't think Luke could stand on his own two feet, but he'd proved him wrong.

'You've done well today, Luke,' Danny said. 'Dad would have been proud.'

'Dad?' Luke said, his voice turning agitated. 'What do you mean, "dad"? Dad wouldn't have been proud even if he knew what we were up to.'

'What you talking about? Whenever he was back from serving, he always put you first.' Danny kept his voice low, lest any other passengers overhear and take it upon themselves to listen in. 'What else has Candice been telling you about him?'

Luke swallowed before responding. 'She told me he was never there. Flew off to Afghanistan to be with some Arab woman.'

Danny chuckled in disbelief. It was laughable, the lengths that Candice would go to in order to deceive Luke and win him over. 'You're fucking joking, right? You've got to be kidding me. How can you turn around and say that Michael and I have lied to you all your life?'

'I'm not—'

'That's exactly what you're saying. You're believing the woman who claims to be your mother – the woman you've met fewer times than the number of fingers on your hand. She's known you for two seconds – of course she's going to feed you stories you want to hear. And you lapped it up, didn't you?' Danny turned to face Michael opposite him. 'Are you hearing this?'

'What's that?'

Danny scoffed. 'This idiot believes the things that woman's been telling him about our dad. He listens to her stories over ours. She has no clue what she's talking about. If he was here to defend himself, he'd—'

'But he's not here, is he? Do you know where he is? I don't?' Luke snapped. 'He hasn't been there all my life.'

'He's more than half the man she claims him to be though.'

Around them, heads started to turn in their direction; he was aware they were raising their voices, but now he realised they were also raising suspicion.

Luke reached into his pocket, produced his wallet and removed a small photo. On it was a heavily pixelated image of a dark-haired man with a thick, shaggy beard. His eyes were as dark as his hair, cavernous, never-ending.

Danny hardly recognised the man in the photo.

'What's this?' Danny snatched the picture from Luke and inspected it. 'This ain't him.'

'Yes, it is. Mum gave it to me. It was the last photo she ever had of him.'

'This man's a pussy. Look at him with his stud earring. This ain't him. Ours was a hero. A *fucking* hero.' Danny clenched his hand into a fist, scrunched the photo in his grip and dropped it. Then he removed his wallet from his pocket. As he pulled it out, the fourth key tumbled out and landed on the floor by his feet. At that moment, the coach seemed to go silent, and the unmistakable sound of a metal key bouncing on the floor deafened them.

Danny reached his arm out, but Luke beat him to it.

'What is…' Luke began as he inspected the key. 'No…'

'Luke—'

'No!'

'Luke, listen—'

'No!' Luke shook his head viciously, and his voice turned deep, almost demonic. 'No! No! No!'

Luke shoved Danny in the chest. The sudden and brute force winded him.

'No!' Luke screamed.

By now, others in the coach had turned round and were glaring at them both.

'What's going on?' Michael asked, leaning across the aisle.

'Nothing,' Danny said. He tried to placate Luke by placing an arm around his body and concealing the key with his other hand, but both efforts were pointless. Luke had no intention of calming down – not after what he'd just realised.

'Luke,' Michael said, 'Luke – listen to me! Shut up and listen.' Michael grabbed Luke by the wrist and, almost instantly, the youngest brother froze. 'You're causing a scene, and you better fucking stop it right now. What's the matter with you?'

Luke shook off both Danny and Michael and brandished the key in the air. The sunlight from outside the bus reflected off the key's surface.

Before Danny could say anything, Michael spoke first. 'Is that what I think it is?'

'Yes,' Luke said, nodding. 'This cunt betrayed us. He betrayed Candice. He's left her there to die.'

'Oh my God,' Michael said. 'You told us you'd left it on the airfield—'

Danny snatched the key from Luke and locked it in his grip. 'Boys—'

'You lied to us. You said she was going to join us at the port, but you knew all along that was never going to happen, didn't you?' Michael said.

'Listen—'

'No. *You* listen,' Luke said, shoving his finger in front of Danny's face. He hissed as he spoke. 'Do you know what you've done? You've killed your own mum.'

'She was already dead to me,' Danny replied, pocketing the key in his jeans.

'But she wasn't to me. And she wasn't to Micky. We were going to restart our lives together, make up for all the time we'd lost, and you've taken that away from us. You selfish bastard.' Luke's eyes turned black with hatred.

'What else have you lied about? What else aren't you telling us, Dan?' Michael said, bringing his voice down to a hush.

'Nothing—'

'Bullshit!' Luke blurted out. 'You're a fucking liar and you always have been.'

As soon as Luke finished, the bus skidded to a halt and dipped to the front left. The three brothers stopped and looked ahead. There was no one standing at the front of the vehicle, waiting to disembark.

'Off! The lot of you, off!' the bus driver called back. He stared at them in the rearview mirror and pointed to the doors as they opened with an eerie hiss.

Nobody said anything, and Danny felt all eyes boring into him.

'I said get off!' the bus driver barked.

'It's fine. Honestly. We won't do anything. We've stopped.'

'This bus isn't going anywhere until at least one of you gets off. Otherwise I'm calling the police.'

Both Michael and Luke glared at him. He knew their intentions, but he wasn't going to concede defeat that easily. He had hundreds of thousands of pounds' worth of jewellery in his bag that he wanted to smuggle out of the country – and more waiting for him at the port. There was no way he was going to miss that opportunity.

As Danny opened his mouth to argue back, Michael hefted his share of the loot from the seat beside him and stood. He stepped into the aisle and stopped beside Danny's knee.

'Come on, Luke. Let's get out of here,' Michael said.

'No. Stay here, we—'

Luke leapt up from the seat and barged into Danny's legs, trying to pass through.

'No,' Danny said. 'I won't let you go. Luke – you have to stay here.'

Luke eventually shuffled past and joined Michael's side. 'No, Danny, I don't. I don't have to do anything you tell me. I don't have to listen to you anymore. I've had enough of you. I wish you weren't my brother.'

'What are you going to do now, eh? You can't do anything? You can't go anywhere. I'm the one with the tickets.'

'So long as we're without you, we'll be fine no matter where we are. I'm sorry it's come to this, Dan,' Michael said.

Without saying anything else, Michael and Luke turned and strode off the bus, keeping their backs to him as the driver pulled away.

CHAPTER 45

CURRY

With them, as Bridger brought the car to a stop twenty yards from the Harbour Car Park, narrowly avoiding a scuff mark on his front near alloy and a hefty repair invoice, was a convoy of armed support in the back of a van that had been called in courtesy of Hampshire Police. In the centre of the car park was the stolen Saab. The bonnet was dented and one of the headlights was missing, the metal bent, car doors left open.

'Must have left in a hurry,' Bridger said as he climbed out of the vehicle.

Jake joined him and together they rested against the bonnet. They were under strict instructions to remain where they were while the firearms team approached the abandoned Saab for any signs of life or threat. It was clear to both of them that they were under Hampshire Police's control now. The baton had been passed, but Jake was adamant he was going to make sure that he'd be crossing the finishing line with them. He felt a duty to find the brothers; not because of their past with one another – although that was a mitigating factor – but because, as time wore on, the pool of people he could trust was drying up very quickly.

After several long minutes of standing in the sun, angling to find shade, Jake and Bridger were given the all-clear by the armed officers. Before they were allowed to investigate the Saab for themselves, they changed into their forensic suits.

Bridger was first to the car.

'What can you see?' Jake asked as he edged closer, fighting with the zip of his suit.

Bridger reached in, out of Jake's sight, and removed something.

170

At first, he couldn't see what it was, but then, as Bridger shuffled around the vehicle, the object came into view.

'The mask,' Jake whispered. In Bridger's hand was the insidious mask that had been responsible for the nightmares, for the weeks of interrupted sleep he'd suffered following that day in Oxford. The sight of it was enough to bring back the knot in his stomach.

'We're close. We can't be too far behind.'

Jake took another step closer to the vehicle and looked through the window, at the handful of glistening jewels and crystals that were buried in the seams of the seats from where they'd fallen out of the brothers' bags. Jake wondered whether they'd been left behind on purpose as a cruel taunt, a middle-finger salute. And then he considered taking one; a single diamond alone was enough to fix several of his financial issues and keep his family in the black for a long time. But the ramifications were too great, and he very quickly realised what a stupid idea that was.

A flurry of liveried police cars skidded to a halt on the outskirts of the perimeter that had been set up a few hundred yards away down the road. It was another patrol from Hampshire Police. Joining them, from the back, was an unmarked car. Two officers disembarked and patrolled towards them.

'What's going on here?' one of the uniformed officers asked them. His full beard shielded his lips, but from the way he spoke and the immediate presence he held over the rest of the team, it was clear to Jake that he was the officer in command. Albeit late to the party.

'DS Bridger. Surrey Police,' Bridger replied.

'We have no need for you here, Sergeant. My team and I can handle this. Let them do their jobs. If I need you, I'll catch up with you in a minute.'

Bridger nodded and smiled graciously in defeat. From the short amount of time that Jake had spent with Bridger, he knew that that was going to bruise the ego, even if it was procedure to follow Hampshire Police's orders from here on. Nobody admired relinquishing control, and Jake just hoped he was better at hiding it than Bridger. They stepped aside and started back to Bridger's car.

By the time Jake reached the passenger side, his mobile started ringing.

'Hello?'

'Jake.' It was Danika. She spoke slowly, as if her brain were still trying to process what she was about to tell him. 'I just thought you should know – I was looking into the tickets for the cruise in Portsmouth. They're all purchased under their Cipriano name. All through the same credit card. They were all registered to the same address in Guildford, near the university – we've organised a team from the office to search the address.'

'Where were they going?'

'Mexico.'

'Mexico?'

'Mexico.'

'Bloody hell. When's the ship leave?'

'It's scheduled to leave at two.'

Jake checked his watch – 1:11 p.m.

'I need another favour,' he said.

It was time for her to prove herself to him.

'What is it?'

'CCTV from the Harbour Car Park and the surrounding area. The brothers are most likely on foot. They'll be much easier to track, so long as they stay like that. Find out which way they're heading, and where they are. Also – are their faces on the news yet?'

'No,' Danika replied.

'Who's the media liaison officer? I would have thought they should have taken care of that by now. Their faces should be all over the television, internet, social media – they should even be on the sides of buses!'

'There's a process, Jake. And remember your place. We can't go around bossing seniors like that.'

Jake sighed and took a step away from Bridger, letting his aggression flow out of his heavy steps on the concrete. He thanked her and then cut the line.

As he lowered the phone, he tried to focus on what was happening in front of him. At the forensics team burying themselves in the seams of the Saab's seats. At the flurry of pedestrian activity to Jake's left, and at the police officers that were struggling to keep the general public at bay. But there was something niggling at the back of his mind. Like why would The Crimsons leave the car in plain sight and with no obvious effort made to conceal the damages sustained to it? Why would they book tickets under their own name and not the alias like Freddy had advised? Had Freddy been pulling him along or was he telling Jake the truth?

Bridger joined his side.

'You know when something's not quite sitting right with you?' Jake asked him.

'You mean like after you've had a curry?'

Jake smirked. 'Not exactly. But when your intuition starts flagging a few things.'

'It's been known to happen. What are you thinking?'

'That it doesn't add up,' Jake said. 'DC Oblak called and said they had tickets booked to Mexico under their original names. But when I spoke with Freddy, he told me to look out for their other name. He said it was likely they would have booked tickets under a name nobody knew they had.'

'What's that?' Bridger asked, putting his hands in his pockets.

'Harrington.'

'Candice's maiden name?'

Jake nodded.

'You think they've booked tickets for the same cruise but just under different names?'

Jake shook his head. 'That would just be stupid.' He paused a beat. 'They're either on a later boat today, or an entirely different one altogether... Maybe even at a different port.'

And then it clicked. The map of Southern England flashed in his mind, complete with its roads and towns and villages and coastal lines and boat routes.

Brighton. Portsmouth. Southampton. Bournemouth.

Southampton.

The storage unit.

The answer was right in front of him all along.

'Jesus Christ,' he said, 'they're going to Southampton Port instead.'

CHAPTER 46

CHANGE OF IDENTITY

Danny Cipriano. That bastard, low-life-piece-of-scum shitbag. Out of all the things he could have done, he'd gone and betrayed them, gone against the plan, gone and effectively killed their own mum. And now he'd deserted them, shown his true colours. Right now, he was as far away from a rainbow as possible.

Something was making Luke shake, and he was certain it wasn't adrenaline. It was an emotion he hadn't felt in a long time – ever since Michael had told him that their dad had left them to fend for themselves in foster care. Luke had been eleven when he'd found out. He'd thought the worst of his dad then, and he thought the worst of Danny now. They were both the same, and for a moment Luke wondered whether all of the Cipriano family members would be like that: completely and utterly selfish, only caring about themselves, ready to throw everything away.

Luke looked up longingly at Michael and hoped his older brother wouldn't do the same. He couldn't stand that.

After jumping off the bus outside Fareham, they'd decided to head into the town, keeping their faces and their features concealed, but in the brilliant sunlight it had proven difficult. Neither of them had been able to count the precise number of witnesses on board the bus, but they were both abhorrently aware that it was a number far greater than they were comfortable with. Discretion, throughout their career, had been their one key factor of success. Without it, they may as well hand themselves in at the station. And so they'd headed into a Boots store inside the nearby shopping centre, positioned just in the middle of the high street, and purchased an electric shaver. Cash. In, out. Without acknowledging or speaking to the cashier. It was the middle of the day and they were in a rush. Nothing to second glance, nothing to query.

Feeling like they'd just stolen it, they hurried out of the store and paced towards the bus depot a few hundred yards away from the centre's entrance. Attached to the depot was a set of public toilets. Men's on the left. Women's on the right.

The brothers ducked into the men's, made a quick recce of the cubicles, and after realising that they were empty, tore open the electric shaver box like a pack of wolves feasting on their prey, destroying its opportunity to escape.

Michael was first. The thinning hair on his head meant that his would take the least time. It was something all of the Cipriano brothers were plagued with: balding. And Danny had suffered the worst. Only a few years older than Michael, his hair – or lack thereof – made him look double his age. With the shaver, they thought they might as well speed up the process and adopt new personas.

Luke's attention waned while he waited, his eyes falling on the crude graffiti in the stalls and above the urinals. There was a lot of anger on those walls, but every now and then they were dampened by the crudely drawn phalluses and vaginas playing with one another. To Luke's surprise, some of them had been artistically done, detailed, realist. He admired anyone who had the bravery and ability to hold a canister in hand and let their fingers do the rest. He'd tried, on several occasions, but each time had been less than satisfactory, and each time had also resulted in a lesson in running away from the police, moving the autopilot from his fingers to his legs and letting them do all the work.

'Oi.' Michael shoved him in the arm. He was finished, his thick bald head glistening beneath the lamp like a polished bowling ball. 'Come on. Your turn. Hurry up.'

Luke took the shaver from his brother, blew the detritus free from the blades and stared at himself in the mirror. Christ, he looked broken, beaten. They both did. Shadows of their former selves. As if the past nine years of solitude and secrecy and being on the run had culminated in this: a man who was a stranger to himself.

'We ain't got all day,' Michael scorned. 'Get moving.'

Breathing deeply, Luke raised the shaver to his head, held it there. Not long, he told himself. Not long until it would all be over. Until he and Michael would be able to start their new lives together somewhere. Somehow. Whether it was in the UK or whether it was abroad in the back of a rubber dingy, they'd work it out.

So long as they were together.

As he grazed the shaver over his scalp, he tried to force the images of the collar currently strapped around his mum's neck from his mind, and then realised that, no matter how hard he tried, they simply wouldn't stop.

CHAPTER 47

MAKING AMENDS

'We think it's a decoy, ma'am,' Bridger said as he tore out of the car park, heading up Queen Street and turning onto the A3.

'What do you mean?' she asked, the static and connection of her voice in the loudspeaker sounding like she was coming from somewhere in space.

'Tanner believes they've booked the cruise tickets from Portsmouth as a decoy. He believes they're really going to Southampton.'

'What evidence do we have?' Pemberton asked.

Jake shifted his arm onto the centre console and leant closer towards the mobile that was tucked into the dashboard vent.

'It's a working theory at the moment, ma'am,' he explained.

'Speculation isn't going to catch these guys. You can't just go gallivanting across the country in the hope that they might be there.'

Bridger opened his mouth but was cut off by Jake.

'With all due respect, ma'am, I have reasonable grounds to believe that's where they're heading. Hampshire Police have sent several officers to search the Portsmouth boat we originally believed they were taking, so if they do show up there – and I turn out to be wrong – then they will be caught. We've asked DC Oblak to find any ticket references that have been booked under the name Harrington.'

A long moment of silence played out in the car as they awaited a response.

'Candice never mentioned anything about Southampton...' Pemberton said.

'Either she's still protecting them and not telling you about it, or she doesn't know that it could be a part of their plan.'

'She's got ten spikes strapped to her neck – she's not going to try and cover for them now, Jake.'

Why do you sound so sure?

'Then there's a possibility that Danny might've only told her half the story. If he's capable of hiding the key from her, then he might not have told her about Southampton. He clearly isn't stupid enough to hop on a boat where he knows we'll be waiting for him.'

Eventually, after another long pause, Pemberton sighed heavily. 'You'd better be right, Jake.'

'Just another one of my bright ideas,' Jake replied. 'There's also something else you should know. She's got a storage unit down there. She's been paying for it for about a year. I think that's where they've been keeping their takings from the previous robberies, and now they're going to pick it up.'

'Why did no one tell me this?'

'I completely forgot about it until now. But I'd have thought DI Murphy would have mentioned it to you, ma'am. Danika told me that she was reporting to him while you're out of the office.'

'Leave that with me. We'll meet you in Southampton. Keep me updated.'

She hung up and, once again, silence descended on the car. Jake used it to dive into his own headspace while Bridger manipulated his way across the traffic. He was finally beginning to feel confident in his actions, in his beliefs, like the wall of white that had plagued his mind so furiously earlier was receding and the colours of truth and courage were coming to the fore. Two years ago, his decisions had been responsible for capturing The Crimsons, and today, his decisions would have the same result. The rope around the brothers' neck was tightening, and he was going to be the one to hold their heads on display.

Bridger slowed as he pulled up to a set of red traffic lights when the radio bleated.

'Echo Bravo Four-Five, Echo Bravo Four-Five, this is Lima Golf, over,' it said.

'This is Echo Bravo Four-Five, reading you, over.'

'Echo Bravo Four-Five, we're receiving reports of an altercation on board a bus in the Fareham area from the driver. Reports indicate three IC1 males matching the descriptions of Luke, Danny and Michael Cipriano. All three individuals were seen carrying large black gym bags at Fareham bus depot. Armed officers are en route. Could you check it out and support?'

'Which bus was it?' Jake asked, feeling the palms of his hands turn sweaty.

'The X4, headed to Southampton from Portsmouth.'

'I don't fucking believe it,' Bridger said, turning to Jake. 'You were right.'

There were people in Pemberton's career that she'd been more than happy to see the back of, and there were others who she'd wished could stay in her life forever, in a professional capacity.

DI Mark Murphy was one of those people. When they'd first met, after he'd been seconded from Brighton, she'd thought he was an arsehole, a selfish, egotistical Lothario who spent more time worrying about his own appearance and himself than finding the criminals that were worsening the county's crime rates. But then, as she'd started to get to know him, she'd realised her prejudices had been wrong, misunderstood and far from the truth.

He was a sensible, honest, kind, considerate human being who'd defended her and supported her when she needed it the most. Not only was he fantastic at his job – when he put his mind to it – but he was also a fantastic friend and potential partner. She trusted him, but now she was questioning her judgement again.

His behaviour in the last few hours had been nothing shy of bullshit and insubordinate. The secrecy, it wasn't on, and as his senior, it was her job to do something about it.

She removed her phone and dialled Murphy's number.

'Everything all right, ma'am?' his deep voice asked.

'Why do I feel like I'm being kept in the dark about everything, Mark?' she asked. 'It seems like I'm last to know absolutely everything that's going on about this investigation, and I should be the first.'

'Sorry, ma'am. I've been managing the information that's been coming in as best I could. I know you're busy, so I've only been sharing the vital bits.'

'I need to know absolutely everything, Mark, regardless of whether it's important or not. You should know that.'

'I do. Sorry, ma'am. It won't happen going forward.'

Pemberton scoffed. 'Yeah, you got that right, and the thing you can do to make amends is give the brothers' photos to the media. I want their faces everywhere.'

CHAPTER 48

RUN

After receiving the news from control, Bridger raced onto the M27 and blitzed through to Fareham with the armed units driving in his wake. Not before long, three lanes melted into two as they pulled off onto the A27, heading south at the mouth of Portsmouth Harbour. Running alongside them, on the left-hand side, was a railway line, and beyond that was Cams Hall Estate Golf Club on the other side of the water. Fluorescent green bounced into the sky, and Jake struggled to keep his eyes from it. He had already been to one golf course today, and he hoped that, should he visit another, it would be under entirely different circumstances. The game, despite never having played, was being eternally ruined for him.

As they drove deeper into town, Bridger departed the A road and headed towards Fareham bus depot, a few hundred yards from the shopping centre. Parking up on the other side of the road, Jake and Bridger disembarked the vehicle simultaneously and met the armed officer in charge of the unit that had been following them. A few seconds behind them was a uniformed officer driving a saloon.

'Where were they last seen?' PS Cavanagh, the officer in charge on the armed unit, asked.

Bridger pointed to the bus depot over a hundred yards away. 'About ten minutes ago.'

'OK,' Cavanagh said. 'My team and I will scout it out. Wait for our orders.'

Bridger nodded in acceptance and Jake watched the four men depart, spreading out in different directions, skulking across the pavement towards the depot in perfect formation, bodies poised, weapons raised.

'You reckon they're still here?' Bridger asked beside him.

'Could be anywhere,' Jake replied, keeping his gaze fixed on the officers as they approached the depot.

At that point, the police constable emerged from his vehicle and sauntered towards them, hands locked in the chest pockets of his vest. He gave them a curt nod and introduced himself as PC Wyatt. Jake offered him the minimal amount of courtesy and then turned his attention back to the depot. A row of First buses were waiting in a line, engines ticking over, spouting filthy fumes and gas into the atmosphere.

As the firearms team arrived, a coach reversed and pulled out of the depot. Jake's heart missed a few beats while he scanned the passengers' faces as the vehicle passed by. Nothing.

A few seconds later the firearms team disappeared out of sight, hidden behind the row of buses. Jake drummed his feet on the floor and scratched the scar on his face as he waited impatiently. It was one of the tensest moments of the day, and he was afraid of what would happen next. A myriad of thoughts raced through his mind. But before Jake was able to focus on any of them, screams and shouts erupted from within the depot. Jake removed his blazer, chucked it inside the car, and started towards the commotion.

'Jake!' Bridger called after him. 'Jake!

And then he saw them.

In the distance, Michael Cipriano forced one of the armed officers to the ground, kicking his weapon away across the concrete. Behind him, Luke Cipriano – smaller, skinnier – sprinted from beneath the bus, heading towards the depot's exit.

Jake raced towards them, the muscles in his legs pumping raw adrenaline through his body. Soon, the soles of his feet began to ache and sent bolts of pain up and down his legs with every step. Wrong activity to be wearing smart shoes. Behind him, he heard the sounds of more footsteps. Jake chanced a glance backward; Wyatt was bounding after him, joining the chase, his vest bouncing up and down as it tried to catch up with the rest of his body.

Both Michael and Luke were lumbered with their gym bags, swinging uncontrollably as they ran, bashing into their legs, hips and back. It was only a small advantage, but it gave Jake and Wyatt one nonetheless.

Ten yards separated them as Luke reached the end of the depot and made a sharp right, heading onto the main road.

Eight.

Five.

And then Jake felt a kick against his legs, buckling him. The world spun upside down and inside out as Jake soared through the air and clattered onto the concrete. He landed heavily on his shoulder and yelled out in pain.

Just as he was about to pick himself up, Michael Cipriano leapt over him. His trailing leg caught Jake in the ribs and knocked him down again.

'Stop!' Wyatt called.

Jake craned his neck and saw the police officer charging after Michael, reaching for his radio and shouting into it. To Jake's left, trailing behind, was Bridger, closely followed by the armed officers. Their shouts and cries were no use. Michael and Luke had no intention of stopping. They were too far ahead.

But then Jake heard another shout. He snapped his neck towards Wyatt and saw the man tackle Michael to the ground, their bodies rolling together as one. Jake staggered to his feet and hobbled after them, ignoring the pain in his shoulder and palms. Both men were panting heavily. Michael was pinned to his front and Wyatt was atop him, wrapping his arms behind his back, pressing into him with his knee.

'Run, Luke! Run!' Michael bellowed, his face eating concrete.

Jake stuttered to a halt beside Wyatt, and as he helped lift Michael to his feet, the armed officers tore past them, their legs and arms pumping hard. They disappeared down a residential road to their right, but Luke was already out of sight. He'd evaded them and there was no way they were going to find him on foot.

A second later, Bridger arrived, breathless. He placed his hands on his knees and bent double, gasping.

'Good work, boys,' he said in between breaths.

'Michael Cipriano,' Jake said, as Wyatt tightened the handcuffs around his wrists, 'I am arresting you for murder, armed robbery, assault and kidnap. You do not have to say anything. But it may harm your defence if you do not mention when questioned something which you later rely on in court. Anything you do say may be given in evidence.'

After Jake finished telling him his rights, the armed officers returned, flustered, yet their breathing remained the same as when Jake had first met them.

'Gone,' Cavanagh said, 'but he's got to be around here somewhere. He must have vaulted the walls.'

'OK,' Bridger replied after finally catching his breath. 'Right now, I want to speak with this one. Let's get him booked in.'

CHAPTER 49

MICHAEL CIPRIANO

'Rupert Haversham,' Michael Cipriano said with a wry smile. 'He's my solicitor. I *want* my solicitor.' His thick, round shoulders appeared to block out most of the light coming from the cheap light bulb overhead, casting a deep shadow across the breadth of the table.

'Tough.' Bridger rested his arms against the edge of the table. 'You're not getting one.'

'On what grounds?' Michael protested. 'I know my rights.'

'You want the specifics? All right then. Code C 6.6 and Annex B. The police may proceed with an interview in the absence of a solicitor if an officer has reasonable grounds that failure to do so will lead to interference with, or harm to, evidence connected with an indictable offence; lead to alerting other people suspected of having committed an indictable offence but which they have not yet been arrested for; or if they have reasonable grounds to believe it will hinder the recovery of property obtained in consequence of the commission of such an offence. So I'd say that covers you straight off the bat, doesn't it? We've got all three, haven't we?' Bridger held his hand in the air and displayed his thumb, forefinger and middle finger in front of Michael's face. 'We've got the evidence connecting you to the crime... We've got your brothers being alerted to what's happened to you... and we've got the jewels and money that your brothers have run away with that are still at large.'

The smirk on Michael's face grew even bigger. 'How many nights did you lose memorising that verbatim?'

'More than you've spent in a nice warm bed.'

'There's just one thing you've forgotten to mention, Detective *Sergeant* Bridger, which is that the law also states that the officer making such a decision must be of the rank of superintendent or above. I don't see those credentials in your title anywhere. Nor your colleague here.' Michael flicked his head towards Jake.

'How many nights did *you* spend memorising that particular part of the code?' Bridger retorted.

'One actually.'

'I've got it cleared with the powers that be,' Bridger replied. 'You don't have to worry about me doing my job properly.'

Jake suppressed a smug smile. The process of getting Michael into the interview room had been expedited, all taken care of by Bridger, while Jake prepared the room for interview, bringing in fresh cups of water and maintaining the room at a comfortable temperature. The tape had been replaced in the recorder, and the video recording was switched on, currently being monitored by someone sitting in the corner of a room somewhere in the recesses of the building.

This was his first interview where he was unprepared. Usually, procedure allowed for time to present the evidence and line of questioning against the defendant. But right now he didn't have that luxury, and he didn't want his inexperience to hinder the proceedings in any way. It was down to Bridger now, and after that small exchange between Michael and Bridger, Jake admired him much more than he had half an hour ago. He was in control of the interview, and Jake was happy to keep it that way... unless, of course, he saw an opportunity for him to strike. And then he'd let his intuition take over.

'It's simple,' Bridger continued after Michael's silence. 'If you want it to be.'

'Leave my brothers out of this.'

'Where are they?' Bridger asked, snapping to the point.

'Gone.'

'Where?'

'Neverland.'

'With Captain Hook?'

'Tinkerbell,' Michael corrected. 'You can always rely on Danny to sprinkle some magic dust on everything and make it better.'

'And you believe that, do you?' The words came out of Jake's mouth before he had a chance to process them. It looked like he'd taken his opportunity to strike without realising it. 'You think he's got the special powder to fix this situation you're in?'

Michael shrugged. 'He knows people—'

'So do I. We meet a lot of people in our line of work,' Jake said sarcastically.

'I'm willing to bet Danny knows the same people you do. If not more. And if not better.' The same wry smile grew on Michael's face again, this time filling Jake with incipient rage. 'Shocking, isn't it? That there's still bent coppers looking for the next pay cheque.'

'I imagine every copper looks for the next pay cheque.'

'You'll never find him,' Michael said, wiping his nose.

'Just the one brother? You have two.'

'I don't need reminding.'

Jake straightened his tie and flattened it against his shirt. 'So what happened with you guys?' he asked. 'How come you separated?'

Michael remained silent.

'Tell us about Luke,' Bridger said, budging his way back into the conversation. 'Where is he?'

'Alone and scared, no doubt,' Jake added.

Michael's breathing increased. The steady rise and fall of his chest turned into a heaving balloon nearing its limit.

'Luke's fine,' Michael said eventually, avoiding their gaze for the first time. 'He'll be fine.'

'You were the one looking after him when you were kids, weren't you?' Jake asked, tilting his head to the side. 'You were the middle child. No mum. No dad. You were the one getting him ready for school. Feeding him. Making his breakfasts, lunches, dinners. Making sure he didn't miss the bus or turn up late. But Danny's role was different – Danny protected Luke when there was any sign of danger, and he left you lurking in the background. Luke never appreciated your help. At least, he never told you he did. So, Danny became the big brother that would always protect Luke, the one he looked up to, and you were cast to the side. And then there was Freddy, wasn't there? Where to begin with Freddy... I bet Luke saw him as the dad he never had, a role model, a father figure. My guess is that it went like this' – Jake held his hand flat in the air, parallel to the ground. He started high, and then gradually lowered it in increments – 'Freddy at the top, then Danny, then *you*. Sound about right?'

'Do you have brothers or sisters, Detective?' Michael asked, keeping his arms folded. A fire of aggression smouldered behind the curtain of his eyes, ready and waiting to burn the stage down and unleash hell.

Jake nodded. 'Younger brother. Older sister.'

'Do you love them?'

'For the most part,' Jake said, his thoughts turning to his siblings and how they had grown distant in recent years.

Michael wrapped his fingers round the edge of the desk. 'Have you ever taught your brother how to steal so he doesn't starve at night? Have you ever taught him how to look out for number one? Have you ever told him never to let anyone else tread all over him? Have you ever told him that, if anything happens to him, he must fight, and he must fight, and he must fight until the other person gets knocked down and never gets back up again?'

Jake hesitated. 'I can't say we ever needed to have that

conversation.'

'Well, we did, Luke and me. I taught him to punch back twice as hard. So don't underestimate him. He's smart. Always was. The brightest out of all of us—'

'Then why didn't you keep him at school?'

'Danny decided to get involved. He always told Luke he needed to stay with us and continue what we were doing, so Luke was always by our sides. He would always wait to be told exactly what to do. He lost his independence. That's Danny's fault. Danny made him that way.'

Jake nodded, absorbing everything Michael was telling him.

'Your actions now will determine what happens next,' Bridger said in an authoritative yet calm voice. 'The past is where it needs to be: left behind. We've all got things we'd like to bury, but right now you should be concerned about your future. Tell us where your brothers are, and things can be made easier for you.'

Michael looked at his lap, exhaled deeply and then lifted his head. 'You know, I read something once. I can't remember where. Might have been from a book somewhere. But there was one sentence that jumped out at me. It said: "All men have one entrance into life, and the like going out." What do you think that means?'

Jake glanced over at Bridger, whose expression was as confused as Jake felt.

'That you're going to kill one of your brothers?'

'Close, but not quite. It means I'm not going to give you what you want unless I get what I want.'

Jake shook his head in disbelief. 'I don't see the correlation, although I'm starting to think maybe you're the smart one. What is it that you want?'

'I was born with one brother, and I'm going to end it with one. I'll give you Danny if you let Luke go. He's had nothing to do with any of this. Detective,' he said, addressing Jake directly, 'this is my act of retribution – I'm wiping Luke's slate clean instead of mine.'

'You realise it doesn't work that way?' Bridger added, checking his watch.

'Yes, but you haven't got long. Time is of the essence for you lot. You need me, whether you like it or not. Otherwise this has been a complete waste of time.'

Jake smirked. 'You're loving this, aren't you? Getting the attention you never had. We don't need you as much as you think we do. We'll find Danny, and we'll find Luke – and when we do, none of you will remember what life was like before prison.'

At the mention of prison, as if reality finally settled in, Michael's pupils dilated and turned into giant black holes swallowing the rest of his eyes.

'That reminds me,' Jake continued, 'I saw Freddy earlier. He was thrilled to see me. He said he'd tried to make contact with you boys but had heard nothing back. Not a single letter. And do you know the most disheartening thing he said to me? He said, more than anything else, he was disappointed in you. *You*, Michael. He expected more from you. I think he even likes me more than he does you and your brothers. But imagine – a few years down the line, you're in prison, you attempt to reach Luke, and he doesn't respond. He's forgotten about you. Nothing but a stain in his memory that he regrets, trying to make his life better without you. If you tell us now what we want to know, we can work something out for you. We can work on something suitable. Perhaps the two of you could share a cell.'

Michael descended into a deep state of reflection. He lowered his head and twiddled his thumbs. After what felt like a long time, he opened his mouth.

'Southampton Port. Danny'll probably be there by now. If I could tell you where Luke was, I would. But you saw him – he ran off. He could be anywhere by now.'

'It's fine,' Jake said, rising out of his chair and straightening his tie. 'We already know where Danny is – you just confirmed it for us. And now we've got a pretty good idea of where Luke is going to be as well.'

CHAPTER 50

GOOD SAMARITAN

The sound of Luke's heart beating in his ears was like a subwoofer. His breathing was wheezy, the result of too many cigarettes and a lack of exercise, and he was bent double, resting his palms on his knees. He didn't know where he was, other than that he was hiding behind a tree and a car. He had sprinted as hard as he could after he saw Michael fall to the ground. He had wanted to stay, fight, defend his older brother, but he knew that would have only made things worse for them both. Michael was gone, and he needed to accept that. He just wished he'd had a proper chance to say goodbye.

Shut up, shut up, shut up. He's not dead. Luke chided himself for thinking such pessimistic and defeatist thoughts. He had been taught better than that.

The sound of police sirens echoed around the town in the distance, and the noise of helicopter blades whirring overhead buzzed in his ears. He was just over a mile away from the bus depot, and as he waited for his body to restore its vastly depleted oxygen levels, he heard a car speeding along the road. He caught sight of it: a police car, replete with reflective stickers and indicia. Panicking, he vaulted the wall and ducked behind it. He closed his eyes as the police car sped past him. His chest heaved, and as the excitement and adrenaline dissipated in his blood, he opened his eyes again.

He was fucked, alone, lost and without any means of getting out of the country. If he was going to succeed, he was going to need help. And fast.

Still keeping himself behind somebody's front wall, he reached into his pocket and produced his phone. He dropped it onto the grass and swore aloud. His body was still shaking. He picked it up, scrolled along the address book and dialled Danny's number.

As he held the phone to his ear, the owner of the property he was outside opened the door and stepped away from the porch.

'Who are you?' He was elderly and was wearing a woollen jumper and checked shirt that had buttons on the collar. On his feet he wore a pair of slippers. 'What are you doing in my garden?'

The call connected, but Luke ignored it. For a brief moment he was frozen, lost for words. As reality began to settle in again, he realised where he was.

'Please,' he said, ignoring Danny who was shouting in his ear through the phone. 'Please – you have to help me. My girlfriend. She's looking for me.'

Luke scrambled to his feet and let the bag of jewellery drag behind him on the grass.

'Why—'

'She hits me.' Luke rushed to the man's side, stumbling as he went. He tripped on a small step and caught the man's arm, pulling the sleeve of his wrist. 'She beats me. Sometimes it's in the evening when she gets home. Sometimes it's in the morning before she leaves for work. But today she left the house unlocked. I packed my bag' – Luke gesticulated to the bag – 'and I got out of there. I need to leave the city before she finds me. You have to help me – please!'

The man peered over Luke's shoulder and glanced into the street. Luke took the opportunity to climb the man's body and cling to his collar.

'Wh— I—'

'Please, man! You honestly don't know how bad it gets. The bruises don't go away. And they're in places you'll never see. Please, man. You've got to help me.'

The man hesitated before responding. 'How… how can I help?'

Bingo. The brief acting lessons Candice had given him a few months ago were paying off.

'Hide me,' Luke said, stifling a victorious smile. 'Inside. She won't find me in there. You have to help me.' Luke pulled up his sleeve and revealed a thick scar he had on his arm from a bicycle accident when he was young. The skin was raised and coloured a lighter shade of pink compared to the rest of his forearm. 'This is what she's capable of. And if she finds me, she'll do it again. If not worse. She… she…' Luke scratched the side of his head. 'She likes to use her hair straighteners.'

The man's face contorted as he fought with himself. His brow furrowed and then the discontent in his expression drained. 'Come on. I'd better get you inside. I'll get the kettle boiled.'

Luke's body tingled with satisfaction, pride. He had succeeded in doing something for himself without the help of either of his brothers. And he didn't even feel guilty about deceiving this old man.

The man spun on the spot and entered the house. Luke followed, closing the door behind him; as he did so, another police car sped past. Luke slammed the door shut and held his breath, listening for any signs that suggested the driver had seen him and was on his way to arrest him. Mercifully there was nothing.

'Sugar?' a voice called, distracting him.

Luke released the door handle, the colour returning to his knuckles, and faced the kitchen at the end of the corridor where the sound of the kettle boiling wafted through the hallway.

'One,' Luke said. 'Thanks.'

He took a moment to absorb his surroundings. The first thing he noticed was that it smelt. Horribly. As if it hadn't been cleaned in a few months, had fallen victim to damp, and a dog had shared its last breath there too. To the right of the hallway was a living room. There was a single armchair in the middle, directly facing the television. Beside the chair was a coffee table with a lamp on it and a collection of fishing magazines.

'You can sit in my chair, if you like.' The man's voice startled Luke. He stood in the kitchen doorway with two mugs full of tea, wisps of steam dancing from the top. He started towards Luke and entered the living room. 'You might struggle to get back up though. It's one of the most comfortable things I've ever been in.'

Luke pulled himself out of his mind and back to reality. Now that he was in the security of the man's house, he could start to plan his next move.

'Yeah. Thanks.' Luke reached into his pocket and pulled out his burner phone again. 'Do you mind if I make a call?'

'Not at all.'

By the time the man finished speaking, Luke was already talking into the phone with Danny.

'You've come crawling back, have you?' Danny said. In the distance, Luke heard the sound of car engines revving.

'Shut up,' Luke replied. The man shuffled past him in the living-room doorway and Luke entered the room. He kept his voice low. 'There's an issue. Micky's been arrested. The cops found us by the bus depot. Two of them got him, but I managed to get away.'

'You're shitting me?' Danny said. 'Where are you now?'

'Emily is abusing me again.'

Luke had only ever had to use the cover once before, when he'd sported an unconvincing display in Leeds following their second heist. It had been Danny's idea originally, to lie and confuse susceptible people into allowing them access to their home, and it had worked a treat, much to Luke's surprise. Emily was the name they'd used back then, and it had stuck as a code word for the situation ever since.

'Does he believe you?' Danny asked.

Luke cautiously glanced beside him. The man had set the cups

190

of tea on the coffee table and then wandered out of the room. As Luke returned his attention to Danny, something caught his eye. The television in front of him. ITV News was playing, and the first thing Luke noticed was Danny's mugshot, taken years ago from when he'd been arrested for possession of drugs. And then Michael's appeared. They were much younger in the photos, but there would be no mistaking them now.

Luke's eyes widened and his lips parted. 'Shit,' he whispered. 'Our faces… they're… they're all over TV.' Luke scrambled beside him for the television remote. He found it on the coffee table and switched the channel.

'You need to get out of there.'

Breathing a heavy sigh of relief, Luke asked, 'Where are you?'

'Southampton.'

'Already?'

'I dipped early. Bus driver was scowling at me. Didn't want the police to catch me on board it so I got myself a cab the rest of the way. Paid him extra to floor it.'

As Luke opened his mouth to speak, the sound of feet shuffling on carpet distracted him. The man was standing in the doorway, holding a small plate of biscuits.

'Everything OK?' he asked.

'Y-Yes,' Luke said, removing the phone and looking at it. 'It's my brother. He can help me. I n-need to get to him.'

'Where is he?' the man asked.

'Southampton.'

The man lifted a finger in the air. 'I can call you a cab.'

'No!' Luke said, shocking the man. He took himself by surprise, and instantly regretted shouting so abruptly. 'You.'

'Excuse me?'

'You. You can take me. I'll pay. I have money. Lots of it. Look.' Luke swung the bag by his side, opened it and grabbed a wad of money they each kept in their bags for emergencies. He waved it in the man's face. 'You're the only person I can trust right now.'

The old man hesitated for what felt like an age.

'It's not about—'

'Please, I wouldn't ask unless I was desperate…'

'I…'

'Please,' Luke begged, clasping his hands together. He sniffled, hoping it would bring a forced tear to his eye.

'Let me grab my keys.'

CHAPTER 51

THUMB

Danny slung the bag over his shoulder, the weight of the diamonds and other provisions almost throwing him off balance. The cabbie had dropped him off in a bus lane, right in the heart of Southampton high street, so Danny could approach the port from a slight distance – just in case. So far he'd seen nothing suspicious, and soon, he and Luke and Louise would board the boat.

All he had to do now was wait.

He checked his watch.

Still another hour until the cruise left.

Still another thirty minutes until Luke arrived.

But where was Louise? She was supposed to be here already. They had agreed to meet at this exact location – just a few hundred yards away from the cruise ship.

Danny checked his watch again, as though it would speed up the ten seconds that had just passed.

He didn't want to upset her.

As he lowered his wrist, his phone vibrated once. He read the text message and swivelled on the spot. Behind him, two metres away, was the most beautiful woman he'd ever seen.

Louise. His Louise.

'Hello, stranger,' she said. Her face and neck were covered in make-up that made her look as orange as the sun, and the layers of fake tan she'd applied stood in stark contrast to the blue hoodie that hung from her shoulders.

She waltzed up to him and dangled from his neck.

'Are you OK?' he asked, letting go of her. 'Nothing's happened to you, has it? I was worried about you. I have been all day.'

'I'm fine.'

'Did everything go all right? The key? The unit?' he said before kissing her. As he released her, she licked her lips, flashing that delicious red tongue of hers.

'Relax. Everything's fine. The suitcases are in my car. It's all there. I just can't believe you made me dress up as a fucking golfer. I've never felt so uncomfortable.'

Danny smirked. 'I've been worried sick. I thought they might've got you. I knew that giving you those extra keys was a bad idea. I didn't think you were gonna show.'

'And miss out on my chance to get my share of everything? You really don't know me at all. Where's everyone else?'

'It's all gone to shit, Lou. We got separated. Michael's been arrested. Luke's stuck in Fareham.'

'More money for us,' Louise said, winking at him.

Danny shook his head dismissively. It was an instinctive reaction – paternal, brotherly – but one that he immediately regretted. His eyes widened and he stared at Louise. Then he lifted his arms in the air defensively, surrendering himself to what was about to come.

'Excuse me?' Louise said.

'I… Luke… I didn't mean anything by it. Don't—'

Louise thrust her hand towards his midriff and, using her thumb, buried it beneath his ribcage and into his diaphragm, cutting him off instantly. A sharp stab of pain squeezed the top of his body. He exhaled sharply, breathing through the discomfort.

'Don't talk to me like that,' she hissed. 'What have I told you?'

'S-S-Sorry,' Danny struggled, the pain too much for him.

'If Luke isn't here by the time we board, that money's mine. You understand?'

Danny nodded. 'Yes, Louise. I under-understand.'

'Good. Where's Candice?'

Danny looked down at the ground. 'She won't be joining us.'

'Is she dead?'

Danny's gaze rose to meet hers. 'No.'

'What happened to her?'

Danny explained, and after he'd finished, she pressed deeper into his diaphragm.

'I knew you hated her, but I didn't know it was that much.'

'I didn't… I do, but…' He inhaled and regained his composure. 'Listen – you don't need to worry about her. She won't be troubling us anymore.'

Louise eased the pressure against his body. 'Suppose it serves her right, innit. Can't believe the stupid fucking bitch didn't approve of me.'

'Neither can I,' Danny replied, breathing slowly, hiding the discomfort in his voice. 'You know, before all of today started, she told me to stay away from you.'

'And what did you say?'

'I told her to go fuck herself. I ain't going nowhere.'

'Good. Because you know what will happen if you do decide to go somewhere.' Louise prodded his body one final time for good measure and then removed her hand. 'What are we going to do now?'

Danny breathed then rubbed the part of his skin that would join the rest of his bruises within a few minutes.

'We wait,' he said. 'When Luke gets here, I want you out of sight.'

'He doesn't know I'm coming?'

Danny shook his head. 'And I'd like to keep it that way for as long as possible. That boy's been through enough today. And he's about to go through a lot more.'

| PART 3 |

CHAPTER 52

DISLOCATION

The spike collar grew increasingly heavy with each passing minute. Her muscles ached. Her back ached. Her entire body ached. She just wanted to rip it free and throw it against the wall, heedless of the outcome. Danny, that sick son of a bitch. She'd known from the moment his finger had hovered over the trigger in the shop that something had been wrong – that something wasn't right about any of this. He'd condemned her to death by adding several layers of complexity to the device, and there was nothing she could do about it. She'd put her faith in her own son, and it had backfired.

The cramped prison cell she was locked in jostled and swayed as the van pulled round bends and weaved its way through traffic, stopping and starting every now and again. There were no windows, no slivers of light coming from the four walls, save for a tiny hole in the ceiling the same width as a paper straw. The cell was grimy, damp and smelt of piss, as if the previous occupant had no other choice but to soil themselves and nobody had bothered to clean it since. Well, she needed to go, but she wouldn't be subjected to such inhumane treatment.

A part of her wanted to scream. Cry. Bawl her eyes out until someone heard her. But she knew it would be pointless; she hadn't heard so much as a car horn from outside. She was alone, and that was the way she was going to die. She had admitted it to herself already. There was no point trying to fight it. The police were keeping her prisoner, and she was starting to feel like perhaps they were all involved with it – an elaborate plan to make her suffer.

The van started off again, startling her. The sudden movement caused her to slip off the small metal block that she'd assumed was a chair and fall onto the cold, solid floor. She bumped her elbow and grazed her right arm as she fell. Her body recoiled and she smacked her head on the wall. A hairpin fell out and landed by her feet.

And then it finally clicked in her head. That tiny little thing was going to save her.

Candice crouched down to the floor, steadying herself with her knees and shoulders pressed against the walls, and picked the pin up using her hands behind her. She worked the metal pin until it snapped in two. And then she remembered something that Michael had shown her when they were preparing for the heist. It was simple, but something that was only supposed to be used a last resort.

If she was going to break out of the handcuffs, she needed to dislocate her thumb. Left or right. Either or. Whichever one she favoured least. It didn't matter.

After a second's deliberation, she decided on the left.

Candice pressed her left thumb against the wall and leant into it, applying pressure on the bone. Pain swelled and throbbed in her hand, and on the count of three, she convinced herself to thrust her hips backward to dislocate the joint.

One.

Two.

Candice screamed out in agony. Hard. Until her lungs hurt and she lost breath, almost dipping her toes into the deep lagoon of unconsciousness. Her cries only made it as far as the ceiling above her. She panted through the pain – now wasn't the time to focus on it. If she did, she knew she wouldn't have the courage to do the next part: slip her wrist through the cuff.

Gritting her teeth and tensing every muscle in her body to draw the pain away from her thumb, Candice wriggled and writhed her hand until it narrowly slipped through the cuff. The metal dug into her flesh, leaving behind red indentations and drawing a little blood.

But she didn't care. The adrenaline was beginning to drown out the pain now.

She had her hand back.

She was free.

Using the forefinger and middle finger on her free hand, she slotted one of the pins into the cuffs and twisted, rotated, fumbling with them both. After a few more seconds, the pin slid inside the lock and the cuff on her right hand snapped open. Feeling an overwhelming sense of relief that outweighed the pain two to one, she brought her hands to her front and rubbed where the cuff had been, rapidly returning the sensation and blood to her wrist. She repeated the same for the other hand as much as she could and, once again, tried to shake the collar free, yanking it from her neck, pulling it from side to side, then apart like it was a stretchy toy. But it wouldn't budge. Her efforts were futile.

She screamed again. But this time she stopped almost as soon as she'd begun. She was acting erratically. Illogically. If she could get out of the handcuffs, then she could get out of the collar bomb. There was no point detonating the device and decapitating herself and removing whatever opportunity she had of survival, no matter how small it was.

She was going to save herself.

She *was* going to save herself, even if nobody else would.

And she had just had the perfect idea of how to go about it.

CHAPTER 53

BETRAYAL

The old man was called Dennis, Luke learnt. He was in his seventies and had been widowed for nearly three decades. After his wife had died, Dennis had decided he would never date again. He thought it was the ultimate betrayal of more than half his life. He and his wife had been soulmates, and anyone new who entered his life would constantly remind him of the past. It wasn't fair on him, his wife, or them.

Luke and Dennis had been talking non-stop since they'd started the journey towards Southampton, and the further they travelled, the more Luke was warming to the old man. He reminded him of the grandfather he'd only met twice when he was younger, and Luke hoped that, when he got out of the car in Southampton, Dennis would just drive away and not ask any questions. That he would get himself out of the area before Luke bumped into Danny. There was the prevalent risk that their paths would cross, and there was no knowing how Danny would react.

Danny was a totally different man today, more like an acquaintance than a brother. Doing things that none of them had agreed on – that none of them agreed *with*. And Luke distrusted his volatility.

They entered Southampton city centre from the east, crossing the Itchen toll bridge, and continuing past Queen's Park at the south of the city. A few seconds later, they approached the Mayflower Roundabout at the bottom of the city, situated a few hundred yards from the Channel. In the distance, Luke spotted the yellow and blue of an IKEA logo. He instructed Dennis to continue straight on at the roundabout and slip into the multi-storey IKEA car park. Luke and Danny had agreed via text message to meet on the fourth floor. As Dennis pulled the car to a stop, Luke exhaled, reached for his wallet and handed Dennis a twenty.

'For the car park and petrol,' he said before he opened the bag by his feet and produced a wad of notes, the smell of old money wafting to his nostrils. 'And this is for your troubles.'

Dennis shook his head, swatting Luke's hand away with his. 'I don't want it. Keep it. I have no need for it… you might.'

A smile crept over Luke's face. 'It's OK, I've got enough. I want you to have it. Maybe you can treat yourself to something nice. That holiday you were talking about.'

'You're going to need it, wherever you're going. Please…'

Luke was about to say something when he noticed Danny standing with his back pressed against a wall, his head low, a hat pulled over his eyes.

Luke opened the door, grabbed his things and stepped out.

'You'll be OK, won't you?' Dennis asked as Luke prepared to close the door.

'I'll be the best I've ever been,' Luke replied. 'Trust me.'

Dennis extended his hand. Luke reached in and shook it. The old man's grip was fierce, a lifetime of manual labour and hard practical work hidden behind the muscles.

'I'll never forget you,' Luke said.

Dennis grinned. 'Likewise.'

With that, Luke shut the door gently, waved goodbye and hurried over to Danny. Luke didn't know what it was, but as soon as he locked eyes with Danny, he felt safe, he felt at home – as though the events of the past few hours hadn't happened at all. As though his older brother wasn't responsible for their mother's inevitable death. As though Danny hadn't shot and killed an innocent shop worker.

It was as if Danny was his brother again.

'About fucking time,' Danny said.

Luke ignored him and embraced Danny's muscular body. When Danny reciprocated the hug, Luke eased into his brother's arms and felt the tension in his shoulders dissipate.

'Stop it,' Danny said, throwing Luke off. 'Making us look like a bunch of poofs. What took you so long?'

'I'm here, aren't I?'

'Were you followed?'

'No,' Luke replied with assurance.

'Sure?'

'Do you trust me?'

Together they started off, heading down four flights of steps. The air inside the stairwell was cold and it was a welcome change from the stifling heat of the car park. They reached the bottom of the stairs and breached into the car park's entrance at the base of the IKEA centre. A queue of traffic had formed by the ticket barriers, and car engines coughed and spluttered as they waited for the vehicle in front to move. A wall of heat suffocated him as he inhaled a large quantity of warm air, taking him by surprise. He coughed across the remainder of the car park until they exited into the open. There, the sunlight blinded him, and his fingers offered little protection.

'Here,' Danny said, placing a pair of sunglasses on Luke's head. 'While I was waiting, I bought these for you. Help keep your ugly mug away from the CCTV.'

'Our mugshots need updating. Yours is from that time with Richard.'

'Richard who?'

'Richard Maddison.'

'I don't even want to think about that guy.' Danny slapped Luke on the back jovially. 'Come on, we've got a boat to catch.'

They arrived at a set of traffic lights. Danny pressed the button and they waited as cars tore past them. After a few seconds, the lights changed, and they crossed the road. In the distance, dominating the skyline along the riverbed, was the Aurora cruise liner. Luke afforded himself the opportunity to appreciate its magnificence. It was one of the largest man-made structures he had ever seen, if not the largest.

He tried to open his mouth, but the words wouldn't come.

'Brilliant, eh?' Danny said. 'In a few hours we'll be out of this clusterfuck, ready to start new lives for ourselves.'

Luke could hear the excitement in Danny's voice. But something troubled him. Danny was too jovial. Too happy. As though he'd forgotten that their other brother had been arrested.

'What about Michael?' Luke asked.

'What about him? He's gone. There's nothing we can do for him. With any luck they'll lock him up with Freddy and the two of them can work on getting out at some point in the next twenty years.'

'Never. They'll never be locked up together.'

'Micky's a big boy. He can look after himself.'

'Just like that?'

'What?'

'Just like that, you're going to forget about him? As though he never existed.'

'Forget about him?' Danny said, coming to an abrupt halt. 'You're the one who left him behind. You're the one who let the cops arrest him.'

'He surrendered himself for me.'

'What a hero,' Danny said, rolling his eyes. He stormed off, leaving Luke to catch up.

As Luke followed, he noticed something irregular about Danny's ensemble.

'Dan,' he called after his brother.

Nothing. No response.

'Dan!'

'What?' Danny snapped on the half-turn.

'Where's your bag?'

Danny's expression dropped. His eyes widened. 'I… er…'

'I don't believe it,' Luke said, stepping away from his brother. '*She's* here, isn't she?'

'Who?'

'Louise. She's here.'

'No. What— Why—'

'*She's* your contact that got all the stuff from the storage units, isn't she? I can see it on your face. That smile. I knew I recognised it. You only smile like that when she's around. I thought you said you two'd broken up.'

Danny bit his nail.

'You lied. Again. You're pathetic.'

'You don't know what you're talking about, Luke. Don't say something you'll later regret.'

Luke shook his head. 'No. That's it, Dan. I've had enough. It's over. I thought coming here would be the best thing, but I was wrong. I thought you'd be able to help. I thought the two of us were going to get out of here. Not three. Not her. She's a cancer to our family, Dan. Don't you see what she's done? You've done all of this for her. I hope she was worth it, because you've just lost two brothers in the process. And a mum.'

'She was not our mum! She never was,' Danny screamed. They were still standing by the side of the road, oblivious to the sea of traffic charging towards them from either side – and the commotion they were causing.

'She was more of a mum to us than all the other women attempted to be.'

Danny pointed his finger in Luke's face. 'Do you know what' – he reached inside his pocket, produced the final key that unlocked Candice's device, and threw it at Luke – 'you can keep this, if she means that much to you. But I want you to know one thing: she wasn't the one who helped put food on the table. I was! Paying for your school lunches and everything else so you wouldn't go hungry. Not her, *me*.'

Luke froze. His mouth dangled like a pendulum. His eyes fell on the key and he fought every will in his body to pick it up. 'You're lying.'

'I always gave the money to Freddy. I saw the relationship you had with him. He taught you things I never could. You were always with him. I didn't want it to seem like I was buying your love.'

'Danny, I… I had no idea.'

'Why would you? Freddy was happy to take the credit for it. He was happy…' Danny choked, regained himself, rubbed just beneath his ribcage and then continued. 'He enjoyed how close you guys were. He knew you always looked up to him. And he wanted to make sure it stayed that way. We never told you because you were too young.'

Luke stopped. He couldn't believe what he'd just heard. What he'd just been told. Everything in his life was a lie. And he had been deceived consistently. It needed to change. *He* needed to change; get his own life back.

'I was old enough to make my own decisions.'

'You were naïve. You still are.'

'For too long I've depended on you and Micky and Freddy. I need to get out of here. I need to clear my head.' Luke bent down, picked up the key, adjusted the strap on his shoulder so it felt more comfortable, then turned his back on Danny and started to walk away.

'Luke!' Danny called back, but Luke ignored him. 'Luke!'

He stopped, turned on a half-twist, and said, 'I hope you and Louise are happy together, Danny. You deserve each other. Enjoy your new life.'

CHAPTER 54

GREEN LIGHT

The search and rescue party that had been sent to look for Luke amongst the streets of residential houses of Fareham – which consisted of an assortment of ten uniformed officers and three armed officers – had been unsuccessful. The youngest of the brothers was still out there somewhere, an invisible moving target, a ghost in a haunted mansion. As expected, from the precarious interview with Michael Cipriano, Jake had discovered that Luke had relied upon his brothers his whole life – they'd protected him, raised him, shielded him from the outside world – and he needed to return to that security. Alone, lost, and with Michael out of the picture, there was no doubt in Jake's mind that Luke was currently on his way to Danny.

He just hoped they'd be able to make it there in time.

'You sure about this?' Bridger asked as he turned the car off the M271 and onto Redbridge Road a few miles from the centre of Southampton.

'Have I been wrong about anything else up to this point?'

He answered the question himself. Yes, he had been wrong: his conduct during Michael's interview had been unprofessional, bordering unlawful, he realised shortly after. He'd lost sight of what they were there for and what they should have been doing and instead had launched a tirade against Michael and his family. And then there was the matter of conducting the interview in the first place, whether it had been appropriately approved by the relevant channels, despite Bridger's claims. But there was nothing they could do about it now; he just needed to prepare his version of events if questions were asked later.

He would have to see how far he could take the maxim 'better to ask for forgiveness than permission'.

'What's our ETA?' Jake asked.

'Hampshire are in the middle of setting up the rendezvous point at the Mayflower Roundabout.' Bridger hesitated for a brief moment as he glanced at the satnav in front of him. 'I'd say we're two minutes out.'

Perfect. That gave Jake enough time to make a call. He removed his phone and dialled Danika's number.

'Jake?' she answered.

'Have you checked the bookings for Harrington at Southampton?' he asked, wanting to keep it nice and concise.

'Yes. Just pulled the reports now. I found four of them. Sean, Alex, Billy and Kate Harrington.'

'Their aliases…' Jake said, thinking aloud. 'Where's the cruise going?'

'Canary Islands. Scheduled to leave at 3 p.m.'

Jake checked his watch. 'That gives us just over half an hour.'

As he thanked her and hung up the call, they arrived at Mayflower Roundabout. Bridger banked the kerb and parked on a small patch of grass near an office block. It was devoid of any police presence, and cars continued to stream past them from four directions. To their right, towering above the office buildings, was the cruise liner they were looking for, unmissable, and to their left was a row of trees sitting in front of Mayflower Park.

'Where is everyone?'

Jake climbed out of the car. The salt in the air licked the skin on his forearms, melting into the thin veil of sweat, already cemented in position by the chilled sea breeze that buffeted his shoulders and legs, as if forming a gelatinous mixture on his body.

'Seems they're late to the party,' Bridger replied, rounding the front of his vehicle.

Just as Jake was about to respond, the sound of sirens pierced the street, followed closely by the shrill pitches of horns and tyres squealing. Around them, an entourage of police vehicles pulled up to the roundabout from every direction, blocking all available streams of traffic. And then an unmarked police car skidded to a halt beside Jake, the front wheel turning away from him at the last moment. The door opened and out stepped a uniformed officer. By the time Jake had registered who it was, the man was by his side.

'PS Hammond,' the middle-aged and balding man said. Hammond outstretched his hand and took Bridger's first. As they shook, Hammond glanced down and nodded at Bridger's watch. 'You gentlemen from Surrey?'

Bridger nodded.

'Glad to have you with us. We've got this under control for now, but if we need you for anything, I want you on hand to assist.'

Jake stepped in. 'Where is everyone? They should be here by

now. Ridiculous.'

'Excuse me?' The uniformed officer advanced towards Jake, but before the situation was able to escalate any further, Bridger stepped in, jumping between the two of them.

'Sorry,' Bridger pleaded, the back of his arm pressing against Jake's chest. 'This is *Temporary* DC Tanner. He's new, joining us on secondment from The Met. Think he's used to things working a little differently up there.'

Hammond peered round the side of Bridger's shoulder and pointed at Jake.

'You'd better know your place, son. You'll learn a few things quicker if you do it that way. Trust me.'

Jake retreated. 'We don't have time to be arguing.' He quickly checked his watch. 'We've got thirty minutes.'

'It's all under control,' Hammond said softly. He seemed to have calmed down almost as quickly as his temper had flared in the first place. 'Firearms teams are setting themselves up now. We're cordoning off the road. And everyone back at HQ is trying to alert the captain to what's happening. But until the firearms team arrive, I can't tell you much more.'

'Has Candice Strachan been cleared to enter?' Bridger asked.

'What do you mean?'

'Our governor, DCI Pemberton, is on her way down here now with Candice Strachan. She's got a spiked collar strapped to her neck.'

'What's she doing that for?'

'Because the only people who can defuse it are inside that boat,' Jake interrupted. 'She's going to die if she doesn't get that key.'

Hammond sighed and placed his hands on his hips. 'I'll have to check whether it's been cleared. Might take some persuasion. Why can't bomb squad defuse it?'

'It requires a key,' Jake said after a long moment of looking deeply into the man's face. 'Danny Cipriano, one of the offenders inside that boat, has it.'

'Has it been confirmed that Cipriano is definitely on board?'

Shit. In the rush and excitement of it all, Jake had forgotten to ask Danika whether all the tickets she'd found had been collected and whether the brothers had set foot on deck. For all Jake knew, they could be anywhere, and Jake was putting all his eggs in one basket in the hope that they were all on that boat.

'We're not sure,' Bridger replied eventually. 'We have intelligence that suggests both Luke and Danny Cipriano are on board, but no confirmation.'

Hammond held his hand in the air, stepped away from the conversation and made a call. While they waited, Jake turned on the spot, cast his gaze around him and surveyed the area. He hadn't realised it, but in the short time that they'd been talking, the uniformed officers of Hampshire police had efficiently cordoned off all access points to the roundabout, blocking the road as far as the IKEA car park in the distance behind him.

But, as he stood there, waiting for the tactical firearms team to arrive, Jake couldn't help but feel like it would all be a little too late.

A cough distracted him. It was Hammond.

'The Strategic Firearms Commander has given the green light for Candice Strachan's arrival. She's good to attend.'

CHAPTER 55

LUKE CIPRIANO

Luke was lost. Physically. Emotionally. Mentally. Everything he had ever thought about his family was a lie, a façade, an act. His entire life had been a tournament for them to fight in. And he was the prize. They'd used him for their own narcissistic gain. He was most hurt by Freddy. They had bonded the most during his childhood. Almost been inseparable. All while Danny was working somewhere, bringing in the money so that they could eat and drink that night. Freddy had been Luke's confidant, his closest companion.

In the space of a few hours, their entire family had crumbled. A mother and their sons split up in the wild, each left to fend for themselves. The metaphor disturbed Luke as he conjured images of blood and massacre and death… and, eventually, a pride of lions being trapped by poachers. Surrounded by weapons. Forced to surrender and die.

Luke closed his eyes and banished the thoughts from his mind.

He found a nearby bench and sat on it, his head spinning as he removed the key from his pocket and rolled it in his fingers. The rusted metal was tinted a shade of green and brown, yet it still managed to glimmer in the sunlight. Luke hoped it was a sign, but he didn't believe in that sort of thing. A higher power hadn't helped him at any other stage in his life, so why would it start now? Besides, it was no use having it anyway. He had no idea where Candice was and no means of getting to her. He wished he'd taken Dennis's number; he could use a somewhat friendly face right now.

Snap out of it, you idiot, he told himself.

A car sped past him, grabbing his attention. Luke's head shot upward, and he glimpsed a police car roaring down the street. His eyes followed it until it parked up beside another police car in the distance. At the sight of the flashing lights, Luke's skin turned cold. The hunters were closing in around him.

And Danny.

Guns at the ready.

A moment of epiphany startled him. It was a farce. It was all wrong. A mistake. The police would find his brother on the ship. Of course they would. Danny was stupid enough to be on there in the first place when they should have had a Plan C, something they'd never needed before. But Danny was too cocksure, too brazen. He had ignored almost all of Freddy's rules – the mantra they had all sworn by when their former leader was still with them. And for what? A stupid bitch who was going to steal all of his money anyway? Luke wished they'd never gone to that pub on that day – that Louise had never entered their lives.

Ifs and buts don't change anything, dickhead.

He stared at the bag of money in front of him. Contemplating. With the amount he had, he could live any life he wanted. Anywhere. There wasn't much people wouldn't give to have that same luxury. And yet, here he was, pissing about with it, considering throwing it all away. His mind turned to the people who had been hurt so that he could have the meaningless sheets of paper and diamonds sat before him. Luke thought of the employee Danny had shot mercilessly, the Audi owner, the police officer.

It was wrong. So wrong. They had gone too far. Too many people had suffered because of their evil – *Danny's* evil. And both he and Michael were complicit, even though they'd never pulled the trigger themselves.

Luke's mind switched to Candice. And then he realised: the police were after *him*, and they were positioned only a few hundred yards away; they would know where Candice was; they would be able to save her. *He* would be able to save her. Even if it meant giving himself up to the police. A small sacrifice to pay for the day's events. A small chance of redemption.

Luke squeezed his head in his hands until everything hurt and glanced at the barricade of police vehicles in the distance.

A moment later, he'd made his decision.

It was better for everyone if he did it this way. Him. Danny. Michael. The families of those that had suffered. Candice. Everyone.

Grabbing his bag, Luke slung it over his shoulder and started to shuffle towards the army of law enforcement that were setting up a cordon in the middle of the street.

CHAPTER 56

NO MAN'S LAND

It didn't take long for Hampshire Police to remove all seeds of doubt in Jake's mind about their efficiency during the operation. Within minutes a plethora of police cars – both undercover and liveried – along with ambulances and fire engines had arrived at Mayflower Roundabout, with some of the vehicles spilling into the park on the other side of the treeline that banked the south side, near the water. They'd evacuated the area and sent the city into lockdown. And, as Jake folded his arms and rested them against his chest, impressed with what he saw, a black van waded its way through the stationary police vehicles and pulled up a few yards away from the roundabout. It was the armed response and tactical firearms units.

Everyone in the area watched in high anticipation as the van came to a halt and six armed officers deftly disembarked from the back of the vehicle. They fanned out, making their way slowly to the front of the van. Two of them approached Jake, Bridger and Hammond. Both of the armed officers were of similar height and build to one another, their features hidden behind helmets and masks.

'PS Grahams,' the man on the left said. 'I'm the Operational Firearms Commander.' Strapped over his shoulder was a SIG MCX 556 Carbine. Standard issue. He turned to his colleague and said, 'And this is PC Radcliffe.'

Radcliffe gave a curt nod at the mention of his name and tilted his visor skywards, revealing a small scar above his eyebrow. On his bare wrist, there was a scorpion tattoo stained into his skin.

Bridger introduced himself and Jake, leaving Hammond till last.

All five men shook hands.

'What's the status?' Bridger asked.

'We've got sixteen plainclothes AFOs making their way on board now,' Grahams said. 'They're going to conduct a thorough and methodical sweep of the boat, searching for the offenders.'

'Do they know what Danny and Luke look like?' It was Jake's turn to speak. In the final moments of the pursuit, he couldn't afford to let his timidity stand in the way of success. Still in the back of his mind were the damaging words of Freddy Miller, gnawing away at him.

We had help from the inside every single time. Someone working against you.

Danika had already proven herself to him, and just because he wasn't certain who it could have been in Surrey Police, didn't mean to say that he hadn't met them yet. There were a lot of new faces in Hampshire Police too, and no time to get to know them.

'They've been sent the visuals, yes,' Grahams said.

'You mean they've seen their mugshots?' Jake asked.

Grahams nodded.

'That's not good enough. Those images are nearly ten years old.' Jake paused for a moment while an idea formed in his mind. 'I need to get on that boat. I can confirm their identities,' he continued. 'Before we arrested Michael, he'd shaved his head. Luke potentially could have done the same. But… this morning I ran into them. I saw Danny without the mask on. I know what he looks like. You'll need to get me on board. The last thing we want is to arrest innocent people and alert them to our presence.'

Just as Grahams was about to respond, the roundabout filled with screams and shouts erupting from behind Jake. He spun on the spot and turned to face the source of the commotion. Fifty yards away, on the wrong side of the police cordon, was a figure sauntering towards them, carrying a bag in his hands that jolted and swayed with each step. Jake's eyes widened. He sidestepped closer to Bridger's car.

'Is that…?' Bridger asked.

'Yes,' Jake replied, unable to tear his gaze from the man approaching them.

'Which one?'

Jake squinted to get a better view of the person's face, and as the man came closer, he recognised the young features. The thin frame. The wiry arms. The red cheeks. The bald head that looked as though the hair had recently been hacked off.

'Luke.'

At the mention of the Cipriano brother's name, Grahams cried out, barking orders to the authorised firearms officers. Radcliffe and the rest of the armed officers raised their weapons and sprinted towards Luke.

Screams of 'Armed police!' pierced the air.

'Wait!' Jake said, rushing behind the officers.

Twenty yards away, Luke came to a stop and dropped the bag by his side. He was surrounded by tarmac on both sides. Behind him was the police cordon, and in front of him were five armed officers aiming their sub-machine guns at him. There was nowhere for him to go.

Tentatively, keeping his hands raised in the air, Jake crossed the threshold into the line of fire and entered his very own No Man's Land.

'Hold your fire!' he screamed, his voice breaking mid-sentence.

He knew that what he was doing was risky, was breaking several procedures, and warranted having his arse handed to him later on, but he needed to step in. Something wasn't right. And it was his job to get to the bottom of it.

After a few seconds of uncertainty and silence, Grahams ordered the officers to stand down. They lowered their weapons slowly.

Jake took a deep breath before beginning. 'What are you doing here, Luke?'

The young man kept his head low and his arms raised, but there was no response.

'Where's Danny?'

Still nothing.

'Luke – we can help you.'

At that, Luke's head lifted.

'Michael's safe, Luke. He didn't get hurt. He's being looked after,' Jake said.

Luke lowered his arms.

'You need to keep them above your head, mate, otherwise these guys have got their instructions.'

Luke did as he was told, although he looked as though he'd given up – as though he'd lost all the fight left within him.

'What's in the bag, Luke?' Jake asked, trying a different approach. It was then that he noticed the undisturbed silence around him. Even the traffic in the far-off distance, the gentle lapping of the waves, the rushing coastal wind, seemed muted.

'Money,' came the monosyllabic response.

'The money you stole from Candice?'

'We didn't steal it from Candice – she gave it to us. She *shared* it with us.' There was a hoarseness in Luke's voice, as though there was a barrage of tears that would come flooding out as soon as the gates opened. All Jake needed to do was unlock them.

'Yes. That's right. She gave it to you. She was your mother, wasn't she?'

'Is,' Luke corrected. '*Is* my mother. She ain't dead yet.' He raised his gaze and stared at Jake. They were of a similar age, yet both had led very different lives at opposite ends of the spectrum. Luke had led a life of crime and constant oppression, whereas

Jake's was normal, civilised. He had gone to school, university, and now here he was. There were opportunities available to Jake that Luke had never been considered for, and he couldn't help feeling like the young man would be in a different position had his upbringing and surroundings been controlled better.

'She won't be alive for long, Luke. And you know it…' Jake brushed his tie and loosened his collar; it felt as though it was strangling him. 'She told us everything. About you. Michael. Danny. The device.' Jake hesitated. 'Help us, Luke. Help us arrest him. He'll be out of your life and you'll never have to see him again. If nothing else, do it for Candice. She's dead if you don't.'

Luke's expression changed to a steely, cold glare.

'How do I know I can trust you?'

'Do you remember Freddy?'

'Yeah.'

'Did you know he had a wife and kids?'

Luke nodded.

'Did you know he's been writing to them and he's not heard a single word from them in return.' Jake swallowed, hoping he was convincing enough in his next few words. 'Well, they're going to see him tomorrow. I spoke with them earlier. Freddy wouldn't talk to me unless I persuaded them to visit. Little Sammy is really excited to see his daddy for the first time. If I can get them to visit him, then I promise you that you can—'

'Where's my mum? I need to see her. I want to see her.'

'And you will. She's on her way down now. All I need you to do is make a call to your brother, and then she'll be allowed to come out. So long as you agree to give us what we want.'

'I'm not helping until I see her.'

Jake pursed his lips.

'Then we'll just have to wait.'

CHAPTER 57

BULLET

A few minutes of nothing passed, the sounds of city life in the distance picked up and moved away by the wind that rolled through the roads. In that time, Luke remained perfectly still, staring up at the sky, kept in place by the numerous SIGs trained on him. Deeming it safe to do so, Jake wandered back to Bridger, Grahams and Hammond.

'What're you doing?' Bridger asked. There was an edge of concern to his voice that, to Jake's ears, almost sounded paternal. 'Do you have a death wish?'

Jake's eyes bounced between Hammond, Grahams and the armed officers. 'Sorry,' he said. 'I needed to speak with him. Pointing your guns at him was only going to make him panic.'

'You don't know that,' Grahams added.

Jake turned to Grahams. He felt like placing his hands on his hips but let them dangle by his side instead. 'Have you ever been on the receiving end of six sub-machine guns, Sarge?'

Grahams didn't have a response. *Thought not.*

'Where's Pemberton?' Jake asked Bridger. 'Every minute wasted is another minute Danny could escape,' Jake said.

'Don't worry,' Grahams added, apparently hoping for a chance of redemption. 'We've finally managed to get through to the captain. He's been made aware and is currently holding fire. He's under strict instruction that under no circumstances is he to move the boat.'

'You're going to leave it waiting there?'

Grahams nodded.

Jake shook his head in disbelief. 'With all due respect, I think that's the wrong idea,' he began. 'Danny Cipriano is dangerous. His actions today have proven that he's irrational and willing to exercise any form of protection against himself and the ones he loves. But the longer you keep that boat idle, the more suspicious Danny's going to get. And the more he's going to retaliate. None of us have any idea what he might have been able to smuggle on board. If he can bring on several million pounds' worth of jewels, then he can also bring on some firepower.' Jake swallowed before continuing. 'Tell the captain to wait until I go on board. I'll be able to identify the right man.'

'We'll get you on board now then,' Grahams said.

'I've got to deal with this first,' Jake replied, gesturing to Luke in the distance.

'How long's that—'

Jake's phone started ringing. He silenced Grahams with a wave of the hand and answered the call.

'Hello?'

'Jake,' Danika began. 'I've spoken with the cruise company. Nobody under the name Harrington has boarded the ship. All four tickets are still awaiting collection.'

'Fuck,' Jake said loudly. Was this another decoy? Was Danny already on his way to another part of the country to escape their clutches again?

Jake thanked Danika for the update and hung up.

'What is it?' Bridger asked as soon as he'd finished the call.

'Harrington. The tickets. They've not been collected so he's not on the boat.' Jake advanced towards Bridger without giving Bridger a chance to reply. He stopped a few feet short from the young, broken man. 'Where is Danny, Luke? He never used the Harrington ticket.'

'I don't know,' Luke said, raising his hands higher in surrender.

'Why isn't he on board the ship?'

'I don't know. I thought he was.'

'Did he tell you where he was going?'

'No.'

'Where is he?'

'I don't know!' Luke gesticulated wildly. 'I don't know, all right? I don't know where he is.' He turned his attention to the white markings in the middle of the tarmac. 'He must have bought another ticket…'

'Another one?'

'Another one,' Luke repeated absentmindedly. 'For him and Louise.'

As soon as he finished speaking, a look of horror crawled across Luke's face, as if he'd just spoken out of line in the classroom and was awaiting his immediate punishment.

'Who's Louise, Luke?' Jake asked, cautiously closing the distance between them one step at a time.

Luke shook his head, avoiding the question.

'Is she a sister?'

No.

'A friend?'

No.

'Girlfriend?'

Luke stopped shaking his head.

'What's her surname, Luke?'

Luke returned Jake's gaze. 'Where's my mum? I want to speak to her.'

'She's coming. She's nearby.'

'You're lying. It's been too long.'

Where the fuck is Pemberton?

Almost as if on cue, a prisoner transport vehicle appeared over Luke's left shoulder. It snaked its way through the traffic and sped the short distance towards them on the other side of the road. As it stopped, the weight of the vehicle tested the suspension, bowing the car forward.

Luke's head darted towards the van. 'Mum!' he shouted, and then sprinted towards the vehicle. At once, he was prohibited by the wall of armed officers who were quicker to react than Jake. They charged at Luke, keeping their bodies low and their weapons trained on him.

'Get down on the ground! Now!'

Luke ignored them, and as he reached the central island that separated the two streams of traffic, a uniformed officer opened the door on the side of the vehicle and Candice Strachan fell out. At the same time, Pemberton alighted the vehicle and rushed to Candice's side, holding the woman's arms behind her back. The sight of her son was too much for Candice – she broke free from Pemberton's restraint and bolted towards him.

'Luke!' she screamed as they collided with one another. Jake was harrowed by the sight of the collar bomb still attached to her neck and a lump swelled in his throat as they clattered together, fearing that the slightest jolt would detonate it and decapitate her right in front of him.

'Get down on the ground now!' the armed officers continued to shout, gradually encircling them both. Their cries echoed around the area. Jake's senses heightened and his body turned taut. If someone wasn't careful, Luke or Candice could be on the receiving end of a bullet.

He intervened, tearing through the throng of armed officers and grappled Luke, clutching the man by the scruff of his collar and pulling him away. In the process, Jake knocked the bag strap from Luke's shoulder and the money and jewels and other precious items inside landed with a terrible crash, some of the contents spilling over the side.

'Luke,' Jake said, shouting into the young man's ear, holding both of them apart, 'if you don't stop right now, you won't ever get to see her again. Is that what you want?'

Luke didn't respond.

'Tell us what we need to know, Luke. Danny… where is he?'

'Let me speak to her please.'

'Not until you answer my question.'

'No. *Please.*'

Jake sighed, looked at Candice, who had her hands cuffed behind her back, and then returned his attention to Luke.

'Give me one second. I'll see what I can do.'

Before leaving Luke behind, Jake gestured for the officer accompanying Pemberton to come over. The man hurried across, hooked his arm beneath Candice's and carried her away. Once there was a large enough distance between the two of them, Jake turned his back on Luke and strode towards Pemberton.

'What the hell is going on, Jake?' Pemberton said, pulling him aside, out of earshot from Candice who was beside the police van.

'Luke won't tell us where Danny is until he's spoken to her. Danny never boarded the boat.'

Pemberton glanced back at Luke in the centre of the street. 'I knew coming here was a mistake. And you think he knows where his brother is?'

'There's only one way to find out.'

'Can they be trusted?'

'Like I said…'

Pemberton sighed and looked down at the ground. She planted her hands on her hips and placed all her weight on one foot, but as she opened her mouth to continue, Bridger appeared, his breathing slightly exasperated from the short run between his car and the van.

'How long until the boat leaves?' Pemberton asked. 'Just in case Danny is on there and we just don't know about it.'

Jake checked his watch – 2:42 p.m. 'We have enough time,' he replied.

'You sure?'

He nodded.

'What do you think, Bridger?' Pemberton twisted round to glance at Candice and Luke before turning back to face the detective sergeant. By now, a sea of police officers had surrounded Luke in almost every direction.

'I say we do it. But someone needs to stay with him. We can't just let them stand there, sharing their own little secrets,' Bridger said.

'I'll do it,' Jake said, keeping his eyes trained on Luke. He ignored Pemberton and Bridger's muted stares.

'Jake, I can't allow—'

'I'll do it.' He hoped the confidence in his voice was enough to convince Pemberton that he wasn't about to budge from his decision.

218

'You're going to need a wire or something,' Bridger added, placing a firm hand on his shoulder. 'I'll find you one.'

As Bridger turned on the spot, preparing himself to go, Jake held him back.

'It's fine,' he said. 'I'll give them a radio.'

'What?'

'If they want to talk, they have to play by our rules.'

Saying nothing more, Jake reached for the radio on his hip, gripping it tightly. He steadied his breathing with long, deep breaths, and then he started, turning down the transmission volume at the top of the device to prevent any feedback and cross-communication over the channels. To his left, he glimpsed the armed officers adjusting their grips on their SIGs, and to his right, he noticed Candice shuffling closer towards Luke. Less than five seconds later, he was standing in front of the young man, with the radio concealed in the sleeve of his left arm.

'What's going on?' Luke asked, eagerly looking straight over Jake's shoulders.

'Lift your arms in the air.'

Luke did as he was told.

'Keep them there until I tell you otherwise,' Jake replied. As he spoke, he turned his body at an angle and clipped the radio to the back of Luke's jeans so that it was out of Candice's line of sight. 'If you touch this,' he said, giving a slight tug on Luke's jeans strap, 'then you lose your privileges. You've got two minutes. That's all I could manage. And then you tell us everything. Nod if you understand.'

Slowly, tentatively, Luke nodded.

Jake breathed a sigh of relief as he stepped to the side and returned to Pemberton and Bridger, maintaining his body angle so that he faced both Luke and Candice at all times. Once he was by Pemberton's side, she gave the all-clear, and the officer guarding Candice released his grip on her.

As soon as the man's hands were in the air, Candice bolted. She leapt across the concrete and up the small kerb, and in an instant, she was on top of him. Luke lowered his arms and embraced her. They squeezed one another, despite the big block of metal impeding them. In that moment, it reminded Jake of his relationship with his own mum. Their bond had never been close before his dad died, but since then, they'd become almost inseparable. He appreciated her more now than he ever had done, and he was paying her back by allowing her to spend as much time as she wanted with Maisie. It was the least he could do.

After a few seconds, Luke and Candice released one another and began talking. Bridger nudged Jake in the shoulder, and together the three of them listened in to their conversation on another radio Bridger had managed to source.

'Where is he?' Candice asked in a whisper.

'On the boat,' Luke said slowly. 'With Louise. I was going to get on with him but then I realised she was here. They must've already bought another set of tickets for the two of them under her name as a backup.'

'That fucking conniving, arsehole… bastard!' Candice breathed heavily.

'Mum. Mum! It's going to be all right.'

'How?'

'I've got the—'

'My handcuffs,' she said, 'they're unlocked. I'm going to find him, and when I do, I'm going to fucking kill him.'

The words struck fear into Jake. Danny. Louise. Tickets. Handcuffs. Unlocked. Jake shot a look at Pemberton.

'Oh fuck,' she mouthed, her words silent.

'But wait, Mum,' Luke began, 'Mum, I have the—'

But before he was able to finish his sentence, Candice shook her hands free from the cuffs and swung herself behind Luke's neck, wrapping her arm around his throat. Jake and the rest of the team watched on in horror. He had been trained extensively to react to even the minutiae in any given situation, but in that moment, nothing happened. It was as if all the hours he'd spent exercising and doing psychometric tests at home were for nothing, his body held back by an impenetrable force.

'Let go of the hostage!' one of the armed officers shouted. 'Lift your hands in the air.'

Candice chose not to comply.

'Candice!' Pemberton called as she stepped closer to the action. 'Candice, for heaven's sake, put your son down. Nobody has to get hurt.'

Candice shook her head. 'You don't understand, do you? He left me to die. I'm done playing games with him. He won't get away with this.'

'We can all find Danny together!'

Candice edged backward, moving closer to the other side of the road, closer to the cruise ship, pulling Luke along with her. The armed officers matched her step for step.

'Stay back!' she screamed.

'Please,' Luke added, 'do as she says. I don't want anyone to get hurt.'

'That's the last thing we want as well,' Jake said, finding the courage from somewhere within him to speak up. Next he moved nearer to Pemberton and maintained her pace as soon as he was by her side.

For the next thirty metres, they followed Candice and Luke across a small expanse of grass, until they stopped between two oak trees positioned like goalposts. Now they were on the other side of the police cordon, and there was nothing between them and the ship two hundred yards down the road. Jake scanned the horizon, searching for anything that could stop them. He found his answer in the form of Grahams. The man was speaking fervently with his hand pressed against the side of his head. Jake's eyes moved to the rest of the armed officers. One of them spoke calmly, his voice inaudible.

Radcliffe.

Jake's gaze darted back to Candice. The woman was snapping her head from side to side, constantly checking the distance between her and the boat, her hair whipping in Luke's face.

And then she bolted, nudging Luke in the back. The young man stumbled forward but quickly regained himself and sprinted after her.

Pemberton cried after them.

Bridger cried after them.

Jake cried after them.

The armed officers cried after them.

They were fifty yards away, rapidly increasing that distance with every step.

And then a bullet rang out, followed closely by absolute silence.

CHAPTER 58

BLACK

Luke Cipriano's mouth felt dry, rough, like sandpaper. He wanted to vomit. He wanted the ground to swallow him up – the patch of grass where his hands were. Anything. Just so long as he didn't have to live in this horrifying, paralysing, painful moment. The bullet had torn through his back and wrapped itself around his organs, crippling him, and as he tried to clamber to his feet, the colours of the world melted into one strange dollop of grey. A few feet away, Candice was standing in front of him, her body twisting and morphing as he dipped in and out of consciousness.

The pain burnt through him. A sensation unlike any other he'd experienced. At first, it started in his front – where the bullet had entered through his stomach – and then made its way to the back before eventually consuming his whole body. As the blood rapidly drained from his system, he became deaf to all sounds around him. The sound of engines ticking over. Water lapping against the boat and sea walls. The screams and shouts from the armed officers for them to remain still. The police sirens bleating in the background. The general hubbub of the city way off in the distance. All of it was replaced by the sound of his heart straining as it gradually weakened and fought heroically – yet naïvely – to keep him alive.

Before he was able to move any further, Candice leapt down by his side and rolled him onto his back. She supported his head while her eyes danced between his stomach and his face, babbling and muttering incoherently to herself. Luke tilted his head downward and inspected the damage the bullet had caused. A flower of crimson had formed on his stomach and was gushing down the sides of his waist, forming a puddle on the grass. He tried to breathe but it was weak. He coughed and spluttered, the pain rising up and down his body like pistons, each movement worse than the last.

In this moment of odd serenity, he should have felt scared, afraid. But he didn't. Instead, he felt calm. He was safe. He was with his mum. Everything was fine. She was going to look after him like she had done when he was a child – from the earliest memory he had of her. She was going to care for him like she had after he'd fallen from the top of one of the garages in the estate when he was three. He'd found himself up there somehow and, when his brothers had tried to chase after him, he's jumped down on top of a nearby bin, rolled off, and nearly broken both his legs.

She was going to cradle him until the paramedics arrived and took away the pain.

'M-M-Mum.'

Candice squeezed his hand and looked into his eyes solemnly.

'I'm sorry,' she said, babbling, her voice barely a whisper. 'I should have… I should have been there… I'm sorry I ever left you.'

Luke's eyes closed as he danced with death. The lure of emptiness was calling him from somewhere, over the weakened beating of his heart. But there was something he needed to do. From somewhere deep within him, he found the strength to open them.

'The key,' Luke whispered, choking on his own blood between breaths and spitting it onto his collarbone.

Slowly, with as much strength as he could summon, he pointed to his trouser pocket. Without needing to be told twice, Candice rummaged through the contents and retrieved the key, quickly soiling it in his blood. She held it triumphantly in the air.

'Use it…' Luke tried. 'Free… Live…'

He gagged and spluttered as his body convulsed. By now the pain had ceased and been replaced with a warm, tingling sensation. He didn't know how long he had left, but he wanted to be able to see her survive. He wanted to be able to watch her remove the collar and use it as a final middle finger at Danny.

Candice's hands shook as she held the key. Running her fingers along the base of the metal box, she found the collar's fourth lock and inserted the key. Luke held his breath as he watched her rotate it, his body freezing as the lock snapped into place.

And then there was complete silence, and the only thing he could hear was his raspy breathing as he waited for the mechanism on the neck to detach itself.

It didn't.

Luke and Candice both glanced at the device, willing it to do something, anything. But when nothing happened, Candice screamed. She clawed at it, beat it, yanked it from her neck, punched it until the edges of the solid metal lacerated her skin and she started bleeding, continuing until her knuckles were covered in her own blood.

Luke watched, paralysed with despair. It hadn't worked. Danny had lied to him about the device. He had assured him – he had assured *everyone* – that the keys would defuse the device, that that was all that was needed. But it had all been a lie. As soon as Danny had put that device around her neck, he had already slammed the final nail into her coffin, while readying himself to start his brand-new life with Louise.

Warm tears filled Luke's eyes and streamed down his face as he lay there on his back. He reached his hand out for Candice to take it. She did. Hers was moist and covered in blood, but he didn't care. So long as he got to hold her and be with her in his last few—

The ticking began. At first it was a few beeps: steady, rhythmic. But then within seconds it intensified.

Beep-beep-beep.

Beepbeep-beepbeep.

Beepbeepbeepbeepbeepbeepbeepbeep.

Luke knew instantly what the noise meant. And so did Candice. But by that point it was too late.

The device detonated. All ten blades plunged themselves into Candice's neck, rupturing and severing her arteries and muscles, breaking her spine and airway, and piercing the brain stem. Small jets of blood erupted from the incisions in her throat and rained down on Luke. Her eyes rolled into the back of her head and she collapsed to the ground. She was dead before her head hit the grass.

Just like that, she was gone. It had been over so quickly, so instantly.

Gasping, clinging on to what little life he had left, Luke rolled onto his side so they were facing one another. Candice's eyes were open, distant, yet, to Luke, it seemed like she was still there, like she was staring at him, ready to read him a story as she nurtured him into his permanent sleep. Luke reached out and stroked her face.

As he watched the colour run from her cheeks and the blood trickle across her throat, anger swelled within him. All his life he'd tried to remember who his mother was. What she'd looked like. How she'd behaved. What she'd done to provide for them. What she'd done with her life. In the few months that he'd been reunited with her, they'd tried to stitch together their relationship, set the foundations in place and build from there. But Luke was never going to get a chance to finish it. And now his final memory of her was tarnished with this image. Dead at the hands of the device. Covered in her own blood.

And it was all one person's fault. *Danny.*

His eldest brother. The one who'd helped raise him had put him in this situation. How could he?

Luke tore his weakening mind from thoughts of Danny and

filled it with the memories that he and Candice had tried to build, and the few he had left of her from before she'd disappeared. As he lay there on the grass, staring into her eyes, a smile grew on his face.

Before the world went black, and before the pain stopped, he was just happy that he'd been fortunate enough to see her come back into his life.

CHAPTER 59

TOILET BREAK

'Hey…' Danny whispered over the sound of pop music coming from the speakers around them. 'Can I go to the toilet?'

'Go,' Louise snapped at him, waving him away with a dismissive hand. 'Just don't be too long.'

'I won't, my love.' Danny stroked her arm; she flinched slightly, pulling away from him. 'Are you going to be all right?'

She glared at him, her gaze more piercing than knives. 'Do I look like a fucking child?' She reached her hand around his body, parked it under his armpit and pinched. Hard. Danny wanted to cry out, but he knew that was a bad idea. For his own sake, it was better to remain quiet and suck it up. The people around them didn't need another reason to look their way.

'I'll ask again: do I look like a fucking child? No. I didn't think so. So why do you insist on treating me like one?'

Danny opened his mouth to apologise but was interrupted by another harder pinch, this time a little higher, grabbing a clutch of hairs. He clenched his jaw, swallowing the pain. There was that fire in her eyes again. The one that always told him she was angry and that she needed to vent her frustrations on him. Sometimes it was a pinch. Sometimes it was a friction burn. Sometimes it was a whipping with his belt. Sometimes it was a punch. But it was always in the places nobody could see, the marks and bruises his little secret, just like the way she treated him.

'Go to the toilet,' she said. 'You're a big boy.' And then she applied more pressure and twisted as a final *fuck you*. His skin throbbed and he felt the onset of a bruise underneath.

She released her finger and a flood of pain narrowed in under his arm. It felt uncomfortable to move, and as he lifted his hand to soothe it, swapping the gym bag to his other hand, she grabbed him.

'No. You can leave that with me,' she snarled, snatching the bag from him.

Danny did as he was told and hurried towards the bathroom, giving one last look at the bags of money and jewellery beside Louise as he entered. Inside, he rushed to the cubicle, slammed the door and locked it shut before leaning back against the door and letting out a heavy sigh. He was safe. Out of reach. She wouldn't dare venture into the men's toilets, that was for sure. But he knew that, if she had, she'd mean well. After all, she was only looking out for his best interests, just like she always did. He had, in a way, deserved his punishment. He'd just insulted her dominance. He shouldn't have likened her to a child. It was wrong, and he'd paid the price for it.

Danny untied his belt buckle, loosened the buttons in his jeans and let his penis dangle in front of him. The cold air chilled him. The rash had been causing him issues all afternoon, but he hadn't been able to do anything about it. Five hours of torture and sitting uncomfortably in the car, wishing he could scratch until the blood came. But he wasn't allowed to touch it – Louise's orders. The rash that she'd given him was his fault. It was *his* fault he'd forced her to cheat on him and contract the virus. It was always *his* fault, and he agreed. He was a bad boyfriend. He did wrong things. He hurt her emotionally. He sometimes wounded her physically by accident. But he never meant any of it. None. And now he was on the final few days of treatment, and as soon as it was over, he could have sex with her again. It had been so long since he'd last touched her, held her, felt her, been inside her.

He started pissing, the lower half of his body tingling as the pressure on his bladder eased. Streams of urine splashed on the seat and ricocheted onto the floor and his legs. After finishing, he pulled his pants over himself and buttoned his jeans, ignoring the wet patch that pressed against his leg, then unlocked the cubicle door and washed his hands, splashing soapy water across his face.

He peered up at himself and resented what he saw. Placing his hands in the sink, he hung his head low and exhaled deeply. He was exhausted – physically and mentally. Drained. But that was all about to change now. Everything. The Canary Islands with Louise. Where they could begin their new lives together. Where everything would stop. Where she'd promised the tormenting and the pain would continue no more.

A loud bang sounded in the end cubicle. Danny froze, his skin crawling. His pulse rose and his chest heaved. *What the fuck was that?* It had sounded exactly like the noise he'd heard a few minutes ago – the noise that had come from outside the ship.

Dismissing it as an example of his overactive imagination, he returned his attention to the mirror and then looked at his watch. He'd been in there for a few minutes. Shit. Far too long for a piss. She would be timing him, he knew, and the beating would be even worse if he delayed any longer. Panicked, he wiped his hands on his shirt and trousers and rushed out of the bathroom.

The door flew open, and as he exited, he bashed into another man trying to enter. The man was twice his size and twice as wide, the same size as Michael. Danny apologised and pressed his back against the wall to allow the man to pass. He didn't want to admit it, but the blow had winded him slightly, and he gasped for breath.

But nothing could have prepared him for what he saw in the waiting room.

Louise – the love of his life, despite everything she'd put him through – was gone. And so were his bags of money and jewels.

CHAPTER 60

ALONE

As soon as Candice's head hit the ground, Jake turned his back on the scene, rushed behind the wheel arch of the nearest car and vomited, the liquid splashing onto his feet and legs while the acid stung his throat, chest, mouth and nose. He wiped his lips with the back of his hand and then rubbed the mess on his trouser leg. The bitter taste lingered in his mouth and made him grimace. Spitting the remnants of the aftertaste onto the grass, he turned to face the piece of activist art that was now Luke and Candice's bodies strewn together.

A team of paramedics surrounded them and began checking for a pulse on Luke's neck. Everyone in the area knew their efforts were wasted, but Jake held a little hope. Luke was a human being, just like the rest of them, regardless of who he was and what he'd done. Nobody deserved to suffer a fate like that.

He allowed himself a moment to process what had happened, so that he had a starting point for when he completed it later that evening. He focused on the collar, the keys, and the order in which they'd been inserted. One. Two. Four. Wrong order. It should have been one and two. Then three and four. And with the third missing — possibly still in Pemberton's pocket somewhere — there was no chance Candice was going to survive. In the heat of the moment, in one final act of desperation, she'd slotted the fourth key into her neck and killed herself without even realising what she was doing.

Jake tore his eyes from the massacre and forced himself to focus on something else: being smart. There was still a job to do – a final Cipriano brother to catch – and there was little time to do it.

An idea formed in his head.

He strode towards Grahams, Bridger in tow.

'I think it's time for me to get on board that boat,' he said.

For a moment, Grahams' face contorted as he considered what to do. Jake could see from the man's expression that he didn't want to be bossed about by someone who had nowhere near as much as experience as he did but also knew that Jake was on the right path. The threat to public life was imminent so long as Danny was still on board the boat. With Jake on there as well he could help minimise the risk.

Eventually, Grahams nodded, raised his hand, and within a few seconds, two armed officers were by his side. He ordered them to strip down to their plainclothes, exchange their SIGs for Glock 17s, and then accompany Jake and Bridger onto the ship.

'You need to put these on,' one of the AFOs said, holding up a body vest.

Jake beamed at the sight of it, more so at the fact that he'd never worn one like this before, rather than the inherent possibility that came with wearing one: he might get shot. It was his first day and there was a first time for everything. Stifling the smile away, he donned the vest and readied himself.

With Bridger and the armed officers behind him, he marched towards the paramedics and reached into his pocket. As he approached them, he removed his phone and opened the camera. He bent down closer to the bodies and began to take photographs of their remains, averting his gaze from the images on his screen as he took them.

Five photos later, he was finished.

'What are you doing?' Bridger asked, rushing over to his side. 'Have some respect…'

'I didn't want to have to do it.'

'It's all in the line of duty, eh?'

Jake ignored Bridger's remark, turned on the spot and started towards the boat, ducking beneath the overhanging branches of a nearby tree and breaching onto the road that led to the cruise liner.

The ramp to the cruise deck was steeper than Jake expected, and he found his legs aching and his lungs out of air after a few steps. After the four of them reached the top, they were stopped by one of the stewards working on board the cruise ship. The woman in front of them asked to see their tickets. Instead, they flashed their warrant cards.

Jake pulled out his phone and displayed the old mugshot of Danny Cipriano's face that had been sent to him by Danika. 'If you see anyone who looks like this, alert us. This man is incredibly dangerous. No one else is allowed on, and no one is allowed off. Do you understand?'

A look of fear struck the woman as she nodded, taking Jake's phone and committing the mugshot to memory. They thanked her and crossed the threshold into the boat, while the steward locked the gate behind them, disabling access for anyone else.

The interior of the foyer was lavish, replete with opulence and extravagance, and it was everything Jake had expected from a mega multimillion-pound cruise line. But there was no time to admire it. Perhaps after all of this was done, Jake mused, he and Elizabeth might have to add another addition to the list of games they played when bored: Cruise Roulette. *Hopefully with this one I'll win big.*

Coming to a stop in the middle of the entrance, Jake turned to his partner and touched his hip, searching for his radio.

'We're going to have to do this on mobile,' he said after realising that it was still attached to a dead man's jeans.

'Fine by me,' Bridger said, brandishing his phone.

'What about you guys?' Jake asked, turning to face the AFOs with him. 'And the rest of the plainclothes officers we've got on board?'

'I can communicate with them on my radio,' Bridger replied.

Jake nodded. 'If you hear anything, let me know.'

'Aye aye, Captain.'

Jake pointed to his left. 'Split up. You go that way. I'll go this. Don't get scared on me now, Sarge.'

Bridger's lips rose. 'That's what makes it so much more exciting.'

Then they disappeared in opposite directions.

Jake headed down a brightly lit corridor. Fluorescent light bulbs hung overhead, blinding him. He hated boats. Had never been good on them. The sense of claustrophobia, like the walls were perpetually closing in around him, an inch at a time. The constant swaying from side to side, the unending motion that sent his mind into a whirlpool of nausea and dizziness and made him want to vomit over the deck or in the toilet – whichever he could find sooner.

Steadying himself with his hands on the wall, Jake ventured down the corridor and, at the end, arrived at an even larger foyer than the one he'd seen when he entered. A large, delicate, ornate chandelier, almost as large as Jake's bedroom, dangled from the ceiling. It trumped Candice's chandelier tenfold.

Cruise chandelier one, Candice chandelier nil.

At the reception desk a member of staff was attending to other clientele, apologising for the delay, promising that they were doing everything they could to get the boat moving as soon as possible. Jake rushed over and barged in front of the next in line, flashing his ID, immediately suppressing any protests before they came his way.

'Excuse me,' he said. 'Sorry, but have you seen anyone that looks like this?' Jake showed the man behind the computer the old image of Danny. 'Looks a bit like this, just a bit older.'

The man leant forward, squinted and then eased back to his

natural position, shaking his head.

'If you see anything, call me on this number.' Jake grabbed a pen and paper from atop the desk and scribbled his contact information on it. Sliding the paper back, Jake thanked the man.

As he stepped away from the reception desk, his phone rang. It was Danika.

'Jake,' she said abruptly. 'I've done some digging and found out the name of Danny Cipriano's potential girlfriend. Louise Etherington. I've sent you an image of her. It's a mugshot taken from a previous arrest.'

'What for?'

'GBH. She almost beat another woman to death in a night club. And she's had a string of related incidences after that but never been convicted of anything. A previous boyfriend accused her of domestic violence, but he later rescinded his statement,' Danika explained.

Jake absorbed the information. In the space of twenty minutes, she'd managed to dig herself out of a hole she didn't even know she was in. And he was glad that she had; he couldn't comprehend the possibility of her being corrupt. Not only would it tarnish his friendship with her, but it would also tarnish his ability to trust anyone in the force, no matter how close or distant his relationship with them.

'You're a hero,' he told her. 'I appreciate it.'

'Be careful,' Danika replied before she hung up.

Jake pieced together the information. Now some of it was beginning to make sense. Perhaps Danny wasn't the mastermind behind this at all. Perhaps it was Louise. Perhaps she was the master manipulator who'd forced Danny into betraying his family and running away with her. Perhaps she was the one controlling everything from behind the scenes, making sure she was kept hidden, unseen until the final moment of glory.

As Jake lowered his phone from his ear, he opened the email attachment Danika had just sent him and showed the phone to the receptionist again. This time he didn't apologise for his intrusiveness.

'This woman. What about her? You seen her?'

The man's pupils dilated. 'Yeah. At least I think it's her.'

The hooped earrings, nose piercing and dodgy fake tan were large giveaways, Jake thought, and from the rest of the clientele surrounding him, she didn't look like she would be fitting in to any country club meetings or University of the Third Age croquet lessons any time soon.

'When?'

The man's gaze flicked to the digital clock on his computer screen. He contemplated for what felt like an eternity before replying. 'About five minutes ago. Maybe more.'

'Which way did she go?'

The receptionist pointed to Jake's left, in the direction of a spiral staircase just to the side of the chandelier.

Jake strode towards the steps, forgetting to thank the staff member, and began to climb. He came to a stop at the top. In front of him was another corridor; it looked almost identical to the first one. Groundhog Day on steroids. Fire Exit signs hung overhead beside directions to different parts of the boat. It was then that he realised how enormous and complex the maze of underground corridors was, and how tiny he was in comparison.

Up ahead, a cleaner pushing a trolley descended on the other side of the corridor. Jake snapped himself out of his thoughts and passed her. As he reached the end, he dialled Bridger's number.

'Louise Etherington. Danny's girlfriend. Possible sighting of her from the reception desk,' he said as soon as Bridger connected the call. 'Heading to seating area one on level two.'

A few seconds later, Jake was there. Although he had no idea where *there* was in relation to anyone – or anything – else. He just hoped Bridger was nearby. Large sofas and chairs were spread across the seating area, with tables and vending machines dotted around. Stands containing magazines and newspapers were situated at the four corners of the room. It reminded him of the time he'd been in the BA lounge once when he and his family had been upgraded for free. High-end. Lavish. Expensive. An insight into how the other half lived.

As Jake crossed the threshold into the area, he caught sight of Louise. She was wearing a thin blue jumper and a pair of jeans, chewing grotesquely on a piece of gum – Jake could almost hear the sounds of the polyol-coated substance from here. In one hand she twirled her hair around her fingers, and in the other she was holding two large gym bags.

And, best of all, she was alone.

CHAPTER 61

LOUISE ETHERINGTON

'Bridger...' Jake said quietly into his handset, holding the bottom of the phone millimetres from his lips.

'Go on,' Bridger replied as softly.

'Confirmed sighting of Louise. Seating area one, floor two. Heading down a corridor towards playroom two now. I'll approach. Danny must be somewhere nearby. She's got the bags of money with her.'

'Understood. I'm on my way now. ETA one minute.'

Jake lowered his arm and kept his phone pressed against his thigh as he continued deeper into the corridor, maintaining twenty feet between him and Louise. At the end of the corridor, she arrived at a junction, stopped, looked overhead and then made her decision: left.

Jake followed, gliding along the carpet as silently as possible. As he arrived at the junction, he crept up to the corner of the wall and peered round. In the short time it had taken him to catch up, she had almost doubled the distance between them.

She was suspicious.

Shit.

He pocketed his mobile – making sure to keep the call connected – and then formed an idea. Immediately opposite him, on the other side of the junction, carrying a handful of suitcases, was a steward and couple. Happy. Bubbly. Possibly on their honeymoon. Possibly on an escape from the mundanity of adult life.

He hurried over to them, flashed his warrant card and grabbed the husband's backpack. Any protestations were stifled by the ID in his hand and Jake's finger pressed against his own lips.

'Stay here,' he whispered. 'I only need it for a second.'

He placed the backpack over his front, shielding the police body vest – and the police insignia on the front of it – from view. He didn't want to give Louise any reason to suspect him. Removing his phone from his pocket, he chased after her. By now she was at the end of the corridor and nearing another expanse of open space. Jake had to move quickly if he was going to catch her.

'Excuse me,' he called.

No response.

'Excuse me!' His voice carried up and down the brilliantly lit walls. He tried to place as much distress in his voice as possible.

The second cry for help worked. Louise came to an abrupt stop, turned and scowled at him. Jake closed in on her. Ten feet. Five. One. He stopped right in front of her, then paused, feigning exasperation.

'Do you work here?' he asked, hugging the backpack against his stomach, spreading the width of it across his body.

'No.'

'Oh.' Jake opened his phone and started to flick through the screens. 'I was wondering if you could help me? I'm a little bit lost. Would you…' Jake paused to open his camera roll. 'Would you be able to help me find someone please?'

'I told you I don't work here,' Louise said, her voice laden with disdain.

Jake continued regardless. 'I'm looking for someone. I think you know him.'

He found the mugshot of Danny and then flipped the screen over. It didn't take long for the shock to register on Louise's face. Her eyes bulged and blood rushed to her cheeks as her mouth fell open and the piece of gum she'd been chewing dropped onto her teeth. It was clear to see from the way her eyes ricocheted between Jake's and the phone that she was formulating a plan, so when she attempted to execute it and run away, she was too slow for him. He grabbed her arm with the right amount of resistance and pulled her back, fighting against her.

'Louise, don't do anything stupid.' She tried to shove him off, but his grip was too strong. 'Where is he? Where's Danny?'

Louise remained silent. She was stronger than he anticipated. She grabbed his arm and dug her inch-long acrylic nails deep into his skin, but Jake ignored the sharp, focused pain that began to swell around his forearm. There was menace in her face, a blazing fire hiding behind the eyes waiting to break free. Jake needed to put it out before it had the chance.

'Where is he?'

'Fuck you.' She spat in his face. The phlegm landed in his eyes and disorientated him. He wiped away the spittle with his free hand and fought every urge in his body to flip her to the ground and restrain her – with a little more force than was acceptable.

'I don't appreciate that,' he said, trying to keep a cool head. 'It'll be easier for everyone involved if you tell me where he is. There's no way out of this. For either of you. Nowhere left to run.'

Louise's expression remained placid.

'Don't make me ask again. Have you let him escape? Are you the decoy so he can run and hide?' As he said it, Louise's face changed. Only the smallest of movements, minute, almost imperceptible, but Jake was sure he'd seen it. A flicker of the eyebrow that confirmed an earlier suspicion.

'No,' he continued, 'of course you aren't. He doesn't even know you're gone, does he? You've just left him.' Jake looked down at the bags in front of him and grabbed one. 'And you've taken the money too. His hard-earned money. But you couldn't have done this without him knowing, could you? You had to wait until he was out of sight and unaware before you took it, didn't you? So where is he, Louise?'

As Jake finished talking, Bridger arrived, out of breath and flustered. Behind him was a plainclothes officer wearing a similar vest to them, similarly out of breath.

'She's taken the money,' Jake said to Bridger.

'Where is he?'

'Alone. He doesn't know it's gone missing. But I've got an idea where he might be. Wait here,' he said to Bridger.

As Jake shoved Louise into his colleague's hand, Bridger pulled him back.

'I'm coming with you.'

'You sure?'

'I can't let something happen to you on your first day. And I certainly can't let you take all the credit.'

With a nod, the two of them set off, leaving Louise in their colleague's custody. Feeling confident and comfortable in Bridger's presence, Jake started back the way he'd come. He'd seen a men's bathroom by the seating area. And there were only a couple of places Danny Cipriano could have disappeared to.

As they rounded the corner, they slowed to a walk and entered the seating area. There, standing in front of the door to the men's bathroom was Danny Cipriano. He was smaller than Jake remembered, and for a moment, Jake just stood there, watching him. How he surveyed the room, his head moving gradually from left to right like a lighthouse. How he wrapped his body tightly with his arms as if he was cold. How he tapped his feet on the floor, waiting for someone. How he looked lost, almost frightened, like a child searching for a missing parent in the supermarket.

And then their eyes locked on one another. It was only a short moment, but it was enough to transport Jake back to Guildford High Street a few hours ago, where everything had seemed to stand still then – time, movement, his breathing, his reactions.

It was funny how cyclical it all was.

Before Jake could do anything, Danny Cipriano bolted.

CHAPTER 62

DANNY CIPRIANO

Jake was first to move. He followed Danny through a new set of corridors, barging past holidaymakers and weaving his way in and out of bulging suitcases sprawled across the floor. Danny was a few years older than Jake but more physically able. His muscles appeared tauter, stronger, and his legs were thicker, more powerful. It didn't take long for him to start pulling away and stretching the gap between them.

As they tore through clusters of people, Danny grabbed one of the passengers and pushed them to the ground. Forced to dodge the unsuspecting man, Jake hopped over him and stumbled as he landed awkwardly on the balls of his feet. His momentum carried him forward and he collapsed to the floor, barrel rolling. Landing on his shoulder, Jake clambered to his feet and continued the pursuit.

All thought of Bridger – who was close behind him – left his mind. One goal, one objective, one chance to make it happen. He chased Danny down another corridor and, as he came to the end, saw him climbing a flight of steps.

'Danny!' Jake called. 'Stop where you are!'

Danny ignored him.

The chase continued to the top deck. Jake breached into natural light, the harsh and abrupt adjustment blinding him momentarily, the heat immediately clinging to his throat. The top deck was covered in wooden panels that stretched the length of the boat. Sun loungers, parasols and suitcases lay against the side of the boat, with some of the passengers already roasting their pale skin as they were eager to get their holiday started as soon as possible. To Jake's left was a swimming pool with two slides at either end. Children were playing in it, using their underwear as swimming costumes. Ahead of him, Danny charged into an elderly couple, knocking the wife to the floor and the husband into the swimming pool.

Jake tore through the crowd once again, screaming, 'Police! Get out of the way!'

Bystanders panicked and dived to the side, affording Jake a clear path through. At the end of the swimming pool Danny made a sudden right turn and climbed another flight of stairs. He was on the outer top deck, and as Jake ascended the final step, Danny came to a stop. He'd reached a dead end.

There was a group of people clustered around one another. At the sight of them both, the group huddled closer in an attempt to protect themselves.

'Danny!' Jake shouted, almost bent double to catch his breath. 'It's over.'

The moment he'd said it, Bridger appeared, just as out of breath, just as fatigued.

Ahead of them Danny lunged at the group of people and grabbed the nearest one. A young woman – mid-twenties, Jake assumed. Fair-haired, with a ponytail. Wearing denim shorts and a Harry Potter T-shirt, looking as though she was indubitably excited about her forthcoming holiday.

She screamed as Danny's hands clasped around her neck. Her arms flailed at his face, but it was no use; he tightened his grip and began to suffocate her in a military position that looked like it had been passed down from father to son.

'Let her go, Danny,' Jake yelled, raising his arms in the air in surrender.

The young woman's screams faded and the air around them switched off, silent. Jake breathed heavily. Beside him, the family whimpered, still huddling together, still protecting each other.

As Jake composed himself, he gradually became aware that the boat was moving. Swaying from side to side. Forward and back. The wave of nausea and vertigo rolling over him until his head swam. 'Danny,' he said, blinking the dizziness away. 'Let her go.'

Danny said nothing.

'She hasn't done anything wrong, Danny,' Jake said. 'She's played no part in any of this.'

He remained silent.

'It's over. You got what you wanted. Now let her go.'

Danny tightened his grip on the girl's throat and pointed at him with the other. 'How do you know what I want?'

Jake considered a moment before responding, otherwise he ran the risk of playing his cards too early.

'Candice is dead, Danny. The device detonated. It killed her. That was what you wanted, wasn't it?'

Danny's hand flinched towards his right pocket, feeling for

something, as if searching for a lost memory. 'That bitch deserved to die! She deserved everything she got!' Balls of phlegm expelled from his mouth and landed on the wooden deck and the neck of his shirt.

Jake took a step closer, keeping his hands raised, ignoring Bridger behind him. It was just him and Danny now. Jake and the leader of The Crimsons. History repeating itself.

'You know, I spoke with Freddy earlier—'

'What?'

'Have you forgotten him already?'

Danny shook his head frantically. 'No. No, no, no. What were *you* doing talking to Freddy?'

'I was doing my job. I was hoping he'd be able to tell me where you guys were heading.'

'That stupid fucking prick,' Danny whispered. 'She couldn't even get that right.'

Jake's eyebrow rose. 'What are you talking about, Dan?'

'That bitch, Candice. She told *you* to speak with him, didn't she? Didn't you think that was a bit odd, a bit out of the blue? Jesus Christ.' Danny shook his head again. 'She thought *you* were someone else. And I can't believe she fell for it. I can't believe she actually thought you were going to be able to get him out of prison and get him on the boat. She was even dumber than I thought.'

Jake paused, his mind racing. It would take him a moment to process what Danny had told him, but that was time he didn't have. He needed to put an end to this now.

Clearing his mind of thought, Jake continued. 'Freddy misses you. Apparently, you've never been in touch. He was like a father to you guys, and you couldn't just forget about him like that, could you? After everything he'd done for the three of you.'

Jake paused, gauging Danny's expression; the man's eyes closed briefly, and he avoided Jake's gaze. Jake wasn't sure of it, but he was nearly certain he'd seen Danny's grip loosen on the woman's throat.

He continued. 'Do you know what else he told me? He said you were different. All of you. This whole operation. It was unlike anything you'd ever done. He said there was something else going on. A driving force telling you to do it like this. Forcing you into it. "He's behaving differently. This isn't the Danny I know" – that's what he said to me…' Jake curled his fingers in quotation marks. Every now and then a white lie could be used for good. 'And do you know what? I think he was right. You *were* forced into doing something you didn't want to do, and then you panicked. You were led to believe that causing as much death and destruction was the way forward, that it was the way to cement yourself in the history books. And do you know who'll get the credit for it? Louise. Not you—'

At the mention of Louise's name, Danny's face morphed into a scowl. He pointed at Jake again. As he did so, his sleeve pulled back and revealed a series of cuts and burn marks on his forearm and the back of his hand. Jake marked each piece of evidence of the abuse. 'It's OK, mate. She's gone. She's not going to hurt you anymore. You won't ever have to see her again.'

'Where is she?' Danny asked, his voice hoarse and weak. It sounded as though he had a catch in it, as though there were floods of tears hiding behind a dam, waiting for a crack to form.

'She's been arrested, Dan. She's with my colleagues now.'

'I want to see her.'

'No.'

Danny repositioned the girl closer against his body.

'I want to see her!'

'OK, OK,' Jake said, lifting his hands higher in the air. 'I can arrange that. I can arrange something. Don't worry. I'll let you see her. But only if you let the girl go. Let her get back to her family… and then we can discuss.'

'What about Luke? Micky?'

This was the part Jake was dreading the most. He didn't know how volatile Danny's response would be. *Only one way to find out. Time to play your hand, Jake.*

'Micky's fine, Dan. He's with us. He's safe.' Jake hesitated, feeling a lump grow in his own throat.

'And Luke? Please. Luke. Please tell me Luke is OK.' Danny took a step backward. Jake matched the step, maintaining the distance between them.

Then Jake fell silent, pursed his lips and shook his head slowly. 'I'm sorry, Dan. They died together. The device killed Candice. And… Luke was shot by armed officers. He tried to protect her.'

Danny choked as he absorbed what Jake had told him. Then he moaned, his voice filled with pain and hurt and raw emotion. Jake felt an odd sense of sympathy towards the older brother encompass him, despite everything the man had done.

'No,' Danny babbled, his mouth filling with saliva. He sniffed hard, fighting to keep the tears at bay. 'No… No. No, it can't— I don't believe— You're lying!' Danny spat as he enunciated the words.

'I wish I was,' Jake replied, reaching for his pocket slowly. 'But I'm not. I really wish I was.'

'How do I know I can believe you?'

'Because you can.'

'Prove it to me!'

'Are you sure?'

'I said prove it! Prove it to me now!'

Jake's hand lowered into his pocket and grabbed his phone.

'What are you doing?' Danny shouted as Jake began to remove the device.

'Just doing as you asked,' Jake replied. He loaded the graphic photo he'd taken of Luke and Candice's mangled remains and waved the phone in the air. 'This is your proof, Danny.'

'Give it to me,' Danny called out.

Reluctantly, Jake prepared himself to launch the phone across the deck. He swung his arm and released, the device soaring through the air. Danny tried to catch it with his free hand, but it bounced off it and fell to the floor.

Danny bent down to pick it up, pulling the girl down with him. As he stared into the image, his eyes widened, his grip loosened on the girl and his hand moved to his mouth; the young woman wasted no time in executing her escape, and rushed towards her family. Once she was with them, the group sprinted away from the deck to safety, where they were greeted by a group of plainclothes officers.

'Luke…' Danny trailed off.

'Danny, listen to me,' Jake began, taking another step forward.

But it was too late. Danny had already made his decision: he dropped the phone, letting it smash on the deck, and then sprinted to the side of the boat, where he climbed over the edge of the barrier and vaulted two hundred feet into the English Channel.

Bridger's heart pounded against his chest, willing itself to break through as he sprinted to the side of the deck. Danny Cipriano had just jumped, and his last chance at salvaging the operation had gone with it. The man would almost certainly die on impact: the fall too great, the water acting like a brick wall as soon his head or neck collided with the surface. Nothing to be done. Two brothers dead, one inside a custody cell.

Today had been a fuck-up from start to finish.

And it was all thanks to one person.

The man standing beside him. The man who, only hours ago, had been shy, timid, reserved, unable to voice his own concerns and convictions but was now the shining light of the investigation capable of handing out orders to senior officers. Jake Tanner had become the true puppetmaster of the operation, and not in the right way.

The job was supposed to be easy. Stall, stall, stall. Allow The Crimsons time to escape and wait for the proverbial dust to settle. But nothing about it had been straightforward. The murder, the abduction, the collar – all just a long list of shitty breadcrumbs he was supposed to follow and cover up, blind. How could he be expected to do a complete job if he only knew half the information?

He couldn't wait for the absolute hiding he was going to receive later on.

Shit. Show.

But there was one saving grace, one opportunity at redemption.

In the two seconds that had passed without his realising, Jake had climbed over the ledge and was positioned precariously on the top, wavering for balance and support. Whether Jake was going to jump, he didn't know. But a little help in the decision-making wouldn't hurt.

Just a nudge. That was all. A little nudge. Not too obvious, but not too weak. Finely balanced. *Nothing your overactive imagination can't lie about.*

The sound of Danny's body hitting the water finally made its way up to them. It was a long, long, long way down.

Bridger raised his head, stepped to the side behind Jake and placed his hands around Jake's waist. He opened his mouth to tell him to be careful but decided against it. Hands clutching the folds of Jake's love handles, he pushed, and suddenly his hands were supporting nothing but air as Jake plummeted into the water.

CHAPTER 63

OVERBOARD

Jake's eyes ripped open as the rush of water assaulted his face. The force of the dive had sent him deep into the cold abyss of the Channel, surrounded by a wall of black, the pressure squashing down on his head.

He searched the murky water for Danny, fearing the worst: that the man had been swept underneath the boat. That he had been knocked unconscious upon impact. That he had vanished completely.

Jake allowed the current to carry him, hoping that it would somehow lead him to Danny. As his natural buoyancy lifted him towards the surface, he flailed his arms and legs about, trying to remain submerged. The body vest and clothes on his back weighed him down but not enough.

And then it struck him. Another one. Worse than before. At first it was the intense claustrophobia. Then the fear of imminent death, followed by the crushing pain in his chest. Jake thrashed his arms violently, kicking out, now clawing for the surface, then opened his mouth in an attempt to scream for help. Water flooded in and he swallowed, coughed, ingesting more salty water. He gasped for breath, choking, gagging, running out of oxygen. But there was none. There was only water, surrounding him from every angle.

Yet the surface was still so far away, just out of reach.

Jake stared vacantly at the sunlight burning through the Channel, as the tide overhead rippled and distorted the light into a dozen different rays. Jake lowered his arms to his side, ready to let the water take him wherever it needed to.

And then he felt something behind him. At first he thought it was the boat running him over, trampling him, crushing him. But then he felt a pair of hands wrap around his chest. The hands removed the Velcro from the body vest, threw it off him and then heaved him upward. The pressure in his head released and a barrage of bubbles distorted his vision.

A few seconds later, he breached into the open, gasping for air and spluttering and coughing water out of his lungs and mouth. Then he scrambled his legs and arms to keep himself afloat. Breathing rapidly, he turned to face his rescuer.

There, wearing a wig of seaweed across his head and brow, was Danny. The man's head bobbled just above the surface and dipped below every now and then as the current pulled him this way and that. How long had he been under there? It had only been a few seconds, but it had felt like minutes, hours. Everything had come at him fast. He didn't know how it had happened – the last thing he remembered was a slip of the foot and Bridger holding on to him. But right now he was grateful he was alive.

'Th-Th-Thank y-you,' Jake said, his body going into shock. He began to shiver as the freezing temperatures of the Channel numbed his skin. His teeth clattered. 'Wh-Why did you s-s-save me? Why didn't y-you let me d-d-drown?'

It was then Jake realised how close he'd come to dying, and how he'd betrayed his promise to Elizabeth that he would stay safe and out of harm's way. If it weren't for Danny, he would have left his daughter in the same position he had been in when he was younger: fatherless. And for that he would be grateful to Danny. Forever.

'Too many people have died today. I'm not adding another to the list,' Danny replied, spitting goblets of water back into the sea.

Jake thanked his saviour again and together they waited, both struggling to stay afloat, until less than a minute later a RIB made its way towards them, bounding over the waves. Their rescuers – consisting of the firearms unit that Grahams had deployed earlier – launched life rings into the water as they approached. Jake was first to be saved. One of the armed officers threw his weapon over his back, leant over the side of the RIB and hefted Jake onto the solid flooring of the boat. For a moment, he just lay on his back, catching his breath, allowing the dark and depressing thoughts of suffocating under mountains of snow to pass from his mind.

He opened his eyes. Light flooded into them and he stared into the sky. In the top-right corner of his vision was a small cloud, thin, delicate, floating through the air, carrying with it the hope of a better day.

The man who'd lifted him to safety suddenly came into view, a wide grin on his face.

'You took your time,' Jake said as the officer helped him to a seating position on the side of the boat. The officer placed a space blanket over Jake's body and handed him a bottle of water.

'We can drop you back in if you're going to be ungrateful about it.'

'You couldn't pay me enough to get back in there.'

'There's a price for everything, lad.'

The remaining officers loaded Danny Cipriano onto the boat and wrapped him in a space blanket of his own. The sun reflected off the aluminium sheet and dozens of shards of foiling danced in Jake's eyes as he stared at Danny while he was arrested and read his rights. The fight in the man's eyes had gone.

He had lost, admitted defeat.

It was over.

And Jake had won.

CHAPTER 64

CONFIRMED SUSPICIONS

A few hours later, after he'd completed the post-incident procedures following the police shooting – which consisted of several tedious and mind-numbing reports, and several rounds of questioning and fact-finding interviews – Jake returned to the office. He'd been given the once-over by paramedics, fed some strawberry and banana glucose in plastic sachets for energy, warmed with a change of clothes and then sent on his way.

For most of the hour-long journey back to Guildford, he, Bridger and Pemberton travelled in silence, the morbidity of the past few hours hanging over them like a heavy cloud. Jake's mind was blank, bereft of any thought while he attempted to process the day's events – the spiked collar, the keys, the bent cop, the gunshot, the death, his near-death experience. It was a lot for his mind to go through, but as he sat there watching the green hills and trees roll past the window, he felt oddly serene, at peace.

At 7:15 p.m., Bridger pulled into Mount Browne and killed the engine. The three of them exited the vehicle and entered the building, signing in their attendance at the reception desk. Jake avoided the receptionist's scowl as he wandered past. It was the same man from that morning, and judging by the disparaging look he shot Jake, he wanted to reprimand him for leaving the polystyrene cup on the table at the beginning of the day.

As soon as the Major Crime Team noticed their presence in the Incident Room, they stopped what they were doing and rose to their feet, clapping. Someone in the background whistled. Jake slowed as Bridger and Pemberton entered, separating himself from them. Despite everything he'd done, how he'd almost single-handedly solved the investigation, it wasn't his place to accept the praise, even if it was bittersweet. He was just training to become a detective. The DCI and DS were the senior rank – they were the ones responsible for the success of the operation, they were the figureheads, they were the ones who should take the credit. Instead he was just going to act as the embodiment of being humble in victory.

As Pemberton and Bridger moved deeper into the room, members of the team rose out of their seats and continued to congratulate them, patting them on the back and shaking their hands. Keeping his head low, Jake stepped to the side and searched for Danika. His friend. His colleague. His closest ally.

He found her at the back of the room where he'd left her. She was on her feet, applauding.

'You all right?' he asked, wandering up to her.

Danika looked like a weakened person, as though the day's events had completely taken their toll on her. A stiff drink was beckoning her, and as she recognised his voice, her eyes widened, and she threw her arms around him.

'You're alive!' she screamed in his ear, drowned out by the cheers of support around the office. 'I heard about what happened to you. I was worried.'

Jake pulled away from her, smiling. 'I won't tell Elizabeth. She thinks you've got the hots for me already.'

Danika rolled her eyes and slapped him on the arm playfully. 'Don't get too cocky, mate. Just because you stopped the bad guys doesn't mean you get the girl as well.'

'Mine's already waiting for me when I get home.' Jake scratched the back of his head and sat on the edge of Danika's desk, folding his arms. 'I'll be honest though, mate. I couldn't have done it without you. You really helped me out there. For a while it felt like I couldn't trust anyone, but you really pulled through and proved yourself.'

Danika brushed a strand of hair behind her ear and joined him on the edge of the desk. She leant closer, touching his shoulder and kept her voice low. 'Have you… have you worked out who *it* is yet?'

'Still working on it.'

Sort of. For most of the journey back to Mount Browne, he'd been processing everything, but on the way back to shore from the cruise liner, he'd dedicated some serious thought as to who the bent cop could be. And he'd come up with a name.

Danika licked her lips and rolled her wedding ring around her finger nervously. 'Was there ever a point where you thought it was me?'

Jake didn't want to lie to her – *couldn't* lie to her.

'There was a moment, yes. Someone suggested it, opened my eyes to the possibility.'

'What? How?'

Jake dropped his head, avoiding her gaze. 'Why didn't you tell me, Dan?'

'Tell you what?'

Jake met her eyes. 'About how bad things are at home with you and Tony? I had no idea...'

Danika's brow tightened. 'What's that got to do with me being a bent cop?'

'Because of Roger Heathcote, the family lawyer. With everything you've got going on, I thought you might have been roped into it somehow. Maybe you were going to take home a large cut of the profits for your help.'

A small grin flashed on her face. 'Dammit. Maybe I should have done. Could have potentially saved me a lot of money in legal fees.' Danika chuckled. 'And I would have got away with it, if it hadn't been for you meddling kids!'

Jake felt a laugh escape his lips, the first in what felt like a long time. It was a strange sensation, one that felt almost alien to him, yet he was grateful he was able to share it with Danika, whom he realised now he should never have doubted.

'I do think it's weird though,' Danika began, 'that an image of his letterhead was on the first set of instructions. Seems like a really strange coincidence.'

Jake tilted his head, as if to drain imaginary water from his ears and check the efficacy of his hearing. 'What letterhead?'

'Heathcote and Sons. The one you photographed and sent in for graphology… Remember, I said on the phone – the impression of the letterhead on the instructions.'

Jake bit his tongue and pulled out his phone from his pocket. He'd forgotten that part of their conversation given everything that had happened. He unlocked the device – which Bridger had retrieved from the deck for him – and scrolled to his camera roll. There, he found the photo of the instructions Candice Strachan had given to him. Pinching the screen, he zoomed in on the image and held it in front of Danika's face.

'Where's the logo gone?' she asked, as if that was the correct question to be asking.

'It was never there.'

'You mean someone added it?'

That was better.

'Who told you the logo existed?' Jake asked.

Danika's response came after a few moments of hesitation, almost as if she were afraid to tell him the answer. Her head slowly turned towards the office, eventually settling on one person, an imaginary finger pointing at the suspect in a line-up.

DI Mark Murphy was standing in the corner of the room, speaking into the handset pressed against his ear.

'You… you don't think that means it was him, do you?' This

time the essence of fear was apparent in Danika's voice.

She knew the answer. And so did Jake.

Before Jake was able to respond, the doors to the Incident Room opened and a man Jake vaguely recognised entered. His head was long and narrow, as if someone had pinched the sides of it and let the excess skin and bone and brain matter stretch. The officer spoke with Pemberton and, after they'd finished, her eyes searched the room until they fell on Jake.

'Tanner,' she called. 'With Bridger. Danny Cipriano's just arrived in the custody suite at Guildford Police Station.'

'You want me to come?'

She nodded from across the room.

Jake hesitated a moment and stared into Pemberton's eyes for longer than necessary, contemplating, deep in reflective thought. His gaze moved towards Danika to his left; they glanced at one another quickly.

'If it's all the same to you, guv, I'd like to sit this one out,' he said. 'The guy just saved my life – I'm not sure how I feel about interrogating him right now.'

'You sure?'

Jake nodded, angled his body towards Danika. 'Would DC Oblak be able to take my place instead?'

'I don't see a problem with that,' Bridger said, appearing from nowhere with two cups of coffee in his hands. He passed one to Danika. 'Come on then. Seems like you're with me.'

Before heading off to the interview, Danika had left Jake with a lump in his throat that immediately made him discount everything he thought he knew. The name of the corrupt officer he'd had in mind had been wrong. DI Mark Murphy was the one who'd been working against him, manipulating everything from behind the scenes – and behind the desk. Not only had he tried to lead the team down the wrong path with the addition of Roger Heathcote's logo to the instructions, he'd also used up valuable time and resources.

Murphy stood for everything Jake hated in the police force. It was the ultimate betrayal of trust. But there was still an issue, something niggling at the back of his mind that caused the knot in his stomach to return.

A word. A phrase. A sentence. Something someone had said to him that made him think it wasn't possible for Murphy to be the bent copper – or to be the *only* bent copper.

Someone else was involved, a tag team, a duo of corrupt officers working together to help The Crimsons flee the country. One on the ground, one in the office.

Jake recalled what Danny had said to him – about Candice

mistaking him for someone else. His conversation with her had struck him as odd as soon as she'd started talking about his watch and how he wore it on the same wrist as one of her sons. In the moment he'd thought nothing of it. Until…

The watch.

The G-Shock.

The sheer unlikeliness of them both wearing the same piece on their wrist.

Bridger.

Then he sat and considered it further. The smell of bleach inside Bridger's car and the obvious attempts to clean Candice's bathroom before anyone entered. The amount of time he'd tried to delay and stall the investigation – with the bomb squad and forensics. The numerous phone calls. Trying to pass the blame onto Danika. The interview with Michael that, it later transpired, hadn't been cleared with Pemberton and was subsequently ruled unlawful.

It all made sense now, but there was just one final piece of evidence he needed in order to confirm his suspicion.

Without realising it, an hour of sitting and contemplating had passed, and Danika returned looking happy with herself – the happiest he'd seen her in a while. It was what she needed right now – a welcome distraction, something to take her mind off everything that was going on in her personal life.

'How was it?' he asked, swinging round to face her.

'Insightful,' Danika replied as she pulled her chair out from beneath her desk. 'Really insightful. He's confessed to everything. All of the previous heists, shooting the employee, shooting the police officer. He even said that, no matter what we'd tried to do, that device was going to kill Candice regardless. There was no way out for her, and the fact she put the fourth key in on her own just sped things up.'

It was hardly a consolation, but that was the least of Jake's worries right now.

'Nice one. Well done,' he said, trying to hide the anguish in his voice. 'Dan… can I ask you something?'

'Yeah, sure.'

'Did you… did you ever hear anything about the traffic accident on the M25 earlier? Was anyone hurt?'

'What traffic accident?'

'Involving a lorry and a busload of kids?'

Danika shook her head. 'Nope. There've been no reports of that. Why?'

Jake dropped his head and looked at the floor. 'No reason. Nothing to worry about. I just wanted to make sure everyone involved was OK.'

It was nearly midnight by the time Jake finally plucked up the courage to knock on Pemberton's door. The majority of the office had gone home for the evening, including Danika and Bridger, and the last few who remained were from the HOLMES team, busy entering the backlog of witness statements and information into the system. It was a tedious job, one Jake was grateful he didn't have to do.

In the four hours since Jake had returned to Mount Browne, Danny Cipriano's full confession had gone on record, the brothers' names had been plastered all over the media, earning them international notoriety, and the team had even had a visit from the Chief Constable, who'd acknowledged and congratulated Jake first-hand.

'Just another day in the office,' Jake had joked to him.

His heart was still beating fast even now, as though he'd just seen a celebrity across the street and spent the rest of the day posting about it on social media and bragging to friends.

Except, now, there was nothing to brag about. His next words had the potential to collapse a career – two, in fact.

He knocked on Pemberton's door and waited. A moment later, she gave him the call to enter.

'Ah, Jake!' she said, waving him in. 'Star of the show. Hope you've not got any more bright ideas for me – I don't think I could handle any more.'

Be careful what you wish for, he thought.

Pemberton put her computer to sleep as Jake sat opposite, giving him her undivided attention.

'I just wanted to say you've done a really good job today,' she began. 'Praise doesn't get thrown around here that much, so you should be proud of yourself. Without your help, I dread to think where we might have ended up. I've been really impressed, and if you keep that up, then we might just—'

'Guv,' Jake interrupted. He kept his head down; he couldn't bear to look at her right now. Not yet.

'Yes, Jake? Is something the matter?'

Jake closed his eyes briefly, inhaled, held it, exhaled. As he opened his mouth to speak, he realised the knot in his stomach was gone. Strangely, it gave him the confidence to look her in the eye.

'I have a few concerns,' he said.

'Oh?'

'While I was in Winchester with Bridger, Freddy told me that, in all of their previous heists, they'd had inside help from a corrupt officer, working to get them out of tricky situations. He said that this heist would be no different, and that someone within the team was working against us.'

Pemberton's face was expressionless, offering no hint of a reaction. He didn't know whether he'd plucked at a nerve, or whether he was confirming her own beliefs.

'I have reason to believe that Freddy was telling the truth.'

'You're suggesting one of my officers is corrupt?' Her voice remained as placid as her face.

'Not one, guv. Two. Two officers.'

'You do realise this is a very serious allegation, Jake,' she said, more as a statement than any sort of question.

Jake nodded. 'I fully understand the ramifications of what I'm saying. But I have proof, guv.'

Pemberton let out a long sigh, like she was getting rid of all the day's stress in one overdue breath.

'Give me their names,' she said abruptly.

'Don't you want to hear the evidence first?'

'No. Names. Tell me their names.'

This was it. No going back now. His reputation and potential friendship with both of them would be permanently tarnished, ruined. And there was certainly one that Jake would miss more than the other.

'Jake?' Pemberton insisted.

'Sorry, guv.' He licked his lips, swallowed, his throat coarse and dry. 'I wish I wasn't doing this, but I have reason to believe that the corrupt officers working with The Crimsons are DS Elliot Bridger and DI Mark Murphy.'

CHAPTER 65

SAMMY

Three days had passed since the robbery, and it had been non-stop, conducting reports, interviews, processing information, submitting it, reviewing it, submitting it again. It had been relentless. But in that time Jake had heard nothing about the small investigation that was being led into Murphy's and Bridger's conduct. After raising his concerns with Pemberton, she had shot him down, denied the allegations on behalf of the accused and called him ridiculous for suggesting such a thing. She was, for some reason, either covering for them or, more likely Jake thought, under their control somehow. That wasn't an environment he wanted to be in, and so he'd started ostracising himself from the rest of the team, distancing himself from the man he'd considered a potential father figure and even separated himself from Danika, who seemed to be growing closer and closer to Murphy, despite Jake's protestations. It was a mess. So when the opportunity for a day off arose, Jake jumped at the chance and decided to use it to clear his head by travelling north to Newcastle and fulfilling a promise.

He pulled up to a desolate car park on the outskirts of Elena Miller's estate, a few miles north of the city centre. Freddy's old partner lived in block ten, floor five, flat twenty-two. Jake removed his warrant card from his glove compartment, exited the car and wandered to the building. On the other side of the car park, a group of kids played on their bikes, swerving around the broken bottles strewn across the concrete. One of them carried a basketball in his hand, and the sound of the ball bouncing up and down sporadically on the ground echoed around the grey concrete walls of the estate.

Jake stopped at a flight of steps, checked the small panel on the side of the wall that told him where each flat was, made sure he was in the right place and started up. The stairs stank of alcohol and sweat and decaying cigarettes. Puddles of liquid drenched the steps, and Jake struggled to avoid them.

His legs began to ache as he climbed to the fifth floor. He made a left turn and walked along the outside of the building, keeping tabs on the children playing and, more importantly, his car. He came to a stop outside number twenty-two. He could hear the sound of a television playing in the background. Jake lifted his hand and rapped his knuckles against the wooden door.

A few seconds later, it opened, and before him was a skinny, almost malnourished-looking brunette with thick black bags under her eyes. She wore a thin grey hoodie with disproportionate drawstrings dangling by her collarbones, and a pair of jeans ripped at the knee. In her hand she held a light blue plate carrying a sandwich. Her expression was blank, clearly unimpressed to see the stranger. Jake tried not to take it personally; he suspected she would have been unimpressed to see anyone.

'Can I help you?'

Jake kept his ID in his pocket. 'Elena?'

'Why?'

'It's about Freddy.'

'Don't want to hear it.' She threw the door shut, but Jake caught it with his fingers before it closed completely, then pushed with all his might, forcing it open a little. He planted his foot between the door and the door frame for extra support.

'Please. I'm a friend of his.' The words felt strange to say.

'The last thing that man has is friends. Who are you?' She hid behind the small sliver in the door.

'My name's Jake Tanner. Would I be able to come in please?'

'No,' she said, scowling at him.

Behind her, from within the house, a call came. 'Who is it, Mummy?'

'Oh, it's – it's no one, Sammy. Just a man who wants to have a chat about adult stuff. Go back to the television.' Elena remained still. She continued to glare through the gap, and he could feel her eyes assessing him, judging him. Eventually, she sighed, stepped aside and allowed him to enter. 'You've got five minutes.'

Jake crossed the threshold and waited in the hallway. Elena closed the front door behind him and pointed to the kitchen.

'In here. I don't want you near my son.'

Jake held his hands in the air. 'It's your house.'

The kitchen was cramped. There was a small table laden with notebooks and textbooks in the far right, barely large enough for two people. Beside it, a fridge that came to the same height as the table. Next to that, an oven, washing machine and a sink. Elena stopped by an overhead cupboard and pulled out a glass.

'What do you do?' Jake asked, leafing through another textbook that was on the surface beside him.

Switching the kettle on, she said, 'I'm studying to be a nurse.'

'That's wonderful,' Jake said.

'But it's a bit difficult with him lying around the house.' Elena nodded towards her son in the other room.

'I commend you for it. I have a lot of respect for people in that role…'

'You have kids?' Elena asked, leaning against the kitchen countertop with her arms folded. He sensed she was beginning to warm to him, becoming less hostile to his presence.

'Just the one for now, though I think we might try for another soon. Let's say I won't be disappointed if we get pregnant again. We were told we couldn't have one in the first place.'

'There's a reason they call it the miracle of birth.'

Jake looked to the ground, bit his lip and decided to move the conversation along. He was conscious of the time. 'He wants to see you… and his son, Elena.'

'You can call me Ellie.'

'Right,' Jake said.

'What do you mean, he wants to see us?' she asked, shifting her weight onto the other foot.

'Freddy. He wants to see you. He wants to see his son.'

'Is that what this is about? He sent one of his mates to come and do his dirty work for him? I've been receiving his letters, and they've been going straight in the bin. That man stopped being a father to Sammy the day I found out what he was.' Elena stepped away from Jake, ignoring the kettle that had just finished its boil.

'It's not like that,' Jake said, trying to ease the tension between them. 'It's not like that at all. I promised him I would come here. I also promised him that you would bring Sammy to see him.'

'Who are you?' she asked.

Jake slowly reached into his front pocket and removed his ID.

'Why's he getting a copper to do his grovelling for him? He paying you? You bent? Wouldn't be the first time I've seen one of them round here.'

Jake pocketed the ID and held his hands back in the air so Elena could see them. 'It's not like that. At all. It's a long story, but—'

'You've got a few minutes left to explain yourself.'

Jake swallowed before telling her everything. He was honest with her. Explained that Freddy had helped him solve the case. That Freddy had proven to Jake he was sorry and was beginning to change – that he was capable of it. That Freddy had lost all of his 'sons'.

'He was like a father to them. They never had their father growing up, so he stepped into the role.'

'And look how they turned out,' she snapped.

'My dad died when I was fifteen, which was worse because we

256

knew him and then he was taken from us. I was the middle child, but I was forced into adopting that role. I looked after my younger brother and I cared for my older sister, who didn't even need me there. But I was, because I loved them. I'm telling you, I didn't know what I was doing. I made mistakes. We all did. I still do. And I can tell you now, we would have been much better off if we'd had our dad in our lives. He would have kept us on the right path, told us when to turn left and to turn right. Not that my mum didn't do a great job – she did.' Jake paused to gauge Elena's reaction; she was attentive, her eyes focused. 'Freddy's not asking for much. He just wants to see him. Maybe even speak with him for a bit. You don't have to tell Sammy that Freddy's his father. Freddy doesn't mind that – he realises he gave up that privilege a long time ago, like you said. Just so long as he's in his life, so long as Sammy knows Freddy exists. I mean, have you prepared for when Sammy begins to get curious? When he wants to find out who his dad is?'

Elena remained silent.

Jake continued without giving her time to answer or think. 'Wouldn't you want to know? I mean, if I could do anything to get my dad back, I would. One hundred per cent.' Jake reached for his wallet, removed a business card that had his work mobile and email address on it, and placed it on the surface. He grabbed a pen from the spine of the textbook beside him and, on the reverse of the card, wrote down the visiting days and hours at HMP Winchester.

'I know it's a long way,' Jake said, 'but if you need me to, I'll be happy to front some of the expense. I can't force you to go, but I hope you'll do what's right for Sammy, because, after all, he's the one that matters in all of this. I'll show myself out. Thank you for your time.'

Jake slid the card closer to Elena, adjusted his wallet in his jeans, then wandered out of the kitchen and out of the flat, closing the door behind him.

CHAPTER 66

BEAUTIFUL BASTARD

The buzzer sounded overhead, and the door clicked open. The prison officer beside Freddy escorted him through the frame and onto his seat. He hadn't been expecting visitors. In fact, he hadn't even known about the visitor – whoever it was – until ten minutes ago. It was out of usual visiting hours but the prison staff had made an exception for him. His assumption was that it would be Jake again, coming back to get help with something.

In the years that he'd been locked inside he had only ever seen a handful of visitors. Mostly solicitors coming to bring him bad news, or the sporadic visit from a deranged member of the family who'd found out he was incarcerated and wanted to put it on their blog or social-media channels. Every time though, whether they were there to exploit him or depress him, he agreed to see them. Prison was a lonely place, and what sort of psychopath would he be to turn down external company?

The visiting room was empty, save for the guards standing to attention in the four corners. Freddy sat there, tapping his knee on the bottom of the table, drumming his fingers on the top. His gaze lumbered to the clock that hung on the wall to his right. It was nearly lunchtime, and he was beginning to get hungry.

A few minutes passed.

'Is this a joke or something?' Freddy asked, facing one of his favourite guards. 'Because I know how you like to think you're funny, Gabe. But—'

Freddy was interrupted by the door in front of him opening. Two people entered. At first he didn't recognise who they were. And then, as the light reflected off their faces, his heart stopped.

Elena and Sammy were right there, strolling towards him. Freddy's eyes were glued to his son. Sammy was growing up to be tall and strong. His hair was well kept, and he looked healthy. Elena had been doing a good job, as he'd known she would.

Freddy felt a sense of raw elation and euphoria crash over him. A lump swelled in his throat and his eyes began to water.

Jake, you beautiful bastard.

Elena and Sammy pulled the chairs from beneath the table and sat opposite them.

'You all right, Fred?'

CHAPTER 67

THE CABAL

Bridger slumped into the front seat of his car and slammed the door shut. He exhaled deeply and ran his hands over the steering wheel, bringing himself to make the call. It had been put off for too long now, and the longer he left it, the worse it was going to get.

The ringer sounded in his ear, sending bolts of panic through his brain and into the rest of his body with every tone. He clapped his knees together as he waited.

The call was answered but he was greeted by silence.

'Hello?' he said, licking his lips. 'It's me.'

There was a pause.

'You've got some explaining to do,' the voice on the other line said. Bridger didn't know his name. He'd never been given one. He didn't even know what he looked like. All he knew was that the nickname the man had given himself was The Cabal. And in the line of work that he was involved in, it seemed apt to Bridger.

'Do I still get my cut?' Bridger lowered himself in the leather seat.

'Depends whether you can convince me you've earned it.'

'Listen,' Bridger began, suppressing the fear in his voice. 'It's not my fault.'

'You were supposed to get them out of the country. That was your one job. They're either dead or in a cell. That's your problem. Your fault. Not mine. No one else's.'

'There were issues. Delays,' Bridger said. 'This new bloke. Tanner. He got in the way every time.'

'He a threat?'

'Nah.' Bridger shook his head and stared out of the window. He glanced up at the police station just as Jake and Danika exited the building, heading off home for the evening. They waved goodbye to one another and headed towards their respective cars. 'Trust me, he won't be an issue.'

'I'll still put him on my radar.'

'He's on mine too.' Bridger breathed in through his nose and out through his mouth. Slowly. Carefully. As if doing it drastically would piss off The Cabal somehow. 'So, do I get my cut?'

'You've still not convinced me.'

'What do you—' Bridger started, preparing himself to release a torrent of anger and frustration, but then thought better of it. This man was the source of most of his income – triple his basic salary from this one job alone – and he wasn't about to burn his bridges over it. If he played his cards right, there would be more.

'I tried to delay Pemberton for as long as I could, but Tanner was all over me,' Bridger continued. 'The keys. The golf course. He was even wearing the same fucking watch as me. Candice mistook him for me – she thought *he* was the one who was supposed to be getting them out. And he even had a little friend to help him as well. Danika. Danika Oblak. She was constantly feeding him information on the phone.'

'I've heard her name before. It's cropped up in a few human resources meetings.' There was a pause. 'What about Mark?'

'He tried to get her onside but couldn't get anywhere with it. He's invited her out for a drink to see if he can do it that way.'

'She on the turn?'

'Doubt it. Maybe. Have to see what sort of magic Mark can pull out of the bag.'

'And what about this other one? Tanner. Same story for him? Can he be swayed?'

Bridger hesitated before answering. In the distance, to his left, a green Austin Mini Cooper pulled out of its parking space, turned right, drove along the road, past Bridger, and headed towards the car park's exit. As the car passed, Bridger busied himself with something in the footwell.

'He's gone to Pemberton about us, Mark and I. Told her about the letterhead, the delays, the unlawful interview on Michael. He even told her about the poxy watch.'

'Is it a problem?' The Cabal asked.

'But the little shit still doesn't know anything about the little push I gave him.'

'Is it a problem?'

'No. Nothing to worry about. Mark's covered his tracks and so have I. Meanwhile Pemberton's backing us to the hilt. She dismissed it as soon as he said it. She's conducting a minor investigation, but it'll be over soon when they find nothing. It's nothing we can't handle ourselves.'

'Sounds like he's going to be a bigger problem than you

thought. You sure he can't be swayed?'

'Tanner's different,' Bridger said. 'He's too keen. Too eager to do his job. But he's a good detective. Thinks of things in different ways. And he's not afraid to voice them either. He'd make a very good asset, but you either want to cut him loose straight away or win him over. There's no middle ground.'

'I do like a work in progress.'

'That one will be one of the hardest grafts of your life.'

'Good. But don't think it's over for you. You're still not done.'

Bridger's brow furrowed and the muscles in his face tightened. 'What?'

'You're not finished. Not yet. The brothers are about to do time. A lot of it. It was your job to get them out of the country. You've made a mess of it. Now it's your job to get them out of jail.'

Bridger sighed. Now he was in The Cabal's debt, and that was the one place he didn't want to be. 'And then I'm done with this job?'

'And then you'll get your cut.'

'What about Mark? Do the same rules apply?'

'Leave Mark to me. There are things that he's probably not telling you. You need to keep an eye on who he's getting close with.'

'But I—'

'By the same token, I think it's in your best interests to find yourself some new talent within the team. You might need it because it's going to get dirty. Oh, and don't get caught. Someone a lot worse than Jake Tanner might make life a misery for you.'

EPILOGUE

Following their arrest, Michael and Danny Cipriano were charged with two counts of murder, aggravated assault, armed robbery, possession of a firearm and conspiracy to pervert the course of justice. They are currently being held in remand in HMP Belmarsh where they are awaiting trial. DS Bridger is in charge of the investigation.

Danika Oblak left her husband and two children and now lives in Guildford as a full-time member of Surrey Police. She's started drinking heavily.

DCI Nicki Pemberton was rewarded with a bravery award for her tactical and strategic decision-making during Operation Corkscrew as the investigation was designated. She continues to live with her husband and children in their home in Liphook.

DI Mark Murphy was lauded for his precise and accurate help throughout Operation Corkscrew. He has since dropped DCI Pemberton and made DC Oblak his next 'conquest'.

After DC Tanner raised concerns regarding DS Bridger's and DI Murphy's conduct during Operation Corkscrew, DCI Pemberton was in charge of investigating the complaint. No further investigation was made, and both DS Bridger's and DI Murphy's records remain untarnished.

Meanwhile, DS Elliot Bridger continues to work for The Cabal in secret.

***

* * *

Jake – and some old enemies – return in *The Community*. Out now.

Enjoy this? You can make a big difference.

Reviews are the most powerful tools in my arsenal when it comes to getting attention for my books. They act as the tipping point on the scales of indecision for future readers crossing my books.

So, if you enjoyed this book, and are interested in being one of my committed and loyal readers, then I would really grateful if you could leave a review. Why not spread the word, share the love? Even if you leave an honest review, it would still mean a lot. They take as long to write as it did to read this book!

Thank you.

Your Friendly Author,
Jack Probyn

ABOUT JACK PROBYN

Jack Probyn is a British crime writer and the author of the Jake Tanner crime thriller series, set in London.

He currently lives in Surrey with his partner and cat, and is working on a new murder mystery series set in his hometown of Essex.

Keep up to date with Jack at the following:

- Website: https://www.jackprobynbooks.com
- Facebook: https://www.facebook.co.uk/jackprobynbooks
- Twitter: https://twitter.com/jackprobynbooks
- Instagram: https://www.instagram.com/jackprobynauthor

Printed in Great Britain
by Amazon